R U ____ D ?

Anne felt the noose tightening about her neck. She tried to swallow. For some time, she stared at her feet. Lord Ruin. Married to Lord Ruin. All this time she'd been frantically searching for some way to stop him from marrying Emily, and here it was. On a silver platter. She smothered a very inappropriate urge to laugh.

At last, she looked up. "Under any other circumstance, I'd be whisked away to the deep countryside never to be heard from again and this meeting would never have taken place."

"Quite true," the duke agreed.

She lifted her hands in a helpless gesture. "But it isn't fair."

"To hell with what's fair, Anne."

"I don't want to marry you, and I daresay you don't care to marry me."

"What either of us wants no longer matters."

She shivered, the proverbial goose walking over her grave. "I know. I haven't any choice."

He regarded her for a long moment, his face devoid of emotion. "The arrangements have been made. The ceremony will take place this afternoon. I am sure, Miss Sinclair," he went on with no conviction whatsoever, "we will get on splendidly."

Slowly, she rose, gripping the chair back for support. All she could think about was Devon. She had lost him again, and this time she would never get him back. "That hardly seems likely, sir."

LORD RUIN

CAROLYN JEWEL

LEISURE BOOKS   NEW YORK CITY

A LEISURE BOOK®

December 2002

Published by

Dorchester Publishing Co., Inc.
276 Fifth Avenue
New York, NY 10001

ISBN 0-8439-5135-4

Visit us on the web at www.dorchesterpub.com.

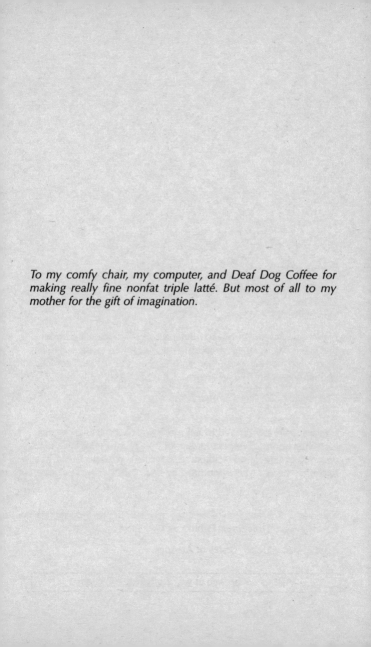

To my comfy chair, my computer, and Deaf Dog Coffee for making really fine nonfat triple latté. But most of all to my mother for the gift of imagination.

LORD RUIN

The mind cannot long act the role of the heart.
—François de la Rochefoucauld

Chapter One

London, 1818

Cynssyr glared at the door to number twenty-four Portman Square. "Blast it," he said to the groom who held two other horses. "What the devil is taking them so long?" He sat his horse with authority, a man in command of himself and his world. His buckskins fit close over lean thighs, and the exacting cut of his jacket declared a tailor of some talent. A pink of the Ton, he seemed, but for eyes that observed more than they revealed.

"The baron's a family man now, sir." The groom stamped his feet and tucked his hands under his armpits.

"What has that to do with anything?"

A handbill abandoned by some reveler from one of last night's fetes skimmed over the cobbles and spooked the other two horses, a charcoal gelding by the name of

1

Poor Boy, on account of the loss of his equine manhood; and a muscular dun. The groom had a dicey moment, what with the cold having numbed his fingers, but managed to send the sheet skittering to freedom.

"Man with a family can't leave anywhere spot on the dot," the groom said.

"I don't see why."

The door to number twenty-four flew open with a ringing crack of wood against stone. Of the two men who came out, the taller was Benjamin Dunbartin, Baron Aldreth, the owner of the house. He moved down the stairs at a rapid clip, clapping his hat onto his blond head as if he meant to cement it in place. The other man gripped his hat in one hand and descended at a more leisurely pace. The wind whipped a mass of inky curls over his sharp cheekbones.

"My lord." The groom handed Benjamin the reins to the dun. Before the groom could so much as offer a leg up, Ben launched himself into the saddle without a word of greeting or acknowledgment. Most everyone liked Benjamin. With his good looks and boyish smile, it was practically impossible not to. At the moment, however, Cynssyr thought Ben did not look like a man who cared for the family life.

"Come along, Devon," Benjamin said to his companion. He spoke with such force his dun tossed its head and pranced in nearly a full circle before Ben had him under control again.

Cynssyr's green eyes widened. "Have you quarreled with Mary?"

"Certainly not," Ben said.

"Well, you look like you've been hit by lightening from on high and still hear the angels singing. What's put you in such a state?"

"None of your damned business." The dun stamped hard on the cobbles, and Ben swore under his breath.

Cynssyr's bay snorted, and he reached to soothe the animal. "I should say it is, if I'm to endure such behavior from you."

"Devon!"

"Is this, by any chance, about Devon's letter?" Cynssyr asked.

Ben's neck fairly snapped, he turned so quickly. "What do you know about that damned letter?"

"He wouldn't let me read it, but it must have succeeded. Camilla Fairchild is too young to be looking at a man that way." Cynssyr's mouth quirked and with the slight smile, his austere features softened. When he smiled, he was about as handsome as a man could get, a fact not lost on him. He knew quite well the effect of his smile on the fairer sex.

Devon reached the curb in time to overhear the last remark. Coal-black eyes, at the moment completely without humor, slid from Ben to Cynssyr. "Disgraceful, ain't it? Her mother ought to set the girl a better example." He, too, accepted the reins of his gelding from the groom. He glanced at the stairs.

"Do you think she will?" Cynssyr managed, quite deliberately, to sound as though he hoped she wouldn't. Christ, he hoped not. He fully expected to soon discover what Mrs. Fairchild's backside felt like under his hands. Soft, he imagined. Energetic, he hoped.

"You ought to know better, Cyn," Devon said. "Even Mary said so."

"You will be relieved to know that at Lord Sather's rout, Miss Fairchild's passion was as yet untempered by experience. I merely provided her some." Cynssyr's smile reappeared. "A regrettably small amount, to be sure."

"You know, Cyn," Ben said, "one of these days you're going to miscalculate and find yourself married to some featherbrained female who'll bore you to tears."

3

"What else have you done, Devon, that's made him such wretched company?" Cynssyr prodded for more information.

"Not one word," Ben said, glaring not at Cynssyr but at Devon.

Devon stopped with one foot in the stirrup to gift the world with affronted innocence. "All I did was—"

"Not one!" Ben turned a warning glance on him. "Not a word from you, either, Cyn."

Dev shook his head and mounted, exchanging a glance with Cynssyr, who shrugged and found himself still mystified.

Only when the three were long out of earshot of the groom and riding toward Hyde Park did Ben speak. "How dare you?" He took a crumpled sheet of paper from his pocket and thrust it at Devon. "How dare you!"

"My personal correspondence is none of your affair." Devon, who had never expected to come into his title, could nevertheless exude more condescension than ever his father had managed, and the previous earl had been a master.

"Give me one reason I oughtn't call you out."

"Now see here," Cynssyr said, more than a little alarmed.

"Frankly, Cyn, if you knew about the letter, I ought to have satisfaction from you, too." Ben turned back to Devon. "Well?"

"I asked permission to court her when we were at Rosefeld for your wedding. But I had not the proper credentials then." Devon laughed bleakly. "I am Bracebridge now."

"Four years ago," Cynssyr said, "Camilla Fairchild all of what, twelve or thirteen?"

"Good God," said Benjamin. "Not Miss Fairchild!"

4

Devon snatched the crumpled paper from Ben's hand. "I won't lose her a second time."

"Lose whom?" Cynssyr drew even with Devon. "What are you two talking about? Devon, I thought your letter was for Miss Fairchild." Two women out for a morning walk stopped their stroll to stare at the men riding by. Out of pure habit, Cynssyr gave them an assessing glance, which made Devon laugh.

"Have you declared yourself?" Ben waved at the paper in Devon's hand. "Besides in that note of yours, I mean."

"If not Miss Fairchild, then whom?" Cynssyr said, by now more than a little annoyed. "Miss George?" When that got no reply, he said, "Not Miss Willowby. Oh, please, no. If it's Miss Willowby, I forbid it."

Devon slid the note into his pocket. "She has not the slightest idea of my feelings."

"Good God."

"Now that she is here in London," Devon said, "I mean to change that." He pulled back on his black, waiting for Ben's dun to draw alongside. Once again, Cynssyr found himself maddeningly excluded. "With your permission, of course."

"It isn't my permission you need be concerned with," Ben said. "It's her father's."

"The old man can bugger himself for all I care." The black-as-the-depths-of-hell eyes that even Cynssyr, who knew better, sometimes thought devoid of life flashed with a violent fire.

Benjamin grinned.

They were at the park now, off the streets and onto the riding paths. "Would one of you," said Cynssyr, "please tell me what the devil you're talking about?"

"Dev thinks he's in love."

"That much I gathered." He looked over at Devon. "In love with whom?"

5

"My sister-in-law," Ben said, throwing up one hand. "That's who."

Cynssyr gave Devon a look. "Which one?" He moved out of the path of a fat gentleman on a white mare. To the best of his recollection, there were four Sinclair sisters and Benjamin had married one of them. That left three. And, if memory served, the Sinclair sisters deserved their reputation for beauty. Ben's wife, Mary, was among the most beautiful women of Cynssyr's rather vast acquaintance. He almost didn't blame Ben for marrying her.

"I don't *think* I'm in love."

"The youngest? Miss Emily?" His green eyes flickered with interest. "If she turns out half as beautiful as she promised, she'll cause a riot at her debut."

"No. And stay the hell away from Emily, Cyn."

"Then it must be the brunette, Lucy." The name rolled off his tongue replete with his recollection of ebony hair and features of heartbreaking perfection.

"No."

"You mean the eldest?" He could not, for the life of him, summon an image of the eldest Sinclair sister. "That's impossible. I don't even remember her."

"Blond? Gray-blue eyes. Yay tall." Ben indicated an inch or so below his chin, which meant a tall woman, perhaps even an ungainly one. "You'll meet her tonight at the ball. Meet her again, that is."

"Why don't I recall her?" Cynssyr glanced at Devon.

"And by the way," Ben said. "Stay away from Lucy, too."

"Why?"

"Because when it comes to women, damn you, Cynssyr, you're a rogue, that's why."

"Mama begins to despair. Perhaps I ought to put to rest her doubts of a succession."

6

Ben snorted. "I'd not curse any of my sisters-in-law with you for a husband."

"Now that," Cynssyr said, "wounds me deeply. When at last I marry, I expect I'll make a most excellent husband."

"Hah," said Devon.

"Et tu, Brute?"

"You can't even settle on what woman to seduce tonight."

"If not for Napoleon, I'd likely be years married. A positive dullard, like Ben here." But Napoleon there was, so Cynssyr wasn't married at all. Love, naturally, would have but a limited role in any marriage he contracted. The war had burned out his capacity, if ever he'd possessed it, for such saving emotion.

"A dullard?" said Ben, spoiling his attempt to appear insulted by breaking into laughter. Devon rolled his eyes.

"Whatever you two think, I'm quite aware I need a wife. A man of my station requires a wife, as my desperate mother so often reminds me."

"God help the woman fool enough to marry you," Ben said.

"Why not one of your sisters-in-law, Ben? It seems an excellent idea." Dozens of suitable candidates were thrown his way every season, this one being no different from any other since the war. But he'd not been able to bring himself to the sticking point with any of them.

"No."

"I'll reform." He grinned. "I promise."

"You'll reform when hell freezes over."

A faint memory tickled at the back of his mind. He tapped his temple. "You mean the spinster, don't you, Devon? The eldest. The one with the spectacles."

"Blond hair, gray-blue eyes. Yay tall," Benjamin repeated.

"What was her name?"

Ben's blue eyes chilled another degree. "Anne."

"Gad. I still don't remember her. Except for the spectacles." He looked askance at Dev. "I have never understood your taste in women."

"You truly want to marry Anne?" Ben asked Devon. Curiosity and relief lingered at the edges of the question, but hearing him, no one could doubt the seriousness of the matter. No doting father could have sounded more cautious.

"Yes."

"I meant to introduce her to Declan McHenry," said Ben, regarding Devon thoughtfully. "Or Phillip Lovejoy."

"I'd be obliged if you didn't."

"Good God, you *are* serious, aren't you?"

"It's been four years. I am done waiting." Amusement brightened Devon's brooding eyes and made his severe mouth curve in a surprisingly warm smile. It did interesting things to his face, the way severity gave way to warmth. At times like this, when he saw Devon smile, Cynssyr understood exactly why women went so eagerly to his bed.

If Devon had really decided the Sinclair spinster was the woman he wanted, then the matter was done. He would have his way. The why of it mystified him. Even as plain Devon Carlisle, he could do far better than some dried-up female who wasn't even pretty enough to bother taking off her spectacles. As matrimonial material, the earl of Bracebridge was nearly as sought after as he himself. Nearly. But, not quite.

"Enough. No more blather about love and marriage, you two," Cynssyr said. With a flick of the reins, he steered his horse past a fallen branch then cantered to the edge of a meadow where he waited for Ben and Devon.

8

"Jade," Ben accused when he reached the meadow.

Cynssyr flashed a brilliantly arrogant smile. "The trouble with you, my lord Baron Aldreth, is you love your wife. And you, Devon. For shame. You disappoint me. You disappoint all our sex, falling for this Miss Sinclair."

"Love," said Dev with one of his wry grins. "A most heinous crime."

"Love." Cynssyr lifted one brow in the supercilious disdain he usually reserved for certain rebuttals in the Lords. "You mean a man's delusion he's not been robbed of his freedom and a woman's that she's gained hers?"

"Exactly," Devon said.

"How can you trust your judgment now?" He lifted his riding whip, but brought it down on his boot leg, not his horse. "Fools the both of you." So saying, he urged his horse to a gallop. "Anne Sinclair," he muttered. He heard Devon and Ben thunder after him and gave his horse its head. They had no chance of catching him now. Only the best horseflesh found its way into his stables. He had the best of everything. Wine. Horses. Women. Friends.

He wanted to roar with disgust and dismay. Devon married. What was he to do with himself then? To the devil with spinsters who set their caps on marriage, he thought as the chill wind whipped past him. "To the very devil with her." Thus did the duke of Cynssyr, so deservedly referred to as Lord Ruin, dismiss the woman with whom he would soon be desperately in love.

Chapter Two

The duke of Sin and the Angelic Sinclair, surely a match made in heaven.

"Well," said Lucy, folding the page from which she'd read out loud. The rest of the paper slid off her lap and onto the floor. "Quite a triumph for our youngest sister."

Mary held out Anne's gloves. "He'll propose to her at Corth Abbey." They were in Anne's room, about to leave for Sussex and Mr. Devon Carlisle's country retreat now that Anne was at last well enough to think of such a journey, illness having kept her abed since the day of the Sinclair family's arrival in London.

"He won't," Anne said, admitting just to herself that in actual fact she prayed he would not. She drew on a glove. She didn't yet know the extent of the disaster, but according to Mary, all anyone had talked about during her three-week sickroom confinement was that man, that awful man, the duke of Cynssyr, courting Emily.

The Angelic Sinclair he dubbed her and, drat the man, the sobriquet stuck.

The only other subject of conversation that even came close to Emily and the duke was how yet another woman had been snatched right from Piccadilly Street. Whispers of the incident abounded, some ridiculous beyond belief. Violence underlay all the speculations, from the probable through to the fantastic. True, ransom had been paid, but no one, it seemed, believed the story stopped there.

"Yes, he will," said Lucy. "Emily refuses to encourage him, but he is determined, is the duke."

Anne turned. She had long ago accepted the unspoken expectation that she would care for their father for as many years as were left him. A pretty woman born to a family of beauties, Anne considered her looks little more than tolerable. With three beautiful sisters, few people, if any, noticed she was not at all unattractive.

"What sort of recommendation is that for a husband?" Fear made her tone sharp. Guilt, too. If only she'd gotten out and about sooner, events might never have come to this unfortunate pass. "Determined." She sniffed. "What about love? Emily must be loved by her husband, and I don't believe for even a moment he loves Emily." She had no doubt whatever that marriage between Emily and Cynssyr would be disastrous. Marriage to the duke would be disastrous for any woman. "Love. He doesn't know the meaning of the word." She gave her other glove a jerk in order to slide her fingers to the ends. "He doesn't. He can't." She tugged hard on the cuff. "He never will."

"He's one of the most powerful men in England, and he wants to marry Emily." Mary tucked a strand of Anne's hair behind her ear. Somewhere between blond and silver-gold, Anne's hair refused to hold a curl. A woman who cared for the fashion of ringlets might have despaired. "Have you nothing else to wear, Anne? Something blue to match your eyes?"

"I'm presentable." That's all a spinster need be: presentable. Her eyes were of little account, not quite blue, not quite gray. Besides, they were too darkly lashed and obscured by a pair of spectacles, gold rims holding narrow ovals of glass. Her features were regular enough, but to Anne, who had constantly the model of her sisters before her, they fell far short of beauty. Rarely did people look past the spectacles, since she dressed like the spinster she was, in plain, sober gowns without concession to style.

"Powerful," she now replied to her sister. "From an accident of birth. It's not as though he earned his exalted position." If she'd known how closely her expression resembled Cynssyr at his haughtiest she would have been mortified. "He's a dilettante who probably cares more for his tailor or his bootmaker than the less fortunate people of England. What does he know of the suffering of real people?" Bartley Green had its share of misery. The duke didn't know a thing about people from villages like Bartley Green. How could he, a man to the manor born, have any understanding of poverty? Or of hopelessness clinging to one's soul like the dampness of mist.

"For pity's sake, Anne, he's not a monster."

"I'll take issue with that." In truth, she knew little of the duke except what she read in the papers and that consisted primarily of melodramatic accounts of his social exploits. Still, if even a particle was true, he was the sort of man a lady avoided at all costs. Satirists rendered the duke's amorous pursuits in droll cartoons, frequently showing him addressing the House of Lords while women swooned at his feet. The caricatures made clear where his interests lay, and it wasn't the subject matter of his speeches.

"Papa is beside himself, you know." Lucy sighed. "Emily a duchess."

"Emily a what?" came a voice from the doorway.

"Papa will not interfere this time," Anne said stoutly, but low enough that only Mary and Lucy heard. "He won't coerce another daughter into a disastrous marriage." What Lucy thought of this reference to her late husband, she didn't care. The stakes were too high for the nicety of silence on a painful subject.

Emily walked in, cooly elegant in a lilac carriage dress. Anne melted a little, as she always did when she looked at her youngest sister. She'd held an infant Emily in her arms, nursed her though illness and soothed her out of unhappiness. Beautiful, trusting Emily would be destroyed by a man like Cynssyr. Her sweet nature and high spirits would not survive the discovery that the duke did not and could not love her. Seeing her sister married to Cynssyr would break her heart. Emily needed love in her marriage. She deserved love. As their parents had once loved. This headlong rush to catastrophe simply had to be stopped.

"A duchess," Lucy supplied.

"If I were a duchess," said Emily, mimicking a regal stance, "you should have to curtsey when I came into the room." Her eyes twinkled. "And Anne would have to listen to me for a change."

"We'll see about that. Lucy, dearest, your bootlace is untied."

"What? Again?" She bent down. "What a nuisance. I am forever coming undone."

"Hurry up, Lucy," said Emily. "Aldreth says the carriage is ready."

Anne smiled grimly and adjusted her cap. "Shall we?"

With dry roads and no rain to slow them down, the

journey into Sussex didn't take but two hours. Too short a drive, thought Anne. And, indeed, they arrived all too soon. She hadn't nearly enough time to lay plans against the duke.

Lucy dropped one of her gloves when the carriage door opened. "Go on, Lucy," said Anne. She dipped her head to avoid being enveloped by Emily's skirt as she descended. "I'll find it."

"Thank you, Anne. You're a treasure." Lucy extended a hand to someone outside and stepped down.

Now, she thought, bending down, where was that glove? Not on the seat. "Come now, little glove," she cajoled. "Blast, do stop hiding. Ah, hah!" There it was on the floor, kicked nearly out of sight beneath the lip of the seat.

"Welcome," she heard a deep, resonant voice say to the others. "Welcome to Corth Abbey."

Inside the carriage, Anne's hand stopped inches from Lucy's glove. She knew that voice. Memories and feelings rushed back, tugging at her heart.

"Anne?" Mary called from just outside.

She snatched the glove and for the space of a breath stayed bent down. Her pulse raced. She lifted a hand to her head to smooth her hair, then stopped. Curse her for her pride. What she looked like didn't matter. Even if she were as beautiful as one of her sisters, what feelings Devon Carlisle may once have felt for her must be long dead. She recaptured her flight of fancy and gathered back the misgivings of her heart. Clutching Lucy's glove, she stepped from the carriage, unnoticed.

Devon stood with Mary and Aldreth but he was bowing over Lucy's hand, distracted, as most men were, by her beauty. Thus, Anne had a moment to compose herself. Though his circumstances had changed dramatically, he had not. His hair was still too long, and he still had that ungoverned air about him, as if he just barely restrained himself from some outrageous behavior. Four years had passed. She told herself she meant nothing to him now. Indeed, she expected he would show her only polite disinterest. He was rich now and ennobled while she was nothing but a spinster of no particular interest to anyone.

He let go of Lucy's hand and greeted her father. Grinning, he gave Aldreth a thump on the shoulder. Then he turned to her. Anne felt her stomach contract with a kind of shivery sensation, equal parts trepidation and exhilaration, it seemed to her.

"Anne," he said in the wine-smooth voice she remembered so well. "How glad I am to see you. You are recovered, yes?" He moved to her, taking both her hands in his and smiling that sinister smile of his.

"Perfectly, my lord." She bent a knee. Papa, when in his cups, tended to talk rather too much. Too late, she learned that four years ago Devon Carlisle had admired her more than a little. She'd returned the feeling, never dreaming that a man of Devon's qualities would think of her as anything more than a chaperon for her sisters. They'd talked for hours in the days before Mary's wedding, when she'd spent more time at Aldreth's estate of Rosefeld than her own home. Then, of course, Devon had been a penniless younger son, and that had been reason enough for Papa to discourage him when he'd called after the wedding and been summarily dismissed.

"Devon," he said softly. "On that I insist."

Her pulse tripped. Lucy and Devon, she thought in a sort of wild panic, would suit. Yes. Suit they would. A perfect match those two. "Yes, sir."

"Devon," he repeated.

Hearing that warm and tender tone, her stomach fluttered with butterflies. Unbidden came the thought that she really could not bear a disappointment. Too much time had passed. Too much had changed. Four years had put marriage further from her grasp. She might as well imagine herself a princess as imagine herself married, let alone married to him. Her place and her future were no mystery at all. She looked to Lucy who knelt over her boot, tying the laces yet again. "Lucy, dear, come along." What she wanted wasn't possible. Matters would end precisely where they had in Bartley Green.

"I own," Ben remarked to Anne, turning his head so only Mary saw him smiling, "Bracebridge here meant to fetch the physic himself when he heard you were not well. He must have asked a dozen times if you were going to come with us."

"We shall be a very merry party, I think," said Devon quickly. He touched the bridge of his nose at the spot where it jogged slightly left rather than continue straight. "Lady Prescott has arrived." Still holding one of Anne's hands, he led them up the stairs. "And the Cookes. Mr. Hathaway, Major Truitt." He gestured. "Breathe a word that the Sinclairs have accepted, and one must deal with all sorts of people desperate for an invitation."

"Has his grace arrived yet?" Sinclair asked with a significant glance at Emily.

Dread knotted Anne's stomach. That man, the duke who was an utterly unsuitable husband for any woman, but especially for someone in her family, would not toy with Emily's heart the way he had with all those other women. No matter what. She didn't know yet how she would prevent an engagement, but she would. Somehow she would.

Devon shook his head. "Alas, sir, no."

Like that, Anne's tension collapsed, the knot in her stomach unraveled. She leaned to Mary. "What did I tell you?" she whispered with undeniable exaltation. "Lord Ruin hasn't even come, the coward. He got nowhere with Emily and has taken up easier prey." A butler moved forward to take hats and cloaks.

"We shall see," Mary said, handing over her cloak.

"Not here?" Sinclair repeated.

"The Privy Council was convened. He's delayed until tomorrow at least. Perhaps even the day after. But there are guests enough for your amusement, sir." Devon hadn't yet left Anne's side. "Major Truitt was kind enough to bring his sister Evelyn, whom I know you ladies will adore, and we are graced as well with Miss Fairchild, her mother and four cousins."

Lucy came perilously close to knocking over one of a pair of celadon vases on either side of the grand staircase. The butler casually repositioned it. Again, that midnight gaze fell on Anne. From pure self-defense, she pretended not to notice. Long practice had made her adept at hiding her emotions. But she couldn't stop herself from thinking that if only her life had been different, she might be four years married. A mother and a countess in the bargain, with every right to hold Devon's hand in hers.

"Pond will show you to your rooms."

No. It simply wasn't possible. Earls married great beauties or heiresses, and she was neither. Anne tugged, and her fingers slipped from Devon's grasp. They were only part way up the stairs, not even half way, when the front door opened. Hearing the sound, they stopped. The core component of the chattering group appeared to be young, unmarried females and their chaperones. A few gentlemen rounded out the group, young men, one or two of them soldiers, Anne guessed, from their posture and serious eyes. Every one of the men gazed at Emily and Lucy, stricken with awe as men usually were with her sisters.

"I saw the carriage," said a woman with iron-gray hair. In the crook of her elbow she cradled a dog the color of snuff and constantly stroked between its pointed ears. "I thought perhaps my son had arrived earlier than expected. But I see it is you, Aldreth." She inclined her head in a queenly nod. "Lady Aldreth." Fixing her dragon gaze on Emily she said, "Do come downstairs, young woman." She pointed at Lucy. "You, too." Emily nodded and returned to the entranceway to offer a curtsey.

Anne's heart sank to her toes. This could be none other than the duchess of Cynssyr and mother to the present duke. No other woman could have such an air of arrogance about her. This was disaster. Complete disaster. The duchess never stirred from Hampstead Heath except on a serious matter. And what could be more serious than meeting the woman her son planned to propose to, the woman who would make her the dowager duchess of Cynssyr?

Lucy made a knee on the step just ahead of Anne, and Anne saw that Lucy's bootlace had come unlaced yet again. "Lucy," Anne whispered. But, too late.

Lucy started down the stairs to join Emily. She stepped on the dangling lace, stumbled and in trying to recover her balance tangled her foot in Anne's skirt. By catching Lucy's arm, she saved her sister from pitching headfirst down the stairs, but the effort cost Anne her own balance.

She grabbed for the bannister and grasped only air. The next thing she knew, she was falling with no hope of saving herself. With a strangled cry as she toppled sideways, Anne felt her ankle give a nasty turn. She landed hard on her side and bounced down two steps to the landing. She lay there, stunned and exquisitely aware of the hush.

Chapter Three

"Are you all right?" Kneeling, Devon handed over her glasses, which had gone flying when she fell. She put them on, relieved to have the world back in focus until she saw herself the center of attention.

"I'm fine. I think." She didn't feel a thing. Her foot was numb from toe to ankle which surely was not natural. "Perfectly all right."

"Clumsy girl."

"Yes, Papa." Sensation returned with a rush, and she bit her lip to keep back a gasp of pain.

Sinclair frowned at her. "Walk it off, my girl."

"Yes, Papa."

"You've hurt yourself." Devon put an arm around her, holding her up.

"Good Lord, man, don't make a blessed fuss," said Sinclair.

Devon lowered her onto a stair and matter-of-factly unlaced her boot. "Would you be so kind, Pond," he told his butler, "as to send for the doctor?"

"Milord."

"I don't believe it's broken, but best have it looked at."

"Nonsense!" Sinclair guffawed.

Anne sucked in a breath as he slid off her boot. From over Devon's shoulder, she got a full dose of her father's glower. "Papa is right, my lord. You mustn't make a fuss." But her ankle didn't just throb, it pulsed with agony. Pride was all that kept away the tears. She managed to stand, but without touching her foot to the floor. "I'm all right."

"You're not." Devon was suddenly close. "Put your arms round my neck." But with her father glaring at her, she didn't dare. "Come now, Anne," Devon said in reasonable tones. "I'll not bite. I promise you that."

"Always been the clumsy one," she heard her father say. For the briefest moment, she resented his glib dismissal. Had Emily or Lucy fallen he would have been the first to demand a litter and a surgeon. She quickly stopped the heretical train of thought. She knew her duty and the respect she owed her father.

Devon lifted her as if she weighed no more than a feather. She imagined her father glaring at her and then she heard him say to someone, "No good comes of coddling."

"It's all right, Anne, darling," Devon murmured in her ear, low enough that in the general commotion no one heard but her.

Her heart leapt. Not entirely welcome, but not unwelcome either. *Darling*. He'd called her darling. She put her arms around his shoulders, for balance, of course, and something deep inside her stirred. Something she'd not felt in four years.

What if he didn't mean it? What if he'd been thinking of Lucy or Emily or even some other woman entirely and the word had just slipped out? *Darling*. In that case, he was embarrassed to his toes, if he even realized what he'd said. Like as not, he didn't know he'd uttered the endearment. But heavens, what if he meant it?

All the way up the stairs, she vacillated between the two possibilities. He meant it. He didn't mean it. My, but he smelled good, she discovered. A faint, lemony cologne and behind that the particular scent of the man. His shoulders felt nice, too. Solid and comforting. She rested her head against his chest and let her imagination take wing.

"Mary," he said, "where shall I put her? I don't see how she can share with Miss Emily and Mrs. Willcott, now. Not with her ankle. None of them will sleep." His arms tightened around her. "Dash it to deuces. When I built Corth Abbey I never dreamed of entertaining so many. Nor that so many would care to visit without an invitation." He turned his head to one side. "My room?"

"Certainly not!" Mary said.

He laughed. "I'd sleep in the parlor, Lady Aldreth."

"Bracebridge," said Mary.

Anne could practically hear Mary's eyes rolling to the ceiling, and in her heart, Anne thought that Devon's glib offer of his room sounded wonderfully wicked.

"Then there's really only one other possibility. You tell me if it will do." He stopped at a door near the top of the stairs and waited for Mary to open it and precede them inside. "Well?"

A moment later, Mary said, "I suppose."

"You're certain?"

"Yes. Yes, of course I am. Bring her in, Bracebridge."

"I feel so silly about all this bother," Anne said as Dev placed her on the bed. If he looked at her, she wondered, did that mean he didn't remember what he'd said or that he did and had intended to say it? Lucy hurried in, kneeling at the bedside.

Anne peeked at Devon. Their eyes met and locked for just an instant. Her heart jumped. Great beauties and heiresses, she repeated. Great beauties and heiresses. "Do stop crying, Lucy. I shall be perfectly all right."

Mary gave Lucy a look. "You are no use to anyone when you are upset, Lucy, dear. Take Papa and see to Emily and the duchess if you would, please. She's probably overwhelmed by now, all alone with Em. Bracebridge." Dev stopped his pacing at the foot of the bed.

"I do not like this," he said.

"It is just for the night, after all."

"Yes, I know, but—"

Mary put her hands on her hips. "I will not put her in your room when you are here, Bracebridge. No. It's out of the question. We'll know soon enough how badly she's injured. Oh, for heaven's sake. Do sit." She pointed to a nearby chair. "Make yourself useful, Bracebridge. Amuse Anne. Take her mind off the discomfort while we wait."

"Major Truitt and Mr. Hathaway can room with me. We'll put her in their room."

From the bed, Anne spoke up. "My lord, honestly. I would not like to have so many people discommoded on my account." She looked away from his black eyes. She had to stop torturing herself this way. He was nothing more than a concerned host. Nothing more and everything but, she thought. She spied a small flagon on the dresser, stoppered crystal rimmed with gold. She concentrated on that instead of her throbbing ankle or Devon's intentions and her own flood of conflicting reactions.

Dark green and gold made the chamber's primary colors. Solid furniture, a sturdy desk on which there sat an escritoire, near that a stack of paper and a mahogany box for pen and ink. A pair of soft leather boots shaped to a man's calves lay near a wardrobe. Near that, a stack of linen shirts, freshly pressed. Hanging discreetly over a stand in the corner, a pair of charcoal trousers. A gentleman's personal effects surrounded her. That was a shaving kit on the dresser, made of pigskin with a crest embossed in shining gold. Not the Bracebridge coat of arms, though. A cockatrice below a duke's coronet. A duke's coronet.

"This is Cynssyr's room!" Anne said, failing to keep the shock from her voice.

"Now do you understand?" Devon jumped from his chair.

Mary threw up her hands. "Bracebridge, you said yourself he's delayed until at least tomorrow, if not beyond. What's the harm? He'll never know. And if Anne's foot is broken, you and the duke may share quarters. I'm sure he'll survive the ignominy."

Anne looked around. Cynssyr's belongings and none other's. He meant to come to Corth Abbey. He must if he'd sent his valet on ahead. She had a sudden and inexplicable picture of herself standing at the open window pouring the contents of his crystal flagon onto the bushes below. The imagined spite made her smile.

Devon leaned forward, reaching for her hand. "Feeling better?"

She nodded. Crowded as she now felt by the duke when he wasn't even here, she suddenly had little hope she could convince him to do anything he didn't want to. Well, she would think of something. She had to, and God help her if Emily thought she loved the man. But she didn't think so. Emily, when at last she loved, would love wholeheartedly and without restraint. She'd know, everyone would know, when Emily fell in love. No, her fear was that Emily might feel obligated to make the marriage.

The doctor's arrival interrupted Devon's tale of the

Italian palazzo that had inspired the layout of the Abbey. Anne sighed. She was sick unto death of doctors. He examined Anne's ankle and concurred it was not broken. Satisfied that her sister's condition, while painful, was not serious, Mary left to fetch some of Anne's things. The doctor filled a glass with water and added two drops of another liquid.

"A small amount for now, Miss Sinclair. I'll leave a stronger dose for you to take if you wake in the night." Under his watchful eye, Anne drank down the contents.

Mary returned with a nightdress discreetly folded over her arm. Lucy was with her. "Go on, all of you men. Out." Mary put down her bundle and made shooing gestures.

Before leaving, the doctor prepared a second glass, titrating several more drops into the water. "There. Should you need it in the night." He pointed to the nightstand.

"Thank you."

Mary sat on the edge of the bed when the sisters were alone. "Was not Bracebridge masterful? Carrying you up the stairs like you were his lover."

"Mary."

"Well, wasn't he? Tell me, are those shoulders as strong as they look?"

"Put that down, Lucy," Anne said. She successfully damped the spark of hope. Just admitting that Devon Carlisle was more than a man whom she happened to know felt traitorous, a betrayal of her father and duty. Frightening and exhilarating both, and neither reaction pleased her. It wasn't wise of her, she thought, to tempt herself with hopes of a husband and children of her own. In truth, a part of her had already accepted the possibility and soared with a giddy happiness.

Lucy sniffed the laudanum-dosed water. "Doesn't smell like much. I think he ought to have given you

24

more. Are you going to answer Mary's question?"

"What question?" The laudanum began to take effect and concentration became difficult. At least her ankle didn't hurt anymore.

"About Lord Bracebridge's shoulders."

Mary laughed. Anne glared at her. "I'm sure I don't know what you mean." She did, though, and despite everything, she joined in the laughter. "Devon's shoulders are broad. And his chest . . . oh, my."

"Do put that down, Lucy," Mary said. "You'll spill it. Go on, Anne."

"He smells good, too."

Lucy put down the glass, not on the nightstand, but on the sidetable by the washbasin. "A fatal case if ever there was."

Mary took her hand. "You could marry, Anne. It's not too late for you."

"Yes, it is." She felt as if she were floating. A magical, wonderful sensation.

"He's waited for you since Aldreth and I were married."

"How could you know that?" She wasn't entirely certain she'd spoken out loud but she must have for Mary answered.

"Aldreth told me so."

"Why do you think he invited us here?" Lucy said.

"So that Lord Ruin could break Emily's heart."

"Nonsense, Anne. Now, we'll manage Papa," Mary said over Lucy's peal of laughter. "Don't you worry about that."

"I predict a marriage." Lucy grinned at Mary as if Anne weren't able to see. "Indeed, yes. A marriage all because Anne has injured her ankle."

"Your injury *will* lead to a wedding," said Mary with a smile. "Yes, I daresay so."

Carolyn Jewel

Anne's last thought as she drifted into the welcoming arms of unconsciousness was that she hoped her sisters were right.

As it happened, they were.

Chapter Four

Ruan saw to his own horse when he made the Abbey at about half past one in the morning. Thank heaven for a full moon and clear sky, or he'd have never tried to make Corth Abbey before morning. Good weather and good luck. The front door was unlocked. He didn't need to rouse the servants. Greatcoat folded over an arm, he went upstairs. He heard voices from the parlor, his mother's among them. Time enough for explanation in the morning, he decided, walking past with a silence learned on campaign. He did not particularly care to hear his mother's reaction to Emily Sinclair tonight. If he made an appearance, he was in for an inquisition. He hadn't the patience for it, not at this hour.

Whenever he came to Corth Abbey, he stayed in the same room. Just as Dev always had the same room if he spent a night at Cywrthorn or at the estate in Cornwall. The idea that by week's end he would be an engaged man buoyed his spirits, quite unnaturally for a man of his temperament. He fully intended to break through that layer of disdain Miss Emily Sinclair had adopted toward him. The girl refused to be easily caught. Well, the hunt was on, and Emily Sinclair was no better than a hapless fox and him the baying hound. She would be his duchess. Lord Ruin ought to marry the most beautiful woman London had seen in many a season. Young, fresh, and so lovely he intended the shortest possible engagement.

His room was closest to the stairs. Dobkin, his valet, had traveled with his mother's servants the day before and had in his usual thorough and methodical manner arranged the room in anticipation of his arrival. A fire warmed the chamber. On the nightstand, a lamp cast a soft glow so he didn't have to fumble for a light. His trunk stood in one corner, and he knew his clothes were laid out in the wardrobe. He threw his greatcoat over a chair and decided not to wake Dobkin. Coat and waistcoat he let drop on a chair. Loosening his shirt, he made for the washstand and sluiced the travel grime from his face and neck. He was pulling off his boots when he realized he was not alone.

Panic had him reaching for his coat, but the fright passed. God knows a woman transformed any room she stayed in, and he did not see a single sign that the one in his bed was there for any purpose but the obvious. Her clothes would be somewhere. Perfume bottles arranged on the dresser, perhaps a pair of slippers near the bed, stockings or a shawl draped over a chair. On a suspicious whim, he threw open the wardrobe. And breathed a sigh of relief. Nothing but his own clothes inside. On the table was his shaving kit, laid out as if Dobkin were about to appear with a cup of foaming lather. Really, there wasn't any doubt. Barefoot, he walked to the bed.

"Dev, you rogue you."

The woman lay on her back, one arm thrown above her head. Sound asleep, despite the noise he'd made undressing. Not beautiful. Nor was she unaffecting. He sat on the edge of the bed. He rather liked her features, framed as they were by a few wisps of pale hair that had escaped a tidy braid. Sleeping, she looked as far from a whore as, well, the woman he intended to marry. The significance of her being in his room was not lost on him. One last hark to the wild life he and Devon were to leave behind.

"This," he said in a whisper as he slowly drew the covers down to her waist, "is what comes of a man owning a brothel." To his surprise, she showed no sign of waking. He adjusted the bedclothes so that nearly the whole of one leg came into sight. A very long, very lovely leg. Her nightdress had slid up while she slept, to nearly the middle of her thigh. The material was fine cambric. No common whore her, but then Devon never did anything the common way.

Thinking she must any moment awaken, he trailed a finger from her knee to mid-thigh. When it came to women, he was patience personified. She stirred, and he waited. But she only flung one arm over her chest. His attention diverted from her leg, he took it upon himself to remove her hand from her torso, gently laying it on the mattress. He shifted just enough to push aside the linens, for they were now most definitely a hindrance to him.

"Sweet Christ," he breathed.

Her breasts were on the large side, more than a palmfull, a sumptuous, overflowing handful. Long and slender legs, small waist and those lovely round breasts that sent heat directly to his groin. He vowed never again to overlook a woman who did not have a conventionally pretty face. A ribbon held together the top edges of her nightdress. One tug on the end, and he was separating

29

the two halves. Not, unfortunately, far enough to see all of her. But even what a man might see in any ballroom impressed him. He slipped a hand inside. With the pad of one finger he brought her nipple to a peak. She moaned softly and with her next breath he had more flesh against his palm than he could hold.

A vision of her calves touching his back prompted him to move his attention back to her legs. He inched the cambric higher. She stirred again, and he checked to see if she'd woken. Her chest rose with another breath, trembling on a sigh, but she still slept. He very much longed to touch her legs at a higher point. Pushing the nightdress up and past her hips called for a combination of strength and dexterity since the woman slept like a log. Now, though, he could not only see but touch the surprisingly dark nether hair. Lord, but her skin was soft. Unconscionably soft. She smelled sweet, felt warm and silken.

That soft skin of hers had him running a palm everywhere he could touch, feather-light strokes. A sigh came from her and with but a little encouragement her legs parted just enough for him to slip a finger between her thighs. His searching finger found the flesh that would make her moan in passion. Another sigh. Would that low sound become another man's name? Devon's, perhaps? He listened, but heard only her breath, faster now he'd brought her close to passion. Tension in her formerly lax body told him she was awake and, easing back a bit so as to both prolong and increase her climax when it came, he whispered, "You're almost there, love." There was nothing better than a grateful whore.

"That's nice." She sounded sleepy, groggy with it. The neck of her nightdress opened wider when she strained upward into his hand.

"Yes, it is," he replied. He stopped, waiting for a protest that didn't come in the form of words. Her head tossed on the pillow when his finger slid inside her just long enough to find heat and wetness. Another moment, and he returned to his slow, stroking motion. He had her quickly at the edge. He left her there a moment longer than he should have because it was such a pleasure to watch her.

When at last he gave her release, she abandoned herself to her body. Not one blessed ounce of inhibition. The long muscles of her legs tightened. Her pelvis arched to him, inviting the intimacy of his hand. A short while later her hands fisted at her sides. Her face in her moment of extremity had a look of wonderment so that a vain man might have thought himself the first ever to bring her to orgasm. Being neither a vain man nor a stupid one, he knew that wasn't so. Devon would have brought her to such a state more than once. All the same, he found the reaction quite appealing.

His fingers curled around her thigh just above her knee and stroked down. "There is something about a woman's well-turned leg," he murmured in a honeyed voice. "The exquisite blending of calf to knee." God knows but her legs were exquisite. She winced, and he couldn't imagine how he could possibly have hurt her. A glance at her foot told him how. A dark purple bruise ran from below her ankle bone forward to the middle arch of her very dainty foot. Probably hurt like the devil. "What have you done to your ankle?" He was only mildly curious, but he asked anyway. His fingers stroked upward, as far as her knee.

"Oh."

His hand inched higher. "Yes, love?"

"Oh." Now he had his hand on her thigh. Her very upper thigh. "You are a wicked man." She giggled and despite it being a giggle, he wasn't put off. The silly sound convinced him all was exactly as he supposed. A lover of Devon's who had injured an ankle. The familiar accent of his own class suggested she was perhaps once a governess now come to a more profitable employment. With her in his room and so wonderfully the flirt, why should he think otherwise?

Devon was just the sort to give up a perfectly acceptable mistress because he fancied himself in love with some old maid from the country. He considered taking her right then, coyness be damned. As wildly as she'd come, perhaps she'd enjoy a hard, fast coupling. He stood up and shucked his trousers, watching as she recovered herself.

A small frown line appeared between her brows. That surprised him. He'd been expecting a soft smile, an inviting pout. Slowly, her eyes focused. She did not immediately look at him. When she did, the frown deepened. She closed her eyes, then opened them again. "Who are you?" she whispered. "A dream? Surely, a dream. A wonderful dream."

"A man who wants you," he replied.

"You aren't Devon."

"No." He softly laughed. "Indeed not." He stepped out of his underclothes and thought about how much he wanted to touch her breasts.

"Lord Ruin." But for the odd vagueness about her, almost a blankness, he might have thought her better than pretty. Some men preferred their women on the feeble side. He never had. At the moment, however, he was more than willing to overlook any defect in her intelligence.

"The very same, my love."

"Oh," she said in a voice that sounded, to his ears, as if she were going to fall back to sleep. "Then it's all right. I know who you are." She laughed. "How fortuitous it's you, though. Quite a stroke of luck. I did so hope to see you in private."

"Did you now?" Even with the rather vague expression, he revised his initial opinion of her looks. Her features were more than a little enticing. Nice mouth, good cheekbones. In the soft darkness, her eyes showed indeterminate color and sleepy passion. Naked as the day he was born, he lay on the bed this time, leaning his weight on one elbow. "Whatever are you doing so far away from me?" He chuckled when he saw her looking at him. As if she'd never seen a man before. "Touch me," he said softly. "Go on," he whispered when she did nothing except gaze at him from half-lidded eyes. "I'd like you to."

Shyly, she reached out. "Lord Ruin." Fingertips traced the ridges of his abdomen down to his pelvis. She kept her attention on her hands. For a time, he watched her face, enjoying the slow increase of arousal in her eyes and the way her mouth curved ever so slightly. He groaned when she arrived at his pelvis, sliding over bone and sinew. He could almost believe her an innocent, the way she looked at him and how she started everything as if afraid she'd step wrong. But no innocent ever took a man's balls in her hands, as the little witch was doing right now.

Devon was a fool. Flat out a bloody fool, to give her up. He wondered what Devon wanted from him that he'd gone to the trouble of finding a woman so unexpectedly to his taste. A specific desire popped into his head, and he rather thought she was just the woman to satisfy it. "Kiss me, take me in your mouth," he whispered urgently.

For an instant, he thought she wouldn't. Then, warm, damp pressure surrounded him, and he leaned back on his haunches. She began with deliberate slowness, learning him, practically committing him to memory, he thought. Whatever it was Dev wanted, he was going to see that he got it. "A little harder." He took her head between his hands and showed her what he meant.

"Yes." He drew in a sharp breath when her tongue went his length, circled the tip until he thought he would expire from the sensation. She had the trick of it now, just the right pressure. Urgency built. Increased. Swelled until he knew she would kill him with that sweet, clever mouth. And then, it was upon him. She did not draw away as he came, offering him the most exquisite pleasure. "Christ. Oh, Christ."

When he let go, she straightened, pressing the back of her hand to her lips. He lifted her onto his lap. "I like to have a woman's mouth around me when I come," he said into her ear while being rather free with his hands.

"I want to do that again."

"And so you shall," he said, laughing as he lowered his mouth to the side of her neck. "Your mouth was very nice indeed."

"That tickles."

He kissed her once more, just to hear that warm, pleasing laugh again, then shifted her off his lap. "Stay here." He went to the washstand and on the way back brought her a glass of water. While she drank thirstily, he availed himself of the chamber pot. Upon rejoining her, he took the now empty glass and replaced it on the nightstand without actually watching what he was doing, so that he did it clumsily. "These, my darling, I cannot wait to kiss them." His hand boldly caressing her breasts made the object of his sentence shockingly plain.

Arching into his caress, she sighed. "Surely, this is a sin."

"Rather late in the game to be worrying about that, don't you think?"

"A wonderful, incredible sin."

"Shall we sin some more?" He grinned and got an admirably bashful look from beneath those too-dark lashes of hers. "Naturally, I am not ready for you quite yet. But, with the proper caress from your lovely hands, or perhaps your mouth, in a shorter time than we expect."

"But. . . ."

"What, my dear?"

She frowned. "I am not myself just now. My mind reels so I can scarce think or speak."

"That I'll take as a compliment. As for anything else, you may trust I'll take care of you." He slipped both hands under her nightdress, molding his palms to the curving of her hip. "I promise you that."

She let out a long breath of air. Not so gently, he pushed her onto her back and moved his hands upward, closer to her magnificent breasts. He kissed her, parting her lips, pulling her to him and shifting so his torso was over hers, and he could feel nothing but softness against him. To his surprise, she resisted his removing the garment. By now his belly touched hers. A mere millimeter of cloth hardly made a difference.

"Let me see you. Just as you've seen me."

"I feel so strange," she said on another sighing breath. "As if I'm floating."

"Darling, please." He couldn't help himself. His mouth came down on hers, opening, delving. After a moment's hesitation, she kissed him back, and he thought he'd died and gone to heaven. God, she kissed like an angel. Or was it a devil? While he took her mouth, he worked at that damned nightdress. At last. With a shiver of anticipation, he had it up and over her head.

The garment fell unnoticed to the floor. For some moments, he just looked at her. She had a figure to make a dead man come to life, and he was far from that state. He'd never felt more alive or aroused in his life. Slender legs, hips that curved to a slim waist. Very nice shoulders and arms, too. And those breasts, really too big for

35

her torso, so perfectly and spectacularly round he ached for a taste.

"You've a flawless body," he told her in a tone made husky by awe. "I've never seen a more perfect one." It was true. Absolutely true. "Where the hell did Devon find you?"

"At the bottom of the stairs," she said.

"What?"

Then she stretched her arms above her head with a motion of such abandoned sensuality that his mind went whirling in another direction entirely. "I'm going to owe him for this the rest of my damn life." He touched one of her breasts. A reverent caress of firm, plump flesh. Lord, he was a man in sensual paradise. He could hardly wait to discover how she felt when he was inside her. Pinning her wrists above her shoulders, he moved over her, letting his weight settle onto her. She did not adjust herself to him, no shifting of hips and legs to accommodate his man's body. But, their skin touched. Ought to be a crime for a woman to be so damnably soft.

He positioned himself between her thighs, making the correct adjustment on his own before driving into her not at all gently. Entering a woman for the first time always took his breath, for he made a particular point of seeing a woman ready for him and this one was readier than most. Because of his ardor and his belief in her experience, by the time he realized that the cause of her discomfort and his difficulty penetrating her was not clumsiness on his part or due to his size and her natural tightness, he was firmly in, having just taken her virginity. Impossible as it seemed, the woman was a virgin. Unmistakably he'd felt the barrier give way.

"I was promised it would not hurt," she said in a voice tense with pain. "I distinctly remember that, being told I would get through the night without pain."

"Hush, love." He nuzzled her ear, wondering if Devon

had thought he needed the practice. "It will soon be all right." A virgin, by God. His sex throbbed in her so irresistibly he forgave her the annoyance. He moved himself the slightest bit forward and inward. She felt good. Reaching down, he brushed the outside of her thigh. As he intended, she bent her knee, and he sank a little deeper in her. "Are you all right?"

"Mm." Not a word, a breath.

He drew partially out then slid slowly in and received the reward of a slow, thoughtful lifting of her hips toward him in that timeless welcome of female to male. Ruan went deeper into her. "My God," he said, catching his breath. "Are you floating still, my darling?" he said fiercely into her ear.

"Oh," she sighed. "Oh, that's wonderful."

"Your body is wonderful. Christ, I can feel myself inside you."

"All the way to my heart," she murmured.

After a bit, his head bent, touching her shoulder while he concentrated on being deep inside her, and she continued to send him mad with pleasure. His orgasm came upon him unawares. The one moment, he was enjoying her pliant body beneath him, at last in the more usual manner, and showing her how to move with him, the next, he was submerged in pleasure so deep he thought he would actually die if he didn't come in her. Now. This minute. He looked away, for the briefest moment distracted by light reflecting off a pair of spectacles on the bed table.

The flicker was caused, he dimly realized, by the fact that someone had opened the door. The distraction was just enough to take his mind off the prevention of conception and had the strange effect of increasing his awareness of being in her. Without warning he was insensible to anything but thrusting into her, the way her

37

passage clung to him, the unholy friction driving him absolutely mad. He howled as he felt his climax peak and shatter him into the most intense sexual experience of his life.

Chapter Five

"You're awake." Mary, on a chair by the bed, leaned forward to stroke Anne's hair from her forehead. "How are you, dearest?"

"I don't know which hurts more, my head or my ankle. Heavens but I feel muzzy-headed. Is it very late?"

"Nearly eleven. I was beginning to think you'd sleep 'til noon."

"Eleven. Good heavens." She frowned as bits and pieces of a dream flashed before her. Shockingly intimate. She could almost believe she'd kissed the duke of Cynssyr, for heaven's sake, that his mouth was by turns surprisingly gentle or thrillingly harsh, that he had told her about parts of his body, and that she had repeated the names to him. Words like *cock* and *ballocks* and even *arse*. Had she really had such an improper dream? Odd, how real it seemed. It was the laudanum, of course, that gave her such unusual dreams.

She sat up a little in bed, but stopped when she jarred

her ankle. Concerned because Mary looked suspiciously close to tears, she reached for her sister's hand. "You, Mary, look like you've not slept a wink. Did you sit with me all night?"

"I ought to have." Mary jumped up, turning her back to Anne. "There's a tray here. Tea. Indian, I think. Some toast and jelly. I'll help you dress. I've brought fresh clothes." She pulled a handkerchief from her pocket and blew her nose. "I do hope I've not got the catarrh that brought you low."

Suspecting what may have happened, Anne sighed. "Did Papa embarrass himself last night?"

Busy preparing the tea, Mary didn't turn around. The cup rattled on the saucer. "No more than usual." When she brought the tea and a slice of toast, Anne ate slowly. "We've been so worried about you. You took such an awful fall. Lucy feels just terrible. Shall I help you dress? I've brought a gown for you. And Bracebridge—" Mary drew in a sharp breath. "Bracebridge sent up a walking stick of his."

Having finished off the toast and tasted her tea, Anne moved to the edge of the bed. Pain shot through her ankle when she put weight on her foot. She leaned backward and hauled herself onto the mattress. The motion dislodged her pillow, but she managed to catch it. With a wry smile at the pillow, she asked, "Is Papa very annoyed still?"

"Papa?"

Anne stilled, for some reason transfixed by the pillow. A residual effect of the laudanum yet lingered, for the duke's face suddenly flashed before her, every detail etched in her brain. His eyes were closed as in sleep, and yet she knew he was vitally awake. Against the pillow, his rich brown hair made a stark contrast to the snowy linen. Strong white teeth showed in his slightly open mouth. The angle of her vision suggested she was

40

above him, looking down at him from a not very great distance.

"Christ, oh sweet Christ, don't make me come yet." The words echoed inside her head. She didn't just hear the husky voice. She felt that caressing, beseeching voice deep inside her wanting to burst out.

"Never mind Papa." Mary gave a strained smile.

Anne dropped the pillow, shaking her head, but the sensation remained, as if she were standing at cliff's edge gazing down.

Mary brushed a few crumbs from the mattress. "Benjamin wants a word with you."

"What about?"

To her astonishment, Mary burst into tears. "Oh, Anne."

"Mary, dear Mary, what is it?" She put an arm around her sister's shoulder.

"His grace arrived in the night, Anne."

Anne stroked Mary's shoulder, giving what comfort she could.

"The worst, the very worst has happened."

Though Anne's heart misgave her, she spoke calmly. "I know," she said, thinking of Emily. Her sweet, young beautiful Emily. "I know. If the duke is here, then indeed disaster has come. Help me dress. I shall deal with this, I promise you."

Mary stroked Anne's cheek. "You are brave, Anne. Braver than I could ever be."

Anne knocked softly on the door frame. As always, Aldreth was impeccably dressed, but this morning his cravat looked as though he'd tied it too tight and he'd just been trying to loosen it.

"What?" he barked. Then he saw her and softened. "Anne. Come in." His hand went to his neck. "Please."

She limped forward, leaning heavily on Devon's walk-

41

ing stick and feeling immediately something amiss. Distress swirled in the air, an all too familiar miasma. The air had turned oppressive like this on the day the magistrate told them how Lucy's husband had died. Something had happened. Indeed so, she knew the signs too well.

"Do sit." Remembering himself, Aldreth brought her a chair.

"What has happened?"

She saw him then. The other man. The duke. A taller man, long-legged and not quite as broad through the shoulders as Devon, stood at the far side of the room. Everything about him announced wealth and rank and consequence. He practically reeked of command, an animus of vitality even Anne found hard to resist. Up close, he was more perfect than her memory of him from Aldreth's wedding. Time had hardened the material from which he was sculpted. The granite core was no longer hinted at. 'Twas exposed for anyone to see. Anne found it suited him vastly.

Enveloped in a tenebrous silence, hands clasped tightly behind his back as if he were still a soldier, he was a breathtakingly handsome man. "Your grace," she said uncertainly. He looked at her and something tightened low in her belly. The impossible green of his eyes held her. A drowning, captivating color. Another fragmented memory flashed into her head. It wouldn't have been so bad except her body reacted to the image, sensations she knew she'd never had in her life. A mouth sliding along her throat, someone's breath hot on her skin. A hand on her breast, holding with a firm grip, another on her backside, bringing her forward. An amazingly clear and intense recollection of a ravenous desire that he not stop.

"A cushion for your ankle?" Aldreth's hands clenched and unclenched.

She looked from her brother-in-law to Cynssyr and back again. She didn't dare look at the duke for long because for some reason he appeared to be the catalyst for the disturbing feelings flitting through her. She brought the whole of her practical nature to bear on the problem at hand, which was whatever Cynssyr had done to her sister.

Feeling ashes in her mouth, she asked, "What has happened to Emily?" With a sharp look at the duke, she bit back rising anger. If he thought Emily could be discarded like all the others, he'd best think again.

"Nothing has happened to Emily," Aldreth said. He'd grabbed a silk-tasseled pillow from the sofa and now stood squeezing it.

"Papa, then?"

"Nothing."

"Lucy?" Keeping her eyes off Cynssyr proved difficult. The harder she tried, the more compelling the urge to look.

"Is fine."

"Mary? The children?"

"Quite well."

"Then what?"

Cynssyr said abruptly, "Do you recall anything of last night, Miss Sinclair?"

Slowly, Anne forced herself to look. The duke stood unmoving, a stark and beautiful man dressed in unrelieved subfusc but for white shirt and cravat. Mourning, it struck her. He lacked only a crepe band about his arm to complete the resemblance. The chest beneath that mourning black was broad and muscled. A scar ran white and jagged along his collarbone. Vividly, she saw his naked chest, could feel the heat of his skin. Impossible. How could she have another woman's memories? Anne Sinclair could not have seen the duke of Cynssyr without a stitch of clothing.

43

She was, she realized, staring at him as if he were some sort of oddity, a puzzle to be solved. Those pure green eyes stared back. Eyes of such haunting familiarity she started to shake. Eyes like gems. Even when she turned away, she felt his gaze on her. Impossible, what her memory suggested. Impossible. "Aldreth?"

"Do you?" Ben asked so gently she had to believe him in earnest. "Remember anything at all?"

"The doctor gave me laudanum." Disturbed and humiliated by the images that danced through her head then disappeared like mist into the air, she stared steadfastly to one side, not looking directly at either of them. "Dreams," she repeated loudly and very clearly. Her mind rejected what her disjointed memories suggested. "I remember dreams," she said calmly. "Nothing more."

"Not dreams, Anne." Staring hard at the cushion in his hands, Aldreth took a breath. "I am so dreadfully sorry." He hurled the pillow. It hit the sofa back and bounced to the floor.

"What do you mean, Aldreth?" But she knew. In her heart she knew the disaster was hers.

"I mean you must be married." He snatched up the pillow and after the briefest of moments tossed it gently onto the sofa. "You must be married to Cynssyr."

"Surely, you're jesting." He had to be. But the sick feeling in her stomach increased, and a tiny, unwelcome voice told her he wasn't.

"Good God, Anne. Do you think I'd be so cruel? I wish it were a prank. I wish it were."

She turned from Aldreth to Cynssyr but words failed to come. All she managed was a mute plea for denial.

Ruan stared at the woman. Dressed in a wholly unflattering gown, without any curls to frame her face, with the spectacles perched on her nose, he could yet see the woman who had made love to him without a shred of inhibition. A jolt of lust hit him when he remembered her mouth and the body that might have been made for his tastes. "I thought you were a whore."

"Damn you." Benjamin whirled and grabbed Ruan by the lapels, jerking hard enough to move him a step or two. "Damn you!" Ruan did nothing, made no attempt to defend himself. Under the circumstances, Ben was showing a great deal of restraint.

"Aldreth, please," the woman said. "I'd hoped for an honest answer. He has given one."

Ben released him with a slight push. "You let your prick do your thinking, that's what happened. If you hadn't been such a randy bastard you might have realized your mistake before it was too late. I warned you this would happen one day. I warned you!"

"Ben—"

"How the hell could you not recognize her? Damn you!"

"It's not the first time some female decided to avail herself of my bed without telling me beforehand. And not the first time Dev has sent me a whore, either. She wasn't wearing her blasted spectacles, which is all I would have known her by. I told you I couldn't remember her. I ask you, what was I to think? There she was in my bed with legs to here and tits like a man only dreams of getting his hands on and—" He stopped because he suddenly remembered the object of his vitriol was listening.

She looked a good deal like he felt; as if the world had suddenly disappeared from beneath her feet. Oh, indeed, Ben had warned him and here sat his future, a bespectacled spinster with eyes that couldn't even decide whether to be blue or gray.

"Anne," said Ben. "I am so sorry. As for you, Cynssyr, if you don't apologize, I'll beat you to a damn bloody pulp, so help me I will."

45

"Miss Sinclair. You have my profoundest apologies. I've no excuse. None whatever. I stand ready to make any and all possible amends."

The woman hadn't any choice but to marry him. He knew that. Ben knew that. But he was interested to see that she did not, for she had yet to show any sign of acceptance of her situation. Better women than she had schemed for just such an outcome as this and failed miserably. Might she actually choose disgrace over a duchy?

"What is your answer, Anne?"

She turned to Ben. "I don't remember," she said, as though by so saying she negated everything they'd told her. "Aldreth, I don't remember. I mean, I remember thinking how odd that Lord Ruin should—" Her hands gripped the chair arms so tightly her knuckles went white. "Then, I felt. . . ." She maintained, just barely, the tatters of her dignity when she saw the duke's complete dispassion. "You weren't here last night."

"I arrived about half past one this morning."

The moment became so deep it threatened to consume them all. She blinked once. Twice. Aldreth tugged at his collar. Cynssyr didn't move so much as a muscle.

Anne spoke into the grave-like stillness. "This can't have happened. It can't," she whispered. "Not to me." Her eyes darted to the duke and found him without any expression whatever. Not compassion or sorrow or anything at all, just a horrible stillness. A sob escaped her but she somehow stifled the impulse to cry. "Dear God." Her mouth had been on him, on his most private parts. "I can't have." She had actually said those words.

"Miss Sinclair," Cynssyr replied in a hateful, matter-of-fact tone. "Collect yourself, if you please."

Aldreth gave him a black glare and snapped, "Have you no pity, man? At least let her get over the shock."

"To what end?" he asked.

"I should have let Devon hit you."

"Devon?" said Anne, horrified. "Devon knows?"

"Hell, Anne. Everyone knows."

Ruan laughed. Amusement without mirth. Dark and quite ugly. Now that he'd recovered from his fit of lust, he remembered the consequences of his indulgence. "At this point, Miss Sinclair, the trick would be finding someone who did not." He caught a glimpse of pale eyes wide with disbelief before he deliberately turned to Ben. He would not feel sorry for her. He absolutely refused. Ben, unfortunately, had nothing to say.

Anne tried to take a deep breath and discovered she could not. "I don't know him, Aldreth. I don't even like him. How can we be married?"

"Naturally, the choice is yours," Cynssyr said.

"The hell it is," said Aldreth.

"You cannot force her to marriage, Ben." She stifled another sob. He wondered if she was going to faint. But, no, she caught her breath, and the tears he expected failed to materialize. She earned his grudging admiration for that. "If you refuse, Miss Sinclair, and later discover I have got you with child, you have only to apply to me and I will settle a sum of money upon you and the child. And," he added as an afterthought, "I will acknowledge it as mine."

She gave Ben a panicked look.

"The possibility exists." Ruan spoke as if he referred to the odds of rain spoiling a picnic, so as not to send her completely over the edge and into full-blown hysteria. Despite her age, despite his having had her lovely mouth on his manhood with him ready to scream he was that close to coming, despite everything they had done, she was so innocent such an outcome stunned her. He wondered if he had indeed made her pregnant.

"Oh, dear God," she whispered. "Dear God."

Ben tugged on his cravat. "An illegitimate child would destroy Cyn as much as it would you."

As for him, Ruan reflected, in such a case, he would spend the rest of his days rusticating far from anything or anyone who interested him. Savage gossip he didn't mind, but under the facts of this case, the loss of his good name was not recoverable, not to be overlooked by the people who mattered. She said nothing, just looked at him as if he were a hunter with his finger on the trigger and her a doe with nowhere to turn. Well. So. Rather apt, actually, he thought ruefully.

"Think of the consequences, Anne," Ben said. "Your father will turn you out, don't doubt that for a moment. You will live the rest of your life in shame and disgrace, and so would the child."

That gave Ruan a start. The child Ben so blithely spoke of would be his child. His flesh and blood. And the child's mother innocent of the shame.

"I do not want to marry him," she said in a sort of hopeless voice.

"Anne," Ben said sadly as he delivered what Cynssyr knew would be the killing blow. He knew Ben loved her too well not to use every weapon, however despicable, at his command. "You were unconscious when the two of you were discovered. If you do not marry Cynssyr, with what he has done, with so many witnesses to your incapacity when it happened, he is finished in society. Forever. He took your innocence." Ben closed his eyes.

What scenes his friend saw behind those tight-shut eyes Ruan knew only too well: him covering Anne, head back in a howl of almost ungodly pleasure; the blood when he rolled off her, baffled by the intrusion; Ben's sister-in-law sprawled on her back, insensible and naked for any and all to see.

Ben's eyes snapped open. Iron crept into his voice. "He will be a man known to have deliberately and maliciously—" He whipped up his hand, cutting off Ruan's attempted protest at his characterization of the event "—*deliberately* and with *malice*, ravished a drugged woman, a spinster of heretofore irreproachable reputation. An innocent formerly innocent of men."

Anne felt the noose tightening about her neck. She tried to swallow. For some time, she stared at her feet. At the bandage wrapped around her ankle. Lord Ruin. Married to Lord Ruin. All this time she'd been frantically searching for some way to stop him from marrying Emily, and here it was. On a silver platter. She smothered a very inappropriate urge to laugh.

"I have no illusions about my importance relative to you, your grace." At last, she looked up. "Under any other circumstance I'd be whisked away to the deep countryside never to be heard from again and this meeting would never have taken place."

"Quite true," he said.

Aldreth walked to her and stood hands on his hips. "I don't give a damn what happens to Cyn. He can rot in hell for all I care. It's you that matters. What will you have, Anne? Wretched poverty or wealth beyond imagining? Which will you choose?"

Ruan saw a flash of frustration. Unexpected spirit. "I don't want to choose."

"You'd risk a bastard when legitimacy is within your power? Think what that means. And not just for you, but for Emily and Lucy, and even Mary." She shook her head, but Ben gave no quarter. "You'd deny your child Cynssyr's birthright? Stop shaking your head like that."

"It isn't fair. Aldreth, please. It isn't fair."

"You haven't the right to ruin a child's life," Ben said in a low, harsh whisper. "You have no right to take that gamble."

49

She lifted her hands in a helpless gesture. "I know that. Aldreth, I know. But it isn't fair."

"To hell with what's fair, Anne."

"I don't want to marry him, and I daresay he doesn't care to marry me."

"What either of you want no longer matters."

She shivered, the proverbial goose walking over her grave, and looked at the two men. "I know. I know I haven't any choice."

Aldreth sat heavily on the sofa, head in his hands. "Thank God," he whispered. He lifted his head, looking at Anne. "The arrangements have been made. Cyn will marry you this afternoon. Right now, as a matter of fact."

"I am sure, Miss Sinclair," Ruan said with no conviction whatever, "we will get on splendidly."

Slowly, she rose, gripping the chair back for support. All she could think about was Devon. She had lost him again, and this time she would never get him back. "That hardly seems likely, sir."

Chapter Six

The ceremony took place in the chapel at Corth Abbey. Ruan had obtained a special license very early in the morning before his bride was awake and knew she was to be a bride. He fetched the parson on his way back. Every wedding had its tearful women, but in this case the tears were in no way joyous. Ruan's mother provided the ring, offering her own wedding band until such time as Ruan could replace it with one of his choosing. Anne's finger was slender, and the gold band slid on too easily. His wife.

Pretending this was a happy occasion took a toll on everyone. Devon, of course, glared murder. Thomas Sinclair glowered, which wasn't so different from his usual expression, and was drunk well before the clergyman stood to read the vows. Benjamin was uncharacteristically subdued, with none of his trademark good humor. A waterfall of tears came from Lucy, and from

Mary a sort of grim acceptance when the parson pronounced their sister a duchess.

Silent, Emily looked stunned, but not, Ruan thought, heartbroken to have lost him to her sister. Miss Cooke laughed nervously, and her mother shushed her too loudly. Clearly Miss Truitt understood too much and her brother too little. For some reason, Lady Prescott, whose single word had dashed the aspirations of many a social hopeful, appeared to have taken a liking to Anne. He assumed this was his mother's doing, for she would know that without Lady Prescott's approval, Anne had few prospects for success in London.

Wearing green satin that did not suit her coloring, the new duchess of Cynssyr stood to one side of the room, pinched and tired as she accepted congratulations. Someone had fashioned a bouquet of tea roses and pansies from Devon's greenhouse. She clutched them and said what was required of her. Nothing more. Pale as death, she smiled only when someone, usually his mother, reminded her she ought. At least her response to Lady Prescott was more than a nod.

He stood at her side feeling curiously protective of her. She had not wanted to marry him. Not by any means. But she had, and so saved him from the loss of the only occupation he had ever wanted for himself.

A celebratory luncheon was served afterward. The pile of cucumber sandwiches and a genoise Ruan was sure Cook had meant to serve for dessert but had hastily dressed up to look like a wedding cake went pretty much untouched. Ruan kept as much to himself as he could but Anne, surrounded by Fairchild cousins demanding to know how long she had been secretly in love, had no reputation to protect her from inquiries she could answer only with evasions or outright lies. Her eyes were mirrors of panic at bay. He saw her father take her aside, letting her hobble painfully to the far corner of the room. Well, at least he'd got her away from those women. Sinclair spoke to her urgently, but he could not tell from her expression what he might be saying to her. Perhaps congratulating her on her conquest, reminding his daughter of her success where every other woman had failed.

He went outside, taking a route that avoided any guests, and thought about his wife who did not like him. Oughtn't he feel as trapped as she looked? He didn't. He stood in the garden wondering why not and smoked three cheroots, one after the other until he felt vaguely sick, then headed inside for a few cucumber sandwiches to settle his stomach. Hoping to find the repast not yet cleared, he went into the drawing room. Devon, the only occupant, stood by the fireplace staring at something, the merest veneer of civility covering his black frown. The cucumber sandwiches remained. He made straight for them. He took a sandwich and ate it.

Devon turned as Ruan dispatched a second sandwich and took another. "Well, Dev, old man?" he said, throwing down the remainder of a third sandwich.

"I cannot fault you for being yourself."

"The answer to a different question."

"It's the best I can do." Silence stretched between them. Devon let out a breath. "Do not make her unhappy." His eyes reflected rare emotion. Anguish. "Swear it, and I'll forgive you anything. Even this. Swear. On whatever soul is left to you, swear you won't treat her like all the others."

There wasn't any question of his obligations in the matter. "I swear it," he said without hesitation. He'd have promised anything to salvage his friendship with Devon.

"You made a vow before God and now me," Devon said. "That ought to mean something. Even to you."

"I'm sorry."

53

A footman appeared in the doorway holding a salver on which there lay a single envelope. "Your grace."

"From Katie?" Devon asked as Ruan took the letter.

He ignored the provoking tone. The seal broke with a soft crack. Not from Katie, which he'd already surmised from the unscented paper. His secretary's precise hand covered half a sheet of paper. "From Hickenson." He scanned the contents and swore. "Hell. The ruddy great fools."

"What?"

"Some damn fool's accused Lord Buckley of assaulting all those women."

"Buckley? That's ridiculous."

"They want to hang him."

"No great loss if they do."

"Something's up. They're moving too quickly. Hell. The Judicial Committee is called to session. Castlereagh is after me for a meeting and Thrale means to stop the pensions bill." He gestured to the waiting footman. "No reply. Tell the duchess we're leaving immediately."

"Your grace." The footman bowed deeply.

Devon stopped the man with a formidable glare. "You can't take Anne to London," he told Ruan.

"Why not?"

"For God's sake, at least let the gossip die down!"

"So, I'll just let Buckley hang."

"Of course not."

"Then what the hell am I to do with her?"

"Send her to Satterfield."

"By herself?"

"It's close enough to town for you to at least maintain the fiction of a blissful marriage," he said wryly. "Besides, you should have this nonsense about Buckley stopped within the week."

Ruan thought of all the matters his precipitous marriage jeopardized by his absence from town. Parliament was in session, he had appeals to hear, a dozen petitions to review, not to mention the Privy Council. No, he could not afford to be away. "No more than a fortnight, anyway. All right then. Have my horse brought round. Henry and Dobkin are to accompany me."

The footman waited for Devon's nod before he bowed. "As you wish, your grace."

"What a bloody nuisance." Ruan stood tapping his thigh. So far, marriage was every bit as inconvenient as he'd dreaded. "I suppose I ought to tell her the news myself."

"Yes," Devon said. "I suppose you should."

Chapter Seven

Ruan found Anne in his room, surrounded by his trunks. Neatly packed by the ever efficient Dobkin, they stood stacked and ready to be sent on to Satterfield. Well, now to London instead. She stood at the window, clutching the damask curtain, head bowed to the darkly rich material. Though he could feel the tension in her, she wasn't crying. No flood of womanly tears. She simply stood there holding the curtain like a drowning man would a rope. "Miss Sinclair," he said curtly because he very much disliked tears and quite plainly there would soon be tears aplenty. Then he remembered she wasn't Miss Sinclair anymore. "Anne."

She slowly turned from the window. No sign of emotion marked her expression. He'd never thought of women as creatures capable of any particular control when under duress, but Anne's composure impressed him. Those damned spectacles of hers made it impossible to see her eyes and even begin to guess what she was thinking. She curtseyed. "Your grace." She wore her wedding gown, green satin old enough to have lost some of its sheen. He still disliked the color on her.

"Urgent business calls me to London," he said abruptly. "I leave within the hour."

"I understand." She pushed her spectacles toward the bridge of her nose in a gesture he thought was pure habit.

"I'm sending you to Satterfield." He walked part way in, and half-leaned, half-sat against the larger of his trunks, wondering why she reminded him of Devon. The moment he and Dev met, he knew they'd be friends. He felt that now, the same unspoken, unquestionable certainty of compatibility. Which made no sense at all, but there it was.

"Yes, of course," she said. Her breath caught, refusing to give voice to the grief he now saw in her eyes.

"What is it?" he asked.

"Nothing."

"Ask me no questions . . ."

"And I'll tell you no fibs," she concluded, a faint, wry smile curving her mouth.

"Then no fibs between us, Anne. I am your husband. You may tell me anything. Anything at all."

She lifted her hands, palms up. "I keep thinking I'm going to wake up and find it's all been an awful dream. Only I haven't."

"We must make the best of the hand fate dealt us."

"I am very good at making the best of things." She returned to the window, staring steadfastly out as if fascinated by the view. "But I want my life back the way it was."

"Put your regrets aside. They do no one any good. Least of all us." Late afternoon sun lit her hair, bringing out subtle shades in her braided bun that ranged from palest gold to silver-white. Not plain hair by any means.

Just a plain arrangement. As with her figure. Plain coverings hid the beauty of her form.

"Never, ever, has it mattered what I want. Not to anyone." She pressed her forehead to the window and spoke in soft, constricted words. "Always, I must accept someone else's decision about my life. First Papa. Then Aldreth. Now you. But I am not a puppet to be manipulated as if I don't matter." She clenched a fist to her throat. "I am not."

"What is it you want? Jewels? New gowns?" he teased, thinking of having his fingers threaded in masses of silver-gilt hair. "A box at the opera? A pretty mare and an elegant carriage round out the usual requests. I'm a generous man and think I can be a generous husband." Midnight blue would be her color, he thought. Yes. Dark and dramatic tones in counterpoint to her coloring. Rich silks and sensuous velvet, as soft and luxurious as her skin.

She turned again, perfectly composed. "I want to go home." They stood close enough that he could touch her. Which he did. A soft, gentle stroke along her cheek. For him, the contact was a lightning strike, a bolt of sensation that leapt from her and shot through him like fire through dry grass. She gasped, and that made him wonder if she'd felt it, too. "I don't want to feel," she whispered. "I want only to get through this without disaster."

"Without inconvenient feelings." He felt a bit at sea because he'd never in his life had so perfect an understanding of any woman. Women as a species, he understood quite well. But any woman in particular? Never. Until now. She was a stranger to him, but not a stranger.

"Exactly," she said.

"In that, Anne, we are in accord." He had the damnably persistent feeling he'd known her for years and could speak to her without dissembling. As if she were a long lost friend with whom he had only to become reacquainted. Again, not what he was used to when dealing with women.

She shook her head. "This cannot possibly succeed."

"I will take care of you. Never doubt that. You are my wife. I take care of what is mine."

"I am not yours." Her spectacles slipped downward, but she ignored them. Lashes black as night made her eyes seem paler than they actually were. Lord, how had he ever thought such eyes lacked spirit? Hers blazed with intelligence.

"Yes, you are." He smiled slightly. "You gave yourself to me when you signed your name on the marriage lines." Christ, her eyes were lovely.

"Papa said you would set me aside."

"So that's what he told you downstairs." He shook his head. "I wondered about that. What else did he say? Never mind. I don't want to know. Your father does not signify."

"He said you will divorce me. That I shall have to live abroad until Parliament grants you a divorce. Then—" She faltered just the tiniest bit. "Then, sir, why, I will to Bartley Green, and you'll never hear from me again."

"I'm afraid that's not possible."

"Bartley Green is my home. Why on earth could I not go back?"

"A divorce. A divorce is not possible."

"You can't mean you haven't the money or the influence."

"I have both, of course."

She lifted her palms. "Well, then."

"Divorce would ruin me. I'd not be welcome anywhere. More important, I'd have to step down from Parliament and the Privy Council. If I were prepared to do that, I would have done as you expected; settle on you a sum sufficient to keep you in the deep countryside never to be heard from again."

"Would that be so bad?"

He met her forthright gaze. "I have responsibilities I wish not to relinquish. There are inequities in England I would see eased, if not erased."

"You mean that, don't you?"

Her surprise pricked his pride. His voice took on a certain coldness. "So much so that there are but a limited set of circumstances under which I would consider so extreme a course as divorce."

"Such as?"

That sounded like a challenge, and he frowned. "The obvious ones. If I had reason to believe any child of yours was not mine, for example."

"Whose could it be, if not yours?"

Ruan felt her innocence like a blow. It kept him from telling her how many married women had come willingly to his bed, how many a woman he knew of who gave her husband another man's brat. Only one thing would be worse than that, and that was no brats at all. "Or if you denied me conjugal rights such that I would not have any heir from you."

He met her gaze head on and was shocked by how intensely aware her eyes were. Aware of him. Aware of his meaning. Aware of the consequences. A woman of parts, he thought, even though he'd never before applied the compliment to anyone of her gender.

"Under those circumstances, yes, I would divorce you. But none other." A rather long silence ensued. He gave up fighting the ridiculous feeling that they had years of history behind them and years more to come. "I'm sorry if you thought otherwise."

"You'll not set me aside. Child or no child?"

"No." He felt—What? Relief. Certainly that. But

while the distant future concerned her, he thought only of the present. At this moment, he had clear memories of making love to her. Memories she appeared not to share, at least not with any fondness. "Can you bring yourself to the marriage bed without disgust?" The thought of her lying inert while he did what he must appalled him.

"If I had a baby, I might not feel so alone. There would be at least some purpose to this mockery of a marriage."

Once again, her thoughts were on the future when what mattered was right now. "You will meet the purpose quite nicely, I should say." She did not look like a woman capable of sending a man insane with wanting. She was not beautiful or seductive, at least not as he'd formerly understood the words. But he knew what he'd felt. He wanted to feel it again. To have an orgasm that shattered him to oblivion and back.

"You make me sound like a prize broodmare."

He acknowledged that with a nod. "I'm certain you will be a good dam to my foals." That made her smile, and he grinned back. "Do you know, until now, I'd only thought of a wife and children in the abstract. As if I'd one day have some sent over from Regent Street. Boxed up nice and pretty to be taken out on holidays and the odd special occasion." He cocked his head. There wasn't a woman alive he couldn't charm if he put his mind to it. "Now that I have you, tomorrow wouldn't be too soon for children. I'd like several." Christ! Where the devil had that come from?

"So would I," she whispered.

"All the dukes of Cynssyr have been born in Cornwall." He took her hands in his, touching the wedding band on her left hand. "At Fargate Castle. It is where my heir will be born." He stood near enough to see the neat stitches in the collar of her gown and an area where

61

satin thread was meant to mimic fabric worn away from long use.

"I'm sure I shall like Cornwall," she said in a determined voice. He rather thought she'd have said the same of Hell. A regular solider, she was. "Is that where you're sending me now?"

"Satterfield is much nearer London than Cornwall." He gave a faint grin. "Did you think I meant to banish you to Cornwall?"

She shrugged in reply. Amenable on the outside she was, but inside, Ruan thought she was not so yielding. He fancied if he pushed hard enough he'd feel the bite of steel beneath.

"Under different circumstances, I might have banished us both, but I'm afraid I cannot stay away long enough for the gossip to die a natural death. So, it's Satterfield, not Fargate Castle. I'll be in town, though. I can't say if I'll be able to join you very often. I shall if I can get away. Christ," he sighed, brushing his fingers through his hair. "I've not been gone twenty-four hours, and I've nothing but disasters to be dealt with."

"Including me?"

He gave her a sharp look, but she smiled, and the tension in him eased. Without thinking what he was doing, his slid his hands up her arms, savoring the warm, silky flesh. "Believe me, you are the least of them." In the back of his mind, he puzzled over how at ease he felt with her. It once again struck him that he might have known her for years. Just like with Devon. An odd, but certainly not unwelcome realization. "So, my dear Anne, only when we have achieved our mutual goal will I banish you to Cornwall."

"Yes, sir."

"I am a practical man." She made a little sound of surprise when he cupped her elbows and pulled her close. He watched her, feeling his interest rising, stirred in a surprising degree. Really, she wasn't a bad-looking woman at all.

"That is not your reputation."

He kept her close. "And that is?"

"That you make women love you."

"I never in my life *made* a woman love me."

"And the moment they do, you are bored and must find another heart to break."

"If any broke their hearts over me, that's not my affair. Now, Anne, surely, there are more pleasant things at hand than whether I am bored by silly women. Do not look away." He put a finger under her chin and brought her head back to face him. "Your skin is soft. Like silk. Everywhere I touch you." He put action to his words and stroked her cheek. "I made love to you. Here. In this very room. *We* made love, make no mistake of that. You were—and are—so very passionate, and you made me feel like a bloody stallion." He ran a finger down her throat, feeling her racing pulse. "The experience was . . . shattering. Last night . . . Last night—I shan't ever forget it. I can't." He hadn't intended to make love to her, but now there wasn't anything he wanted more.

And she, sensing the change in him, went stiff. Her hands made fists at her sides, and she clenched her jaw.

Her perfume floated to him, light and pleasant, with a hint of citrus. "I will be gentle." But her body shook, and her eyes locked onto his, wide and panicked. Thinking to calm her, he kissed her. Tenderly. A lover's kiss. The sort of kiss he had used to great effect on dozens of other women: soft and just the least bit eager. With his fingers now buried in her hair, he tasted her, feeling the shape of her mouth under his and, regrettably, absolutely no indication that she knew what to do to help things along. "Have you never been kissed?" he asked, pulling back from her. "Well," he amended, remembering the likely answer to that. "Other than by me."

"No."

After a moment's consideration, he said, "I think I like that." He drew her closer. "Do you feel it?" he whispered. He could tell she had no idea what he was asking. "When I'm this near you, the very air thickens with desire. I could reach out and grab a handful, it's so thick, and all I can think of is kissing you and feeling your maddeningly, wondrously soft body against mine."

Anne's head came just under his chin which meant he had only to tip her chin to his to brush his lips over hers once again. As he did so, he slid a hand between them and lightly touched his thumb to the crest of her breast. She nearly jumped out of her skin. He summoned all his patience, which wasn't much but would have to be enough. His hand fell away from her. "I won't hurt you."

"I am sorry, I am sorry, I am sorry." She gasped for air and got very little. "I don't know you," she said with a soft hiccup. "I know you are my husband, but in fact, I don't know you at all. I thought you would send me away until the divorce. Now you're not, and you expect me to . . . do . . . do whatever it is you intend."

"You are my wife. And I must have an heir. We will do this often, you and I."

"I know," she whispered.

"Kiss me, Anne." A moment passed before he felt her lips press briefly against his. Catching the nape of her neck before she could back away, he kept her close. "Not like that. Like you did last night. Like this." And he lowered his mouth to hers and kissed her until her lips softened under his and she responded. He kissed her until he was completely taken away by the sweetness of her. Leaning back, he touched his fingertips to the side of her face. "You surely do kiss like an angel."

Behind them, a servant coughed. Her eyes darted

past him, but Ruan didn't look away. "Ignore that." The moment he heard the door discreetly close, he gathered handfuls of her skirts. "I adore women. I adore making love. I'm told I'm very good at it, but I think you're better because God knows I've never wanted a woman the way I want you." Slowly, he brought the material up and up and up until he touched the bare skin above her garter and was stepping forward to let his body trap the material between them. "I'm harder than a stone," he said as he opened his trousers to the imperative.

He knew he should save the more interesting variations of sexual congress for later, but he just couldn't. She set him on fire. He took her there, against the wall, sliding inside her, nearly undone by the soft exclamation that accompanied his entrance, lifting her thigh to open her for him, feeling her not as ready as he might have liked. "Christ, but you are perfect. You are so hot inside." Moving in her exposed the head of his sex to her depths and almost immediately, pleasure coiled in him, threatening to take over. "Oh, God." He couldn't believe the intensity of his every sensation. He'd not been abstinent long enough to feel everything so sharply, but he did.

She put her arms around him, palms touching his back and holding him close. Her earnest and thoroughly unschooled intent to please him did just that. He groaned into her ear, briefly caught the lobe between his teeth before sliding his mouth to the hollow at the base of her throat. Determined to make her want him the way he wanted her, to have her the way she'd been last night, he held her waist and then her upper thigh and for all of five minutes concentrated on her. The effort ended in failure because she made a small sound, an intake of breath, and then he was gliding in her more and more easily and his urgency built. Their hips found a rhythm and there wasn't anything left of him but desire. The siren call of release beckoned. "Oh, sweet Christ."

While he moved from orgasm to an otherworldly pleasure that threatened to turn him inside out, she whispered his name. He heard it low and soft, an undercurrent of tenderness beneath the roar of his climax. Cynssyr. *Cynssyr.* One moment, he clung to the edges of himself, in control, if just barely, of his pleasure, and the next he was gone. The sweetest death he'd ever felt in his life.

When he let her go afterward she began to slide to the floor as if only his body, his manhood, had held her up. Then, she gathered herself, adjusting the hem of her gown so that it once again fell to her ankles. She arranged her face with as much care as her skirt. No other description would do. The chin firmed, her back straightened and her mouth curved in a gentle smile. Her hands, though, trembled and gave away the emotion so carefully concealed.

He still didn't have his breath or his customary equilibrium back. The pleasure lingered, but he wanted it back at the same time he wondered if he would survive it if he felt it again. When he could stand no more of the silence or his inability to gather logical thought, he gave his attention to his clothes.

She tried to repair the damage to her hair, but he'd made a such mess of her braid she had to start over. With deft fingers she twined her hair into another braid. This was not at all what he had intended. She'd had little satisfaction from him. No release at all. At the very moment she ought to be wrapped around him in the aftermath of mutual enjoyment they were a thousand miles apart. Her face once again settled into mute amiability.

Appalled by the magnitude of his failure with her— Did he not pride himself on finesse?—he said, "Forgive me. I am not usually a clumsy or selfish lover." Lord almighty, he had taken her up against a wall like she was some practiced courtesan. "Next time, I assure you, I will see to your thorough satisfaction." He walked to her, standing behind her with his hands on her shoulders, deciding that a change of subject might help relieve the tension. "I'll place the notices when I arrive in town. Shall I send you copies?"

"I should like that."

"Devon is right. It's better that you stay at Satterfield. Let Mama and your family combat the gossips until I send for you."

"I don't want to go to London." She faced him, clutching the curtain in a fist. Pleading as much as he suspected she was capable of doing. It wasn't much. "Can I not stay there?"

"I'm not about to travel all the way to Satterfield whenever I want to make love to my wife." Which he now began to think might be often. "Besides, when the time comes, my duchess will be expected to entertain, so you must."

"I don't care for parties."

"There's no help for that."

"Than I shall." She shrugged. "I shall."

"I'm sorry," he lied.

"As am I." He wondered if she knew they weren't talking about the same thing at all.

Affairs in London kept him frantically busy, so he didn't get to Satterfield even once in the next three weeks. Even after settling matters with the Council and saving Buckley's fat neck—the man had been in Germany during three of the assaults of which he'd been accused, and dead drunk at Boodles during another, and further, he had in his possession uncollected vouchers from half of London and so no motive for ransom—there arose crisis after crisis that demanded his attention.

Urgent appeals required his presence at the Justice Courts, and since he was in town, he attended the sessions, which proved just as well because had he not, the pensions bill would surely have been killed. As it was he managed nothing better than to delay the vote.

In deference to his marriage, he accepted no invitations, made no calls and was, in general, unavailable and not at home. His butler, Merchant, was under strict orders to leave the knocker off the front door to keep up the appearance that he was staying at Satterfield with his bride. At Whitehall, he kept Hickenson on guard at his office door. He stayed away from his clubs, except for Brooks, because most political compromise took place at Brooks. When he rode in Hyde Park, he did it at an ungodly hour of the morning. Several times he thought about calling on his mistress, Katie, but never did.

Four weeks into life as a married man, Ruan decided it was time to call Anne to London. Having her in London seemed far more practical than enduring the bother of a journey to Satterfield. Besides, more than once he found himself thwarted by the distance when he discovered himself in a mood for her intimate company.

This particular evening the parliamentary sessions had extended to nearly three in the morning but as soon as he came home, he told Merchant to have Anne brought to London tomorrow. Quite satisfied with his decision, he went to his room. Dobkin glided from his dressing room, a fresh jacket in hand. Gratefully, he changed into clean clothes.

At his desk, he quickly sorted though the afternoon post. Of all the correspondence, only one item interested him. He was by now so used to watching for Anne's letters he no longer questioned why he so looked forward to one. Ignoring the stack of papers Hickenson had given him on his way out of Whitehall, he took her letter and sat down to read.

Though mostly she penned polite recitations of the weather, Anne had a knack for deft descriptions of village life and of his staff at Satterfield, so he expected her missive would amuse him. Which was why he wasn't at all prepared for what he read.

"Cynssyr," she wrote. "I believe I may be with child." He went to Satterfield himself.

Chapter Eight

Slowly, reluctantly, Anne surfaced from deep sleep. Exhaustion pulled at her, clouding her mind. She didn't know where she was or even who she was with. Someone shook her shoulder. "Anne, my dear." The voice, a man's rich and silky voice sent a thrill along her spine. Not her father, which it ought to have been. "We are home."

Cynssyr. Even before she fully recalled her situation, she felt a curiously physical recognition of the man. Electric. My God, the duke of Cynssyr was her husband, and she had been asleep, truly and deeply asleep with her head and hands on his lap. His warmth had seeped into her, she felt it still, could not shake it off. Her hands and cheek retained the feel of his thighs. A man's legs, firmly muscled, and yet she had been quite comfortable. She sat slowly, letting her aching body resign itself to wakefulness. Her stomach roiled. She saw him make a sharp motion in the direction of the open carriage window.

"Are you ill again?"

"I don't mean to be a nuisance." She swallowed hard and still felt sick. He handed her one of the biscuits they'd discovered fended off the worst of her nausea. Gratefully, she nibbled on it.

She tried not to be obvious about staring at him, but she couldn't help it. If the duke of Cynssyr had physical imperfections, she had no idea what they were. She had, during her time at Satterfield, read everything even remotely connected to the duke. *The Times*, *The Court Journal*, anything at all. Her husband, she soon learned, was brilliant. She had good reason to feel intimidated. And embarrassed to have dismissed him as a dilettante. He was anything but.

"Better?" he asked after a bit.

"Yes."

"Good." He opened the door. A footman held it open, gray periwig and tricorn hat misted with light rain. Cynssyr stepped down and, boots crunching on the gravel, turned with one of those carelessly melting smiles on his face. He held out a hand.

Something inside her reacted to that breath-robbing, heart-pounding smile so that for a moment she sat frozen on the seat, leaving her husband with his hand extended and the footman holding the door and both getting wetter by the moment. Down she stepped. Another footman hurried forward with an umbrella, ready to escort them inside. Cynssyr moved to her side as grooms led away the coach, and she saw for the first time her husband's home.

Cywrthorn melted into a backdrop of low gray sky. Somewhere above, a flag whipped in the breeze, but fog shrouded all but the bottom of the flagpole rising from a central dome. Mullioned windows on the lower floors would let in whatever light there was on such a chilly, rainy day. The upstairs windows were wide and sashed. Brass gleamed atop the wrought-iron fence enclosing the courtyard.

Behind her, the gate clanged shut with a hollow ring. Turning, she saw portions of the Cynssyr coat-of-arms fashioned on the black curves. Growling stone lions glared at the street from the gateposts and from the pillars flanking the stairs, holdovers from the days when the Bettencourt titles had not yet included the duke-dom.

Cynssyr took her hand and led her up the stairs. On cue, the massive front door opened. Two unsmiling footmen in powdered wigs, green frockcoats and knee breeches bowed at either side of the entrance. Above their heads loomed the lintel and the stone-carved crest of the ducal title. A butler as distinguished as he was severe inclined his head in a respectful bow. Cynssyr released her hand to peel off his gloves. She tried to keep her eyes off a monstrous stuffed tiger positioned so its snarling, glassy-eyed glare confronted anyone entering the house.

Her knees shook, they actually shook because any moment, any moment at all, someone would declare her a fraud. She was no duchess. But the footmen stood at military attention, eyes forward, necks stiff. If they had such thoughts, Anne couldn't tell. She didn't dare move from Cynssyr's side. His gaze shifted from his hands to her with a small sideways glance. The corner of his mouth curved just so. A flare of heat danced in the green eyes, unmistakable and intensely hot. When she looked away from him because if she didn't she wouldn't be able to breathe, she caught the butler staring. The man had no expression whatever, but he was staring. He was shocked by her, she felt, because she was not the beautiful princess they had been expecting of Cynssyr.

"Merchant." Ruan nodded as he led Anne over the threshold. Merchant, he saw, had been knocked back on his heels by the look he'd just given Anne. He'd been with the family for years, and Ruan was expert at reading his shades of expression. A layer of mist covered the coat and hat he handed to his stiffly standing butler.

"Castlereagh sent several messages." He deftly caught the gloves Ruan tossed him. "All urgent, your grace. There are two from Lord Eldon and one from Norfolk."

"No others?"

"None important, your grace. Lord Buckley sent a case of champagne."

"A good vintage, I trust."

"An excellent one."

"Tell Hickenson I will see him first thing tomorrow. Put the knocker on the door, but we are not at home tonight."

"Yes, sir." Merchant edged toward Anne, effortlessly positioning himself to take her pelisse. She slipped free of the garment and took several steps ahead.

Ruan spent a long moment appreciating the sight. The woman walked as sensuously as she smiled. He couldn't help thinking of her hips moving to meet his. Christ, he fairly itched to have his hands on her intimate places, the insides of her thighs, that lovely, ravishing backside. How had he gone a month without that? Since the end of the war, he'd not lasted a week without making love, and now he'd gone an entire month. Even after indulging himself at Satterfield, he felt eager as ever for his wife's bed.

Merchant cleared his throat. "May I offer the duchess felicitations on your marriage?"

"You may, thank you," Ruan said.

"Madam, your grace, best wishes for your future happiness."

"Thank you, Merchant." Her fawn gown did no great service to her appearance, Ruan thought. Recent developments had taken their toll on her appetite and the dress hung limply on her shoulders. He knew she must feel much like she looked: tired, slightly crumpled, and glad to be done with the traveling. The journey to London had exhausted her, that was clear from her shadowed eyes and her pale, pale skin. She'd slept like the dead until he'd awakened her.

Merchant bowed, his face devoid of emotion. And yet, Ruan thought as he watched Anne, she possessed an air of serenity that must impress his butler, who considered composure among the highest of accomplishments. The three then walked forward into the great hall in which upwards of a hundred servants waited to meet their new mistress. Merchant began the introductions.

Anne was glad of Cynssyr's presence. The gathered servants looked a stern bunch, wary and no doubt wondering just what sort of mistress the duke had brought home to them. "I am glad to meet you," she said when the introductions were over. She raised her voice so the kitchen maids and stableboys arranged in the back could hear her. "All of you." The corner of her mouth quirked as she glanced around. "And I thought Satterfield large. I shall certainly become lost in this house. If I shout, 'hullo,' I hope someone will come running to show me the way." The moment she finished, she wanted to take it all back. How provincial that sounded. Unsophisticated and every bit the rustic she was.

Cynssyr leaned close and softly said, "Well done, Anne." He gestured to Merchant. "The duchess and I will dine in her rooms tonight." That incandescent smile of his appeared, and Anne turned from the sight.

"Your grace," murmured the butler. Anne's heart

thudded, and she nearly missed Merchant's gesture. "This way, Madam Duchess, to your apartments."

Anne walked at Cynssyr's side. He kept a hand on the small of her back, and she felt the gentle pressure like sparks from a fire. They followed Merchant through the marbled great hall, the gleaming parquet upstairs, over thick wool carpets, past carved paneled walls, under high ceilings painted, molded or decorated with gold.

Gilt-framed dukes watched sternly from beneath powdered wigs, high lace collars and the gleam of polished armor. Crystal chandeliers that must take a team of maids an entire day to polish sparkled from cavernous parlors and withdrawing rooms just glimpsed as they passed. Lovely side tables bearing exquisite vases and marble niches containing figurines of alabaster, marble or bronze decorated the passageways. Rococo mirrors and oils painted by a master's hand hung from the walls. Through an arched doorway she saw a richer room yet, an entire wall carved with gold-tipped columns.

They stopped. She felt bereft when Cynssyr removed his hand from her waist. For a deathless moment, they stared at each other, oblivious to Merchant. Oblivious to anything but each other. Impulse had her brushing a lock of mahogany hair from his forehead, as if she'd known him for years and was entitled to a gesture of such intimacy.

He caught her hand in the moment before she would have snatched it back. Slowly, he brought her fingers to his lips. "Rest, Anne. I will join you later." And then he let go and strode briskly down the hall as if he couldn't wait to get away from her.

"Your apartments," Merchant said, opening the door for her.

"Thank you." Without Cynssyr so near and addling her wits, she recovered her sensible, practical nature. In she went, through a private sitting room done in ivory and gold. On the far side, an interior door led to a small withdrawing room. To the right of that was a dressing room in which young Tilly, who had agreed to leave Aldreth to take on the position of Anne's ladies maid, and another servant unpacked her trunks.

"To your left, your grace," said Merchant, opening doors, "the bathing room and watercloset." Directly forward was the bedroom, also decorated in gold on ivory and big enough to hold two of the largest rooms she had imagined would be hers. "To summon a servant." Merchant indicated a gold-embroidered pull. "Another by the bed." Silk gauze tented the bed, falling in delicate ivory curves from a spot high over the center of the bed. "Through here," said Merchant, opening another door, "the boudoir."

"Where does that door lead?" She pointed to the opposite side of the room, by now expecting a private library or office, perhaps.

He coughed. "To the duke's rooms, madam."

"Yes, of course." She felt herself go horribly red.

"Shall I send tea?"

"Thank you. Please do." Tired to the bone, she sank onto a chair covered in gold-striped ivory silk. She thought of Cynssyr and his ease in this huge house, walking past an army of servants as if it were nothing. To him, it was. None of this was out of the ordinary for him. He took no notice of the luxury and splendor. Simply put, he belonged here, and she could not image she would ever feel at home. And yet somehow she must find a way to manage. "Merchant?"

"Madam?" He stopped at the door, his expression as starched and friendly as his cravat.

"You must see I am hopelessly over my head with him."

Merchant's face did not change, but she would have sworn his eyes softened in some indefinable way. She grimaced. She needed something to nibble on, something to ease her stomach, only there was nothing at hand. The biscuits had been left behind in the carriage.

"I do not wish to embarrass him," she said. "Will you at least help me to master the household?"

"Madam." He bowed and when he straightened, his expression was once again impassive.

"Thank you." She clenched her teeth and willed the nausea to vanish. If she did not succeed, there was always the washbasin. An entire room distant. "One more thing."

"Madam."

"Perhaps it would be wise to have several basins on hand. In different rooms." She rose, her stomach now in full revolt. The washbasin would have to do.

"Basins, Madam?"

"I am not well. It is, I fear, unpredictable when I shall be ill." She did not hear Merchant depart, nor see his pleased and knowing smile. Later, when there came a soft tapping on the door between her room and the duke's, her heart beat just a little faster than it had been.

Chapter Nine

Ruan opened the door and found Anne standing midway between the door and her bed, a look of utter panic on her face. She wore another dreadful gown. Periwinkle muslin in a countrified style; no lace, only a wide grosgrain ribbon beneath her bosom and limp ruffles in two rows straining toward her chin. For all its lack of fashion, the color smoothed the pallor of her cheeks and lent her eyes a sultry lavender cast.

That her figure was an excellent one could not be entirely concealed. Could he think of nothing but taking her to bed? She'd removed her hat, he could see the bedraggled thing sitting on a side table, and run a comb through her hair. Her shoes lay sideways on the floor, near the fireplace. Though her bare feet sank into the carpet, he saw her stockings nowhere. From the rumpled state of the bed, she'd only recently been sleeping. Her disarray appealed to him enormously.

There was a knock on her door from the hallway side,

and she jumped like a quail to wing after the hunter's gunshot. "Our supper," he said, walking in. He raised his voice so as to be heard from the hall. "Enter."

The door opened, and they waited in silence while servants set linens, china and silverware on the table and placed trays of food on a side table. She watched, twisting her hands in the folds of her drab skirt. An intimate arrangement, true. The table was, after all, in full sight of her bed, but he was damned if he was going to cater to any niceness about such matters. One of the footmen opened a French Bordeaux smuggled in from Calais by way of Sweden and Cornwall during the height of the war.

"Thank you, we'll serve ourselves," he said when the plates and trays were arranged. The servants bowed or curtseyed as appropriate and vanished without a sound. He came around the table and pulled out a chair. Having helped her to sit, he found himself admiring the pale back of her neck while she did her best not to accidentally touch him. It was all he could do to stop himself from caressing that soft, white nape. He forced himself to release her chair and walk to the sideboard. "Shall I fetch you a plate?"

"Just bread, please."

"You should eat more." He uncovered a tureen, breathing in the scented steam. He felt unduly conscious of her sitting at the table, her back stiff, hands clenched on her lap. "Excellent. Jubert has sent up his lobster soup."

"Please, I can't." He knew it was early to be certain of her condition, but Ruan had no doubt she was with child. He knew with an absolute, terrifying and joyful certainty that he had made a child in her.

He covered the tureen. "Jelly or marmalade with your bread?"

"Nothing, if you please. Thank you," Anne said when

Cynssyr returned with the bread. He was a young man to have accomplished so much, and young for the weariness she sensed in him. Urbane, self-assured, and so far never once condescending, beyond all her expectations of him.

Dressed informally in trousers, soft boots and a white shirt without waistcoat or cravat, he still commanded attention. His hair fell straight and thick to just above his collar, the color of aged wood, a rich earthy brown and slightly mussed, as if he'd recently run his fingers through it. Relaxed though he was, she felt the vigor of him. No wonder women fell so hard for him. The man's ease with himself was just as attractive as his physical appearance.

After fetching his own plate and a bowl of steaming soup, he settled on a subject as bland as her meal. "There is the small matter of your wardrobe. Wine?"

She nodded. "My things arrived from Bartley Green last week."

"So I am told." He filled a crystal flute for her and another for himself. "Did not that damned papa of yours outfit you for London?"

"The expense wasn't necessary." She didn't get her wine halfway to her mouth when the smell sent her stomach into rebellion. From the label, she knew the wine was French and probably a better vintage than she'd ever had in her life. If things went on this way, she'd find herself subsisting on bread and biscuits. He seemed to understand the problem, for he whisked it away without comment.

"Most of what you have is remade from several seasons past. Expert work, I grant you, but the fashion for lace fichus is long gone." He grinned. "I expect you hoped to disguise your bosom with such a trick." Her cheeks turned pink, and pinker yet when he let his gaze wander below her chin. She felt like a favorite pastry about to be devoured. "Can't imagine how it could have worked, though it must have."

She evened her expression to cover the uneasiness inside. "I'm sure I don't know what you mean."

"What I mean is you'd have been hounded if any red-blooded man had noticed." He turned sideways on the chair. "One of them would have at least kissed you by reason of your magnificent bosom, alone. The best thing you've got," he continued as if discussing her bosom were no more interesting than the weather, "is that green frock you were married in."

"I wear that to church."

"You haven't even a ball gown." He applied himself to the tender slices of beef on his plate. "That I saw, anyway." His shoulders lifted, and Anne had the oddest sensation that she could actually feel muscle moving beneath the fine lawn of his shirt.

"To be sure, the list of my deficiencies is a long one," she said, smiling just a little.

His eyebrows lifted. "Be that as it may," he said with a slight smile, "the raw materials are there."

"I am an excellent seamstress. I'm sure I could have a ball gown made up before too long." They looked at one another, and quite suddenly Anne was out-of-breath.

He picked up fork and knife. "You're a pretty woman, Anne. You must know that. You've good bones. The spectacles disguise it, but you won't wear them in public. You've a figure, too."

"A figure."

"Yes." His eyes, partially hidden by the downsweep of his lashes gleamed in the light. "Indeed, yes. A figure that makes a man insane."

Anne stared, unaccustomed to finding herself so completely out of her depth. Control of the conversation seemed to have been wrested from her if, indeed, she'd ever had it. "What perfect rot. I am too tall by far."

"Not for me." He ate the last of his *haricot verts*.

She crumbled a bit of bread. "I'm not dainty like Emily, or elegant like Mary nor have I the drama of Lucy's coloring. I'm not anything men much admire."

"Your father tell you that?" He leaned toward her. "The truth, my dear," he said in a voice pitched deliberately low, "is that put you in a proper gown, something bright and low cut, and your sister Emily would have a few admirers the less."

She laughed because she didn't know what else to do. "You're mad, your grace. Quite mad, if you believe that." But she was surprised to feel pleased he'd even thought to flatter her.

Ruan dismissed her laughter with a wave. She'd eaten an entire slice of bread. The restorative effect on her cheered him as much, if not more, than it did her. "There." He pointed at her with his fork.

"What?"

"You're pretty when you smile. That dimple in your left cheek is most charming, I assure you."

Another bit of bread found its way into her hands and it, too, was shredded.

"I have made arrangements for a modiste to visit you tomorrow at three, if that does not discommode your schedule. My apologies. I ought to have seen to it while you were at Satterfield. But, what with one thing and another I never did."

"I do not as yet have a schedule."

"You soon will. I have mentioned your condition to the modiste in confidence. She will see to clothes to fit you later on." He leaned against his chair. Odd that he should feel so at ease with her when in fact he barely knew her. "Do you drink coffee? Jubert's coffee is unparalleled anywhere in England. I am happy to pour you some if you indulge."

"No, sir." The very thought made her stomach object.

"We'll get on well together, you and I." He took up his wine, inordinately pleased by her lack of pretension. He'd never given much thought to the sort of wife he ought to have. Anne, though not the woman he'd chosen, had qualities that suited him better than most women of his acquaintance, and that included her sister, Emily.

"I'm sure we shall."

"Oh, I am absolutely convinced it's true." He successfully resisted the impulse to reach across the table and take her chin in his hand, but the urge to know everything about her overcame him. "You are twenty-five, yes?"

"Twenty-six on the ides of May, sir."

"Women of more tender years are rather a trial. Silly creatures. Spoiled and self-absorbed." Why, he wondered, had he never considered an older bride? First saluting her with the glass, he drank. "Which you are not, thank the Lord."

"I do not think I am."

The more Ruan talked to her, the more he saw how incomplete was his picture of her. There was depth to her. Unexpected depth, for she'd certainly met his rather terrifying household with equanimity. Strength, too. Character. Complexity. She was, in many ways, more than a match for him. She would not bore him anytime soon. In fact, he couldn't imagine ever being bored by her. Not sexually or any other way. "The modiste will see you have a proper wardrobe. I will see you have the proper background before we begin entertaining." He put aside his wine. "I suspect you already know a good deal that will prove useful to me."

"Such as the price of beeswax or tallow candles?" She held back a smile, but he heard it in her voice. "Or how to make fine soap?"

"Don't be impertinent. No." His forthright gaze challenged her. Would she rise to his bait or shrink away? "I mean you know who votes the Opposition. Or who heads the Privy Council Judicial Committee."

"You, sir."

"Am I Tory or Whig?"

"Tory, sir."

"What of lord Thrale?"

"The Opposition."

"Aldreth?"

"A Whig, sir, but he's voted with you on occasion. As has Devon, but him less often than Aldreth."

"You," he said, "are a bluestocking."

"Sir, I am not."

"Anne, it's not an insult. I cannot long endure the company of a stupid woman."

"Have you often found yourself on the horns of such a dilemma?"

"Oh, ho!" With a laugh of approval, he slapped the tabletop. "That's bold of you to prove my point with such wit." He leaned against his chair, stretching out his long legs. "Dr. Carstairs will attend you tomorrow at one. Does your maid, what is her name? Tilly? Yes. Does Tilly know what we suspect?" She nodded. "She will attend while Dr. Carstairs examines you."

"Sir."

"There's to be a ball in your honor. In two weeks."

Instead of looking delighted, she became thoughtful. "Two weeks is hardly sufficient time to plan a ball." She shook her head. "No. That's too soon."

"But necessary. Mama and your sister, Mary, have done their part. Now we must play ours. Besides, if it's true you're in an interesting condition, we oughtn't wait too long."

"But, two weeks!"

"Merchant will assist you. Invitations should go out

tomorrow, although the day after will probably suffice. Consult with my secretary, Hickenson, regarding my schedule before you fix a date, but not beyond the end of next week. Mama can help you draw up the guest list. I will, naturally, provide you with several dozen names. Let's say, no more than a hundred or so to supper, three hundred for dancing? You will find Jubert's advice on the menu invaluable. We'll need to use the Confectioner's for so many guests."

She nodded, unfazed by the numbers. "Gunter's, I presume? Aldreth uses them, too."

"Yes," he said, nodding. He liked a woman who dealt so pragmatically with what life served up. She'd have coped if he'd said invite a thousand guests.

"A turtle dinner," she mused, tapping the table near her empty bread plate. "Twenty courses? Served à la Russe, but cooked à la Française."

"I knew I could rely on you." And, in point of fact, he *had* known. "Now, in the meantime, I might manage supper two or three times a week if I am not otherwise engaged with parliamentary matters. Restrict your own calls until after the ball. You may visit your sisters. Mama, of course."

Cynssyr left his chair for the fireplace. Anne watched the play of muscle beneath his shirt, took in the way his upper back narrowed to his hips as he bent to the hearth. A nervous flutter started in the pit of her stomach.

"Continue your acquaintance with Lady Prescott," he said as he stirred the coals then added more. "I encourage that, if it can be done."

"Yes, sir."

He replaced the andiron and repositioned the fire screen. Every movement had a fluid grace. No wasted motion, just power and efficiency. "I'm given to understand the Viscount Wilberfoss has offered for your sister,

Emily." Watching him, Anne tried to decide what gave Cynssyr his beauty. Not just the shape of his cheeks and jaw or the extraordinary eyes. Something else made him compelling. Something far more elemental made her stomach soar when she looked at him.

"Mary wrote me."

He faced her. "I do not wholly approve of Wilberfoss either, but there are advantages to the match."

"His support on the pensions bill would be invaluable." Women, she thought, probably admired and envied his hair and eyes, but she began to think they fell in love with his vitality.

"Yes," he said thoughtfully, walking toward her. She wondered why she'd ever thought him a dandy. There wasn't anything frivolous or inconsequential about the man. "It would. If I have Wilberfoss, at least a dozen others are bound to follow, and Castlereagh and his like be dashed." He stopped behind her chair.

Quite abruptly she recalled he was her husband. Not only did he expect intimacy between them, but she was required to oblige him, and she wasn't at all certain she was ready for the life before her.

"You are well-informed." His voice dropped a notch. "I do like that. I wish I'd brought you to town sooner." The light touch of his fingers on the back of her neck was like lightning, it prickled the skin and left nothing but heat in its wake. "You please me a great deal, Anne."

"Emily will not marry a man she does not love." Lord Ruin, she told herself, had never loved any woman. He seduced them. He made them fall in love with him, but he never felt a thing. But, maintaining that low opinion of him was more difficult by the moment. He wasn't frivolous. Nor vain, though he had every right to vanity. As for his intellectual gifts, she had foolhardily underestimated them.

86

"Mm." His hands slowly traced a line down her spine. "Your father has given his permission."

She steeled herself against the melting of her will. "Did you ever love Emily?"

"No."

By then, he was unfastening the back of her gown and coherent thought ceased.

Chapter Ten

"You're a clever girl," the dowager duchess of Cynssyr said to Anne. A helmet of gray hair surrounded a face of stern lines and steely eyes pinned Anne to her chair. On her lap, she cradled Caesar, a dog about the size and shape of a modest teapot. His chocolate eyes constantly followed his mistress's hand in hope of a treat.

"I'd be pleased if you thought so." Anne pretended to drink her tea, but held her breath when the cup came near. The smell of tea, like wine and an ever-growing list of food and drink, threatened to turn her stomach inside out.

The duchess stared down her nose and watched Anne through half-lidded eyes. "Yes. A very clever girl. I thought so the moment I heard your sister, Mary, was to wed Aldreth. I was convinced of it when my son told me of your sister, Emily."

"More tea?" said Anne. By the far wall a footman stood solid as an oak, his green livery clashing with the lilac wallpaper. She thought he must get quite tired of standing.

The duchess extended her cup, and Anne dutifully poured. Caesar lifted his head, sniffing eagerly. "Whatever he thinks of you," the duchess said, stroking the dog with her free hand, "and I don't imagine it's much, he will stand by you."

"Three lumps, am I right? Here are the best."

The duchess stirred her tea into a whirlpool. "Young women these days have their heads stuffed full of nonsense. Their fathers do not discipline them and their mothers daren't. In consequence, they make bad marriages and even worse wives."

"Do have this last cake."

Her lips thinned, and Caesar, too, seemed to stare at Anne with a jaundiced eye. "A marriage of opposites so seldom succeeds." She fed a bit of cake to the dog before her attention landed once again on Anne. "I wonder, will my son's?"

Anne lifted her cup and smiled. "Does it often rain in London this time of year?"

"The boy's been between the sheets with half the ladies of society." Much to Caesar's disappointment, the duchess ate the last bite of cake. "Ah. Jubert. A genius." Her eyes closed while she savored the taste, then she laid down her fork. "Have you enough starch in you to manage my son?"

"I have no wish to manage him."

Caesar yipped, and the duchess cradled him to her chest, stroking his chin. "There, there. Such a willful boy," she said, addressing the dog more than Anne, so that for a moment she wasn't entirely sure if the duchess meant her son or the dog. "And proud."

"Pride is not one of Cynssyr's vices."

"He's a handsome devil who knows too well how women admire him. But, he was born to greatness and

God has seen fit to make him capable of achieving it."

"Some would say he has."

"He has not been happy since he came home from the fighting. He changed after that, and though war made a man of him, I wish he had changed less." She bent her head to the little dog, and Caesar stretched up his nose toward her. "The joy went out of him." A moment later, the iron eyes once more studied her. "I have long prayed he would find solace in marriage. Well. Perhaps he may find it in his children."

"I hope, your grace, that will be true for us both."

"What kind of woman are you, I wonder. Have you malice toward my son? Can you make him happy?"

"My tears are shed, Duchess. As for his happiness, that is in his control, not mine."

"And your happiness?"

"Is my own affair."

The duchess rose, tucking Caesar into the crook of her elbow. "I take my leave of you. The hour grows late and you must be at your best tonight."

Anne returned to her room after the duchess left, and though the ball was hours away, she found Tilly beside herself with anxiety. In her bath, with Tilly's strong fingers working on her scalp, Anne could not stop thinking of the duchess. Could a mother feel anything but disappointment for a beloved son so unsuitably married? How sad, she thought, to have such lofty, loving hopes bitterly dashed. And yet, the duchess had made no personal attacks. Who could blame a mother for wanting her son's happiness? She wondered if happiness was now beyond both their reach.

The delicate scent Ruan had come to associate with Anne wafted to him when he entered to a blizzard of petticoats, chemises and stockings. Four silk shawls draped various surfaces. No fewer than five pairs of slippers were scattered about the floor. He plucked a lacy garter off the mantle and dropped it on a chair heaped with frilly drawers. He rescued a sheer white stocking from the fireplace grate and deposited it with its mate on an ottoman. Well did he recognize the results of a woman preparing for an important event.

His wife appeared surprisingly calm. Tilly, however, hovered like a robin over its nest, picking up a stocking and dropping it somewhere else, smoothing the lace on Anne's sleeve, adjusting the tiny yellow roses atop her head or realigning the ribbon wound through her hair.

Madame Louise had earned her steep fee, which pleased him both financially and personally. Anne's ballgown fit like a dream. His dream, anyway. Deliberately, he slid his gaze over her, letting her and even the maid—he didn't care what Tilly thought, though he should have—see his admiration. The gown was not anywhere near as low as it might have been, but it was low enough to more than hint at her shape.

"Cynssyr," Anne said when her husband stood there fingering the clasp of the box he held. Closely tailored clothes suited his leanness. Nothing so tight as to be uncomfortable, but there wasn't any doubt of his superb condition, either. Time in the saddle shaped the muscles of his thighs and taking a hand at the ribbons of a coach-and-four gave his shoulders and arms breadth. He wore no hat and in the light cast by the lamps, his hair was an intensely deep brown. She'd begun to think she'd never get used to him. He didn't wait for an invitation to sit, he just cleared a chair of a petticoat that had not passed muster and sat as if he had every right. Well. In fact, he had.

"There was another incident."

"Oh, no." Though he spoke in a singularly uninflected tone, she understood how deeply the violence affected him. Personally, even. Her heart went out to him.

Truly. But she knew better than to let him see the weakness.

"This afternoon. At Marylebone Gardens." He settled himself on the chair. "However, this time, they did not succeed."

Tonight his eyes were greener than ever. His coat was the deep red of port wine, his shirtfront and cravat snowy white. "Thank goodness." He was like a cat, sleek and even motionless, wholly confident of his strength. "How did it happen?"

"She believed she was to meet an unknown admirer. A *gentleman,* though I hesitate even to use the word, who these last two weeks has been sending her poems declaiming her beauty and his adoration."

"But it must be a gentleman."

His eyes snapped to hers. "No gentleman would do such a thing."

"Who else could it be but someone who passes for a gentleman?"

"God help us if you're right. The girl jumped from the carriage and broke her head in the fall. I called on the girl's family, but she was not conscious. In any event, her father would have refused my request to interview her." One hand curled into a tight fist. "They'd already found the letters and burned them all. Every blessed one."

"Will she be all right?"

"Uncertain. They're preparing to leave town the moment her condition permits. She saw them. The girl saw them, and she's as lost to me as Miss Dancy, whom even Devon cannot find. Never mind that this scoundrel will surely go on to another innocent woman."

"You will stop him. I know you will."

Cynssyr shuddered, and slowly his fingers unfurled. "Forgive me, Anne, for broaching so distasteful a subject." He drew a deep breath and like that, all the emotion she'd sensed was smothered. "On this night in particular." His glance took her in from head to toe. The man who stole hearts as easily as a thief stole a purse vanished in his cold, assessing gaze.

"Mary helped choose my gown," Anne blurted out. From some impulse she didn't fully understand and could not explain to Mary, she'd tried to match her gown to Cynssyr's eyes. The pure, piercing green of his eyes wasn't easily duplicated.

"She has excellent taste," he said, bending one leg so that his ankle rested across his knee. He popped open the box's clasp and immediately closed it. He'd not meant to tell her about the girl, but the words had just come out. However inappropriate it was to tell a woman his affairs, he now felt the better for his indiscretion. Even as he resolved never to fail again to keep his counsel, he wondered if he could. Damn, but he must constantly remind himself she was only a woman.

She glanced at him, swept over the box in his hand without really seeing it. "What of Bow Street?" she said. He was like the devil, she decided, luring souls to their eternal doom. Luring her. "Would not a Runner be of help?"

"So far they've turned up nothing. Perhaps this time they'll have more success. I leave that business to Devon, for he's contacts there I haven't." Her spectacles perched about halfway down her nose, low enough for him to see the jet black lashes. Eyes a man could watch forever and never tire of the sight. They changed constantly; on a whim, for the color of her gown, for deep emotion such as she held back from him in the marriage bed and elsewhere. Tonight, the color was more gray than blue. Slate with a hint of sky. "Enough of this unpleasant conversation, Anne."

"I'd like to help." She knew his body now, the shape, the feel, even the taste. The times when his needs forced him to her bed, and he stroked her and called out her name, when his mouth and hands and body took hers, why, he almost convinced her she was beautiful. When he was inside her, she felt with such richness, such completeness, that it took all her control not to simply hand him her soul and her heart with it. She wanted to cry that a man who did not want her should make her feel like that. She needed a good deal of control around him. Perhaps more than she possessed.

He lifted his hands. "How?"

"Perhaps you need a woman's point of view."

"This is men's business." He rested a hand on the box. "Though if any woman could help, it would be you."

"Then let me."

"I am forever telling you things I ought not."

"You take on too much, sir." She touched her chest, but she meant him. "I would ease the burden on you, if only I could."

"Do not attempt to manage me." He hated himself for snapping at her. "I despise women who think I can be managed." Her eyes filled with hurt and then shuttered. Hell, he thought. He was a brute, and damn himself for that.

"I am not managing at all, your grace." She walked to her dressing table where she gathered up a ribbon and stood twining it in her hands. After a bit, she threw it down. "Not a bit, sir."

"Yes, you are. Come now, Anne, and tell me you forgive me."

She faced him. "Of course."

"You manage me quite well, the deuce take it." He eyed her. A pair of dainty satin slippers, green like her gown, covered her feet and put a deadly feminine curve to as fine a pair of ankles as he'd ever seen. He felt the stirring of arousal. "Damnation, but you do manage me."

"Green, I know you dislike it, sir, but it matches your eyes almost exactly." She squeezed a handful of her skirt. "Madame Louise warned me, but I thought—" She touched her skirt, facing him again. "I never had so fine a gown in all my life. I feel out of place wearing it, and I thought, what difference will it make if it's green or orange or any color in the world?"

"You are exquisite." And wasn't that the bloody truth? "Venus incarnate. I can't take my eyes off you." Most particularly, off the swell of her bosom, that creamy, rounded flesh he so adored. Or was it the tiny waist? He ended up staring at Anne's reflection since she'd turned to let Tilly adjust a petticoat. He sure as satan in hell did not understand why she affected him this way. But she did.

"Find the satin, Tilly," she said. "The pink."

"The gown you have on is perfect," he said.

"You once said yourself green is not my color."

"No." His wife wasn't beautiful. He knew she was not, but his nether parts didn't seem to notice. They never did. Once, the arrangement of a woman's features had been the sole criterion by which he judged her beauty. But more and more Anne pleased him better than any beauty he'd ever known. Her physical shortcomings were numerous. Her mouth a bit too wide. Her face not a perfect oval. Nose ordinary, chin ordinary. And yet he couldn't remember wanting even Katie as badly as this. Hell, his dainty, fragile beauty of a mistress had never intrigued him like this. Much as he appreciated Katie as a woman, it was pure and simple the case that he *liked* Anne. He liked her, and he wanted her to like him in turn. Unsettling. A bit. He'd never cared before whether a woman liked him. What mattered, if he wanted her, was whether she could be made to want him, too. Invariably the answer had been yes.

Anne faced him serene as if she were going for a walk to the corner and back. He was beginning to hate that amiable expression. He much preferred Anne when she had less control of her emotions. "Changing won't take long."

"No."

"But—"

"I forbid it." He stood. God, he wanted to touch her, to have her melting in his arms as she had at Corth Abbey. Though she hadn't Emily's exquisite features, nor Lucy's ethereal beauty, nor Mary's outright charm, she beguiled all the same, especially when that uncertain smile hovered around her lips. "You're lovely," he murmured, holding out a hand for her to take while he started her in a slow turn. "Quite lovely."

"Acceptable, anyway. And I thank you for your compliments."

"I was wrong to insist green was not your color."

The woman had no idea what a rarity she'd just heard from him. The duke of Cynssyr admitting he was wrong. All she did was nod, as if she did not entirely trust his honesty with her. "Thank you, sir." He did not release her hand, but let her fingers slowly slip from his of her accord.

"Always so formal. Please, not 'sir.' Cynssyr would suit me. Cyn, if you like. Better yet, Ruan."

She pushed her spectacles upward. "Nerves. You unsettle my nerves," she said.

"You needn't be anxious, Anne." He really couldn't keep his hands off her.

"I can't help it."

"I dislike your formality." Deliberately, he kept a stern expression, knowing she would take the remark to heart and would be that much nearer to the Anne beneath the pleasant exterior. When she had, he took a step nearer. "Your formality keeps us at arm's length when I want not even a hairbreadth between us."

She guessed his intentions for she backed away, saying, "Tilly, you may go."

Whether the maid saw them mattered not a whit to him. The door wasn't closed before he had his arms around her waist to pull her close. Anne's face was but inches from his, long black lashes making her eyes impossibly clear by the contrast, and that mouth enticing him to bold action. "I have no control whatever," he complained.

He bent his head. His mouth touched hers softly, a whisper of a kiss that came a breath away from flaming out of control. The air turned thick, combustible almost. He was gunpowder, she the lit match. He brushed his lips over her bosom. Without conscious thought, he cupped her breast. The hunger he always experienced with her rose up, sharp and demanding he sate himself. Sliding his fingers into her hair, he pulled back, exposing her throat to his searching mouth. Her arms gripped his shoulders for balance.

Frantic to have her breasts under his hands and in his mouth, he unfastened her gown to her waist, unlaced her corset and generally made a mess of her chemise. He knew her breasts were tender, and it was pure deviltry that delighted in her moans and her back arching toward him as he slid his tongue across her nipples.

"Lift your gown," he growled, not at all certain she would comply. He sank to his knees, leaning back and using one hand to unfasten his trousers. When he looked up, Anne stood above him, her upper gown in complete disarray, holding her skirts above her knees. She stood that way because he'd told her to, not because she understood the first thing about the power she had over him. It made the moment all the more arousing.

He put his hands on the back of her knees and pulled

forward. She sank down, they adjusted and met unerringly. He went deep inside her, stroking hard, sliding in her heat. Holding her was like holding heat itself. Christ, but she knew what to do. Every atom of his being balanced on the point of orgasm. Release danced just out of reach, unendurable and unbearable.

"Now. God, now. Anne." He lost himself completely, became wholly absorbed by the demand for release. "Now or I'll die." She did something with her hips and pleasure roared through him.

When he gathered himself enough to open his eyes, he saw he'd undone a good deal of Tilly's efforts. "Christ, woman." He sat forward and kissed her mouth, a hard, brief kiss. "What you do to me is beyond comprehension." One deep breath, and he was as under control as he could be around her. His own clothes were easily restored. They set themselves to repairing the damage to her hair and dress. No one but him would know her chemise was damp from his mouth. One stocking was ruined, but he found a replacement. Fortunately, he knew his way around hooks and hairpins and before long, she was once again presentable.

He remembered the box he'd brought with him and that now lay somewhere on the floor. The bloody reason for being here. Under the damn ottoman. He retrieved the box. "My wedding gift to you." He handed it to her without the fine words he'd planned. "A bit tardy, perhaps, but here it is at last. Open it."

She did.

The diamonds glittered with that inner fire so peculiar to the finest gems. Tiara, necklace, bracelets, three rings, ear drops, two sets, long and short. There were plenty of gems in the vault, but Anne must have something given by him, not one of his ancestors. He was, for some unfathomable reason, a bit on edge. Fancy that. Presenting a woman with a generous gift was something with which he had a great deal of experience. But he wanted to please her rather than impress her, and he had no guarantee of that. Anne fell far outside his experience of women.

Time passed with exquisite slowness.

About now, Katie would be beside herself with gratitude. An excited squeal, a delighted clap of the hands. A passionate kiss as a prelude to other displays of appreciation. Anne uttered no squeal of excitement. No delighted clap of the hands. No passionate kiss. He ought to have known she would not like gems in such abundance. Katie, or any of his past mistresses, would have loved them, but if he knew anything at all about the woman to whom he was married, it was that her tastes did not tend to the extravagant.

"If you do not like them, there are other jewels," he said. "There's just time to choose something else. The emeralds, if I am not mistaken, will go well with your gown." His father had ordered the emeralds reset to a more modern sensibility, which meant the settings were twenty years out of fashion, but the stones were close to flawless.

"Emeralds?" Slowly, she lifted her eyes to him. "But, your eyes are peridot. Not emerald."

He reached for the box. Her face became a perfect picture of misery when he took the velvet case from her. She started to speak, faltered when he lifted one eyebrow, then said with complete sincerity, "They take my breath, Cynssyr."

"As you have taken mine."

"Will you help me?"

He lifted the tiara from the box, finding pins to secure the piece on her head. Then, he scooped up the necklace and fastened it about her neck. The lowermost stone hung barely half an inch from the swell of her chest. She turned when he finished and let him fasten the earrings, too, the long ones. "The queen herself could not look more regal," he told her, meaning every word, too.

She ran her fingers over the necklace. "I never dreamed of anything so beautiful." She went on tiptoe and kissed his cheek. A peck. A dutiful peck. Progress. A week ago, she wouldn't have dared even that much. "Thank you, sir. Cynssyr." Her hand slipped down and touched his fingers.

He reached for her spectacles and removed them. "Come, my dear. London awaits."

Chapter Eleven

Anne's first experience of her husband's mastery of all things social did little to soothe her nerves. Just standing in the receiving line Cynssyr was a sun around whom others hoped to orbit, and she was simply no match for his brilliance. The sheer number of people whose names he knew overwhelmed her. And he always knew some personal detail about each one, some bit of information that made each feel welcome. A grandson inquired after, a favorite dance promised, a passion for painted plates recalled. All manner of looks came her way, from frankly curious to disdainful, but very few were friendly. By the time she and Cynssyr left the great hall for the dining room, her hand felt wrung out and her foot had gone to sleep.

She knew she'd not made much of an impression, perhaps even so small an impression as to constitute a bad one, but dinner, thankfully, was a complete success. Gleaming candelabra and gold-rimmed crystal amid arrangements of white roses and Cynssyr's best porcelain service elicited more than a few admiring nods.

Footmen worked with military precision bringing in one course as another was cleared. The wine never ran out and the food, large unstinting portions, was sublimely prepared. She bowed her head and gave a prayer of gratitude for Jubert's genius in carrying out the menu. Best of all, someone had contrived to see that the blandest of victuals were constantly at her side. Bread, clear consume, buttered potatoes so that she could easily conceal her tepid appetite.

Aldreth sat on her right; to her left was none other than the marquess of Thrale. Lady Prescott made a friendly neighbor and the countess of Vale, another. Devon sat close enough to frequently join in so that Anne, who had dreaded having to make conversation with strangers, was quickly at ease. Thrale she particularly liked for he took pity on her schoolgirl French and replied in English often enough that she did not seem hopelessly the country miss. And once the marquess discovered she had a more than passing knowledge of music, they gave up French entirely.

At the opposite end of the table, Cynssyr held court with the expected elan. Once or twice she caught him watching her with an impenetrable gaze. Honestly, she was always aware of him on some level, but on one occasion when their eyes met, he, leaning against his chair, lifted a knuckle and absently rubbed it across his lower lip. He might as well have been touching her, for there she was once again standing at cliff's edge looking down. Her stomach fell at Cynssyr's intimate caress. Her breath simply stopped. The noise dampened, the clatter of silver against china ceased. Then Lady Prescott, who sat at Cynssyr's right, rapped him on the arm and all was as it had been. The moment shook her to her toes. She managed to finish the meal without further incident, and even, so she fancied, to improve the impression she made.

Ruan danced the opening minuet with Anne and from then on, he lost his wife to a crowd of men eager to officially meet Lord Ruin's wife. The marquess of Thrale, who had practically usurped her at supper; William Fenney; Portland; Brenley Cooke; Julian Durling; Sather; Kinross, the old goat; and too many others to name.

His mother found him during one of his rare moments of solitude. "You are brooding, Cyn," she said.

"I am not." But he was. He was brooding because he'd had Anne to himself these past two weeks and sharing her was not much to his liking. His mother, however, mistook the cause of his black silence.

"So far she's done well."

He watched Anne dancing with Benjamin. "A bit too subdued in the receiving line," he replied blandly.

"I like her. She will do you good."

"Agreed." He gave her a wry smile. "I've surprised you. Well, it surprises me, too. The question, Mama, is whether I shall do her any good."

His mother gave him a considering look. "She dances better than I hoped."

"Yes." The pleasure she took in dancing was seductive, quite apart from the other qualities he found appealing in her. As he stood there with his mother, a rousing jig followed a reel, and there Anne was, in the thick of it, a smiling, laughing goddess. Rhythmically stomping feet and clapping hands nearly drowned out the pipes and fiddles. People joyfully made their own music. Anne shook her head so that the light caught the diamonds and scattered a halo of rainbow light. She was his, and he liked that state of affairs. Only his. Just watching her he wanted to take her off and make love to her.

"She's been noticed," his mother remarked.

"Yes," he replied. Indeed, the men noticed her. Before his very eyes his wife transformed herself from old-maid-forced-into-marriage to the woman Cynssyr had been lucky enough to catch. He decided, at last, to be amused by the notion.

"Well, my dear boy," she said, sounding amused, too. "I think I'll rest my tired bones."

"Mm," he said. Anne carried his child, he thought. Her first concern must be her health, not dancing with that lecher Cyril Leander, who only wanted one thing from any woman between the ages of twenty and forty. "Excuse me, Mama."

He strode toward Anne and she, as if she sensed his presence, turned and broke into a smile of unreserved joy.

"Well, well, Cyn," someone said. There were other greetings from men he'd gambled with, drank with. Men he'd fought with, too. They surrounded Anne like bees around a hive. He ignored them all. All he noticed was her delight that he was with her. Pleasure on his account. He reached for her hand. Really, she was too sweet for the likes of him. He'd probably go straight to hell for being so fiercely unrepentant for what he'd done at Corth Abbey.

"Cynssyr." She smiled again, and for a moment he thought his heart would never start beating again. "I'm having such a grand time."

"The duchess," he heard someone say, "dances as if on air."

"Why, thank you, my lord."

Ruan opened his mouth to demand that she rest.

"Do you hear?" she said, breathless. "Oh, it's wicked, isn't it?" Her eyes lit mischievously. "Cynssyr, you didn't order this did you? What will people say? A waltz."

In fact, he had ordered the waltz, and he was about to tell her so when Fenrother interrupted. "Dance with her, your grace."

"Go on, Cyn."

"Can't deny her," said a baron he remembered as an even harder gambler than he was a drinker.

"Hear, hear."

He held out his hands, and she floated into his arms, her body supple and responsive. Usually, dancing bored him, a necessary evil visited upon men who craved the intimate company of women. This was different. Music and Anne flowed through him, becoming a part of him. This, surely, was what dancing should be. Effortless. Captivating. Bewitching. A world in which only two people existed. He didn't want ever to let her go.

A final cord echoed, fading into the background of conversation. In the beat before the orchestra began the next dance someone could have fired a pistol, and Ruan wouldn't have noticed. The blue-gray eyes of his wife held him fast, the wistful smile on her face enthralled him, struck him dead-on, a shot straight to the heart.

Until now, this very moment, he'd not understood how a man could make a fool of himself over a woman. The abyss loomed deep and ominous. What next for him but flowers and insipid poetry and him tripping happily to his fate? She'd changed him, Anne had, and he was not at all certain he liked the result. His old life had been perfectly comfortable, with Katie never causing him a moment's concern. Not one moment. He sometimes forgot Katie for hours on end. Days even. Katie came to mind precisely and only when it was convenient for him to think of her. Not so with Anne. She'd not been long out of his thoughts since Corth Abbey. Devil take it. What sort of man wanted to save himself from his own wife?

Chapter Twelve

"I adore dancing," Anne said to cover the nervousness caused by Cynssyr holding her so close. He moved with wicked grace, all polish and perfection.

"With four girls, I imagine the Sinclair family attended its share of dances."

"Oh, yes, indeed."

"Did you waltz often?"

"Never, I'm afraid. Papa always said I oughtn't dance."

"Why not?"

"Well, what would have been the point?"

Pulling her closer, he stared as though he wanted to see inside her, a look that made her insides shiver. "To the devil with your papa," he said, and effortlessly whirled her in a tight turn.

A fortnight in London, and Anne knew exactly why so many women had loved Cynssyr. A similar fate awaited any incautious woman. Already she wanted badly to believe he cared for her more than a little.

"Anne," he murmured, a low sound that felt like water to a parched throat. The sound caught at her, ensnared her. She lifted her gaze, met his eyes and was trapped there, too, willingly drowning in the peridot depths. A smile curved his mouth and her breath stopped, simply stopped. He was so lovely when he smiled.

Seeing the shadow of exhaustion in her eyes, he cursed himself for his selfishness. "You are fatigued." He touched a finger to her cheek, tracing a line from temple to just beneath her eye. At the contact a jolt of awareness sped through him, of her strength of character, her scent, her wholly unanticipated charm, and of his body's response to her, sharp and hungry, which he had damn well better learn to curtail.

"A little," she admitted.

"Are you hungry?"

"No, not yet. Soon I imagine."

"You need to rest. Shall we go to the card room?"

"All right."

Tables set up in the Octagon room were already crowded with guests. Footmen in the Cynssyr livery of green and gold circulated with bottles of wine, champagne and glasses. There were discreet and not-so-discreet looks when Ruan strolled in with Anne on his arm. The men eyed Anne speculatively, pausing at bosom level before moving on or returning their attention to cards or dice. The few women present patted their hair, adjusted their gowns or arranged their positions to better advantage.

He didn't dare hold Anne as closely as he wanted. For one thing, he had no intention of making a spectacle of himself with her. Anne deserved a dignified introduction to his circle. For another, he feared if he did he'd soon drag her off to some secluded spot and make love to her again. God knows she needed some respite from him as much as he needed to exercise restraint.

"Thank you, Cynssyr," she said, after he saw her to a chair at one of the tables.

"What do you think, my dear?" God, how he wanted to touch her, to have his hands around her waist helping her ride him to oblivion. "Faro? Whist? Hazard? Backgammon?" He leaned down and put his mouth next to her ear. "I wish you were sitting on my lap right now." She tilted her head in a quizzical motion. "Wearing nothing but those diamonds." The tip of her ear turned red, and the color spread slowly downward. She looked around, trying to gauge whether anyone had overheard. "I wish I were inside you right now," he whispered. A vision of the two of them doing exactly that nearly sent him cross-eyed.

"Hush!" she said in a low voice.

He straightened, caressing her shoulder while he nodded at a lanky man whose pale hair fell in ringlets to his ears. "Whatever you choose, Mr. Durling will have a game with me."

"Backgammon, if it pleases you, sir." When he sat, she refused to look at him for quite a bit.

As predicted, Julian Durling eagerly assented to a game. Sky-blue eyes lingered at Anne's throat then swept downward to take in the rest of her. He fancied himself a gamester and a lover both, and Ruan did not object to the suggestion of a small wager on the outcome.

Durling drew up a chair next to Anne. While playing, he kept up a running account of his failed attempt to learn the guitar, which skill he had intended to use in wooing a woman who'd caught his eye. The man managed to get his fill of Anne's figure and so did not play well. Anne appeared fascinated by his insipid story. If she wasn't, she was an actress the likes of which had never been seen outside Drury Lane. Several times Ruan caught Durling staring at her waist and lower down where the act of sitting had tightened her gown over her hips and legs. After one such lingering perusal, he caught Ruan's eye and gave an appreciative nod.

"Y'know, Cyn," Durling said in an unaffected manner that proved Anne had gotten to him, too, "she's not at all what I expected."

"Really?" Fierce desire to toss the man out on his ear made Ruan's voice dangerously flat. Durling had a reputation for chasing other men's wives, and he was getting that look. Ruan knew that look all too well. A gleam of appreciation. Anticipation of conquest, as it were.

"You never cared for substance before." He seemed to get himself under control for the drawl reappeared. "Tell me again, Duchess, that you think I might learn the guitar."

"I am convinced you could learn to play wonderfully."

"Dashed if I've never met a woman to make me think better of myself than you." He brushed at his cuff with a perfectly manicured index finger. "Remarkable. I am a renowned ne'er-do-well, as Cyn will tell you. Do you know I once took up painting, too? Gave it up after a week. I've no talent for art."

"I don't believe it, Mr. Durling. No one who dresses with such a splendid sense of color could be a failure at art."

"You don't say?" His eyes flashed with a distinctly lecherous light. With a flourish, he produced a set of dice. "Cynssyr?" When he looked at Ruan, his expression was far too innocent. "Another game?" He closed a loose fist around the dice and vigorously shook them. "You'll give a kiss for luck, won't you Duchess? What do you say, Cyn?"

Her eyes danced with humor and earned a look, more

admiring yet. "Against my own husband? I think not, sir."

Ruan nodded. Durling lost on the first toss. The stakes quickly streaked upward from a few pounds to a few hundred pounds, with the other man losing more often than not. Forty minutes later, he wrote out his note for nine hundred thirty pounds.

"I needed that kiss, Duchess," Durling said, grinning as he handed over his voucher. "Brilliant play as always, Cynssyr. Your grace. Think I'll go see if Miss Sinclair will dance with me." Rising, he took Anne's hand. "Once again Cynssyr comes away with the best. I am heartbroken." He placed a hand over his heart. "Inconsolable to be the loser again."

Anne laughed. "Hardly that, Mr. Durling."

He bowed and clicked his heels, still holding Anne's hand. His eyes flicked up, settling on something past Anne's shoulder. "Well, well. Your brother-in-law approaches. Such a serious look on his face. I fear your husband is to be called away. Matters of state, perhaps." He put a finger to his chin, aping deep thought. "No, that cannot be. The subject is something else entirely, for Bracebridge is with him." He waved a hand, still holding her fingers in his other. "I depart, dear Duchess. I am not in the mood for the fright I get whenever I see that brutal face."

"You disappoint me, sir," Anne said, pulling her hand free. "I do not find Devon brutal in any respect." She missed the suggestive rise of his brow in response.

"Ah, Duchess," he said archly, "but then you are his particular friend, are you not?"

"Indeed I am, sir."

He bowed once more, contrite. "Forgive me if I offend. Good evening." Durling vanished just before Ben and Devon reached them.

"Aldreth. Devon." Anne extended a hand to each,

taking in their expressions and feeling sharp curiosity mixed in with a goodly portion of disappointment. "It's true, I see. You've come to take Cynssyr away."

"If we may," said Devon, lingering over her hand.

"Stay away from Durling, Anne," Ruan said, hearing too late that he sounded accusing of her.

Anne's expression smoothed out. "Yes, sir." She bent a knee and was gone.

The three men walked to Ruan's study. "Well?" Ruan asked when he'd lit a lamp and closed the door.

"You might at least pretend to care about her feelings." Devon planted himself, legs apart, arms crossed over his chest.

"You might pretend to care less."

"Gentlemen. Gentlemen." Ben walked between them. "Let's not quarrel. Though frankly, Ruan, you could have been more chary of Anne than you were."

"I don't like the way Durling looks at her."

"Well," said Ben affably. "Deal with him."

"I will," he said.

Devon cleared his throat. "As I was saying—"

"You weren't saying anything at all," Ruan said. He spoke sharply because he knew Devon loved Anne, and he didn't like it.

"Please!" Ben said. "Stop baiting one another."

"There may be a gentleman involved," said Devon. "I'm hearing only whispers. But I have the names of men who've recently been in—and out of—dun territory."

"Who?" Ben asked.

"You might not like the list."

Ben laughed. "I'll wager I can guess three-quarters of the names."

"Get on with it."

Devon ticked off the names. "We can start with our friend Julian Durling."

"No doubt he still spends his allowance before the quarter's ended." Ruan glared in the direction of the door. "And is in debt to his ears."

"So does most every gentleman in London," said Ben.

"Hell," Ruan said. "He owes me nearly a thousand pounds."

"There's also Kinross and Jamison. Wilberfoss, too, but he solved his difficulties some time back. Been in the clear ever since. But, were either of you aware that John Martin is in town?"

"Indeed?" Ruan imagined the man as he'd last seen him. A whipcord-thin man whose generous mouth, ready smile and warm eyes disappeared entirely whenever he drank, which was often. Not particularly successful with women, though not at all a bad-looking fellow. His indolence was a flaw of character that had ended Martin's otherwise promising military career. A pity. But for that flaw, he would have been an excellent solider.

"Tempting as the notion is," Ruan said, "if Martin has only just arrived in town, we can't consider him."

"What if he hasn't?"

"We'll find that out soon enough. At any rate, Wilberfoss has always paid his debts so I doubt it's him. Besides, his mother had money, too, and she left him everything. Durling's a convincing suspect. Perhaps too convincing," he reluctantly conceded. "Kinross surprises me though. I've heard he has certain tastes. Think he could be our man?"

Devon stroked a finger down the length of his crooked nose. "There's one more name."

"Who?" said Ruan and Ben together.

"The marquess of Thrale."

"Impossible. I won't believe it," said Ben. "Thrale's bloody rich."

Devon shook his head. "His father was bloody rich. And jolly good at spending his money, too. It's been what? Six months since the present marquess came to his estates? There are whispers the title's bankrupt."

Ruan felt a shiver of dread. A gentleman responsible for the brutal assaults? Inconceivable. And yet. . . . It explained so much. How easily the women were lured away. With the exception of John Martin, any of the men Devon had named possessed sufficient knowledge and familiarity with society to concoct the tricks played on the victims. Without doubt, the man responsible knew the Ton and the men and women who moved in it.

"There's more," said Devon, thrusting his hands into his trousers' pockets as he leaned against the wall.

"What?"

He gave Ruan an inscrutable look. "Katie is here."

Chapter Thirteen

Anne scanned the crowd, looking for Cynssyr like a child who knows she will have a treat and is constantly on the lookout for its arrival. Farther than twenty or thirty feet distant she recognized people mostly by shape or coloring. Despite not having her spectacles, she'd feel it if Cynssyr were in the room, and he wasn't. She rubbed her eyes. Not having her glasses made her head ache. Her temples throbbed with the effort of trying to see. She felt more tired than she'd ever been in her life, and not just from dancing. The fatigue never really left her anymore, and now, with the late hour, she felt ready to collapse.

"Duchess?"

Recognizing the voice, she turned, smiling. "Lord Thrale."

"I've come to claim my dance." The marquess had a smile to rival Cynssyr's, surprising for so grim a man. He took her arm, preparing to lead her into line. His

114

slate-gray eyes swept over her, and he stopped short.

"But, I'm done in," she said. "Would you mind terribly if we sat this out?"

"Not at all."

Thrale walked with her to a crowded salon where he somehow managed to find her a chair. She sank gratefully down. "I'll fetch you some punch." People who'd come for dinner had left, others who'd not been invited to dine had just arrived, and judging from the number of people crushed everywhere she looked, a good many people who'd not been invited at all had come. Quite a different mix than earlier.

"My lord," she said when Thrale returned with a glass of orgeat. She motioned for him to bend close so she could speak softly. "Who is that?" Anne pointed to a tiny woman holding court at the far side of the room. Hardly five feet tall, she was surrounded by admiring men, and with reason. Brilliant blue eyes flashed in a heart-shaped face and shining auburn hair made a striking counterpoint to her pale skin.

"Which?"

"There. The woman in the exquisite gown." Snow-white silk gauze set off rubies the color of blood. They encircled her slender throat and sparkled on her wrists, fingers and delicate shell-like ears. "I've seen her several times tonight, but we've not been introduced. She must have come late, for I don't recall her from the receiving line."

"Mrs. Forrest."

"She's beautiful."

Thrale gave her a penetrating look. "You've been a married woman for all of six weeks now."

"Is that all? It feels as if I've always been married. No, that's not quite it. Inevitable." She moved a hand in a gesture that encompassed the whole of the scene

115

before them. "That this all was inevitable. Isn't that strange?"

"Yet you are innocent. Among the Ton, that's a rare commodity."

"You mean unpolished, but I thank you for your tact." She smiled, expecting him to smile back, but he didn't.

"I mean innocent. He must find that fascinating."

"Cynssyr?"

"Shall we take a turn?" Thrale rose. He tucked her arm under his and began a slow stroll around the perimeter of the crowded salon. "Tell me what you think of London. Do you find it as tiresome as I do?"

"Honestly, I've not seen much. Queen Anne Street and Portman Square. Once to Hampstead Heath for tea with the duchess. Goodness, what an ordeal that was."

They continued their circuit, coming quite near Mrs. Forrest. The woman saw Thrale and lifted one fragile hand in greeting. Every finger glittered with gems and filigreed gold. As close as they were, Anne saw no flaw in the porcelain skin, no imperfection in her features or figure. Thrale acknowledged the gesture with a nod, but he continued past.

"Will you introduce us?" Anne asked.

"No."

"Why not?"

They'd reached the door, and as he led her back to the ballroom, he said, "May I give you a word of advice?"

"I should welcome it."

He pressed Anne's forearm. "Your husband can be very charming when it suits him. I expect just now it suits him to be charming to you."

Anne laughed. "Charming to me? No, I'm afraid not."

"Not at all?"

"No."

"How unlike him."

"Cynssyr is himself around me." Anne knew that for fact because this evening she'd seen him charming the ladies and it wasn't anything like how he behaved with her. She'd know if Lord Ruin ever set out to deliberately charm her.

"Now that, Duchess, astonishes me."

A stir distracted them and they both turned toward the salon they'd just left. They saw him at the same time. Cynssyr. Anne shivered inside, and she smiled without realizing she did it. Goodness, but he was handsome. The crowd near him parted so that he appeared to move effortlessly where everyone else had to start and stop and jostle one another. Cynssyr lifted a hand in greeting to someone off to his left and continued his course toward the salon.

Thrale glanced down. "The moment he holds your heart in his hand, he will crush it. That is his way." He gave a very Gallic shrug. "I have seen it happen so many times. To so many women. I should hate to see you hurt that way."

"Oh, I'm safe from that danger."

"Ah!" someone called. "I say, Thrale, it's not sporting of you to try to hide her away."

"Wilberfoss." Thrale greeted the man with a somber nod.

"It's my dance now." He wasn't a particularly tall man, nor terribly handsome either, but he reminded Anne of Aldreth, with his look of perpetual good humor. Wilberfoss reached them and bowed, a trifle too deep to keep his balance. "Your grace."

"Now, I really should let you go," Anne said to Thrale, taking the viscount's arm. "I need a word with Lord Wilberfoss." She tapped his arm. "If he wants to marry my sister, he'll have to prove himself worthy."

Wilberfoss nodded gravely. "I very much hope to, Madam."

"You've been kind." She touched Thrale's sleeve. "Thank you."

"I would be glad if you called me Richard."

"Then you must call me Anne."

Thrale bowed, and with one brief glance at Wilberfoss, left.

"Lovely Duchess," Wilberfoss said, speaking so that half the consonants disappeared into the vowels. "You will honor me with a dance?"

"Delighted, my lord." She sent one last look toward Thrale and had the very briefest glimpse of the exquisite Mrs. Forrest leaving the salon with Cynssyr at her side.

"There is Aldreth with his beautiful lady," the viscount remarked as they started out by narrowly avoiding the lumbering pair of Mr. Julian Durling and Miss Camilla Fairchild. He spoke carefully now, producing crisp syllables. He was not half the dancer Cynssyr was. Grinning, Wilberfoss swung her around a half-beat behind the music. "Been looking for you all night. Ought to get to know each other better, don't you agree?"

"I admit I'm curious about you. Emily's not told me much." He was younger than she expected, no more than twenty-three or twenty-four, and quite exquisitely dressed, though he hadn't Cynssyr's natural flair or Thrale's austere elegance.

"Your sister mentions you quite often. Can't praise you enough. Got me worried, her having a paragon of perfection for a sister. What if she expects me to be as perfect as you? It's been fretting me no end."

"I assure you, I'm far from perfect."

"Good." He feigned relief so comically Anne had to laugh. "Now I see why Cyn married you." His hand, which had rested very properly on her back during a chasse exerted a slight pressure. "Magnificent," he murmured. As she and Wilberfoss passed each other again, the viscount's focus shifted from her eyes to her mouth then down to rest below her chin.

"Your jewels are lovely."

That made her look. For the briefest moment, she could have sworn to a salacious intent. But his face was all innocence and smiles. They moved past, dipped away, then back to one another.

"A gift from your husband?"

Of course, he meant the diamonds. "Yes." What else could he have meant? Fewer couples hemmed them in since they had somehow ended up at the edge of the ballroom.

"The duke has always had excellent taste in women and in jewelry," he said to her diamonds.

"Has he?" She backed out of his arms, giving up the pretense of dancing since Wilberfoss had stopped any attempt to guide her through the steps.

He drew a flask from his pocket and took a long draught. "Give anything for his knack of matching the gem to the woman," he said. "I keep thinking, what ought I to give my beautiful Emily? Have you any suggestions for me? I confess I'm at a loss." Daintily, he wiped his mouth with the side of a pinky. The smell from the open flask sent her stomach into near revolt. "What is it I heard him say once? Ah." He lifted a finger. "I have it. A rule, he said, by which he ordered his most private affairs. Diamonds for a blonde. Emeralds for a brunette. Rubies for a redhead."

Anne forced a grin because what leapt instantly to mind was Mrs. Forrest's rubies, and it was really too bad of Lord Thrale not to have made an introduction.

"Were you my wife, I would look no further for companionship. Tonight or any night." Wilberfoss put a hand on her shoulder, gazing at her with concern. "Why,

Duchess, you're flushed. Are you faint? Air. You must have fresh air."

She seized the excuse because her fatigue had quickly worsened with even their little bit of dancing, and her stomach pitched unpleasantly. "Yes. Do forgive me." She wanted to like Wilberfoss, she really did, but she couldn't entirely approve of him, though she wasn't able to pinpoint the reason. They'd stopped near a wide corridor leading eventually to the gallery, and she walked out, heading for a marble bench about halfway down the hall. She never reached it, for Wilberfoss followed her.

"My dear Duchess," he said, all cloying concern. He walked into the corner of a side table. "Damnation!"

Anne stopped. "Are you all right?"

"Your servants appear to have been lax." The flask appeared once again. "Have I made a hopeless muck of things?" His disarming smile made her think that perhaps he and Emily would suit after all. She was learning the value of a partner with whom one might laugh. "Don't tell me you didn't know about the rubies."

"For redheads, you mean?"

"Rubies for redheads. Yes, indeed. Magnificent rubies for a magnificent woman. Cynssyr is a man of the world. 'Deed he is." He raised his flask, smiling cheerfully so that his round cheeks became rounder yet. "I drink to men of the world." He opened a door just to his left. "This should do nicely."

"For what?"

"Come, come, now," he said impatiently. He gripped her elbow.

"There's nothing in there, my lord. Cynssyr does not use that room."

"Even better."

She dismissed her alarm as absurd. Wilberfoss was a

puppy, and practically engaged to her sister. "You wish to speak to me about Emily?"

"Yes, that's it." As he came closer, fingertips brushed her bosom. Anne backed away. "Duchess," he said. "I assure you your husband is well occupied at the moment."

"What would you like to know about Emily? I fear she's strong-willed, but I'm sure you'll agree it's a good deal of her charm."

After another sip from the flask, he held it out with an inviting nod. "No?" He shrugged. "Then how about a kiss for your future brother-in-law?"

She crossed her arms beneath her breasts, saw him become completely distracted by the movement and immediately uncrossed them. She knew she was naive, but not so much that she could misinterpret that look. "You're drunk."

"Lively, my sweet. Merely lively." Again, his eyes swept her. "Honestly, of all the lovely bits here tonight, you are the morsel I should most love to sample." He stood close. Far too close. Instinctively she put a hand on his midriff.

"You have drunk too much, my lord. You are not in your right mind."

The boyish smile reappeared. "Oh, I dare say I am very much in my right mind."

"Let me go."

"There's a love." He slid an arm around her waist and pulled her to him. She reacted on instinct. Her palm connected sharply with his cheek, and his head snapped back. "Why, damn you!" He touched his face, red where her fingers had landed.

Now that it was too late to take it back, she wished she'd not done it. "Forgive me."

"I suppose I deserved that," he said, easing back, though not enough for her to walk away.

121

"As a matter of fact, sir, you did." She tried to slide past him, but his hand shot out, grasping the nape of her neck and trapping her between him and the door. "My lord. Please. Let me pass." She pushed again, but he didn't budge. "Lord Wilberfoss!"

His fingers brushed over her breast. "Luscious."

She rationalized what he was doing. He didn't mean it. Or else he did not understand that she objected. Somehow, she'd not managed to make herself clear to him. "Please," she said in her most reasonable tone. "Let me go. You must let me go."

"I think not." He pressed her hard against the door, hard enough that she felt his aroused state.

"Let me go," she said, still not able to believe she might actually be in danger. "Please. You must let me go."

"Don't be difficult." He addressed her bosom. "God, but I want a mouthful of you." She shrieked when he kissed her there and pushed his shoulders hard enough and unexpectedly enough that he stumbled back. She darted past, but he swung around, stopping her with a hand on her wrist. He gave a good-natured grin and tightened his fingers. "God knows why he wants another woman when he's got you."

"You're hurting me."

"You make even her seem positively spindle-shanked." He dragged her closer, and she could do nothing to stop him.

"My Lord Wilberfoss. I said, you're hurting me."

His eyebrows drew together. "Am I? Do forgive me." His fingers dug into her wrist.

Under no illusion now of his bad intentions—whatever the motivation—she struggled to free herself before he overpowered her. He now held her so tightly that she bent slowly to the pain. Catching at her neckline, he said, "They're the prettiest I've seen for ages."

"My lord." She tugged on her wrist. Fear shot through her when he thrust his fingers down the front of her gown. "Please. Stop."

"Stand up." He hauled her to her feet. She lifted a palm to slap him again, but this time he was prepared, and he caught her other wrist. With a forward lunge, he pinned her between him and the wall. "No more coy nonsense. I don't like it. A husband's got to expect these things when he neglects his lovely young bride." Though she tried, she could not avoid his roving hands. Disbelief warred with outrage. She did not want to accept what Wilberfoss was doing, she kept thinking that any moment he would come to his senses and stop. But he didn't. "Stop wriggling about. Damn me if you ain't teasing me! I tell you, I don't like it."

"Stop this" she cried. "Stop this moment." Frantic, she struggled, but his grip on her tightened. Panic took over completely. She shouted. "Cynssyr!"

"What will you tell him if he comes?" Holding her tight against him, he brayed with laughter. "That you're a deceitful little bitch?"

She tried to kick him but missed badly.

"Why, you little bit of skirt!" He grabbed her by the shoulders and slammed her against the closed door hard enough to dislodge a nearby painting from its mooring. Her head snapped back and hit the wall, stunning her. Drunk he surely was, but he still outweighed her, and Anne could do nothing to stop him. Reaching around her, he opened the door. The sudden lack of support unbalanced them both. She stumbled, but kept her feet. Wilberfoss fell hard.

Terror gave her speed she didn't know she possessed. She bolted. But the blow to her head slowed her reflexes. He caught her only steps from the ballroom, spinning her around and holding her tightly, face to face. His hand over her mouth kept her from calling for help.

"Quiet!" he hissed. Drink was strong on his breath. "Someone will hear you. Do you want to rouse the household?"

She kicked out, and this time she connected with his shin. He was not, thank goodness, wearing boots that might have protected him.

"Damn you!"

His grip on her loosened, and she bolted again. Wilberfoss followed, letting out a shout of outrage. His fingers just caught her sleeve. She jerked. The fabric tore, and she was free and dashing into the ballroom. As luck would have it, she careened into Henry, the postilion who had, for the evening, been cast in the role of footman. For all his hulking size, Henry was the sweetest, gentlest man she knew. Fortunately, Wilberfoss didn't know that.

The footman caught her shoulders but released her as if he'd been burned. "Here now, Madam Duchess!"

"Henry." Her heart pounded and though her knees felt like water she wanted to run and keep running. She glanced behind her. Wilberfoss took three steps more, saw Henry and skidded to a stop. She turned back and grabbed the servant's hand. "Have you seen the duke?" In her moment of terror, when she'd believed Wilberfoss would overpower her, she'd called for Cynssyr. That fact stayed in her head and refused to leave.

"Yes, Madam Duchess." Henry essayed a bow as he pulled at his forelock, or where his forelock would have been had he not been wearing a powdered wig.

"Where?"

"The French Parlor, Madam Duchess."

"Show me the way, if you please."

"Such a large house, Madam Duchess," he said, taking such deliberate and careful steps she wanted to scream for him to hurry. It wasn't a royal procession, for heaven's sake. "It's no wonder a body gets lost.

Why, I once was lost nearly a week 'tween the kitchen and the scullery. Here we are."

"Thank you."

Blocking her way, Henry harrumphed loudly and tapped on the door. "Your grace?" he called out.

Anne reached around him and opened the door, walking in without waiting for an answer to Henry's announcement. This was one of the more intimate parlors, her favorite because of the shades of damask rose and heather. Lord, she was shaking still from her encounter with Wilberfoss. Please, she thought, let Cynssyr be there. She wanted him to hold her. To tell her all was well. She needed him.

He stood by the sofa, straightening his coat. She had the impression he had just risen.

"Anne."

"A word, sir."

Cynssyr nodded toward the door. "You may go, Henry."

Now that she stood confronted with her stern, too somber husband, she didn't know how to start, how to tell him that Wilberfoss had frightened her, or how badly she wanted him to reassure her, like one of those armor-clad ancestors of his might once have done for his lady.

His eyebrows shot up. "Yes?"

She took a steadying breath against tears. "Do not think for one moment, sir—" She covered a sob with a breathless hiccup. "Do not think my sister will ever marry Lord Wilberfoss." She wished she had her spectacles. Not being able to see put her at a serious disadvantage.

"Doubtless you are right."

She recalled the viscount's groping hands on her, the stink of alcohol on his breath. "I will do everything I can to prevent it."

"We will talk of this later, Anne."

She moved toward him because she wasn't close enough to see his face, coming farther in so as to stand between him and the sofa. She got herself under control. "He's a drunkard, sir," she said in a low, fierce voice mercifully free of quaver, "who I have had the misfortune to discover becomes violent when under the influence of spirits." On the verge of tears, she stood clenching her hands and then lost the fight not to throw herself into his arms. She stepped toward him. Someone coughed. She turned.

Mrs. Forrest reclined on the sofa, one pretty foot dangling toward the floor, looking very much like a woman who has just enjoyed the embrace of her lover.

Chapter Fourteen

Anne backed away from the sofa. "Forgive me, Cynssyr. I did not know you had company." She had every reason to expect this of Cynssyr, so she didn't understand why the sight of them together felt like a dagger to the heart.

"Perhaps in future you will wait for an invitation to enter," he said irritably. Nothing in his expression betrayed the slightest guilt for being closeted with another woman. This woman. One of the most beautiful women she'd ever seen in her life.

Eyes on Cynssyr, Mrs. Forrest stroked the rubies around her throat, awaiting her cue. Anne understood now why Thrale had refused to introduce her. He'd tried to warn her. What must everyone think to see Cynssyr's mistress here? At a ball in honor of his bride. Cynssyr's arms remained crossed over his chest. What he thought was anybody's guess.

Mrs. Forrest laughed, a sound of tinkling crystal, pure

and insufferably delicate. "Cyn was just telling me how highly he thinks of you, Duchess." Slowly, she sat, making a great show of rearranging her gown. She had the grace to look at least a little uncomfortable. "Had I known an ability to do sums would so impress him, I would have paid more attention to my governess."

"Katie."

She'd counted on finding him alone, on being able to tell him what had happened, on having his advice. Perhaps even his sympathy. Instead, he was vexed, and she was humiliated. Emotion threatened to choke her. She, stupid, besotted woman that she was, had refused to hear anyone's warnings. "I am sorry to have disturbed you," Anne said, backing away. Oh, good gracious. She was going to be ill. She looked around for one of Merchant's basins, praying she would not embarrass herself further. The basin sat discreetly in a corner, and Cynssyr stood between her and complete disgrace.

Seeing the direction of Anne's gaze, his eyebrows lifted. "Perhaps, Katie, you will give me a moment alone with my wife."

"Of course."

Anne's stomach turned inside-out. Only Cynssyr's quick reaction saved the lovely carpet. "Poor wee wren," he whispered.

"So," came the woman's soft voice.

She felt him stroking her back while she bent over the basin, embarrassed, ashamed and too sick to care. Her stomach heaved again. "Darling," he said gently. Not to her, to Mrs. Forrest. "Ring for a servant."

Silk rustled, then all was quiet but for the sound of Anne sniffling.

"Congratulations, Ruan."

"Thank you. Leave us now."

The servant came, saw immediately the problem and took away the basin without a word. Anne sat on a chair, miserable to her core while Ruan went to the door. He returned with a glass of punch. "A sip only."

She pushed away the glass when she'd had enough to wash out the taste of bile. "Thank you, sir." She wanted to scream. To scratch out his eyes. She wanted to run away and never see anyone again. Of course she did none of those things.

"Better?"

"Much."

"Now, Anne," he said gently. "Exactly what did you mean with that outburst about Wilberfoss?"

"She's in love with you."

He replied with a shrug that could have meant anything at all. He knew. He didn't know. Or he just didn't care.

"She's so small. Fragile and beautiful. It's a wonder you don't worry you'll break her." She left her chair because Cynssyr was too close, and she could not concentrate on anything but him. A book lay on a small cherry table, and she opened it, flipping pages. None of the words made any sense. Her husband and his mistress. "I had no idea. She must think me a perfect fool, walking in on you like that, and you, too. Everyone must. I'm not used to how things are done in society. What a fool I am. I just wouldn't see it." Oh, for heaven's sake. The book was in Latin. No wonder she couldn't make sense of it.

Ruan gave her an odd look. "She has her congé from me, Anne."

Out of habit, she touched her nose. Her spectacles were not there which briefly disconcerted her. "What on earth for?"

"She has bored me, and I dismissed her."

"Her? Bored you?" Tension coiled heavily in her chest, a threat of tears, but she ignored it. It was never very pleasant to know one's been made to look foolish. "That hardly seems possible."

"Nevertheless."

She looked into his face, that lovely, beautifully masculine face and remembered what Thrale had told her. "It's all right." But it wasn't. Not really. "I understand you need a diversion from everyday dullness."

"Diversion?" One mahogany eyebrow arched. "No. Not a diversion this time."

"It's all right. Honestly, it is." Her heart contracted. She told herself to be grateful for the reaction, for it meant she would be protected in the future. Better a mild hurt now than a worse one later.

"Mrs. Forrest is in my past, Anne. And there she shall stay." He sighed. "I should like to know why you came in here." He went to her and took her by the shoulders. The contact rocked her, for she felt the difference between what happened to her when Cynssyr touched her and when it was Wilberfoss. That same shivery apprehension, but with her husband, it wasn't sick-making. The feeling still frightened her, but not at all in the same way as with the viscount. With effort, she reined in the reaction.

"What did Wilberfoss do or say to disturb you? The truth, for I know you would not be angry or upset without cause." He thought that damn dress of hers fit too well. It hugged her bosom, clung to her thighs and knees, and distracted him from what she was telling him.

"He . . . he, he is no fit husband for Emily."

Ruan frowned. Normally, Anne kept iron control of her emotions, but now he sensed a crack. Tempered steel taken beyond that metal's endurance. Even considering she'd just been ill, she was too pale. Her fingers worked nervously at a seam of her gown. Undoubtedly, something had happened, and she was keeping it bottled up inside like she did so much else. "If you wish me to keep Emily and Wilberfoss apart, I will."

Her chin lifted and a bit of her spirit flashed in her eyes. "Would you do such a thing? Could you?"

"Yes."

Anger tightened her mouth. "Then do it. Do whatever it takes."

He nodded. "Consider it done. But, Anne, I don't think it's unreasonable to ask why."

"No," she whispered, looking at the floor. Her fingers resumed their worrying of the seam. "It's not."

He saw the torn lace of her sleeve and did not at all like the way the puzzle came together. Not a small tear such as one might easily get by accident, but practically a rend. He felt himself go dead inside. "Did he make an advance?" He needed that deadness to keep the rage from overwhelming him. Had he ever been so murderously angry in his life? Indeed, how long had it been since he'd felt anything as deeply as this?

She kept her head bowed, refusing to look at him.

"Did he?"

"Yes, sir," she whispered.

"Are you all right?" He put a hand to her chin and lifted her head, waiting patiently until she met his gaze. "Are you all right?" She nodded, but he could see the effort it took her to maintain her composure. "He's a boy," he growled. "A harmless boy. Damnation, Anne. Tell me what happened." Her inability to see herself as the object of a man's lust made her vulnerable to the wolves constantly on the prowl for a new amusement. If Wilberfoss had so much as laid a hand on her, he would pay. Dearly.

Cynssyr's flat, chill eyes made her shudder. Carefully, she blocked off her emotions until she felt just like her husband's eyes. Chips of green ice. Arctic. "With all the dancing and, and the excitement, and, well, you know

131

I am so tired, Cynssyr. I wished to sit down. I left the ballroom. He followed me. Lord Wilberfoss, I mean. And he seemed to think I wanted to be alone with him, but I didn't. I didn't at all."

"Did he touch you?" Speaking casually took effort. He dared not let her see the rage. She must at all costs think her answer was of no great consequence. But her luminous eyes reflected a battle between giving him an answer that would exonerate the viscount and the truth. Whatever she said now, he already knew the truth. "Did he?"

Her eyes were huge in her too-pale face, but she spoke serenely. "Yes."

Cynssyr went absolutely still. Anne's lungs refused to draw air. She wrapped her arms around her waist, hugging herself as if that would protect her from his anger.

"I was frightened. He frightened me. He was mean, and awful and I don't understand why he—I couldn't bear to have him near me. Even though he was drunk, he was bigger and stronger, and I couldn't get away." She stopped, appalled that she'd resorted to excuses. Best come at the thing straight on. "I struck him, sir, and then he tried to push me into the room, but he stumbled and, and I didn't. I ran, and he ran after me, and I wanted so badly to find you I just kept running until I found Henry and I made him take me to you." She let go of her waist and stood again, drawing herself up with a terrifying control. "I'm sorry. I don't know what's got me so upset. How ridiculous I am tonight. I assure you, I am not usually so excitable."

He put his hands on her shoulders, and he felt her flinch. "I am not your father, scolding and disapproving at every turn." Studying her, he said, "You aren't concerned about having struck him, are you? You defended yourself. It was brave of you."

"Ruan." Devon's voice, a low, velvet utterance.

"Christ!" Ruan whirled. "Am I to have no privacy whatever?"

Ben coughed into his hand and hung back while Devon walked straight in.

"What do you want?" Cynssyr barked. His tone of voice was definitely dangerous. He meant it to be, but neither Devon nor Ben took heed.

"It's about what happened at Marylebone Gardens," Ben said, strolling past him and Anne. He exchanged a look with her, then sat.

"What about it?"

Anne moved away, but Ruan's hand shot out and grabbed her wrist. All this time he'd been worrying about Julian Durling, and it was Wilberfoss who had actually tried something. "I've not done with you, Madam." Fury bubbled up. Not at Anne. Never her. At Wilberfoss having the gall to put his hands on her. At himself for not protecting her from the sod. At Thomas Sinclair for coming so damn close to breaking his daughter's spirit.

"Last night," Devon supplied.

Ben stood to his full height. "Let her go, Cyn. You're hurting her."

Cynssyr glanced down and saw his fingers tight around Anne's wrist and then saw her face. He was hurting her. Abruptly, he released her. "My apologies."

"I was not hurt, Aldreth." The way she rubbed her wrist revealed the lie.

Ruan found himself the object of two malevolent glances from Ben and Devon. They blamed him for Anne's pallor and her tension. Not knowing how often she was ill nor that her early pregnancy was the most immediate reason for her chalky complexion, nor that Wilberfoss had laid hands on her, no wonder they put him down as the cause. Particularly since the effects of her encounter with Wilberfoss showed plain in her face and eyes. "Will the woman's father let me see her?" he asked.

Both Ben and Devon looked at Anne and remained silent.

"I don't think it's Durling," Devon said too carefully. "Thrale's our man."

"Thrale?" Anne repeated, guessing immediately what they meant. Ruan silently applauded her quickness of understanding. "Surely not," Anne said. "He couldn't be."

"Be what?" Ben said with exaggerated innocence.

"The man you're after."

"Who said we're after anyone a'tall?"

"Oh, please, Aldreth."

"Why couldn't it be Thrale?" Ruan asked, interested to know the reason for her certainty.

"He's not capable of violence."

"Given sufficient compulsion, every one of us is capable of violence, Anne," Ruan said. He lifted one eyebrow. "Did you not learn that for yourself just tonight?"

"Not the marquess," she protested over a furious blush. "He simply could not."

"That's a quick defense for a man you hardly know." For the second time in one night, he was jealous and not equipped to deal with a reaction so entirely foreign to his experience. Anne didn't reply. She just accepted what must to her have seemed a rebuke.

"Enough of this," Devon interjected. "This is a ball, and we are keeping Anne from her triumph. Besides—" He bowed, eyes and voice rich with sensual undertones. "I've yet to dance with you."

Ruan scowled. Was he going to have to kill his best friend, too?

"May I?" Anne asked with a carefulness that struck to Ruan's heart and brought a frown to both Ben and Dev.

Ruan summoned all the calm at his command, a niggardly portion that didn't feel like nearly enough. "Dance with whomever you like. If you are up to it." It wasn't enough. He came off sounding like he'd couched a criticism of Anne in a sarcasm directed at Devon. He could not fathom how the evening had turned so horribly wrong. He'd not minded so much that Anne had been leered at by every damned man present. Dressed as she was, a man would have to be blind not to look and keep looking.

Looking was one matter. Having Anne preyed on by Wilberfoss was another, entirely. But worst of all was having her walk in on him and Katie. Though she pretended otherwise, he'd seen the betrayal in her eyes. Of all he'd done to Anne, this was by far the worst. Tonight, he'd damaged something precious. Really, he didn't see how the evening could get worse except, to top it all off, Ben and Devon believed he mistreated her, and he'd had enough trouble with those two over Anne.

Ben grasped Ruan's arm when he would have followed Anne and Devon from the room. "You are my good friend," Ben said in response to Ruan's questioning expression. "You have my admiration and esteem in almost every respect. But I tell you honestly, the thought of you taking Anne to wife made my blood boil. If I'd seen any other way—any way at all . . . What happened at Corth Abby was entirely your fault. My God, man, you violated her. You stole her innocence. You robbed her of the chance to marry someone not afraid to admit his feelings for her. And yes, I do mean Devon." Benjamin jabbed his finger in the direction of Ruan's chest. "You owe her. Good God, man, don't you see she did *you* the favor, not t'other way round? She deserves better from you than damnable gossip about how much time you spend with bloody Katie Forrest."

Ruan felt the chill of those clear blue eyes. "Are you quite done?"

"No."

"Pray continue." Ruan waved one hand toward his friend in a hurry-up motion.

"Anne has spirit. Real spirit, Cyn. The kind that runs deep and true. A man doesn't often find a woman like that, and when he does, why"—he made a grabbing motion with one hand—"he snatches her up before it's too late. I know, for Mary got her spirit from Anne. Anne's the best of the lot. For all that I love Mary, that's plain truth."

"Then why didn't you save me a pack of trouble and marry her yourself?"

Ben drew a silver case from his coat pocket from which he extracted a slender cigar. Ruan refused the offer of one. "Don't think," Ben said, examining his cigar, "that I didn't notice her." With elaborate care, he lit the end and watched Ruan through a cloud of smoke. "Those exquisitely long legs. Good God, I love to watch her walk." He shrugged, and tossed his spent match into the fireplace. "I wanted to take her to bed the moment I laid eyes on her. But by the time I met Anne, I was hopelessly in love with Mary. I didn't admit that, of course, but I loved her madly." Another column of smoke went spiraling to the ceiling. "Doesn't Mrs. Forrest bore you to tears by now? She ought to. I should think Anne would be a breath of fresh air."

"She is."

"If ever you harm her—If ever I see a mark on her—"

"Damnation!" He faced Ben with fisted hands, itching to lay into him, to anyone at all. "I will not have this. Not even from you."

Ben shifted his balance to the balls of his feet. "Go ahead, Cyn. I'd like to see you try."

Ruan turned on his heel and went to the fireplace. He gripped the mantel, staring into the embers. He would die before he hurt Anne. Or let anyone hurt her. The certainty consumed him like fire devoured tinder. "Have I so far managed this marriage well?" he asked of the fireplace. "I'm the first to admit I have not." He faced Ben. "Have I given Anne anything like the affection she deserves from her husband? No, I admit I have not. But harm her physically? That I have not done. Nor shall I ever. Do not believe me capable of lifting a violent hand to her."

"If you harm her in any way, Cyn, I'll come after you."

"Be my guest, Aldreth." Ruan laughed. "From the look of things, there'll be a long line."

Ben drew on his cigar. "You poor bastard. If she didn't hate you before," he said, "she must by now."

The hell of it was, Ruan was afraid she might.

Chapter Fifteen

Ruan lasted three hours at his Whitehall office before he gave up believing he could concentrate on anything meaningful. So far, he'd snarled at anyone who came by and sent more than one man running to safety. Hickenson hadn't left the anteroom since the last time Ruan had practically taken off his head for his pains. He shoved away the pile of papers before him. He'd made no inroads in the height of the stack.

Plainly, working was an unachievable goal. Going to one of his clubs didn't appeal. He didn't want the company of men. Blast it. He wanted to be with Anne. Read her a poem, perhaps, or just talk. He wanted to see her lovely, seductive smile. For pity's sake, he was a fool and nothing else. But he still wanted to be with her. He grabbed his coat and stalked out. Anne, unfortunately, wasn't any too pleased with him. Ever since she'd seen him with Katie, she'd been cool as ice. Cooler, even. And he didn't blame her for it, either.

Hickenson shot to his feet. "Your grace!" He pulled so hard on the lapels of his coat the garment fairly snapped to his shoulders.

"The afternoon is yours," Ruan said.

"Good day, your grace." Hickenson quickly bowed but not before Ruan saw the man's relief.

"Good day."

He found himself on the street outside Whitehall with no notion of what to do with himself. Finding himself at loose ends for an afternoon, he would normally call on Katie. Perhaps even spend through the late evening with her. For the last three years, Herriot Street had been his home away from home. He made a mental note to send Hickenson to fetch his things. Half his clothes and his best boots were there, yet to be collected. He didn't regret the break with Katie. No other woman interested him. Only Anne.

He went home.

Calling cards with corners bent to convey one meaning or another filled the salver on the table kept by the door for the very purpose of collecting such mementos. He put his hat on the table and glanced through them. A veritable register of London society. Lord Eldon. Lord Fenrother. Sather. Kinross. Brenley Cooke and his wife and daughter. Richmond, Portland, Essex. Lady Prescott. Sir Reginald Dinwitty. The Fairchild mother and daughter. Julian Durling. Durling, the great ruddy sod, had scrawled an extempore poem on the back of his engraved card.

To Anne
The duchess, for whom, whatever
my desires, alas,
I cannot rhyme a poem
that will not roam
all over the d——d page.

139

Durling had written the last line so that it curled around to the top right of the card. "Precocious bugger," Ruan muttered as he climbed the stairs. He paused outside Anne's door and wondered why he knew she was inside. Ridiculous, to feel so certain. All the same, he knew she was.

"Come in," she called out when he rapped lightly on the door.

His heart beat a familiar drum when he saw Anne. She rose from the desk where she'd been writing a letter. Her violet gown fit well. Not low cut, but nipped tightly under her bosom and narrow at the hips and of a flattering color that deepened the blue of her eyes. Slipping Durling's card into his pocket he inclined his head. She looked delicious. Delectable. He wanted to take her in his arms and make love to her right now.

"Anne." His pulse raced as he watched her lean over to blot the page.

"Sir."

It struck Ruan that Anne, who of late existed on a diet of toast and porridge had lost weight. "I must consult with Dr. Carstairs about whether it's usual for a woman to be so ill and tired."

"I'm fine."

"If there is cause for concern, I want to know. You are pale. Are you certain you are well?"

"Yes, sir." Anne could not help staring at Cynssyr. He moved with the lithe, powerful stride that always threatened to strike her dumb. No weakness, she chided herself. From now on in, she would be strong and as impervious to feeling as ever she'd been in Bartley Green. And she tried to be. She really did. But she felt so out of place in her clothes, the ridiculous violet silk more suited to one of her sisters, and Cynssyr so impossibly beautiful that it was difficult to maintain her equanimity.

She retreated to her desk, sitting to fold her letter and write a direction on the outside. Cynssyr did not leave. Nor did he say anything, but she could feel him standing there, a vital presence. She closed her eyes, trying to make herself feel nothing. "Someone called while you were out," she said.

"Indeed."

"A man." Having gotten herself under control, she turned on her chair and faced her husband. "My sisters were here. He told the most amusing stories you can imagine. Even Emily laughed at him. But I could not make myself like him. Something about him unsettled me. He claimed he knew you from the war. But he did not strike me as someone with whom you would have an acquaintance."

"Who was it?"

"Mr. John Martin."

"Martin? A bad bargain."

"I thought he was not much a gentleman."

"I was his commanding officer in Spain and Portugal. He cashed out when the fighting got rough. No one was sorry to see him go. Least of all me."

"I cannot say I am entirely surprised. She took up something on the desk. "Someone else called, too. She gave me this." She held out her hand and dropped the object onto Cynssyr's palm. A signet ring.

His long fingers turned the heavy ring over and over.

"You recognize it, then," Anne said, determined to keep her distance, physical and otherwise. But, dash it all, he was in her room, and he just took over the space.

"Who gave it to you?"

"A—woman." She faltered because she had known the woman was no proper lady. "A, a loose woman."

His eyebrows shot up. "You received a prostitute?"

She matched his aplomb. "I give alms to anyone who asks. If Merchant is not present, then another is."

141

"And this—woman gave you the ring?" He looked at her sharply. "Why?"

"She said she'd heard you were paying for information."

"True enough. What made her think I would pay for this?"

"About a month ago, her best friend was beaten."

"Not so uncommon among her class, I'm afraid. The life is often violent."

She pressed her lips together, gathering herself. "She died, Cynssyr. The woman's friend died. And this woman, she was frightened to her very soul that she'd been followed here. A month after the fact, she was that frightened. She refused me her name, but once I'd given her money, she gave me that." She pointed at the ring. "She told me it belonged to the man responsible for beating her friend."

"Did she see him? Get a look at his face, perhaps?"

"Briefly. When he chose her friend over her. But she had no details other than he was a gentleman. With gold buttons on his coat." She watched Cynssyr's face, his intense concentration as he examined the ring. She took a step back. How easy it was to be drawn in again.

"Talbot passant," he said, brushing a finger over the medieval hunting dog engraved in the burnished gold. "With trefoil, bar dexter and coronet of rank." He closed his fist around the cold metal.

"I looked it up," she said.

"Then you know it's Thrale's crest." He held the ring so the golden carving faced her.

"Yes."

He looked at Anne. "It doesn't fit the pattern. She was a cyprian, not a woman of society. And, as I've said, the life is often violent."

"If money is the reason behind the attacks, why hurt any of them? Why not just ransom?"

"I don't know." He bowed his head, but after a moment he spoke in a low voice. "You have something there, Anne. I don't think money's the reason he does this. He didn't start asking for ransom. It's only the last few he's done that. He's more like a hunter taking the tail of a fox for a trophy. He's taken something from each of them."

"To remember the moment."

"This is perfectly clean. Not a speck of blood." He frowned, thinking of how, among the victims, the injuries were progressively severe.

"Of course," Anne said slowly. "There are any number of explanations for this. Perhaps it's not his. Or he lost it and someone else found it."

"It's his. He may have worn gloves. Or removed it first, and then forgotten it."

"I can't believe Richard would do something so awful."

He looked up sharply. "Richard, is it?"

If tomorrow's affair of honor left him dead, he wondered, would Thrale and Devon fight over Anne? And which would win? Either result opened up a hole inside him so wide and so deep he swore he'd come back from the flames of hell to fill it.

Chapter Sixteen

Predawn gloom cast the planes of Ruan's face in a chiaroscuro of tension-marred beauty. Still as granite, he stood at the open window like some Greek-carved Apollo. Behind him, the room remained shadowed in night. His perfectly made bed did not beckon as it should have to a man who'd not yet been to sleep. He meant to put a bullet into Wilberfoss come dawn. A fatal shot. Hell, he'd done as much before and on less provocation, too.

No one would blame him if he killed the man, not with so much more than honor at stake. Yet, he felt shooting Wilberfoss would be a betrayal of Anne. Nonsense, of course. After all, he was, in effect, doing it for her. But she hadn't meant killing when she'd asked him to intervene. Killing she would not approve, and he found it mattered. Damn it to hell and back.

Dobkin moved into the approaching light, brushing a last speck of lint from the heavy black coat in his hands.

Knowing better than to disturb the duke's silent reflection at such a time, he said nothing and walked softly. Ruan slipped into the garment and resumed his window-side vigil. When the fog and the sky became one indistinguishable gray, he stalked out of his room and into his wife's.

As he had at the window, he stood silently at Anne's bedside. At this hour, half past four, he had just enough light to see her sleeping, the gentle rise and fall of her chest, the faint gleam from the wedding band on her fourth finger. He came often to watch her sleep, as if by staring at her he might divine the sort of woman who so slowly ensorcelled him.

Not so long ago, he'd possessed perfect control of his life. Once, he had no feelings but those he trusted. Now, his emotions were a shifting tide, constantly in flux. His friendship with Devon and, to a lesser extent, with Benjamin, which he had considered solid as rock seemed more like sand, uncertain and uneasy. Lust for beautiful women, for Katie in particular, had once been a source of comfort to him. Predictable, ever-present. Not even two months he'd been married, and he still wanted only one woman: Anne.

How or why escaped him, leaving him only the bare truth of his predicament. Women lusted after him. Even when he didn't try, women wanted him, they flirted subtly or outrageously. Anne didn't at all. In fact, he doubted she even knew how to flirt. Anne had changed everything he ever knew or believed about himself. He was a man familiar with lust, and honesty forced him to admit that what he felt for his wife was considerably more than that. The very underpinnings of his existence were gone.

As he looked at his sleeping wife, he knew Ben was right. He ought to have known his mistake that night at Corth Abbey. Well, he was not so sure he hadn't. He'd never asked her name. He recalled the enticing picture of her in his bed, her lovely purity and the soaring delight of taking what she had never offered before. Once he knew he was first, he hadn't stopped. And now she would have a child by him. By rights, she ought to hate him just as Ben predicted. He didn't think she did, not exactly, anyway. But she didn't revel in being a duchess or care much for the trappings of her exalted position as the wife of Lord Ruin. He didn't know what she felt for him, except it probably wasn't the hatred Ben had predicted. Nor was it love. As for lust, that, too, seemed gravely in doubt. His own state was not.

He had no innocent motives about her. He wanted her. Pure and simple, he wanted her in the basest, most carnal way a man could want a woman. The women he bedded knew quite a lot about men. Anne knew very little. He had always preferred experience to green exuberance. Yet now he suddenly preferred Anne's innocence, which he would have thought about as likely as a leopard changing its spots for stripes. Christ, he wanted her. Warm and giving and luxuriously sensual. Once, he'd been a man without vulnerability. Another weakness he could lay at Anne's feet.

The urge to wake her with a slow and tender kiss nearly overwhelmed him. A last goodbye, if need be. Realistically, the likes of Wilberfoss posed no threat, but anyone could have bad luck. Perhaps Wilberfoss would return the victor. With a muttered imprecation, he turned on his heel intending to leave as silently as he'd come.

He knew immediately when she woke, though she didn't move or make any sound. Her breathing altered, and his awareness of her deepened. He stopped and faced the bed once again.

"Cynssyr?"

"Yes."

146

She sat. The covers pooled around her waist. For a moment, quiet predominated. He heard the clock on the mantel ticking away the seconds.

"Don't go," she said. In the dark, her voice sounded small, pleading even.

"I must, Anne."

"Why? For your honor? Honor won't open the gates of heaven for either of you."

"Anne." He stared at her for a moment. "If I'm killed, will you shed tears for me?"

She drew a breath. "That is unfair."

"So?"

"He'll be drunk."

"Likely so."

"Where's the honor in that?" She pushed at the sheets. "You need not kill him."

"For once, what I must do and what I want to do are in perfect accord."

"You are not so cold as that."

It was a reproach. To which he replied, "Oh, but I am." And this time he did leave. Before his doubt exceeded his conviction.

The affair did not go exactly as expected. Not on his account. The moment he saw the viscount's carriage arrive at Wimbledon Common a glacial calm descended. Nothing pierced the layer of ice that surrounded him. A familiar insulation from emotion. He welcomed the cold.

Devon, who had insisted on being his second, nudged him when Wilberfoss threw open the door and fell to the ground. The marquess of Thrale stepped out after him. Thrale looked at Ruan and shrugged as if to say, "What can I do?"

"The fool," Dev whispered, staring at Wilberfoss clumsily brushing off the mud that clung to his coat. "Well, try not to kill him by accident."

"It won't be an accident."

Devon fell momentarily silent. "Seems somehow unfair, with him in that condition."

Ruan left off watching Thrale and Wilberfoss. He strode to Devon. "He mauled her as if she were some chambermaid who'd caught his fancy."

"Like you did?" Devon shot back so quickly there could be no doubt his anger came from the heart.

"To the devil, Bracebridge," he said, turning. "To the devil."

"Ruan." Devon stopped him with a hand to the shoulder. "My apologies. That was uncalled for."

"When did you ever not speak your mind?"

"I shouldn't have. Not today."

"Gentlemen?" The marquess of Thrale called them to attention.

Ruan looked at his best friend and saw nothing was settled between them. "Well, then."

The first shot was Ruan's. He listened to Thrale counting the paces and turned on ten, ready. Anne's reproach of him was like a tangible thing. He lifted his arm. Wilberfoss did too, weaving on his feet. "Damnation," Ruan said, and aimed to the right.

Chapter Seventeen

Wilberfoss fired on the run and into the dirt at Ruan's feet. Unfortunately, the viscount's escape path placed him to Ruan's right. Hit by a shot that ought to have missed by a good six inches, he yelped and fell to his back screeching. With a shout, the physician raced toward his patient. Ruan strolled to where Wilberfoss writhed on the ground and bent over him.

With a soldier's eye, he assessed the wound. Not a fatal shot. A painfully deep crease across the forearm, but no more. Ignoring Thrale, he waited until he had the viscount's attention then said slowly and clearly, "If ever again you lay a hand on my wife, you won't be able to run fast enough. I will kill you."

"Well, damn me," Thrale said, disgusted. "I was given to understand the circumstances of offense were quite different."

"Oh," Ruan added. "Should you so much as speak to Miss Emily Sinclair, your regrets will be the last ever you have." Wilberfoss's eyes rolled in his head. "Have I made myself clear?" He waited for a nod. "Good."

"My lord," said the physician to the marquess, looking up from his groaning patient. "If you would help me get him into the carriage?"

Thrale signaled to a footman. "See to him. Look here, Cynssyr, I had no idea he'd insulted the duchess."

"He did more than insult her." He'd done what Anne wanted, and now he was sorry he'd not killed the man.

The marquess nursed a sore hand, himself. When Ruan gave an inquiring look, he said, "Nicked it in the carriage, trying to stop Wilberfoss from jumping out before we even got here." He winced as he slowly made and released a fist. "An old injury. Reopened it. You're a lucky man, Cynssyr."

"Because of Wilberfoss?" he said, incredulous. "Make no mistake, if he'd not been drunk, I'd have put a period to his existence."

Thrale almost smiled. "I meant because of your wife. Anne—the duchess, I mean, is an extraordinary woman."

"Yes, she is."

"I admire her a great deal."

Unflinchingly, Ruan met that iron-gray stare. Jealousy was not an emotion he liked at all and here he was, jealous again. He knew Anne liked Thrale. He'd seen them talking as though they were friends of longstanding. He was jealous of their nascent friendship. "I've no compunctions about killing you, too, if need be."

"I think," Thrale said with that same hint of amusement, "that you would find me a more challenging opponent than my Lord Wilberfoss."

"Oh, I don't doubt that. But I would still kill you." With a slight bow, he turned his back on Thrale. "Dev, old man, are you ready?"

Dev retrieved his coat from the groom who held it and settled the heavy garment on his shoulders. "Ready."

In the carriage, silence predominated. At first, it was the sort of easy silence as falls between close friends. But when they reached the outskirts of London the atmosphere had changed from comfortable to decidedly awkward. Devon leaned forward and said, "A favor, Ruan."

"Anything. You know that."

"I saw how you were with Anne. At the ball, I mean and a few times since."

"Look here, I admit I spoke too sharply to her, but Durling was getting ideas."

"That is hardly her fault."

"She is too innocent to understand what he's after."

"Well, at any rate, I didn't mean that. I meant when you were dancing. I saw how you looked at her. How she looked at you."

"We danced. That's all."

"Are you certain?"

"Yes. I am quite certain we danced."

Devon's mouth thinned. "Have you any feelings for her at all?"

"She's my wife."

"Restrain yourself," Devon said. "Just this once."

"Meaning?"

"She is already too desperately impressed with you."

"So far as I can see, Anne is impressed with very little where I am concerned."

"You can't be as blind as that. For the love of God, do not let it go further."

Ruan replied without thinking. "Further than what?"

"You made me an oath."

"Which I have kept."

"Too well, Ruan. Too well."

"Damned either way."

"You will break her heart. As you have every woman before her. I won't have her hurt. Not like that. She does not deserve it."

Devon's rejoinder caught him unprepared for his almost giddy reaction to thinking of Anne in love with him. If she loved him, he would be safe. "It is not," he said at last, "as if I can throw her over for another." Nor, he thought, as if he wanted to. Or that he believed for a moment Anne was in any danger of falling in love with him. But if Devon were right, what then? He rested against the seat. What if she learned to love him?

Dev pinched the bridge of his nose as though he took strength from the gesture. "There is a good deal of talk."

"There's always talk." Crossing his legs, he imagined Anne gazing at him with soft, devoted eyes, hopelessly in thrall. "I pay it no heed. Nor should you."

"About you and Katie. She ought not to have been at Cywrthorn."

He shook his head at that. "I know."

"Camilla Fairchild is telling everyone you kissed her."

"Weeks ago, Dev. Weeks ago." His recollection of the moment felt empty. Had he really been so callous and shallow that he bothered with the likes of Camilla Fairchild? Well. He had kissed her. And longer than he should have. He remembered enjoying her eager, unstudied kiss enough that he'd given brief consideration to something more. Then, she giggled and effectively quenched his desire. He laughed. He had Anne to thank for freeing him from Camilla Fairchild and her ilk. "What a silly chit."

"People are saying you and I have quarreled."

"Hm."

"Over Anne."

"Why?"

"Why do you think?"

"So long as it's not so, I won't concern myself."

The carriage stopped at Devon's Cavendish Square home. "Perhaps it's time you did concern yourself."

"Anne," Ruan said, "would never play me false." She simply wouldn't. "Nor do I believe you would either."

"She would not."

"What about you, Dev?" He wondered how much Devon knew about him and Anne. Had he guessed Anne's condition? Had she told him? To his mind, her pregnancy made her all the more his. Or was Devon still so in love with her, he didn't care one way or the other? The groom opened the door and pulled down the step. Once Dev stood on the ground outside, Ruan could read nothing in the black depths of his friend's eyes. "Can I trust you?"

"Anne isn't like other women," Devon said.

"I know."

"You don't understand the first thing about a woman like her."

"The hell you say."

"You aren't capable of the tender emotion she deserves, Cyn. You can't give her what she needs. I can. We both know that. It's I who should be her husband. Not you."

"Can I trust you?" Ruan repeated.

"You can trust her, and that's all that matters." Devon turned without another word, and Ruan let him go. It was the first time they'd parted on less than amicable terms.

Anne was waiting in the foyer when he returned to Cywrthorn. Merchant was nowhere in sight. Nor any other servant. He went to her and folded her into his arms.

"Cynssyr," she said.

He touched her face and felt his heart melting. "You're crying."

153

Chapter Eighteen

"Please. Anne." He stared helplessly at a teardrop caught and glittering in the sable sweep of her lashes. "Don't cry."

"I'm not."

"That is patently false." He fished a handkerchief from his pocket and dabbed at her cheeks. Plenty of women had resorted to scenes of despair with him, some he'd even say were heartrending, but Anne's silent tears unmanned him as even the most histrionic sobs never had. "Why?" He brushed a finger beneath her eye. He would have given a great deal to have some of Devon's ease with her or for her to have with him some of the ease she had with Devon or even Thrale. But he was never sure how best to deal with her. A more complex woman he'd never met.

The moment Cynssyr touched her Anne felt a shock of awareness. In her imagination, she heard the bark of a gun, smelled acrid smoke. Heard a man's shout as a tall, lithe form slowly crumpled. No matter her determination not to let him ensnare her as he had so many others, she was desperately, resentfully, caught up anyway. Drowning in the green depths of his eyes, she felt her will ebb away. She said the first thing to pop into her head. "I'm homesick. For Bartley Green."

His fingertips moved over her cheek, and he gave a tender smile. She wanted him to stop touching her. She didn't think she could bear it if he did stop. The feeling made her despair all the sharper because she wanted him to mean it, that inviting glance and magical smile. She hated the way her heart sped up when he was near.

She told herself it was only a physical reaction. One she could control with enough effort. A good deal of effort. Lord Ruin. A well-deserved name. Deliberately, she drew away from him. She would *not* humiliate herself. About all she had with him was his respect. What would happen if he found out she was no different from any other silly woman who fell in love with him? "I miss my family, that's all."

"Understandable." He walked to the table, pushed aside the salver and his hat and leaned against the edge, arms crossed over his chest. One look at his face and the hint of curve to one side of his mouth was enough to see he didn't believe her. She wished she were a better liar. "You should entertain them here more often. I won't object if you do."

She shoved her spectacles higher on the bridge of her nose, then clasped her hands. "Thank you, your grace. I shall." He was staring at her, and she really wasn't sure how long she could take it.

As often happened, Ruan found himself focusing on some aspect of her features. The back of her neck once. Another time her lovely throat. Her eyes were perhaps her best feature. Unless you were looking, you didn't notice they were large and perfectly shaped. What a pity the spectacles hid her thick lashes and that soothing and gentle blue-gray. Her mouth, too, he thought, was lovely. A shape that made a man think of kissing. Slowly, thinking of kissing her, he smiled.

Anne's breath hitched, and she stepped back. "I take it," she said with some struggle for repose, "that your matter of honor this morning was settled satisfactorily?"

"You are my wife. You belong to me. I will never let you suffer insult without retribution. You are mine, and I will protect you with my life, if need be. That, Anne, is all you need to know. I will challenge any man who dares what Wilberfoss did."

Her worst imaginings rushed in like an incoming tide. Without another thought, she closed the distance between them and clutched his shirtfront. "What if he'd shot you?"

"It wasn't very likely."

"Cynssyr," she whispered. "Cynssyr, do not tell me you killed him."

"No." He dabbed at her cheeks again. "Though it was damn hard not to."

Tears. Betrayed by tears. He would, and probably did, despise her for the tears. How tiresome and childish. How like all the others. She collected herself. "It's time I went to Cornwall, Cynssyr." One emotion rose clearly above all the others she kept at bay with such poor success. Ruthless by necessity, she dismissed it. "To Fargate Castle."

"It's too early to begin your confinement. I've not even told Mama of your condition."

"Mary has already guessed. Heaven knows who else," she said.

He put his hands on her shoulders. "My dear, whatever is the matter? What are these tears? You have never been emotional before now."

"I don't know," she said, miserable because she was

lying to him. "I don't know, Cynssyr." She leaned against the hard expanse of his chest. And what a bit of stupidity that was. She ought to have moved away, not come closer. If she did not leave him, she would be hopelessly lost. Cornwall seemed her only escape.

Taking her chin between thumb and forefinger so that she had to look at him, he said evenly, "You may say anything to me. Anything at all."

"I don't know what's the matter." She drew a ragged breath, tremendously aware of him gently stroking her cheek with the side of his thumb. He did this to her without trying. Made her want to tell him her cares when she never had to anyone before. "I have always been the levelheaded one. A woman to be counted on in crisis."

Ruan drew her closer. "It's the child." His thumb stopped moving on her cheek to rest along the side of her face.

She pressed her palm to her chest. "When Lucy's husband died so horribly, I never felt helpless or that my world might come apart at any moment."

"You feel helpless now?"

"Everything is such a muddle." Despairing, she wiped at her cheek again. "This business with Wilberfoss . . ." She shook her head because emotion choked off the words that might express how she felt. Besides, it was far safer to say nothing at all. God knows what she might reveal in her present state.

"Come, Anne." Though he did not reach for her, he spoke with such genuine concern she felt he had. Her body reacted to the very thought of his hands on her.

"I am lost, Cynssyr, and I don't know how to get back to the woman I used to be. I've always known my own thoughts, and now I don't."

"Anne, my dear."

"I want you not to always regret I am your wife. All

I can do is cry like the sort of silly woman you despise."

"Believe me, you are nothing like the women I despise."

She swiped at a stray tear, determined not to make a greater fool of herself than she already had. The thought of his life's blood staining the cold, hard ground tore at her. "You could have been killed," she blurted out. "My God, you could have died." Without her there to hold him and tell him she would be desolate without him.

"So, that's what this is all about." He was relieved to find the solution so near at hand. "Wilberfoss upset you. Rightly so. But I have put an end to it, so no more of this nonsense about Cornwall. It's too soon."

She sighed and turned away, but not before he caught a glimpse of her despair. He couldn't have this. This effect she had on him.

"Anne." He made her face him again. "Had I made your acquaintance in a more normal fashion, we wouldn't have this awkwardness between us."

She smiled sadly. "If we had met like any two people might, you would be married to my sister."

"But *you* are my wife." He let his voice drop. "And I am dying for want of you."

She looked away because she was afraid of what he might see if she didn't. "Never say so."

"Your innocence goes straight to the core of you, doesn't it?" He cupped her face between his hands, staring at her. Her eyes slowly closed. He kissed first one eye, then the other. Without thinking what he was doing, he pulled out a loose hairpin and let it fall to the marble floor. "Wilberfoss was drunk. Just as you said. I kept thinking of you telling me not to put a bullet through him as he deserved. As it was, I believe he thought he would die from his wound."

Her eyes popped open. "Wound? What wound?"

158

"An accident. The fool walked into my shot." Another pin, then another came free until her hair spilled over her shoulders.

"It would have been wrong to kill him."

He shook his head. "I could feel you there, disapproving."

"Cynssyr." She lifted her hands to her head, trying to gather up her hair. "The servants."

He pushed away her hands. "Never mind them." A river of silver-gilt fell over his fingers. He ran his hands though the tresses, discarding the occasional hairpin. "I love the feel of your hair." He breathed in the scent of her. "You always smell good," he whispered. He didn't even know what scent she wore. "What perfume is that?" When he found the last pin, he filled his hands with her soft, silky hair.

"*Eau de Naphre*." Her nervous eyes followed the downward spiral of the last hairpin. It clattered on the floor, a faint echo of sound. "My mother wore it."

Desire burned through him, an inferno as unexpected as it was undeniable. He was finished waiting for her to do more than accept him. He would make her lose control. His thumb moved to her lower lip. "I might have done a good deal worse than you. Left to my own devices, I would have." He tipped her head and gently brushed her mouth with his.

"Please. Do not say things to me you don't mean."

"Agreed, Madam." He released her hair. "But I wonder, if I spoke nothing but unvarnished truth, would you believe me?" His hands trailed to her shoulders, a feather-light touch that continued to her waist. She drew in a ragged breath. "Will you believe any compliment I pay you?" he asked.

"Can I or will I?" she asked faintly, having trouble catching her breath.

He moved closer. "You tell me the answer to that."

159

She met his gaze and told him the naked truth. "Yes. When you look at me like that, yes."

He lifted her onto the table and stepped between her thighs. She stared at him, never taking her eyes from his while he worked his hands beneath her skirts. "I have this image in my head I can't dismiss. Exactly this. Of making love to you like this." He glanced over her shoulder. "Thank God, that tiger is gone." His fingers touched her calves, stroking upward and around to her thighs until he was gripping both her legs.

"Cynssyr." She whispered the protest.

"We'll not be disturbed."

"How do you know?"

He gave her a slow, blood-boiling smile and lied. "I do not pay my servants to disturb me when I am occupied with important matters." As he said this, he released one of her garters and slid her stocking down. Then the other. He watched himself push up her skirts and then followed the slow glide of his hands along her bare thighs. "You have beautiful legs." Some years back, before Katie, before he'd gone off to join the war, he'd had a mistress close to his physical ideal. Not as perfect as Anne, but very close. He'd broken with her sooner rather than later because, quite bluntly, the woman had all the intelligence of a turnip and so little imagination he could endure no more than the briefest conversation with her.

He moved forward and released one of her legs so he could unbutton his trousers. Her eyes, when he looked up because he was free of his clothing, were wide and aware, locked onto his face. Her hand rose and clutched the front of his shirt. He got a palm under one of her thighs and lifted it. "Look at me," he told her. "I want to see your face when I come into you." She was ready for him. She gasped when he was at her entrance and

160

sliding in and in, as deep as he could get into heat and wetness.

Her fingers tightened in his shirt, her head fell back. "No," he said. He caressed the side of her face, bringing her head back to him. His lips hovered just over hers. "No, you must look at me. I want you to see my face." He took in a long breath as he pulled out and rocked back, very much at the edge of climax. Too much. "Can you not see how much I want you?" He stared into her eyes, willing her to give herself. The pent up emotion was there, so palpable he might damn near taste it. "What are you thinking?" he rasped. "Tell me." She held him close, arching toward him. She was not unaroused, but not abandoned to him as he wanted, as he knew she could be. "Tell me," he insisted.

"You are beautiful, Cynssyr." She touched his face, and he saw in her eyes what she would never say. That she believed herself his inferior and worse, that there was probably nothing he could say to make her believe different.

"It's you who's beautiful, Anne. Inside and out, you are the most beautiful creature on earth." He moved deeper into her, changing the tempo of his strokes until he hovered at the precipice. He could feel her tighten around him, the contraction of her body around him, and still she held back, fought for control as if she dared not let go. She did not know, or recall, what she might feel with him if only she gave in. Even so, it was good. Very good. Enough to create a storm in him and drive him past all concern.

"Cynssyr," she said in a lost and wistful voice. He drove into her one last time before a shattering release made him shout to the ceiling. The sound echoed off the painted dome above their heads. He did not come back to himself at all quickly. Sheer pleasure wrung him out. He gave not a single thought to where they were or the fact that anyone who might open the door would see his naked backside until she moved in an attempt to relieve her by now uncomfortable position on the table.

A lovely pink tinted Anne's cheeks while they put their clothes to rights. He retrieved her slipper which had ended up several feet behind them, but she had to put it on a bare foot because her stocking was a shambles, and he'd somehow managed to break her garter. Grinning a little, he put stocking and garter in his pocket. Her hair spilled down her back, hiding her face from him as she knelt gathering scattered hairpins. "Anne," he said.

"Just a few more."

He brought her to her feet. "I'll buy you a thousand more."

Her fingers fisted around her hairpins. "I don't need more hairpins. I've plenty, thank you."

"No hairpins, then. But, what do you want from me, Anne? What do you want most of all? Jewels? More gowns? Name it. Whatever I have, it's yours." How many women had longed to hear those words from him? He'd never said them to Katie. No, instead, he'd served himself up to the one woman most likely to refuse him.

Her eyes darkened to stormy gray. "Truly?"

He nodded despite the likelihood that he did not want to know the answer. If she asked for the world, he'd do his damnedest to give it to her. But, somehow, he didn't think that's what she'd ask for.

"I want to go to Cornwall."

He steadied himself. "My dear, we cannot leave London until the Sessions are over."

Slowly, she stooped to retrieve another wayward hairpin. "You must stay, but I have no such obligation."

Unimaginable, letting her leave him. "I need you here." He simply wasn't an unselfish man.

"Why?"

For a moment, he was flummoxed, at a complete and total loss for a reply that did not reveal more than she was prepared to accept. Desperation spawned inspiration. He didn't consider the implications of involving her in his private affairs, he just did it and was glad for it. "Because," he said, "I need you to interview the women who've been assaulted."

"I see."

"They count on me, you know," he said. "Whether they say so or not, they expect me to put a stop to this. All of them. Husbands and fathers alike. They trust me to protect their wives and daughters. Their lovers. And I have let them down. I need your help, Anne."

Behind the careless drawl, she heard despair. "Oh, Cynssyr." She put a finger over his mouth and knew giving in was a terrible mistake. "I will help you. Whatever you ask."

Chapter Nineteen

Ruan, Devon and Benjamin waited two interminable hours for Anne to return from Mrs. Featherstone. Ruan couldn't sit. He paced while Devon and Benjamin lounged on chairs near the fireplace. They were in a corner parlor that overlooked Queen Anne Street to the front and Wimpole Street to the left. Mostly Ruan watched rain drip down the windows and counted cobbles in Wimpole Street below. Nine hundred fifty-five. Four wagons, five hansom cabs, three nannies with young children, one pickpocket, twenty-six gentlemen, ten tradesmen, eleven servants male and female, including those glimpsed through windows. He lost count of ladies with their companions.

"Taking a bloody long time," Ben complained for the dozenth time. Devon had long mastered the art of silence. He'd not spoken in the last hour at least, surrounding himself in brooding quiet. Ben glared at Devon for not agreeing and spoke in an irritated voice. "Stop that infernal pacing, Cyn."

"I don't like this at all. We have ill used her," Devon remarked from his sullen slouch on the sofa. "Dragging her into this sordid affair."

"We ought to have involved her sooner." Ruan was completely unapologetic. "If I'm right, and the women tell her things they could not tell a man, then we'll stop this all the sooner."

"I have to say I agree." Ben reluctantly nodded.

Ruan resumed his pacing. He analyzed the tightness in his chest. A sense of anticipation. And it wasn't just because he wanted to hear what Anne learned from Mrs. Featherstone. He wanted to have Anne in the room with him now. He missed the way he felt when they were together. He thought her fascinating. In all his life, he'd never known what it was like to admire a woman until Anne. To appreciate the physical and the intellectual at one and the same time. To be so entirely enthralled.

"Cyn?"

He looked at Ben and had the impression he'd missed something. "What?"

"What do you think?" he asked, very slowly, as if annoyed that he had to ask.

"About what?"

"Anne."

"I don't see it's any business of yours."

"Well, you can't just send her off to talk to the others without consulting us, Ruan," Benjamin said.

Ruan kept still. Dear Christ, he'd completely misinterpreted the question. "Of course I will not," he replied. "Withers next, I should think."

"Yes," said Devon stirring slightly on the sofa. He gave Benjamin a look. "Withers next, just as he said."

165

"Twenty pounds to your one, Devon," Ben said casually lifting a hand, "that Cyn here was thinking of Anne when he was off woolgathering."

"Well," Devon said sourly. "He was thinking of a woman, at any rate."

Ben made a show of adjusting a cufflink. "I fought it when it happened to me, Cyn, old man. But I swear to God, it's not half as bad as you fear and much better than what happens if you don't admit it."

"What in hell are you babbling about?"

"Love, Cynssyr. I speak of love."

"Love?"

"Don't repeat that rubbish about love and delusion." Ben's amiable face rearranged itself to something edged with anger. "You can live without love, I won't deny you that. But what a horrible life."

Devon laughed softly but without amusement. "Of course, Aldreth means mutual love. He loves his wife, and she loves him in return. Any other state of affairs, I assure you, is truly miserable."

"My condolences, Bracebridge," said Ben.

"I don't accept them."

"That's enough," Ruan softly said. Hell. Hell and bloody hell. His own freedom was fast becoming mere illusion. It ought to matter more. "To the devil with you," he told the window. "To the very devil with you both."

The carriage he'd put at Anne's disposal appeared on Queen Anne Street. His heart sped up, a purely involuntary reaction. "She's here." He watched the carriage draw up in the driveway. Henry jumped from the back and ran around to wait with an open umbrella. A footman flipped down the step and opened the door. Anne descended and Henry surged forward to make sure the umbrella protected her from the wet.

It seemed forever until she arrived in the salon. She

Join the Historical Romance Book Club and GET 4 FREE* BOOKS NOW!

A $23.96 Value!

Yes! I want to subscribe to the Historical Romance Book Club.

Please send me my **4 FREE* BOOKS.** I have enclosed $2.00 for shipping/handling. Each month I'll receive the four newest Historical Romance selections to preview for 10 days. If I decide to keep them, I will pay the Special Members Only discounted price of just $4.24 each, a total of $16.96, plus $2.00 shipping/handling ($23.55 US in Canada). This is a **SAVINGS OF AT LEAST $5.00** off the bookstore price. There is no minimum number of books I must buy, and I may cancel the program at any time. In any case, the **4 FREE* BOOKS** are mine to keep.

*In Canada, add $5.00 shipping/handling per order for the first shipment. For all future shipments to Canada, the cost of membership is $23.55 US, which includes shipping and handling. (All payments must be made in US dollars.)

NAME: _____

ADDRESS: _____

CITY: _____ **STATE:** _____

COUNTRY: _____ **ZIP:** _____

TELEPHONE: _____

E-MAIL: _____

SIGNATURE: _____

If under 18, Parent or Guardian must sign. Terms, prices, and conditions subject to change. Subscription subject to acceptance. Dorchester Publishing reserves the right to reject any order or cancel any subscription.

looked quite neat in her royal blue pelisse. "I've ordered tea," she said, walking in.

"Well?" Devon said when Ruan helped Anne to a seat.

She pushed back the trim of her hat. "You must stop them."

"We will," Ruan said.

"Good." She searched her reticule for her glasses. "Here they are." Ruan experienced an uncomfortable spark of arousal when she looked at him, outraged, spectacles perched firmly on her nose. A handkerchief, well used, fell unnoticed from her sleeve. He lifted his eyes from the tear-stained bit of silk. The spectacles slipped down her nose long enough to show eyes faintly red, as if she'd been up too late the night before, only he knew she hadn't been. She replaced the frames with a determined motion. "It is as you suspected, Cynssyr. She did not tell you all that happened."

"The woman did not," he said brusquely, "tell me a damn thing."

She looked at Devon and Ben. "Two men assaulted her." Speaking crisply, she drew herself up, back ramrod straight. "Not the same men who accosted her in the street. Those men were ruffians, they spoke in street cant and were in need of a thorough bath."

They fell silent when the merchant brought in tea and sandwiches. Anne ate a slice of bread while the others set to. "One is certainly a gentleman," she continued. "His accent was educated and from London. The second spoke well but with a country accent, very slight, but there. Liverpool. Or some such place in Lancashire, she thought. The second man, the one with the country accent, was slender with dark eyes and dark hair. His mouth is thin, his cheeks and chin narrow." She hesitated, a thoughtful quirk to her mouth. "He is a violent man and cruel. He does not like women, Cynssyr." She made a face. "I'm sorry. That is my interpretation. Mrs. Featherstone did not say that."

"You did well."

"Extremely well," Devon echoed.

"Thank you." Anne practically glowed with pleasure. Deep inside him, Ruan felt an answering pleasure. They did well together. Remarkably well.

"When she revived, the other was—" She reached for her handkerchief but of course did not find it. Devon handed her his. "Thank you. The other was taking liberties." A flush, anger and embarrassment both, colored her cheeks. "With her person. He wore a sort of mask that hid his features. He told her, the man did, that she ought to enjoy what he was doing as his associate—that's the exact word he used," she said, crushing the handkerchief. "His *associate*—had been so cruel by comparison."

"Blackguard," Devon said.

"Very much so, Devon." As always, her aplomb roused his admiration. "She believes she was held outside of London. She was not assaulted until very late the night she was taken, very nearly morning. She could hear livestock. Cows and pigs. A rooster. Her room contained only a bed. A house, not a cottage was her impression."

"Did she say how far they traveled from where she was abducted?" asked Ben.

"She didn't know."

Ruan pushed away his tea and jumped to his feet. "What did the two ruffians look like?" Intent on these new facts and getting them to fall into a sensible pattern that would lead him to whomever was responsible, he fell by habit into the steely voice he'd employed with his soldiers during the war. He paced before her, hands clasped behind his back. Anne met his iron gaze with a steel of her own. She was utterly reliable. Steady as any man. More dependable than many men he'd known.

"She did not have any more detail than I have given you."

"The carriage. Was it a hack or did she think it a private vehicle? Was she able to see anything inside?"

"No. She was blindfolded."

"The one with the mask. Did she notice distinctive jewelry or physical characteristics?" He concentrated on the flood of information and on uncovering every last detail to be had. "Anything besides voice that made her think him a gentleman? His clothes? A monogram embroidered anywhere? Engraved buttons? Perhaps an unusual watch fob? A scent or hair oil?"

"Slow down, Cyn," Ben softly warned. "She's not one of your soldiers."

"A ring, Cynssyr. She saw a ring. Carved with some sort of animal. A signet ring. Worn on the small finger of his left hand."

"What kind? A bird? Beast? Real or mythical?"

"She didn't remember any more than it was an animal."

"T'was someone she knows," he said. "That's plain."

"Yes."

"Why else would he go to such lengths to hide his face from her when the other man did not?"

"So I concluded, as well." She twisted the handkerchief, holding one end in either hand. "I cannot believe this of Richard. He is kind and gentle." She looked at all three men. "I like him. He loves Emily."

"Do not let emotion cloud your judgment." Despite Ben's admonition, he spoke to her exactly as he would have to a promising officer. "Emotion prevents reason. You must suppress emotion at any cost." The moment he spoke, he wanted the thought back, but the words had flown. Emotion unleashed was precisely what he most wanted from his wife. He thought of the victims and what they had suffered. He thought of husbands and fathers frantic with worry, impotent with rage. What if Anne were next? A hole opened inside him that nothing could fill except Anne. He did not like even a taste of what those men had felt. God, it would be living hell. "There must be something more!"

Ben put a hand on Ruan's shoulder. "Cyn. Please." To Anne, he said, "Who do you think it is? If you had to pick someone, whom would you chose?"

She answered without hesitation. "Lord Wilberfoss."

"He's a boy."

"Not a boy," she replied. "A spoiled, immature man."

"That's as may be." Devon adulterated his tea with a healthy dose of cream and three lumps of sugar. "But he doesn't need the money."

Anne sipped the weak tea she'd brewed herself. "Money isn't his reason. Whoever it is, Lord Wilberfoss, or Richard or someone else, he enjoys it."

"But why Wilberfoss?" Ben again. More gentle than Ruan, but just as relentless. "Because of what he did?"

"Not entirely." Leaning back, she fiddled with one of her gloves, eyes shuttered and unreadable.

Ruan restrained himself from pacing anew. He drew a deep breath and asked, "Why else, then?"

"I don't know why, Cynssyr." A distant church bell chimed the hour. "But I feel it. Perhaps I am prejudiced." She lifted her hands then let them fall to her lap. "What have you heard about Richard?"

"Very little." Devon took a long draught of his tea. "Rumors. Nothing I can substantiate. But I've heard even less of Wilberfoss."

"Wilberfoss?" Ben shook his head. "I just don't see it. He's harmless."

Ruan studied Anne's face. Composed and calm as ever. He trusted her judgment and instincts. "Devon, how soon can you get someone to Liverpool? Have him nose around the larger estates thereabouts."

"Quickly enough."

"Do it." He stopped before the tea cart and poured himself some tea. Unlike Devon, he drank his black and just short of bitter. When he turned back, Devon had moved to the sofa next to Anne. His arm circled her shoulder, and he murmured soothing words in a low voice. As he watched, Anne leaned toward him until her forehead touched his shoulder. The truth was, Ruan thought, silently watching his best friend comfort his wife, Anne had found something in him he thought didn't exist. Damnation, but she had him hopelessly trapped.

Devon glanced up to meet Ruan's eyes. Even Ben watched in silence, saying nothing. Well, then. He saw but one way out. He must turn the tables, as it were, and make her fall in love with him first. The solution to his predicament was as simple, and as difficult, as that.

Chapter Twenty

Anne left Cavendish Square quite late. For some reason, she'd expected Cynssyr would appear at Devon's afternoon rout. But he hadn't, and then she and Devon had got to talking until long after the last guest took his leave, and the time simply flew away. Just as it had four years ago in Bartley Green. Full dark had fallen by the time she recalled herself and made her excuses. Devon refused to hear her apologies for taking so much of his time. He walked her to her carriage and stood in the pouring rain until the carriage left the drive.

The rain made a lake of the street and soaked everything: her shoes, her cloak and her hat. Poor Henry. He took the rain as a personal affront to her dignity and his. Once in the coach under the flickering light of the interior lamps, she wondered what to do about Emily. The loss of Lord Wilberfoss's suit hadn't affected her at all, which relieved Anne no end. But she didn't seem to care for any of her other suitors. Not even Thrale, to whom she was in fact well-suited. Unless Anne missed her guess, and she didn't think so, Thrale was half in love with Emily, and without encouragement, either.

Indeed, Anne spent the last hours of Devon's party watching her youngest sister act as if London's most eligible and charming men annoyed her by their very existence.

A snarl of vehicles heading for the opera or Vauxhall or one of the dozens of entertainments to be found in town brought the carriage to a stop. The coachman roared at someone to move on. There came an answering shout and they rocked and at last advanced, but no more than the length of the coach. Anne peeked out the window. Raindrops flashed like tiny diamonds past the lamps to dash themselves onto the street. The carriage lurched again and instead of the black mass of another coach, she saw the street and two men at the curb.

While they inched forward, one of the men peered from under an umbrella that served as poor protection against the downpour. His companion remained lost in the edge of shadow. The first darted forward, directly toward her. Her heart leapt and with a cry that stuck in her throat, she let the curtain fall back.

"Duchess!"

She knew the voice. Leaning forward again, she flicked back the curtain. "Mr. Durling?" The massive shape that was Henry jumped from position at the back and took up a rather threatening posture opposite the two men. "It's all right, Henry. It's Mr. Durling," Anne said.

"At your service." Durling glanced over his shoulder. "May I introduce my friend?" A heavy cape shielded the man from the wet and from scrutiny.

"Yes, of course."

"Duchess, I present Mr. John Martin."

"We've met," she said.

173

At last, Martin came forward to stand under Durling's umbrella. He bowed and then Durling stepped into the street to avoid being skewered by some passing umbrella. Martin once again stood in the rain. Durling peered in the carriage. "What's this?" He affected astonishment. "You are alone?"

"My governess has the night off, sir."

Martin laughed.

"Might we trouble you for a lift, Duchess?" Durling asked. "I've not a coin in my pocket, and we don't fancy walking, Martin and I." He put a hand in his trousers' pocket and turned it inside out to demonstrate his lack of funds.

She opened the door. She did not care for Mr. Martin, but Durling amused her, and really the rain might drown them. For the sake of Durling, she supposed she could tolerate Martin. "Come along, then. Where to?"

"Dorset Street." Raising his voice for the benefit of the coachman, he said, "The home of Mr. Frederick Merryweather. I believe you know the way." He fell onto the seat across from her, shaking water off his umbrella with a motion low to the ground. Martin joined them soon after. "He's having a party, and we are sure to get a decent meal and failing that, a decent drink." He placed his hat on his lap. Martin did the same.

"Besides," Martin quipped, wiping rain from his forehead. "His servants are always extremely pretty, and I find that ever the mark of a man with excellent taste."

"Mr. Martin, you've made friends quickly for a man who only just arrived in town." She knew nothing of him, really, except that he had influential friends, a talented tailor, and that Cynssyr did not like him, which meant more to her than his having all the friends in the world.

"Oh, Mr. John Martin," Durling drawled, "is the sort of amusing young man who gets himself invited to the best parties despite his lack of wealth, inherited or otherwise."

Martin grinned. "I am never five minutes without a friend, madam."

"How many minutes ago did you meet Mr. Durling?" she asked.

"Twenty, at least."

"Martin and I are old friends. We met years back." Sighing, Durling lovingly stroked the leather seats. "Ah, to have the money to indulge one's good taste."

"Nothing but the best for Cynssyr," Martin said.

"Well." Durling crossed his legs and clasped his hands behind his head. His mouth turned up at one side. "I shall enjoy the ride, but it's the view that has me enthralled."

"Mr. Durling." She had to move her feet because Martin had stretched out his legs and did not move even when the toes of his boots touched her slippers.

"Julian. Do please call me Julian." Suddenly, he leaned forward. "A renowned beauty whose name I'll not repeat has been summarily dismissed from the company of her longtime lover, and I have it on good authority she will be at Dorset Street tonight. All the gentlemen are agog with the news. Who shall next be cradled in her alabaster arms? Tell me, Duchess, shall I aspire to such heights?"

"You're incorrigible," Martin said, laughing. By now, Anne's feet fit smack against her side of the seat. In the semidark, she could just make out his smile and shadowed eyes.

"I'm told women like a man who's a bit of a challenge," Durling replied. "Tell me, Duchess, what think you?"

"I'm the very last person to give you advice."

"Shall I ply her with roses and sweetmeats? Amuse

175

Carolyn Jewel

her with my wit? Pen her poems? Well, not poems. Poems fail me most miserably, I fear."

Anne laughed. "Try them all. One of them is bound to work."

He sighed, rolling his eyes heavenward. "I fear some fellow with more blunt than I will succeed in capturing her affections. I haven't the funds for extravagant gifts."

"It's not extravagance that matters."

"What them? My inestimable person? It's all I have to offer."

"You're a woman," Martin said to her. "Tell the poor man how to woo his beauty, for I tell you, I am tired of his complaints." His grin reappeared. Anne was sure he meant to charm her, but she felt quite the opposite effect. "By the by, I shall take notes as you do, for the advice is bound to come in handy."

"I'm afraid I've no head for romance."

"What would win your heart?" Martin gave her an arch glance.

Durling leaned forward again, waving a hand to silence his friend. "What if I told you my heart flutters when you are near? Would that persuade you to me?"

"If ever a man said such a thing to me, I should tell him it seems a most serious matter and that he ought to consult a physician for a remedy."

"I cannot sleep for thinking of you?"

"Warm milk is a cure."

"A cooing dove is cacophony compared to your dulcet tones?"

The carriage stopped. "Dorset Street," called the coachman.

Durling put a hand to his chest. "What am I to do, Duchess? My case seems hopeless."

"It is," Martin said.

"Surely not, sir." She touched Durling's arm. "But I should not mention cacophonous doves, were I you."

176

Durling and Martin sat unmoving while they waited for the groom to pull down the step. Martin, apparently thinking she did not notice in the dim interior light, stared hard at her. She did not like his assessing look. She could feel the calculation coming up short. As Martin put on his hat, his coat sleeve bared perhaps an inch of skin above his glove, revealing a poorly healing gash. "I have a balm that might help that," Anne said.

"It's nothing. A scratch." He tugged on his sleeve, covering the wound.

"Let me send you some."

Martin laughed. "Don't I know what Cynssyr would say if you did!"

"Cynssyr never condemns a kindness, if that's what you mean."

"As you say." He nodded his assent. "Send what you wish. Durling will see it gets to me."

"I wish," Durling said without any of his facile drawl, "that I had met you before Cynssyr married you." The glimpse of the man he might have been intrigued her. "You might have saved me from myself." That made Martin guffaw. Durling elbowed him and the sound abruptly stopped.

"How could I save you when I cannot even save myself, Mr. Durling?" Anne said lightly.

The carriage door opened, and the two men stepped down. The rain fell as hard as ever. Martin pulled up his collar again. Durling bowed. "My compliments, Duchess, and my thanks."

"Good night, Mr. Durling. Mr. Martin."

Durling stared into the coach, never minding the rain. Martin, however, sunk his hands into his pockets, hunching his shoulders against the wet. "It's true, you know," Durling said. "He's given up the most desirable woman in all of England. Well, almost all of England."

"For another."

Durling gave her a quizzical look. "Is it possible you're the only one who doesn't know for whom?"

"Good evening, gentlemen."

Henry came to close the door. "Home, Madam Duchess?" he asked.

"Yes," she said. "Home."

He touched the brim of his hat and closed the door. Home. When, she wondered, had Cywrthorn become home? The moment she walked into the grand foyer, she knew her husband hadn't yet returned from his day. Something in the air tingled when he was in residence, and she felt nothing now. Upstairs she changed from her damp things and went to the library to fetch a book. A comfortable sofa by the fireplace invited her to sit, which she did, curling up in one corner.

Sometime later, a shiver of awareness sped along her spine, breaking the pleasant concentration of reading. Cynssyr. Without doubt, she knew it was him. Hardly a moment later, in he walked. Hickenson stood behind him, holding a heavy leather case and looking anxious. Anne was beginning to think anxiety was Hickenson's perpetual state.

"Good evening, Anne."

"Cynssyr." The sound of his voice, deep and smooth as silk, sent liquid heat flowing through her veins. Seeing him had much the same effect. "Mr. Hickenson." The short man bowed.

"Please." Cynssyr lifted a hand to stop her from rising. "Don't disturb yourself. Hickenson." Turning, he addressed his secretary. "We'll finish up tomorrow."

"The Livingstone brief, your grace?"

"Put the writ in my study. I'll read it later tonight." Hickenson bowed. "Your grace."

Once Hickenson made his exit, Cynssyr walked to the sofa where Anne sat. "I'm surprised to see you home. I thought you'd be at Portman Square." Sighing deeply, he sat beside her.

"I wanted to rest. Something you don't do often enough."

"Surely, that's the truth. This Livingstone matter has everyone all worked up. Quite the legal knot. The hearing is in three days, and I've a stack of papers as high as you are tall to digest before then." She lifted a hand to rub the back of his neck. "Mm." He bent his neck to give her better access. "The Cabinet is making noises about sending someone to Belgium. Every time Eldon looks at me now, I fear he'll ask me to go." Anne gently kneaded up the side of his neck and got a soft groan for her trouble. Even that small sound contained an undercurrent of silk. "Thrale won't see reason on the pensions bill, I've lost Norfolk entirely, and I've no support but from Canning on reform, and little enough from that quarter."

"Lie down."

"I've no time." But he stretched out his legs and rested his head on her lap. His eyes closed in ecstasy when she pressed her fingers to his temples with a gentle circling motion.

"Stop worrying for just five minutes. Hickenson will survive five minutes, and probably a good deal longer, alone with the Livingstone brief."

"It's heavenly, Anne, but my beard is growing," he said, eyes still closed. "It must feel like sandpaper on your fingers."

"Hush." Since his eyes remained closed, she drank her fill of him. The strong lines of his face, vital even at rest. She liked his mouth best of all. Firm, and he would never admit to it, with more than a hint of sensitivity. He really was too lovely for words. A furrow remained between his eyebrows, and she circled a finger there until that at last smoothed out.

"Keep that up, and I'll fall asleep." He moved one hand between her back and the sofa so that she fit into the curve of his arm.

"You should. I know you didn't sleep last night. You had another nightmare."

"Did I wake you?" His eyebrow arched. "I'm sorry if I did."

"You didn't." After a bit, when she realized he wasn't going to fall asleep, she said, "I saw John Martin tonight." Cynssyr's eyes opened. "He was with Julian Durling. Mr. Martin said they'd been friends for some time."

"Durling keeps worse company than I thought."

"I like Mr. Durling."

"Really?" Which sounded a good deal more like *Why?*

"He's amusing. But I don't like Mr. Martin at all."

He turned a little, pulling her toward him so that his face was nearly hidden by her gown. Her pulse jumped. "I don't wish to discuss any of the men who admire you more than I like. I have been cradled here on your lap, Anne, thinking that just this once I will keep my hands off you. Just once I will demonstrate some restraint. Turn around." He moved them both to face the rear of the room. "This way. Hold on to the back of the sofa." Anne's body responded so quickly she would have been ashamed had she the wits to think of anything but his hands stealing beneath her skirts. His front pressed against her back and then she felt the whisper of air on her lower parts. "Let's give these books a tale to tell, shall we?"

Anne laughed—she couldn't help herself—even though she was nearly out of her mind with the sensation of him slipping inside her.

He drew in a breath, running his hands from high above her stockings to her garters, then upward along the back of her thighs until their joined bodies forced his hands over her hips. "Anne. Lovely, lovely, Anne." His voice dropped lower and softer, to a drugged whisper that somehow worked its way inside her. "I want you to love me. Will you? Will you, please?"

She pressed her hips backward. "Like this?"

After a moment's silence, he said in that same low, drugged whisper, "That will do for now."

Chapter Twenty-one

Ruan came awake with a start. He sat, taking in deep breaths of air against the pounding of his heart, disoriented because he had no idea where he was. His skin felt slick and fever hot.

A woman's hand touched his bare shoulder, cool and comforting. But this was not Katie's familiar room. Her room he knew like his own. Nor was it Katie next to him in the bed, and that panicked him. She said something, but he heard only the sound. A foreign language perhaps. If not Katie, then who? If not Herriot Street, then where? The woman's hand left his shoulder.

Eyes squeezed tight shut, he heard linens rustling, felt the mattress shift and guessed she'd wrapped the duvet around her then slipped off the bed. With her leaving, a sense of loss smothered him, a haunting, drowning bleakness that shook him worse even than not knowing where he was. A moment later, she was at his side of the bed, holding a cup.

"Here. Cold tea, but it's something."

His bearings returned. He was in his wife's room. She was naked under that duvet because he'd all ready made love to her once. As he had every night since she'd come to London. Not so long ago that was, yet the time when she hadn't been with him seemed ages ago, another, bleaker lifetime. "Thank you." He took the cup and tossed back the contents in one swallow. A chill shook him.

"You'll catch your death." Anne leaned in to straighten what remained of the bed covers, pulling them up and over his waist, then padded to the fireplace. "You were shouting in French," she said as she stirred the embers. "Too fast for me to understand much. You're more than fluent."

"I've a facility for language." If he'd shouted in French, then he'd dreamed of Quatre Bras.

She poured half a bucket of fresh coal on the fire. The duvet draped down in the back, exposing a length of delicate shoulder and mid-back. Her independence captivated him. No helpless female she. Katie would have lain shivering more and more dramatically until he rolled out of a warm bed himself. Or called a servant and been cold the meanwhile. "No doubt you speak Spanish and Portugese as well."

"Enough to get by." His heartbeat was calmer now, the dream further from memory. "A smattering of Flemish, too."

"I have only a little French. Well, you know that." Still clutching the duvet around her, she came back to the bed. Instead of getting in, she stood uncertainly. She bent down, momentarily disappearing from his sight. When she straightened, she had his robe. Carefully, because she insisted on a lamentable modesty, she folded it over a chair. He held out his empty cup. She took it. "More, sir?"

"No."

"Are you sure? It's no trouble."

"Come back to bed, Anne." He snagged a corner of the duvet and tugged. She resisted his effort to draw her to him, but eventually she had to practically hop forward. "I can't believe I want you again." Christ, did he want her. His need for her actually hurt. He pulled her onto the bed with him. Quatre Bras receded as he set himself the task of unwrapping his wife.

She tried to scoot away, but he followed. "What are you doing?" she asked.

"Trying very hard not to be a clod."

She slapped his hand. "Whatever are you about?"

"Kissing you."

"But, it's nearly morning."

"You don't need darkness to kiss." He had a hand beneath the duvet now. Ah, her hip, lovely. His body clenched. The way she felt against him was going to drive him mad.

She laughed, a low sound in the back of her throat. "You don't?"

"No," he murmured, bringing himself over her and sliding his hand from hip to waist. How he loved the way she laughed. "Now, open your mouth. Just a little." He touched her lips with his. Gently. "Just so."

When he drew back, she said dreamily, "Your lips are soft."

"So are yours." He nuzzled her cheek, breathing her scent. "You kiss well, Anne."

There was a very brief pause, then: "I have an excellent tutor."

Her wit, unexpected as it so often was, made him chuckle. He could not see her smile but he heard the lazy grin in her voice, the dreamy, sensual breathlessness. Not one inch of his body didn't burn. "If you like," he said in her ear, "you may kiss me now."

"Haven't I been?"

"No, my dear. I kissed you." She hesitated, and he said, stroking a hand along her bare thigh, "It's going to be my life's work to thoroughly corrupt you." He was fully aroused. By now, Anne knew enough to adjust when he sought her entrance. Her hips lifted. He guessed most of what he did embarrassed her, but she never complained or refused, and quite frankly, by the end, he never cared if she was in agonies of shame, because there wasn't another woman who came close to making him come apart like she did. Like he was right now, teetering on the edge of reason.

He reared up enough to see her face. Ragged breaths parted her lips, the back of her head pressed into the mattress bared her throat and lifted her chin toward him. He circled his hips, a tight, deliberate motion intended to elicit another sharp intake of her breath, which it did. Slowly, as if her eyelids were weighted, her eyes opened and met his.

"How does it feel when I am inside you?" he asked.

She wrapped a hand around the back of his neck and tried to bring his head down to hers. Since she did it only to avoid the embarrassment of making him a reply, he removed her hand and pinned it to the mattress.

"Answer me, Anne." He moved deeper inside her and for a brief while the room had no sound but the breath entering then leaving their lungs, two bodies moving on the mattress, of skin touching skin, silk sheets sliding to the floor. The moment he felt her anxiety ease he put his mouth close to her ear and demanded, "How does it feel? Tell me."

A small cry of frustration escaped her. "I haven't the words, Cynssyr."

"Your sex is hot and deep and tight. You have this trick—Oh, God—of closing around me with such wet and greedy eagerness I am quite taken away. Shall I give you some words? Marvelous. Astonishing. Magnificent. Sublime. Oh, hell, Anne. Christ. Bloody damned good." He caught her other hand. "Do not do that yet. I'll be damned if I come before you do."

A bit later, he lay over her, sweating, heart thumping, breathing like a man desperate for air. "I would never hurt you, Anne," he said, holding her tight. He stroked her back, keeping her in his embrace.

"I know."

"Then let go when I've made you come. Shout, scream. Call my name. Call on God, if you are so moved." He dropped a kiss on her shoulder, tasting their mingled sweat, then rolled so he lay on his side with her nestled in the curve of his body. She didn't say anything in reply. He was hot and sticky for a different reason now, but he had no inclination to let her go. He needed the contact with her, couldn't bear to let go.

"Manly," she softly whispered.

After a bit, he repeated, puzzled, "Manly."

"You feel manly when you are inside me."

He gave a grin she couldn't see. "Well thank God for that." He waited until she fell asleep in his arms before he slipped from her bed and returned to his room. This hour of the night rarely passed with him asleep, and he did not want to wake Anne with his restlessness. He knew the dreams would be back.

A bloodcurdling shout cleared Anne's sleep-fogged mind. That horrible, anguished call came from her husband. Worse, far worse than any previous nightmare. Throwing off the bedcovers, she hurried through the connecting door and into his room. The muffled sound of limbs against bedcovers raised the hair on the back of her neck as he thrashed in the bed. He hit the drawn hangings. She dove past them and was enclosed in black. The air swirled as if with the demons that tortured Cynssyr.

"To me, men!" One flailing arm tangled in the covers.

"Sir? Cynssyr?" She grabbed his free arm, trapped the other with her body and did her best to hold him. Steel-hard muscles contracted with the effort of his dream.

He sat bolt upright, Anne sprawled across his lap, and thundered, *"Hold your fire!"*

"Sir," she cried, falling head-over-teakettle off the bed to land, thud, on the carpet. From the floor, she said, "It's all right. You've had a dream. Another dream. That's all." She climbed up again and just missed an elbow to the forehead. His open eyes stared, a gaze so stark and true she wanted to weep. Sweat slickened his skin and made her fingers slip on his wrist. "Cynssyr."

"No. No. No, damn you." With chilling abruptness, he fell against the pillows, his voice low and anguished. *"It isn't so."*

"Hush."

"All dead," he whispered. *"All of them."*

The desolate whisper told her he remained in the grip of his dream. "It's all right, Ruan. My love."

He gasped once, and the tension went out of him. He was awake.

"It's all right," she repeated, touching a hand to his cheek. "I am here. It's all right." His arms went around her, holding tight. "You are safe," she soothed. "No one will hurt you now."

Ruan clung to his wife as he emerged from the bleakness. He was safe in her arms. Whatever he felt for her, whatever he did or had done in all his long empty years without her, he could trust her with his soul and know he was safe. "Anne."

Strange, she thought, for the low, breathy sound of her name to have such an effect on her. The word sent a shiver coursing up her spine.

He released her and sat up. Shaken by the lingering

187

immediacy of his dream, he wasn't sure where he was. His bed. Yes, despite Anne's presence. Cocooned in bed with his wife whose breath warmed his shoulder she was that close.

"Did you dream about the women again?"

He thought of the cold, dank place inside him. "Belgium." She stroked him softly, tenderly, a gesture of which he was certain she was unaware.

"When you almost died? I heard," she hastened to add, "that you were nearly killed in the war." The fire in his room had burned to little but tiny red-orange eyes glowing in the darkness.

"In Spain." Where he had lain wounded, sweltering in the heat, frenzied with thirst, nearly insane with the relentless pain of a bullet wound and a broken collarbone. Absolutely certain of his death. "I came through Belgium without a scratch."

Curious, Anne thought, how he spoke casually of Spain yet the way he said the word "Belgium" fairly froze her blood. Just as her whispered name resonated with undercurrents she did not comprehend, Belgium was a word fraught with dark and terrible meaning. "But you dreamed of Belgium."

"Yes," he said. Not exactly curtly, rather, choked off.

"What sort of dream makes a man cry out like that?"

"Not a dream." His words made a soft confession. "Memories. I don't admit them during the day, so they haunt me at night." In the dark, his fingers curled around hers. When she didn't object to the contact, he pulled her hand onto his lap. "Stay awhile, Anne."

"Was it awful? Belgium, I mean."

"I never talk about the war." Long habit shut down his emotions, and he welcomed the blessed lack.

She held his hand and waited. Inexorably, the accepting silence drew him past the wall he'd constructed between himself and feeling. She did it easily. Gently.

Effortlessly. Without a shred of remorse. She stripped him to nothing just as he had known, he thought, that she would. If he spoke, he would tell her what he had not told anyone else. If he let this woman inside him where not even he dared go, everything would change. Irrevocably. Her fingers tightened around his hand. She would never love him if he did not share himself, his innermost thoughts and fears. The pity was he had so damn many private fears.

"You were in the thick of it, weren't you?"

"The very. Were I to be killed—" His throat closed. Go slowly. Not all at once or she might refuse to listen. That she should listen to him and really hear him, seemed terrifyingly important. "Were I to be killed, I wanted to die from a clean shot. Quick. Through the head or the heart. I didn't want to linger for days like some of them did." He lifted her hand onto his lap as insurance against her escape. "Belgium, Quatre Bras, that is, was different, but in Spain I tried to kill cleanly. Sometimes I couldn't. Combat in close quarters means bayonets. It's a rotten thing to do to another man. You're damn lucky to stop a man on the first thrust. Generally it takes a few, all the while someone else is trying to gut you himself. I ought to have insisted on a command from the bloody start."

Once begun, he could not stop. Every awful memory poured from him. The heat, the smell of blood and dust and sweat and rotting men. Gaping wounds, the look in a soldier's eye just before he died. Swirling, churning lust for death and survival. Screaming men and horses. The god-awful sound of swords and guns and cannon booming. Metal piercing flesh. Quicksilver judgments and near instantaneous reactions that meant a man's life or yours. Winning or losing. Life or death.

Anne said nothing, for Cynssyr spoke to her. The man. Not the aristocrat. Not the dandy. Not the politician. Not even the soldier, but the man who was all those things. Nothing stood between them. The power and depth of his emotions humbled her. Occasionally, she touched him or murmured something comforting. Heaven help her, he was so much more real to her this way, telling her of his experiences in the war, binding her to him with his sharing. A man like any other. Like Aldreth or Devon. Not at all intimidating. A man with fears and imperfections. A man reaching for comfort and afraid he would find nothing.

"It's not the same dream every time. Sometimes I've been shot in the belly. Something that takes a while to snatch you away to hell, and I've been left for dead." He shuddered. She felt his tremor in the dark. "Sometimes I am dead. A corpse on the field while that damned Lieutenant Martin steals my watch and cuts the buttons off my coat. I keep shouting 'I'm alive. I'm alive!' Only no one hears me." His voice dropped to a low, raw whisper. "They go on about what a pity it is I got myself killed. A man of such promise, they say. Whatever it is, it ends with me surrounded by dead men. They grab me, beg me to save them, and I can't. There's nothing I can do but listen to their curses. No matter what I do, no matter how many Frenchmen I murder, there are too many. I never save anyone. Least of all myself."

Images of men fighting, going down, bleeding from mortal wounds filled her mind. Cynssyr grasped her head between his hands, peering into her face like a man desperate for an answer. "What?" she whispered over the fear in her heart. That look stole her breath, her will, the very core of her.

"Until you, I wondered if I really was dead. All this time, I thought I might be. Until you."

In the semidark, she brushed a crescent of hair from

his forehead. "I've always thought no one was more alive than you."

"Until you, I didn't know what it was to be alive. You've shown me something I didn't think existed." His voice fell so low she wasn't sure if she heard the words or just absorbed them. *"I am not dead."*

She stroked his face. "Cynssyr."

He let out a short breath of air and spoke in a normal, almost dispassionate tone. "You are good to sit here listening to me tell you of my night terrors."

"How could I not?" A deep sadness filled her. When he came out of this mood, he would see her. The woman he did not love. The wife he never wanted. She leaned away only to encounter the heavy silk hangings that cast them both in shadow.

Air moved across her forearm, as though he'd meant to touch her then changed his mind. "I am so often awake past dawn I've been a dolt and forgotten you are used to country hours yet. Go to bed, Anne."

"What is it like for you?" The question came out impulsively. Obscurely. Too abrupt and too blunt.

"What?"

"When you're with a woman." She could not bring herself to ask the question she wanted answered. What was it like for him to make love to her?

"That very much depends," he said in a quiet voice. Had his emotions ever been in such turmoil? Anguish. Gratitude, then amusement. Admiration. Lust. Inevitably, lust.

"On whether the woman is beautiful enough?"

"I used to think so."

"What then?"

He shook his head. "With you it's different. I come like a bloody bull with you. I want to reach inside you and make you feel what I do, to know heaven and hell and pleasure so intense you can't tell if it's agony or pure bliss." He touched her cheek and decided he had nowhere to go but forward. "When I make love to you, I am yours. You own me body and soul."

"Cynssyr." And in that one word he heard doubt and anger and fear.

"You don't believe a word I've said, do you?" he asked.

"I don't know."

"You are always honest with me."

"Usually," she said.

"I'm not sure I care for it."

She laughed at that, and then they laughed together. He drew her closer, grateful for her impossibly even temper.

"Tell me, was there truly no one ever to court you?"

"Never."

The swiftness of her reply sent an alarm through him. "Bartley Green must be full of fools." She must have been courted. A woman like her would have been noticed by someone. And, of course, she had been.

"No more than any other place, I imagine," she said with altogether too much caution.

"No one you longed to kiss?" he asked. She tried to squirm free of his embrace, but he kept her close. Jealously cut astonishingly deep. The reality that Anne, his Anne, had longed for another man, had dreamed of another man's embraces pierced to his soul. "Was it Devon?" He hated himself for asking, but he had to know. Ben and Devon had both talked as if Anne had no notion of Devon's intentions. But she must have. She would have.

If she felt the edge to his question, she didn't let on. She laughed. "I might as well wish to fly as think of any of Aldreth's friends. There were so many handsome men at Mary's wedding. Besides, no one ever paid that sort of attention to me. Why would they?"

"Anne," he said. "I forbid you to talk in this fashion. You are not a crone. You crack no mirrors when you look in them. Nor is it true no man paid attention to you. Devon did."

"Not the way you mean," she said. She didn't sound surprised. No, of course not.

Oh, Christ, he thought. Jealousy twisted in him because he knew Anne too well to believe she hadn't at least suspected Devon's feelings. "Ben had no intention of letting you molder in Bartley Green. Do you think he brought you to London solely to chaperone your father?"

"That's perfect nonsense."

"You knew he had someone in mind."

"Cynssyr," she said reasonably, even though he had her decidedly off balance, guessing things she'd not wanted to admit even to herself. Not openly, anyway. But, he was right. "Why does it matter? I would never have married."

"Not even if you were in love?" He gave her a full minute to answer, and she didn't. "Were you in love?"

"Why does that signify, Cynssyr?"

"Let us just say that it does," he whispered, terrified he was too close to the brink, terrified that he had lost himself to her and that she would never accept him because she'd loved Devon first and still did.

In the darkness Anne could not make out his expression. But she didn't need to see him to know his mood. His voice sounded like steel, so hard and unyielding that his hand on her cheek gently tracing a line down to her throat startled her. She tried to still her racing pulse. "Papa refused to give his permission, and so I put him out of my thoughts."

"And what of your heart?"

To this, Anne made no reply.

"Who is it?" he asked. "Some other man I'll want to kill? Or is it black-hearted Devon?"

Chapter Twenty-two

"Did you dream of kissing him?" His arms crept around her, still gentle. "Of having him hold you like this?"

"I did not dare."

"Do you love him still?"

"He is my friend, Cynssyr. I don't know what I'd do without him."

"He loves you."

"Yes," she said after a bit. "I know."

"Not as a friend, Anne. He does not love you as a friend."

She tried to pull away, but he wouldn't let her. She turned her head, staring at the silk bed-hangings. "I know."

"He wanted to marry you. He intended to."

"I know that." With an anguished cry she faced him again. "He waited for me all this time. He waited when no one else did. When he stopped being just Mr. Devon Carlisle he wanted me still, and he waited. But Papa hates him. Even after he had money and his title and was a gentleman whom everyone wanted to know, Papa still hated him."

"Especially then, Anne." He cupped the side of her face. "Devon meant to take you from him. And your father knew he could do it this time."

"Don't you see, Cynssyr?" Her voice broke. "I knew it was impossible."

"And now it is."

"Yes," she said. "Now it is."

"Do you hate me for it?"

"I should." Her voice fell to a whisper, like silk against air. "I should."

"You are mine, Anne. You don't belong to your father anymore, and you never belonged to Devon. You are mine." His fingers slipped from her shoulders to her waist. He shook with his want of her, with an almost violent need to make love to her.

He wanted to make love to her. But he wanted more than sexual release. Physical intimacy was the only way he knew to express what he felt for her. Ruan, who had once looked upon sexual relations as akin to food, a corporeal need that since it must be satisfied had as well be satisfied by only the best, glimpsed a frightening truth. He'd wasted something precious with those other women, and had certainly never truly made love. Though he had always satisfied his partners, and by some accounts magnificently, he had in fact been a selfish lover.

Anne's breath caught in her throat when his mouth grazed her neck, a tender, lingering touch at odds with the tension she felt in him. Gently, he moved aside her braid, exposing more of her neck to his mouth.

"Mine," he murmured. "Mine."

His lips warmed her skin. There was that feeling again. That nervous ball in the pit of her stomach. And,

Lord save her, anticipation, too. She felt his lips brush her shoulder and a corresponding disturbance in the rest of her body that centered itself in the core of her womanhood.

"This is mine, too." He put a hand on her breast and found the peak.

She bowed toward him, completely undone by his fingertips on her. And then it was his mouth. "Cynssyr."

Anne's heart jumped in her chest, her body fevered from the inside out. She pressed herself against him, offering herself to him with helpless desperation. One of his hands was on her knee and stroking upward beneath her nightdress. His mouth was on her throat, tracing a hot, damp line toward her belly. Sensation buried her. She didn't care what happened to her or what he did so long as he continued to touch her. He devoured her, and she let him. She wanted him to. One of them gasped, she thought it was probably her.

"Are you all right?" he whispered.

Honestly, she didn't know. She felt dizzy and out of breath. He held her even more closely than he had before this started. "No," she said. "You've stopped kissing me."

"Let me remedy that." His mouth felt wonderfully greedy, taking what she gave and then coaxing more from her so that she teetered constantly on the brink of another discovery about just how hot her blood could burn. Her arms were around his neck, clinging to him while his lips sliding down her throat sent trails of fire to her belly.

Christ, she had that soft voice that had so pleased him at Corth Abbey. The passionate witch was summoned to his arms. And here they were, so conveniently in his bed. His mouth caught hers, and his chest quivered. Heat flashed through him because he knew he would have her this time. All of her. Everything. The heat settled at the base of his spine and between his legs at a distressingly specific spot.

A spark shot through him at her bewitching surrender. He took her mouth again and urged her lips farther apart, wanting every bit of her sweetness. He tasted her, drank of her with his mouth and body and mind. His hand cradled the side of her face while he swept his tongue past her lips and into her mouth, bent her over his arm, kissing her with what his fogged senses dimly recognized as desperation. He ran his tongue over her teeth and along the inside of her cheek, exploring, luring, capturing.

Hunger rose in him, needy and overpowering. The hand on her cheek slid around to the back of her head and brought her closer yet. He burned for her. For Anne. He held her tightly, taking her mouth like a starving man. He wanted to devour her and thought maybe he would. She answered his passion, arching against him until he was certain he would go up in flames. Her kiss seared him, burned him to ashes, melted him and put his life and future in his lover's hands and heart.

He turned so that she was beneath him, his body over hers. Her legs parted, whether from the weight of him or some happy accident of their position or even instinct made no difference. Whatever the reason, their respective parts were suddenly touching. He took her heat into him. His mouth left hers to search downward, along her neck to the soft skin above the neckline of her nightclothes. She moaned her longing and pleasure. One of his hands found her bare knee and stroked along her thigh. That brought on another moan, another arch of her body into his. He adored her with his mouth and his hands and then, just when he was going to reach for his own nightclothes and begin the all-important lesson about her passion for him, she stiffened.

"Anne, what's wrong?" Christ, his fingers were tangled in her pubic hair. "Have I frightened you?" Hell. Hell and damnation. Was he destined always to be a clod? "I'm sorry."

"The door."

"What?" The fog of passion began slowly to dissolve. She touched his cheek. "Merchant," she said with gratifying breathlessness. "The door."

"Your grace?" came his butler's voice.

"What?" he shouted. Merchant, he decided, had just spent his last hours of employment at Cyrwthorn.

"My lord the earl of Bracebridge is here, sir. He is most insistent upon seeing you."

Devon. He shot a look at Anne and saw her lips swollen with his kisses, her hair disheveled, nightclothes loosened, the flush of passion still there.

"He wouldn't insist if it weren't important," she said.

Another five minutes and he would have been between her lovely thighs, losing himself to her. And she would be losing herself to him.

"In my study," Ruan called to the door, pushing himself away from Anne. He hung his head, drawing in a calming breath. "Ten minutes."

"Very good, your grace."

He caught Anne's hand just as she slid off the bed, modestly pushing her nightclothes below her knees as she did. "Don't leave." She stopped, a look of inquiry on her face. Against his better judgment, he leaned in for another kiss, catching her lower lip between his. "That," he said, pleased because she moved eagerly into the embrace, "must sustain me." He left the bed and after lighting a lamp, gathered his clothes. "I woke you, Anne. Sleep here. If you like." The essentials only, underclothes, trousers, shirt, boots. Could he stand the thought of knowing she was here? In his bed.

"I couldn't sleep now," she said. "Not with Devon downstairs on urgent business."

He threw a glance at her as he drew on his trousers. Strands of her silver-gilt hair fell about her face, her hands rested palm down on his rumpled sheets. Without the spectacles, her eyes were vivid blue-slate. A wrinkle formed between her brows as she squinted to see him.

"Merchant didn't say it was urgent," Ruan said.

"But that's what it means, his coming here at this hour. He must have some news."

"Yes, I expect that's so." He held his shirt, poised to pull it over his head. It struck him that she was beautiful. But he saw far more than her physical beauty; he knew the woman who lay beneath her strengths and weakness, which when it happened with other women generally sent him quickly on his way. Not with Anne. If she turned to a crone before his very eyes she would still be beautiful to him. "If that's why he's come, you ought to hear, too. We'll be in my study. Join us there when you've dressed." But he caught her hand before she could leave. "You *are* mine."

"Like a toy to be tossed aside when you've grown bored?" She did not smile or laugh this time.

"He is my best friend."

"I know." Briefly, she pressed her palm to his cheek. "I know." And then she was gone. He dressed quickly and went downstairs to see what his best friend was up to.

Devon turned when Ruan stalked in. One black eyebrow shot upward. "Good morning to you, too, Cyn."

"I was making love to my wife," he said, throwing out the declaration like a challenge.

"My timing has always been execrable," he said wryly. "I trust you gave a good account of yourself."

Ruan took a deep breath and sat heavily behind his

desk, waving at Devon to find a chair of his own. "My apologies for that, Dev."

"So," Devon said softly, stretching out his legs and crossing them at the ankles. The question in his tone was obvious.

"I barely remember meeting her." He held his head in his hands. How could he have met her and not known? There ought to have been bells tolling or a ray of light shining from the heavens to her. Some damn premonition anyway. "I won't even tell you what I thought of her when we met her at Aldreth's wedding."

"I know what you thought."

"However you look at it, I've been a worthless bastard."

"Well, now," Devon drawled. "I wouldn't say worthless."

A soft tap at the door interrupted Ruan's tart reply. Anne came in carrying a tray of tea and hot cross buns straight from the oven, judging by the fragrant steam. "I thought a bite of something might do us all some good." She smiled at Devon, and it was like an arrow turning between Ruan's ribs. "Good morning, Devon."

"Anne."

She set out the cups, wondering what they'd been talking about that made the air thick enough to cut with a knife. Once, for so brief a time, she had let herself love Devon. He would have been a good match for her, she thought. Or maybe for the woman she used to be. Somewhere in the back of her heart's regrets she felt sad for the loss of that future. She served each of them tea and a bun, then settled down with one for herself. No tea, though. The smell bothered her. "What have you learned?" she asked Devon. "Do you know who it is?"

"Cheeky little thing, ain't she?"

"Yes." Cynssyr gave a very slight smile. Anne stared at his mouth. Those lips had been on hers. Doing won-

derful things to her. Worrying things. Fretful things.
Shamefully splendid things. Things to enslave her.
Thankfully, they'd been interrupted, because she'd
been close to disastrous surrender. In truth, she had
surrendered. She knew he would have shown her no
mercy.

Devon unfurled from his chair and rose. Where Cynssyr moved like a cat, graceful and sinuous, Devon was
feral, a wolf to Cynssyr's lion. With a brief glance at
her, he threw a letter on the desk. It hit the polished
mahogany surface and slid toward Ruan. "Waiting for
me when I got home. Intercepted quite by chance."

"What is it?" Anne asked.

Ruan read the letter. Twice. The first time quickly,
the second more slowly. "I'll not keep anything from
Anne." He looked at her from over the top of the letter.
"It's from one Richard Harrow. To Miss Fairchild. Pro-
claiming, among other things, his undying adoration of
her."

"Richard." Anne echoed the name.

"Thrale," said Devon. "He means the marquess of
Thrale."

Anne couldn't imagine the stern man she knew becoming infatuated with Camilla Fairchild. "Camilla
Fairchild is a perfect goose."

"There's been talk, just lately," Devon said, "that
Thrale has certain tastes. For violence."

"Has he a mistress?" Anne asked. The question met
with shocked silence. "Well, has he? Perhaps we might
ask her if Richard ever shows her any violence."

"We?" Devon asked.

Cynssyr cleared his throat. "Much as your help has
been invaluable, Anne, that is not a conversation you
ought to have with anyone of that sort."

"Well, I think someone ought to."

"That may not be necessary," Ruan said. "In order

201

to prove his love, our devoted Richard, he begs her to meet him. A clandestine meeting."

Anne rose. "I don't believe it."

"You seem very certain of Thrale."

"He is a decent man. As I know Aldreth and Devon are decent men. Just as I am certain that you, Cynssyr, are a decent man. Richard would no more turn violent than you or chase after a silly child like Camilla Fairchild. Than any of you."

Ruan leaned back and tossed the letter onto the desktop, his face a mask. "What if you're wrong?"

She leaned across the desk to snatch the letter, then froze as the truth came home, for she understood the man better now, the pampered, hardened, damaged aristocrat constantly searching for the love he believed did not exist. Without a thought, not even thinking of Devon, she touched Cynssyr's jaw, brushed a lock of mahogany hair from his forehead. "I wouldn't believe it of you, Cynssyr, and I don't believe it of Richard."

He held her gaze. Then, in a moment that seemed to last forever, he took her free hand and brought her palm to his mouth. His lips molded to her skin, warm and soft. "Thank you," he murmured. Unnerved, she backed away from the desk. Devon remained settled in obdurate silence. Cynssyr, too, stayed silent for a time. Taking the sheet of paper, he refolded it, pinching the creases of the folds. "I'm sorry, Anne. I know you think him a friend. But right now, things don't look promising for Thrale's innocence."

"It's happened before." Devon put his hands on his knees and levered himself to his feet. "Just as you suspected, Cyn. Forty miles from Liverpool."

"I don't understand," Anne said.

"Thrale's estates are in Lancashire," said Cynssyr. "About forty miles from Liverpool."

Chapter Twenty-three

"That proves nothing," Anne said.

"In itself, no," Ruan agreed. "But the concatenation of what we know is ever more damning."

Anne finished her bite of hot cross bun. It was excellent. Warm and buttery, comforting to her inconstant stomach. Devon drank the last of his tea and took a second bun.

"One of these days, Cyn," Devon said, "I will steal Jubert from you."

"You are welcome to try."

"What will you do about this, this supposed tryst of Richard's?" Anne asked while Devon, rolling his eyes heavenward, took a mouthful of Jubert's exquisite version of an English staple.

"Go, of course." Ruan took her measure. Once, and not so long ago, that look would have had her pulse racing with fear rather than desire.

Carolyn Jewel

Devon casually wiped his fingers on a linen napkin. "Shall I come along?"

"No," said Ruan, thinking Anne looked tired. "I need you to keep an eye on Thrale. In case it's a trick."

"I tell you, so far the man lives a monk's life." Devon rose with a sigh. "I don't know why I bother. I could follow Miss Emily Sinclair and know Thrale is close by. He dogs her every step."

"Half the bucks in London dog her steps."

Anne looked between the two men. "Do you think Emily's in any danger?"

"Not so long as we know where he is," Ruan said. "Aldreth will stay with Emily."

Devon nodded. "I'll show myself out. Cyn. Anne."

"Good morning, Dev." Anne stifled a yawn.

When they were alone, Ruan went to her chair and stood over her. "You're exhausted." He brought her to her feet, and she stepped unhesitatingly into his arms. Imagine that, feeling comfortable in Cynssyr's embrace. "Go to bed, my love."

She rested her head against his chest and yawned again. "I'm to make calls with Mary this morning."

He pushed her back just enough to look at her, a long and searching stare. Anne drank in his features, the straight, strong nose, firm mouth, the pure green eyes. A face that had, to her, once represented all that a woman ought to avoid. "You have good sense," he said at last. "I trust you'll use it."

"I'll be careful."

"Go nowhere alone. Nowhere without me or Henry."

"Of course not."

"I want to take you upstairs and finish what we started." He traced a line just beneath her eye. "But you need rest, not a randy husband in your bed."

An impish grin flashed across her face. "Perhaps I need both."

"You are an impertinent minx."

Anne spent her morning making calls with her sisters. Breakfast with Lady Prescott, a levee for the duchess of Cumberland, an appearance at Lady Kinross's salon and several at-homes at which she managed to find food sufficiently bland to keep her stomach settled. Finally, they arrived at Ormond House for a recital featuring a French tenor in magnificent voice. She met Devon at most of the affairs because, as he'd predicted, Thrale, and a host of other admirers, followed where Emily went. Neither Devon nor Thrale, however, was present here.

Brenley Cooke and his wife and daughter came in as the tenor concluded a second glorious aria. Emily and Miss Fanny Cooke had become bosom friends, and Fanny immediately left her mother's side to sit by Emily. The two whispered to each other as young women do when there are beaus to discuss. Anne was content to listen to Monsieur Faurer. Her sheltered life in the country meant she was not terribly familiar with opera, certainly not as it was sung by this man. His voice wholly captured Anne's attention and took her mind off Cynssyr and her increasing awareness of him as a man. As her husband. Of herself as a woman who could arouse a man. And be aroused herself. A major revelation, that, for she'd believed herself incapable of passion. Now she knew she wasn't.

"Duchess?"

"Mm?" Enthralled by the music, she didn't look.

Someone tugged on her sleeve. "Your grace." The voice, urgent and clipped beyond the point of rudeness, belonged to a woman. "I should like a word with you. Now."

"Yes?"

"A word, please." The woman's eyes flashed.

Even while she wondered what she could have done

to make the woman angry, Anne tried to place her. "Mrs. Fairchild?"

"In private, if you would be so kind." She pulled on Anne's sleeve again. Anne stepped out of her reach. "It's important that we speak." Mrs. Fairchild took a deep breath and said, "Please?" in a voice that trembled with her attempt at politeness.

"All right." They went to an empty parlor a few feet from the salon where she could even now hear the clear, liquid notes of song. "What is it, Mrs. Fairchild?" She was a lovely woman, nearly forty, but still a beauty. A woman, she thought, in whom Cynssyr would take an interest.

"This." She thrust a note into Anne's hand.

"What is it?"

"Read it, and you shall see." She picked up a bit of carved ivory from a table and turned it in her hands.

Anne opened the note and read the opening paragraph. She looked at Mrs. Fairchild from over the top of the sheet of paper. "A love letter."

"Exactly."

"The sentiment is a bit overblown, but should not every letter from a beau be exactly so?"

" 'Eyes of soft brown, lips of red rose,' " Mrs. Fairchild quoted as if the phrase had some deeper meaning for her.

Anne scanned the lines then said, "I'm not sure why you've shown this to me."

Mrs. Fairchild's thumb pressed one side of the carved piece. "I thought you might like to know what sort of letters your husband is writing these days."

"My husband?" Anne checked the signature. Indeed. Her husband's name was signed at the bottom. Cynssyr. A bold flourish. What she would expect of him. She lifted her eyes from the page. Had all of Cynssyr's fine and touching words last night been empty? Likely, she

Lord Ruin

decided, or, rather, he may have meant them only in the moment. But the letter bothered her, struck a note discordant with what she knew of him. "You are his diversion?"

"His diversion?" Mrs. Fairchild threw down the piece of ivory. "Just long enough for him to write this bit of filth to my daughter."

Camilla Fairchild flashed into her head. A beautiful girl, but silly and an incorrigible flirt. Far too young to be Cynssyr's lover and simply not the sort of woman Richard would pursue. "No, that's not possible."

"Thank God I found out before it was too late. Camilla would have met him. The girl's convinced herself she's in love with the man. And your husband, well, he's convinced her he loves her and means to leave you for her. And he would have ruined her. I did not dare show it to Mr. Fairchild, for I know he would demand satisfaction. And Cynssyr would kill him without an instant's hesitation."

Quickly, Anne read the rest, down to the final, chilling, entreaty to meet him at a particular address. A familiar address. One she'd heard just this morning. "Cynssyr never wrote this letter."

"You're as dazzled as Camilla." Her lower lip quivered, and Anne thought of herself a few years from now, just as protective of her own children.

"What would you have me do?"

"Tell him to leave my daughter alone. You're his wife. Keep him away from innocent girls."

"Mrs. Fairchild. I am so sorry. It's a trick. This letter is a trick. A base trick as has been played on others, to their sorrow."

"You don't strike me as weak-minded," the older woman said in a voice fully capable of freezing water on the spot.

"Attend me, Madam." Anne adopted her best stern

nanny voice, throwing in a measure of Cynssyr at his most imperious. The basic tone had worked well with her sisters, and it worked with Mrs. Fairchild. "This morning, my Lord Bracebridge brought Cynssyr a letter he'd intercepted. A letter to your daughter, Camilla. Not from Cynssyr. From someone else. That letter asked her to be at this address." She shook the page, willing the woman to understand. "At five o'clock. Not three o'clock, as this one does. Don't you see? It has to be a trick. Why else would there be two such letters? Cynssyr was meant to see the other. Not this one." Quite plainly both letters had been sent to cast blame on an innocent man, and never mind at what cost.

Mrs. Fairchild gave her a scornful look. "I see why he chose you. The perfect little wife. Just pretty enough. Respectable. Sensible. You're probably hopelessly in love with him, too, which only feeds his vanity. All he needs to do is show you off to his friends, and they'll all think he's turned over a new leaf. Well, he's not fooled me. He's on to girls now he's safely married."

"Your daughter is lovely, but her youth is not to his liking," Anne said grimly. "You know that. You know his tastes. The letter is a ruse, Mrs. Fairchild. Cynssyr never wrote it." Anne's foreboding increased. "There is to be a certain man at this address, and Cynssyr is intended to come upon him and, well, it was to be Miss Fairchild he's to discover him with." She began to pace. "Only, Bracebridge and my husband would have been too late to do anything but blame an innocent man." Mrs. Fairchild was no fool. She couldn't be, if she'd been Cynssyr's lover. Cynssyr didn't choose foolish women. Anne waited for her to come to the correct conclusion.

"So you say," she whispered.

"You must believe me."

"Why ought I?"

"You were his lover once." Squaring her shoulders she faced Mrs. Fairchild and saw she'd guessed correctly. "Tell me, is Cynssyr the sort to write a letter like this? He'll give expensive trinkets. Gowns, perhaps. Jewels, certainly." Mrs. Fairchild touched her throat, remembering, Anne was sure, a particular gift from him. "But writing letters of such sentiment, mawkish or otherwise? You know him at least a little. He is not capable of that."

"Dear God. Oh my dear God." She sat down clumsily, her anger vanished. "Camilla," she whispered in a voice so tortured Anne felt tears rise up. "Who would do this to her? Why?"

"That's what Cynssyr is trying to find out." She touched Mrs. Fairchild's shoulder. "Camilla is safe. Give thanks for that." The older woman looked at her, and Anne, with fear like a lead ball in her chest, said, "Are you absolutely certain you prevented her from going?"

"I think so. But she's a headstrong girl, and she believes herself in love."

"Go home. Go home and be certain she's safe."

With Mrs. Fairchild gone, Anne picked up the bit of ivory scrimshaw. She feared the reason Devon and Thrale were not at Ormond House, and more, she feared if she did not do something, an innocent man would find himself accused of a crime. She considered going directly to Cynssyr, but changed her mind. Even with Henry along, going alone courted danger she had to balance against the passing of time.

The first thing she did was summon her carriage. Then she made her way back to the salon and found the only man she knew well enough to plead for her favor. Julian Durling.

"Please, you must come with me," she said when she'd pulled him aside.

"Why, Duchess, I should be delighted to go away with you." His eyebrows waggled in a ridiculous arch.

"Don't be a fool, Mr. Durling. I daren't go alone. Cynssyr would have my head if I did."

"The question is whether he would also have mine."

"There's no one else. It's urgent. A matter of a young woman's life."

He dropped the dandy's drawl. "As you wish."

"I'll just tell Mary I've been called away. My carriage is outside. Meet me there." He nodded, and they parted ways.

"What's this about?" Durling asked when he'd joined her in the carriage.

She showed him Camilla's letter and explained the matter and the trap she thought had been set for Richard. "Lord Thrale will have been lured into coming, Mr. Durling, with Cynssyr to arrive just in time to find him with the poor girl. No doubt the murderer intended to brutalize her first."

Durling rested a fisted hand on the edge of the window. "I don't approve of you being involved in this. Cynssyr ought to know better."

"While I appreciate your concern, you are not my husband, Mr. Durling. Besides, Cynssyr trusts me."

He gave her a depthless look. "You were right to fetch me. A neat trick, if you're right. Girl or no girl, my Lord Thrale showing up at all looks bad. It's fortunate her mother discovered the letter."

"What if some other girl hasn't been as lucky?" She saw from Durling's expression that he had already asked himself the same question. "What if he's found someone else?"

He leaned out the window and shouted, "Faster, John Coachman. Faster!"

The address was a modest flat off Tottenham Court Road. Dead and shriveled leaves remained of the geraniums that had once grown in a window box. Though the windows were shuttered, and the knocker had been removed, the door was unlocked. Durling put out an arm, blocking her way up the stairs. "Stay outside. You there!" He waved to Henry. "Watch out for the duchess."

"Don't be ridiculous, Mr. Durling."

"Look here," they heard someone shout. "All I want to know is what the blazes are you doing here?"

From the landing, Anne heard Cynssyr calmly reply, "I'd rather have the answer from you."

She caught Durling's arm and tucked her hand under his elbow. "Remind me," he said with uncharacteristic solemnity, "to tell His Grace that a husband must be firm enough with his wife so as to obtain her complete obedience even when he is not present."

"Cynssyr," she said softly and with complete innocence, "is firm precisely when a husband ought to be." At Durling's sharp look, she gave smile of wicked innocence.

He colored. "Ahem."

They strolled into a darkened parlor like a couple without a care in the world. Manifestly, this was not a house in which anyone lived. Sheets covered the furniture. Carefully rolled up carpets lined the floor along one wall.

"Oh, I say," Durling said with a wooden surprise not meant to fool anyone. "Sorry to intrude, Cyn old man."

The marquess of Thrale whirled. "What now?"

"Anne." Cynssyr faced her. "Always a pleasure to see you, my dear." His expression spoke volumes, and Anne's anxiety on that account vanished. He knew she would not be here except for good reason. A tightness in her chest eased. "And Mr. Julian Durling."

Thrale bowed to her. "Duchess."

211

"Richard." Anne nodded curtly. "Is anyone else here?"

The marquess threw up his hands. "I should very much like to know if there is."

"Have you been upstairs yet, Cynssyr?" she asked.

"No."

She pushed Durling toward the stairs. "Mr. Durling, have a look."

"Right-O!" But he didn't move until Anne prodded him yet again.

"What the devil is going on here?" Thrale demanded, looking daggers from Cynssyr to Durling on his way to the stairs.

Ruan saw Anne to a chair before drawing one of the heavy curtains. Late afternoon bathed the room in gray light. "Much better." He rested a hand on her shoulder. His fingers gently caressed the nape of her neck.

Hands on his hips, Thrale glared at the open door. "This just tears it. I oughtn't to be surprised. Do come in, Bracebridge."

"Thank you." Devon entered and arranged himself on a chair, not bothering to uncover it. He slouched, a deceptively casual position, Ruan knew. "Thought I'd follow when I saw Anne come with Durling there." Dev spared a look for Thrale. "As for him, I lost him. Don't know how he slipped away, or even when." He lifted a hand. "Now, Thrale, I don't mind if you do answer Cyn's question. What are you doing here?"

"I own this house."

Ruan took up position behind Anne's chair. "Do you, indeed?"

"I own this house, but as you can see, I do not use it. It is presently let out. The family to whom the house is leased has gone to Scotland to sit vigil at the side of a relative I was given to understand was quite ill. This afternoon I received notice someone had broken in and might be living here illegally. I came to investigate. And find you."

From upstairs, Durling shouted, a high-pitched cry of alarm that made Anne's blood run cold.

Thrale, Devon and Cynssyr rose as one. "Mr. Durling? Where are you?" She led the way upstairs.

Durling met them near the top of the stairs, white-faced. "It's Cyril Leander's girl." He stopped Anne from going past him. "There's nothing to be done for her." His voice tightened. "Nothing."

"I'll fetch the constable," Devon said.

"I had a message," said Thrale. "From a child off the streets who claimed to be from my solicitor. Said I needed to come right away." He sat on the stairs, palms on his knees. "But I was late getting here."

"Your hands are bruised, Thrale," Ruan said. "Mind telling us what happened?"

"What?" He lifted his hands and flexed his fingers. The skin was broken in several places. "I was at Gentleman Jack's."

"True enough," Dev said. "That's where he was when he disappeared."

"Got the worst of my bout, I'm afraid. I was relieved when that dashed boy interrupted." Slowly, he looked from Durling to Ruan to Anne. His brows drew together over tempest-gray eyes, but he calmly shook his head. "No. I did not do this." Every word came out clear and distinct.

"Take the duchess home, Cynssyr," Durling said in a shaking voice. "She doesn't need to see this." He came down a step looking ready to collapse, himself.

"I shall deal with this," Ruan said.

Thrale shot to his feet, body taut, fists clenched. At the very moment Anne was sure he would strike out, he suddenly controlled himself. With terrible effort, he said, "I have never struck a woman. Ever. But I won't say as much about a man."

"We arrived at the same time, Ruan," Devon said.

"He could have left and come back."

"Could have."

Anne was grateful for Cynssyr's hand on her shoulder, for she could not imagine Thrale was so vile a man, and yet it seemed she must.

"His hands give him away," Durling cried. "They're bruised and bloody, and that poor girl—"

"If you are searching for a man capable of such a monstrous act," said Thrale, "you should consider John Martin. And you, Cynssyr, have more reason than most to understand why."

At Anne's questioning look, Cynssyr explained. "As I said, he was briefly under my command in Spain. If he'd not cashed out on his own, I'd have had him cashiered. Not after being discovered rifling the pockets of the dead or near dead, though I argued that was grounds enough, nor for his acts of brutality against the Spanish, particularly women, but for failing to lead a charge after a direct order. Worse, I found him drunk afterward, and upon interviewing several of his men could only conclude that he'd been drunk during battle, too."

"I often thought my father would have preferred him for his heir." Thrale gazed at the three men, then at Anne. "Martin is his natural son. But you know that."

"Yes," said Durling softly. "But it was not Martin who did this."

"His mother was married." Thrale examined one bruised fist, running fingers along the ridges of a gash with an oddly languid care. "A farmer's wife. Common as they come, but my father always did like them close to the earth. They passed off the child as legitimate issue of her marriage. My father paid for his education and then for his commission, too. I was glad to see him in the army for it got him out of the parish. Nor was I surprised to learn he'd cashed out. He wrote me for money a while back, a few months since. I replied his commission was inheritance enough, and t'was not my fault if he'd squandered it. My father had been giving him money off and on for years and once he passed away, that stopped."

"But he's in town now." Anne thought of the exquisite clothes. "How does he afford it?"

"He was a charming boy," Thrale supplied. "Carefree, a daredevil with whom no one could long stay out of sorts, and I expect that's not changed. There's always someone taken in by him. But it won't last. For all his gifts; charm, wit, education beyond his station, John is a wastrel. Just like my father. My father paid to get him out of several unfortunate scrapes, most of them involving women."

"Just so," Cynssyr said. And Anne could not help thinking of the girl upstairs, the life forever gone from her.

"Yes." Thrale glanced at the top of the stairs. "Just so."

Until now, she'd been able to think of what lay upstairs as an abstraction. A regrettable death for which she was very sorry. It no longer felt abstract. That young girl's life was tragically gone, and Anne wondered how her parents were to survive the loss. She thought of her own child, as yet unborn, of her sisters and how her heart would break if anything happened to them.

"Anne?"

She turned her heard in the direction of Ruan's voice and found she could not clearly see him for the tears. She reached for him but his arms already surrounded her. "Cynssyr." And then she was ill.

"My wee wren," he whispered to her. He gave her his handkerchief. "Henry will see you home," he said

215

when she had done what she could with the handkerchief and a pitifully small amount of water. Before she could protest, he held up a hand and said in a voice so cold and so utterly lacking in compassion for that poor dead child, a chill went up her spine, "Wait for me at Cyrwthorn, Anne. I shall come home presently."

"Yes, sir."

The dinner hour had long passed before he returned. She was in the front parlor embroidering more roses on a shawl for Lucy. The work provided a way of keeping her thoughts from wandering to Thrale and what he might prove to be, or to her husband and the sort of man he was. Or wasn't. Her hands stilled on the fabric as she listened to Cynssyr mount the stairs. Then, just when she was certain he would walk past, he was there. A tall, lithe shape in the doorway. "Have you dined?" she asked, heart pounding because that was always the effect he had on her.

He came in. Every stitch of his clothing was perfect, every movement of his body indisputably masculine. His eyes alone betrayed his only flaw. They were cold and hard. "I'm surprised you're still up." Even his voice felt cold. His slow entrance eventually brought him to her side.

"That poor girl," she said in a choked voice.

"I don't want you ever to take such a risk again. You must promise me you'll let me manage this affair from here on out."

"You asked for my help."

"I was wrong to involve you in this," he said, lowering himself next to his wife on the sofa. Though no stranger to grief and sorrow, he didn't think he'd ever reacted so strongly to someone else's emotions. Anne wasn't ever to hurt like that again. He wouldn't permit it. He couldn't bear it. The horror of the Leander girl's death still resonated in her. At Fargate Castle, she would be safe. She peered at him, and after a moment, he heard her catch her breath, a sound of recognition, of what he'd no idea.

"Were you the one to tell her parents?"

"Yes." He took a section of the shawl in one hand and let the silk flow through his fingers. Tiny stitches formed roses so perfect he half-expected them to move. "Exquisite work, Anne."

"Cynssyr." She touched the edge of his jaw, and Ruan felt the now familiar leap of passion. "Has there ever been anyone to comfort you?" A pair of tiny scissors fell to the floor. "Leave them." But he bent to retrieve them for her anyway. She took them. "I'm glad you involved me," she said fiercely. "We will find this monster and stop him." She leaned her head against his chest, placing one hand over his heart. "Promise me vengeance, Cynssyr."

Cornwall. Yes, he would send her to Cornwall just as she'd asked. But even as he planned how and when he would tell her of his decision, he knew he couldn't bring himself to make so selfless a move. "Yes, Anne," he breathed into her hair, "we will have vengeance." He slipped his arms around her and brought her close.

Anne listened to his heartbeat. She knew exactly the danger he posed, but if he would hold her like this, tenderly, as though he cared and felt deeply for her, she might just walk headlong into the inevitable heartbreak. Taking one of her hands in his, he kissed her palm. Her body reacted, she opened to him like one of her embroidered roses come to life.

Then he kissed her, not opening his mouth until she leaned into him and opened hers. The warmth flamed into heat. She didn't care if he did break her heart. When at last he drew back, she said, "How can we, when that poor girl lies cold and alone?"

"How can we not?" Gently he covered the back of

217

her neck with one hand. "No, love, don't close your eyes. Look at me." She could scarcely breathe. His fingers stroked over her. "Does this frighten you?"

She shook her head. Not in the way he meant, anyway.

His fingertip brushed across the aching peak of her breast. She felt melting, bone-deep heat in response to that touch. "This material is very thin. I can feel you almost as if you were naked in my hands."

Every nerve in her body was on fire. His thumb rubbed over her nipple. Her eyes popped open. A familiar panic rose when she saw the half-lidded green eyes and his sleepy, almost drugged, concentration. She would lose herself to him if he made love to her now and that frightened her enough to pull away.

"What?" He gazed at her with a lazy curiosity but she saw smoldering fire underneath.

"I don't like the way that makes me feel." Lord, his hand was still on her, still touching.

He stopped his caress. "Does it hurt?"

She shook her head.

"Are you afraid I will hurt you?"

"I don't understand what's happening to me." In fact, she feared she understood all too well.

"Anne," he said softly. "Anne, you are a passionate woman who denied her nature for too long. For years you had to. No longer. You've no need for dreams, now." He took her head between his hands. "Let go, my dearest heart. Let go and I will catch you however far you fall. Let go, and I will show you a whole other world."

She could only stare mutely, brought low by frank longing.

"Anne," he whispered as he dipped his head for a kiss. He edged her toward pure sensation. An existence where she knew only the heat in her blood. His hand slipped between them, searching and finding, it seemed to her, every part of her body that might respond to him. "Hold still. I don't want to tear your gown." He laughed, a quiet rumble of private amusement. "Unless I have to." Quite suddenly, he was inching her gown down her arms. "Sweet Christ. You truly are magnificent."

The sleeves of her frock trapped her arms at her sides. She wasn't anything now but a mass of longing. His fingers touched her bare skin, lightly skimming her shoulders. She could only pray he would not stop. Fingers caressed along her collarbone. Sensation. Nothing but sensation. First one, then both his hands at once, molding her, teasing her into mindless submission.

"When I made love to you at Corth Abbey, Anne, you moaned just like that. And when I touched you like this—" His fingertips touched her breast briefly, oh so briefly. "—I was in heaven. I had to have you, and so I took you. Because it's what I wanted." Then his mouth was there, where his hand had been, through her chemise, tongue sipping, teeth nipping, her own body dissolving. "Are you well enough for this?" In response, she tugged his head to hers. He picked her up and pulled her onto his lap. Her head swam when he bent over her for a long, deep kiss that seemed to go on forever and then, when he stopped, not at all long enough. "Open your legs, darling," he whispered.

His hand under her skirt slid determinedly up her thigh. Molten lightning streaked upward from her toes to her belly. His tongue flicked out, teasing her breast. Desire filled her to bursting. She arched toward his mouth.

"That's it," he crooned. She didn't know or even care what he meant by that until his fingers touched the curls between her legs. "Trust me," he whispered. "I will take care of you." A finger pressed there, circling gently.

Pleasure of exquisite depth stole over her. Cynssyr continued to kiss her, a long, sensuous kiss while his hand stroked. Once, he stopped, but only to bring up her knee so that she was opened farther for him. Her legs were exposed to the air, the very core of her welcomed him and the magic he worked on her. "Let go," he said. "I am here." His finger slid inside her. Her breath hitched in the back of her throat. And then, before she could do anything to prevent it, an incredible tension broke over her like a wave and sent her spinning onto a tightrope of desire. She couldn't stop any of it. "My love," he whispered. "My love. I am here."

"Ruan." That long, anguished moan came from her. He had a hand on her breast again. She lay across his lap, her legs bare to nearly her thighs while his fingers stroked between them. Her arms reached to catch him and hold on because he had her balanced at the cliff's edge and she really was falling. When he gently tugged on the peak of her breast, she came apart, fractured into a thousand pieces.

He pulled back to look at her. "Darling," he whispered, not to her, but to himself. "Exactly so." She felt the heat of his eyes on her, as green and bright as any gem could ever be, and was surprised when he reached to wipe tears from her cheeks.

She wasn't sure how long they held each other, each wrapped in their shared silence. But even when someone tapped on the door, Ruan did not release her.

"Your grace?" came Merchant's muffled voice.

"No," Anne moaned, still bespelled by what he had done to her. The sofa, positioned as it was to face the fireplace, was at least partially hidden from someone standing in the doorway.

He lifted his head, but his hands continued a soothing stroking of her. "Do not come in, Merchant."

From the doorway, the butler cleared his throat. "Your engagement with Lord Eldon?"

"Thank you for the reminder. Tell Dobkin I must have the charcoal suit."

"Very good, sir."

Ruan helped Anne fasten her gown, then took her in his arms. "I prefer to tarry in your warm embrace, my dear, but I can hardly put off the lord chancellor at my convenience."

Anne pushed away from him, rising. Emotion paralyzed her, suffocated her. The feelings were so big and so dangerous she didn't dare acknowledge their existence. "I told you once," she said. "I do not wish to feel. We get along quite well without any of that. You've said so yourself. We are two entirely different people, Ruan. We've nothing in common, and I am trying my hardest not to fail at this." Her breath caught in her throat. "And you persist in this . . . this. . . . In breaking me to your will."

"Breaking you? That's absurd." But Ruan felt more than a small twinge of guilt. Wasn't that his intent?

"That's what it feels like." She dissolved into sobs. "Leave me alone. Stop making me feel this way."

"And what way is that?"

"Like your current diversion soon to be discarded. You have no right to be so tender when you do not mean it for me." She rapped her chest with her fingertips. "You do not mean it for me, Ruan, and I cannot bear it. Save such words for Mrs. Fairchild, for she at least wants to hear them." She clasped her head. "My God. Listen to me! I'm raving. Stark raving." She looked into his face. "What have you done to me?"

His mouth twisted. "What have *you* done to me?"

221

Chapter Twenty-four

Ruan's meeting concluded earlier than expected. Castlereagh was there, among others, along with Lord Sather, who'd also fought in the war. The subject concerned a suitable candidate to send to Aix-la-Chapelle. Whoever went would conduct the negotiations concluding the division of Napoleon's failed empire. Before Anne, Ruan would have expected to go and been more than eager to put forward his name were he not approached. Had someone else been chosen in his stead, he would have felt slighted. His reluctance now even to be considered surprised him. A bit.

"Cynssyr," Sather said, "I've heard you might welcome an opportunity to go abroad."

"You have misheard."

"Indeed?" said Sather.

"I am but recently married." With a meaningful glance at Castlereagh, he said, "Even if I were not, there are men who will more ably represent Britain's interests."

"You might take along your bride," Eldon offered.

"My heir will be born at Fargate Castle. On English soil. Not foreign."

"Quick work."

Ruan shrugged. If Castlereagh or anyone else was annoyed at him for yet another reason, he didn't give a tinker's damn. His decision was made. He would not willingly leave Anne. They danced around the issue a bit longer, but at last it was agreed Castlereagh, himself, would go. By three in the morning, Ruan was back at Cyrwthorn. Early for him and far too late to hope Anne was awake. He dismissed Dobkin once he'd changed from evening clothes and had a glass of brandy and a book in hand. His intention was to sit before the fire until dawn came and went, but compulsion took him into Anne's room.

With each passing day he wanted her more desperately. He wanted to think they had forged a respectful friendship, a first for him, having the sort of friendship with a woman that he had with Devon or Aldreth. But her accusation that he wanted to break her to him became a gnat at his ear, persistent, refusing to be ignored. She was right. He did want that, and one did not do such a thing to a friend. Anne was his friend. If he was to capture her love, he must come by it honestly so that when he had it, he would keep it safe.

Anne slept on. After a minute longer or so of him staring at her form in the dark, she stirred and lifted her head from the pillow. In a soft, lazy voice she said, "Cynssyr?"

"Yes." His body tingled, anticipating his desire for her.

She slipped from the bed and moved in front of him,

a slender, white-clad shape. Her spectacles gleamed in the dimness when she retrieved them from the table beside the bed. Though her figure was but faintly suggested, he knew what he would find if he undressed her. Full breasts, long legs, the swell of feminine hips. Perfect. Absolutely perfect. His body reacted to the image. She was like a drug to him, he thought. No opium eater could be more in thrall to his mistress drug than he was to Anne.

"Is aught well?"

"Castlereagh will go to Belgium."

"An apt choice."

"I came to make love to you."

"Oh."

"It's useless unless you want me."

She came close. Stood inches from him. "You are my husband," she said in her quiet, reasonable voice.

"Scores of wives do not want their husbands."

"There are husbands who do not want their wives."

"I am not one of those men, Anne. You are more than any husband could want in a wife." He trailed a finger along the line of her jaw. "Kind. Intelligent. Clever with a budget. Resourceful. There's only one thing you're not."

"Beautiful," she said. "I never cared before, but now I do. I wish I were."

He held back a flash of anger. "Ordinary."

"Yes. I am quite ordinary."

"It's been said a woman is not a beauty until I have pronounced her so."

"You are a connoisseur."

"I tell you now, of all the women I have known, you are the only one who deserves to be called a beauty. Only you, Anne. No other." God help him. He meant every word. With a start, he realized he'd put a hand on her belly. His fingers spread between her hips as if measuring. "You are so miserably ill."

"Mary assures me it will pass."

He stroked her belly. "Ah," he said, thinking he detected a swelling. "Are you quickening?"

She put a hand over his. "It's too early for that."

He thought she did not sound entirely certain of her denial. They stood a foot or two apart. Not particularly near, but intimate all the same because of his hand on her and hers over his. "Make love with me, Anne. Because you want me. Not because I'm your husband." Desperate to bridge the widening chasm between them he said, "Or must I add disobedient to my list of your failings?"

At first, she did and said nothing. His request shocked her, he thought. Perhaps even appalled her. But, then she closed the distance between them. Since he had come to her wearing only his robe, when she reached for him the silk separated, and her palm touched his naked torso. "You're wrong about me," she said.

"I am judge and jury both. You *are* a beauty."

"I meant," she said, laughing a little, "that I am obedient." The room felt suddenly very small. "What would please you?" she asked in a tiny voice.

Ruan didn't move. He hadn't expected this. Not at all. She'd never asked before, just done what he showed her or asked her to do. "Your mouth again," he said. "Your mouth hot and wet around my most intimate part. Your lips on me everywhere you can reach." Her palm stayed flat against his chest until he took her hand in one of his and kissed the tips of her fingers. "Your beautiful backside," he said. "Your breasts beneath my hands. Your legs, your knees, your arms. Most of all, I want what's inside you. I want all that passion let out and overwhelming us both."

"Ruan," she whispered, although she might have said *Lord Ruin*.

He went absolutely still when she freed her hand and stroked his naked chest again, sliding her palm so that she no longer touched any part of his robe. Her hand moved slowly, experimentally. For once, his thoughts didn't leap to his pleasure but instead lingered in the momentous present. The pressure of her hand turned his blood to fire.

"Your skin is warm."

"Yes, love."

Her fingers slid upward. In the faint light, her spectacles flashed once. He was going up in flames. He knew it and fought it because he wanted her to control their passion. He closed his eyes and immediately felt sensations doubled. Her fingertip reached his nipple and glided over it.

"Should I stop?"

"Christ, no," he said, breathless with the effort of holding himself in check. She had to have time. Time to want him. Time to accept what she felt and give in to it.

The silk of his robe slid over his shoulders. Both her hands touched him now. Liquid heat poured into him. Every part of him was sensitized to the moment. Slowly, her hands moved over him, tracing along his ribs and the muscles of his side, upward to his heart. He balanced at the edge of control, quivering with the effort of his restraint.

A groan escaped his tight shut mouth. Anne increased the pressure of her fingers over him and drew him that much closer to the inferno. His hands hung clenched at his sides, but when she leaned forward and pressed her mouth to him he could not help himself. He grasped her head and guided her to his nipple. "Here." His voice sounded gruff, but her tongue flicked out. "Sweet Christ, yes." She drew back and, beyond anything but desire, he cupped the side of her breast.

"Oh."

"If Merchant or anyone else knocks on the door," he ground out, "there will be no reply." She shook her head, and blast it, he did not know what that meant. Agreement? Disagreement? "Hold nothing back, Anne. Shout if you wish. Scream my name. Caress me however you desire. I promise I'll do the same."

"Yes," she breathed.

"Excellent." Coming in for a kiss, he bumped his cheek on her spectacles. None too gently, he reached for them.

"Please," she said breathlessly, taking them from him, fearing, and rightly, that he might toss them across the room.

He spent all of half a second watching her walk to the dresser. She gasped when he put his palms on the dresser top, one on either side of her to effectively trap her. "Anne," he said, choking with desire. "Anne." The spectacles clattered onto the tabletop. "My beauty, Anne."

Time stopped, filled with nothing but silence and the tension he felt in her body. Then, she leaned back and gathered her nightdress in both hands. As she raised it, his body thrummed in anticipation, tingling, hardening, but he did not touch her until she'd brought it over her head and let it fall to the floor. He covered her breasts with both his hands. "You are exquisite." Fire raged in him, shot through his veins when she leaned against him, reaching back to stroke the side of his legs. Her nipples peaked and became pebble hard under his fingers. A low moan came from her throat. Memories of Corth Abbey rushed back; her supple body, soothing hands, and a wickedly tender mouth. Lord Almighty, what a mouth. He'd exploded into her.

"I want you inside me," she whispered. "Now. With us standing just so."

He separated her cheeks with the palms of his hands and came into her, instantly at a peak of unendurable tension. Forcing himself to do nothing, he savored the heat that enveloped him, the shiver of fire that coursed through him. Only when he was sure he wouldn't lose himself entirely did he pull her hips hard against him, wanting the feel of her backside. She made that sound again, that drawn out "oh" that was half groan, half moan and without a drop of protest. She accepted him easily despite being tight inside. He could see in the dresser mirror her pale torso and his own body behind hers, but mostly he felt his engorged sex moving in her, the thrill of a too-rapidly approaching orgasm.

Now, that would be disaster. He subdued the impulse to drive into her, to satisfy his own urges. Instead, he leaned against her, one hand around her waist and slipping upward, the other seeking between her legs, his fingers curling in crisp hair. She had to support her weight and some of his with both her hands flat on the dresser top. He meant to bring her to climax before he took his pleasure and that was fast seeming an impossibility, especially when she matched the circling of his hips, her pressure outward against his inward. She made an inarticulate cry when, summoning the absolute last shred of control he possessed, he withdrew from her.

She shivered at the loss of his warmth then turned around, breath coming rapidly. Eyes of dark-blue smoke hinted at the fire within. With him standing just inches from her, he could feel desire coming off her in waves. He was at the brink himself. A mass of dawn-lit hair fell over her shoulder, and he pushed it back.

"It's not too fast, is it?" he forced himself to ask. "I'll slow down if you think so." He wondered if it would kill him if she said yes. But she shook her head. "Good."

Too close to release, himself, he knew the pain of his denial now would only double his pleasure later. He sank to his knees, got her to spread her thighs and pressed his mouth to her. It didn't take long.

She convulsed, crying out, "Dear God, Cynssyr!"

Eventually, she simply collapsed. He had by then regained some of his self-possession, though the bed seemed altogether too far away. Her fainting couch was much closer, easily within reach. He got them both onto it. He was Lord Ruin, a man expert in the seduction of women, and he called on every ounce of his fabled finesse so that Anne would be bound to him. Only him.

She met all of his passion and more. She cupped his behind, pulled him closer to her as she arched toward him, seeking and offering at one and the same time. Sweat beaded on their skin. His belly slid easily over hers as they found the rhythm of mutual need. Her face was a study in passion, her mouth slack at the edges. All that was lacking from his fantasy was her spectacles. He regretted having made her take them off. A slow, forward circle of his pelvis against her made her moan and bow upward. Her knees bent on either side of his hips, her hands gripped his forearms while he watched her climax with gratifying intensity. He gathered her into his arms and carried her to bed. She fell asleep in his embrace, with his heart beating slow and steady against the curve of her back.

The experience, a lightness of spirit, still resonated with him the next day when he managed to leave Whitehall early enough to attend one of Anne's at-homes. Ruan slipped quietly into the drawing room. Enough people crowded the room that the feat was quite possible. Leaning against the wall, he crossed one foot over his ankle and his arms over his chest, content to surreptitiously watch Anne for the few moments he managed to

229

stand unobserved. Several gentlemen, among them Julian Durling and Thrale, engaged in lively conversation with her, the men holding hats and riding whips to satisfy the social fiction of a brief visit. Even Emily, the divine Sinclair, rarely laid claim to a greater number of fascinated gentlemen.

Though Anne smiled frequently, he soon noticed a certain tension in her shoulders that suggested discomfort. She shifted her weight from one foot to the other and slowly waved an ivory fan under her chin. Her gown of peach sarcenet and satin lent such feeble color to her complexion, odds were good she wasn't feeling well. Lord Sather joined the circle, completing a veritable wall around her. Ruan caught only a glimpse of her fan quickly moving, a flash of peach and ivory.

Intending to rescue her, Ruan left his place against the wall and was promptly waylaid by Lady Prescott. As he watched over her shoulder, the throng of men around Anne parted and she appeared, walking urgently toward the door. Seconds later, a man whose face Ruan could not see peeled away from the circle and strolled out. The man, whoever he was, stood in the doorway, peering down the hall before walking out. He didn't turn toward the stairs, but moved further down the hall.

Chapter Twenty-five

"Excuse me, Julia," he said to Lady Prescott. "I need a word with my wife, and I see she's just left."

"Not the first time I've seen her suddenly absent herself." One side of her mouth lifted. "Is she perhaps . . . ?"

"Shy?" he supplied, straight-faced. "Why, yes, she is."

As he bowed, she murmured, "Such a virile man you are. Are you certain you wouldn't . . . ?" She finished the sentence with a tiny lift of her eyebrows. "For old time's sake?"

"No. Forgive me, no."

Ruan pushed his way though the crowded room to the hallway. He saw no one. Not Anne. Not the man who'd followed her. If Anne were ill as he suspected, she'd not have gone far. He scanned the hall. No open doors. The nearest room was the Red Salon, seldom used since his mother had decamped to Hampstead Heath some years before. He opened the door. The

231

Carolyn Jewel

scene registered instantly and yet seemed to last forever: Anne with her back not quite opposite him, bent over a basin and heaving up the contents of her stomach. A man walking toward her. Anne moaning and pressing a hand to her stomach. Near the basin stood a washbowl and near that a stack of towels. "Oh, God," she said, and lost her stomach again. The man reaching for one of the towels, stretching it to its full length.

He didn't think he'd ever moved so fast in his life. In one movement he crossed the room, grabbing the intruder and whirling him around. Ruan slammed a fist into his face and let momentum send the man crashing to the floor. Anne shrieked once, very briefly, then had herself under control.

Still sprawled on the floor and holding a hand to his cheek, Julian Durling said, "Look here, Cynssyr. It's not what you're thinking. Not at all."

"What are you doing here?" Anne said to Durling.

"Yes," Ruan said. "I am sure you won't mind explaining yourself."

Durling rose gingerly to his feet and with a look at Ruan, handed her the towel he clutched. "I should much rather go home. If you don't mind." He stumbled when Ruan pushed him to a chair far opposite from Anne. "This is an outrage."

"My sentiments as well."

"There's a perfectly innocent explanation, I assure you."

"You are at leisure to provide it."

Durling scowled and made a show of straightening his clothes. "Perfectly good coat ruined," he muttered. "Are you feeling better, Duchess?"

She squeezed the towel and nodded at Ruan. "I didn't know he was here. Nor you, Cynssyr."

"I saw him follow you."

"Why?" She asked the question of Durling.

232

"I'm waiting," Ruan said, leaning against the fireplace mantel like a cat ready to pounce. "For your innocent explanation."

Durling gave Anne a pleading look. "Under the circumstances, I didn't dare speak with you directly, Cynssyr. Not after you had that hulking great footman throw me out on my ar—"

Fire leapt to those peridot eyes. "I'll thank you to mind your language."

"Well, yes." Durling coughed. "Of course. You know what I mean."

"He threw you out of—What are you talking about?"

"Told me he didn't like the way I looked at you."

As usual, Cynssyr's impassive face gave away nothing. He stood by the fireplace, one arm on the mantel. Durling, on the other hand, was amused.

"You're a handsome woman, Duchess," Durling said, shaking his blond curls, "and if your husband goes about threatening every man who admires you, he'll have to step down from Parliament to have the time. I've every reason to fear him. The man shot Wilberfoss, who was supposed to be his brother-in-law. He'd bloody well kill me for wanting to speak with you when twice now he's told me not to. He was bound to get the wrong idea. And he has."

"Twice?"

"Just start explaining," Ruan said gruffly.

"The duchess is in danger."

Ruan pushed off the mantel. "What do you mean?" Watching him, Anne thought she wouldn't care to be on the receiving end of that stare. The pale eyes glittered with an unsettling light.

"Played cards night before last. Least I think it was then. Dice too, though my luck with dice has always been wretched."

"Where?"

233

"Does it make a difference?"

"Yes."

"In a place a gentleman should not frequent."

Ruan leaned an arm on the fireplace mantel again. "A name, Durling, if you would be so kind." Had she not come to know him, Anne might have thought her husband utterly at ease. But she knew he was not.

Durling swallowed hard. "The Three Swans."

"I know of it."

"As I said, not a place a gentleman should frequent." He fingered his cheek, found the rising bruise and shuddered.

"It is not," Ruan said.

"On my honor, your grace, I shall never go there again. I do beg your forgiveness, Duchess, for being indelicate in your presence." He regained a bit of his indolence. Her father would have called him *one of those damned fops*. "Your husband is such a bear. However do you manage him?"

Ruan took a step forward, hands clenched.

"Cynssyr," Anne said. "Please."

"You're a lovely woman," Durling said. "And loyal, too. But I adore you anyway." He threw up his hands with mock horror when Ruan scowled. "I refer, of course, to that most noble emotion such as a brother feels toward his sister."

She had to smile. "And when you are not too much the dandy, I do like you. As a sister would a brother."

"Thank the Lord for that," he drawled. "I'd be in a pickle for sure if Cyn's wife fell in love with me." He winked at her. "Not even a twinge?"

She shook her head.

"Pity."

Ruan made an impatient gesture. "I'll have your heart on a platter, Durling, if you don't start explaining yourself."

"A thousand pardons, your grace." For a moment, the dandyish drawl vanished. "One of the men I played with last night fell rather deep in his cups and said a few things about the duchess."

"Such as?"

"Such as she's a beautiful woman." His eyes fell to Anne's bosom. "And Insincere Cynssyr is remarkably protective of her."

Cynssyr tensed. Anne didn't think Durling noticed, but she did. "She's my wife," Cynssyr replied shortly. As if that explained everything.

"Attentive, too. Everyone's noticed." He threw up his hands. "T'was not me, your grace. I merely repeat what I heard."

"Go on."

"One of them said, er, some rather specific things. Involving him and the duchess."

"Such as?" Cynssyr prompted.

"Such as I refuse to repeat."

Cynssyr examined his nails, to all appearances at ease with the response and the ensuing silence. Eventually, he fixed Durling with a look sharp as the edge of a sword. "I grow impatient."

Durling wilted. "Didn't think 'til I got home the fellow might have been serious." He waggled his fingers in an airy manner. "Bluster and too much ale. You know how these things are. But, listen here, Cyn." Durling sat forward. He touched a hand to his cheek and winced. "The remarks I overheard might be interpreted to mean the man plans revenge on you through the duchess, and after what I saw at that house—" He shuddered. "I wanted to warn her."

"Revenge for what?"

"With you, who knows?" He leaned back and crossed his legs. "Any number of husbands or fathers after a piece of your hide."

Carolyn Jewel

"Against whom are you warning me?"

Durling frowned, glancing at Anne and then looking back at Cynssyr. "I don't know his name. But he was slender, brown hair, brown eyes. Drank like a dashed fish." He returned his attention to Anne. "I should think a man like your husband would take care to know his enemies."

"I should think," Ruan said, "you'd want to know the name of the fellow who might owe you money. Or the other way round."

"We were drunk, I am sorry to say, and I was close to winning enough to—Well, never mind about that, too. I do not know the man's name. But he made it quite clear he feels he has a score to settle with you and that he has friends in high places who will help him. Very high. Oh, not so exalted as yourself, Cynssyr, but nearly as high. Men like that, like you, are so often vindictive when crossed. As my Lord Wilberfoss learned, much to his detriment. Did you know he's been told he may never regain full use of the arm?"

"Then, I suppose, you understand the danger you are in."

"You'd imagine Cynssyr grateful," Durling remarked to Anne, to all appearances unmoved by that low, dangerous voice. "I might have kept my mouth shut, you know." Again, he touched his damaged cheek. "He's ruined my pretty features for a fortnight, at least." With a sigh and a shrug, he said, "Now, that's all I know, your grace. Or all I remember, anyway. May I go, or am I to be held further against my will?"

"Leave," Cynssyr curtly said. "By all means, leave. But be warned, if ever you lay a hand on my wife, in jest or otherwise, I'll put a bullet in your head." He waited for a nod, it came quickly, then he rang for Merchant.

"He *is* protective, isn't he?"

"A cold compress on that cheek will help, Mr. Durling," Anne said.

He rose, grimmacing. "Thank you."

"We're grateful for the warning."

"Yes. Well." He sent a cautious look at Cynssyr. "Grateful is as grateful does."

"Take care, Mr. Durling," Anne said.

"Now I've your husband on my tail." Another look went Ruan's way. "Bracebridge and Aldreth, too, I should think." Hand to his chin, he pretended to consider his predicament. "Well! Never let it be said I cannot make out the silver lining. I'll be safe from my creditors. Yes, I shall. Safer than a rat on a sinking ship. Why, my cup simply runneth over." He grinned, then winced because of his damaged cheek. "Too bad it's poison, eh?" He bent over her hand in an elaborate show of manners. "Your husband, Duchess, does not deserve you."

"Get out." Cynssyr took a step in his direction. "Merchant!" he bellowed.

"Stay away from the hells, Mr. Durling," Anne said, "and you will stay away from trouble."

"No worries there." He sidled toward the door. "I've spent my quarterly allowance. Nothing for it now but to hit up the maiden aunt for more funds or else rusticate in the wilds of Lancashire until the old bird gives me money to go away."

Merchant came in, just a hint of haste in his step, and Anne couldn't help but wonder how many times past the butler found occasion to show out a guest who wasn't entirely sure what had happened to him.

Cynssyr took a chair when Merchant and Durling were gone. Anne patiently waited. "I don't trust him," he said after a bit. "You're not to see him. Not for any reason." He placed his hands on her shoulders and peered into her face. "Not so pale, now. Are you better?"

"Yes. Much."

"Good." He pulled his watch from his waistcoat. "You've an appointment with Mrs. Withers later tonight, yes?" He rose with that arrogant elegance that seemed to define masculinity.

"Seven o'clock, sir."

He kissed her, only briefly and on the cheek. The contact made her pulse speed. She hoped he didn't notice. Probably he did. Very little went unremarked by her husband. No matter how she fought it, she would look at his mouth and think, those lips had kissed her, had been on her breast, his teeth gently tugging, his breath hot on her skin, his tongue doing things that turned her insides to fire so that all she could do was clutch his head and hope to survive the conflagration.

Together, they returned to the salon. From almost the moment Cynssyr walked in, the dynamic of the room changed. The men seemed less charming, the women more flirtatious. And everyone wanted at least one word with him. Many hoped for nothing more than to later say in passing that they had been speaking to Cynssyr, you know. And he held thus and such an opinion, or he had listened most carefully, or that the cut of his coat might never be duplicated. She knew because she'd overheard or even been party to many such breathless accounts. Cynssyr awed just about everyone. Men and women alike vied for his favor. And of all the brilliant sycophants surrounding him, it was to her, Anne Sinclair, that he revealed himself. Such an awesome, overwhelming circumstance could not last, Anne thought. How could it? How would she bear it if it did not?

With the salon concluded and the last guest was seen off, Anne went upstairs while her husband closeted himself with Hickenson and the morning's post. Her present life, she decided, was lived on borrowed time. An interlude to be savored whilst she struggled to protect her heart. She dressed for her calls and met Cynssyr on the landing. He, too, was heading out for the evening. He wore a frac of hunter green, buff trousers cut close to the thigh—he had the legs for it—and carried a greatcoat and beaver hat. Hickenson paced at the bottom of the stairs clutching a leather case to his chest.

"Where to, my dear?" Cynssyr asked her.

"Portman Square. Then to Mrs. Withers."

"I'm to Whitehall. Come. I'll walk you to your carriage." He tossed a look backward as he caught up his coat and settled it over his broad shoulders. His hand stayed on the back of her arm all the way outside. Hickenson trotted behind but discreetly found his way to the duke's coach. True to his word, Cynssyr waved off the footman to help her up himself. He turned away, frowning. "With the duchess, Henry," he called to the postilion waiting in position at the back of Cynssyr's coach. "You're not to let her out of your sight."

"Aye, your grace." He jumped down and ran to Anne's carriage.

She reached to straighten the lay of his cravat over a stiff collar. His beauty had become as familiar as if it lived in her, a part of her. "Cynssyr," she said softly.

He caught her hand and brought it to his lips. "I shall be home early tonight, unless the sessions keep me late." She knew what that meant, or thought she did, and it made her smile. He smiled in return, murmuring, "You are a minx."

When the carriage door closed on her, she fell against the seat, eyes closed, hearing the echo of her husband's voice. If she wasn't careful, she would find herself just as helpless as all the other women in love with Lord Ruin. If she did not find a way to stop herself from feeling, she saw nothing in her future but heartbreak.

Chapter Twenty-six

Mrs. Withers and her husband lived on the border of Mayfair, not one of the best addresses, but nevertheless a good one about thirty minutes from Aldreth's, under normal circumstances. Tonight, with another of the prince's lavish entertainments open to the public, traffic clogged the streets, and the drive was over an hour. She could have walked faster.

A rotund servant showed Anne to a parlor decorated in unrelenting pink. Polly Withers sat on a chair like the stem of some pale rose doomed to break in a strong wind. A spray of egret plumes dyed a faded ruby adorned her hair, her fingers moved nervously around a gold chain. She was delicate with sharp elbows and parchment-pale skin wrapped tight around vein and tendon. Her youth came as a surprise, much younger than Anne. Emily's age. Seventeen or eighteen at the most. With her waiflike features she ought to have been pretty and was not.

"Duchess," she said in a lisping tone Anne at first thought an affectation but soon understood to be her normal speaking voice. Anne's calling card rested on a table, aligned at a precise diagonal to Polly's chair.

She still wasn't accustomed to the precedence she now took, nor the rapt attention paid her as Cynssyr's wife. "Do sit, please." She waved to head off another curtsey but found herself gazing at a crown of champagne curls. Mrs. Featherstone was also a blonde.

"Your grace. An honor to meet you. May I offer you tea?" Nerves and fatigue haunted eyes of a lovely golden brown.

"Tea would be splendid." The parlor was immaculate, nothing out of place, no brick-a-brak to lend character to the room, just a vase of blush roses on a sidetable and over the mantel a portrait of a stern, bewigged man. Exactly the sort of spare look the house in Bartley Green took on once Anne had sold everything that might fetch a pound or two.

"My husband should be here shortly. Tea?" Polly served enthusiastically but without attention to detail, leaving the cakes just out of reach and, without asking, adding a large amount of cream to a dark tea Anne knew she'd never be able to drink. "What lovely dishes," Anne said of the rose-painted service.

"Thank you," Polly said as the door opened to admit an elderly gentleman. She peeked over her shoulder.

"Duchess," he boomed in the manner of the hard of hearing. Anne extended her hand to the man in the portrait, expecting to be introduced to Polly's father-in-law, for he was several decades Polly's elder, sixty if a day. His dry hand trembled against hers. "Mrs. Withers," he said sharply, "you are remiss in making introductions." He bowed. "I am Mr. Withers, madam, at your service."

"Sir." Anne looked at Polly uncertainly. Surely this

241

man wasn't her husband? But Polly had wilted onto her seat as though all her strength had just drained away.

Withers released Anne's hand. "I have already told your esteemed husband what happened to my wife." The sparse gray whiskers that covered his cheeks disappeared entirely at his jowls. "This interview isn't necessary. Ask me if it's not a complete waste of time."

"Do have a seat, Mr. Withers," Anne said. He gave a curt nod and sat by Polly, one hand gripping the other over his paunch, trying, Anne realized, to hide the tremor of his right hand. "Cynssyr and I appreciate your allowing me to visit your very charming wife. The duke," she added with deliberate emphasis, "hoped Mrs. Withers might recall something else." She looked at Polly. Busy pouring tea for her husband, she might have been his grandchild rather than his wife. "I assure you not a word of what she tells me will find its way to anyone but Cynssyr."

Some of the tension left the man's shoulders. "My wife is a foolish girl, as you've no doubt divined." Polly gave him his tea. He pressed his right palm into his belly and accepted the cup with the other hand. "Had she better wits she would never have been tricked."

"I'm sure it's true," Polly said, retaking her seat. "I did believe the fellow to have been sent by Mrs. Halifax." She darted a look at Anne. "Eugenia is my bosom friend, and if she. . . ." She caught sight of her husband's scowl and left the thought incomplete.

"She allowed herself to be overpowered." From that point on, Anne heard little more from Polly. Her husband's version was not remarkably different from Mrs. Featherstone's, if lacking in detail. Occasionally, he lifted his hands, and she could see the tremor had become more pronounced. She listened politely, nodding as appropriate. Had she ever seen a couple less suited than these two? He was far too old for Polly, a man long past his youth and well past his prime, too set in his ways to adapt to a child-bride and too resentful of her youth.

Anne could not help making the comparison to her own marriage, certainly hers was also a match of opposites. But Cynssyr didn't treat her like a child, and he never condescended to her as did Withers to Polly. She felt an unexpected but familiar shiver streak along her spine and knew it for desire. Lord, but she didn't think Withers had ever made his wife feel passion like Cynssyr roused in her. Much as she and Cynssyr were mismatched, the fact was, he could have made her quite unhappy, and he hadn't.

"And now," the man concluded. "You know all there is to know. Mrs. Withers will see you to the door."

"Oh, but she's not finished her tea." Under cover of refreshing Anne's untouched tea, Polly leaned forward and spoke softly. "One of them was from the country. The north. He's in service somewhere here in London."

Anne, who had given up hope of learning anything new, forced herself to calm. "In service?"

"In a fancy house, I gathered." She glanced at her husband. "He made disparaging remarks about his employer. Thought him a dullard. A vain dandy." She laughed, a weak, joyless sound, the rustle of leaves in the breeze. "Aren't all the dandies vain?"

Anne spoke softly, too. "Is it possible the other man was his employer?"

"In truth, I thought so."

The parlor door opened to admit the butler. "We are not at home," Withers bellowed.

"Begging your pardon, sir." The card on the salver the butler extended to Mr. Withers was Devon's. "The earl of Bracebridge."

Withers took the card, silver eyebrows arching. His hand trembled. "You don't say?"

Devon strode in before a refusal could be offered. Hat under one arm, he went straight to Polly. "Madam." He bowed, taking her hand but quickly releasing it.

"My lord," she said with a dainty sigh and an uncertain glance at Anne. "Will you have tea?"

"How gracious, but, thank you, no."

Withers stuck out his hand. He, too, gave Anne a sideways look. "Honored, my lord. Honored by your visit."

"What is it, Dev?" Anne asked. She could hardly help but be aware of a new undercurrent of tension. Though she didn't know why, plainly Devon's visit had some special meaning.

"There's been another abduction. Late yesterday evening."

"Is she all right?" Polly breathed.

"Never mind that," Withers rumbled. "Have they caught the man?"

"No, to both, I fear. The physician does not expect her to survive." He gave Polly an assessing look then addressed Anne. "It was Cynssyr who found her. He is with her now, or was when he sent me to fetch you."

Polly shivered, clasping her arms around her waist. "Take her home, my lord. She should be with the duke at a time like this." She sounded, for some reason, accusing.

"You are, madam," said Devon his voice a bit too smooth, "quite right." He took Anne's arm. "Shall we collect your things, Duchess? I've sent your carriage home," he said when they were on their way out. "I'll take you in mine." He held her arm as they walked down the stairs. Devon's curricle was at the curb, but he'd been lucky to get the spot. Carriages jammed the streets every way one looked. None were moving with any dispatch. Raising his voice to be heard over the din, he said, "Damn Prinny and his wretched parties." He helped her into his coach, a handsome vehicle with green leather seats. After thirty minutes they'd not even made it out of sight of the Withers' home, and Anne felt the beginnings of nausea. The biscuits were in her carriage.

She concentrated on taking slow, deep breaths. "Really, I think we ought to walk."

Devon cursed and threw open the door. "You're right." To the coachman, he called out, "Make your way home as best you can." He took Anne's arm. "Pull up your cloak. For certain we'll have rain before we make Queen Anne Street." At first, she didn't mind the cold for the fresh air settled her stomach. A quarter of an hour later the damp had penetrated her heavy cloak and frozen her nose, hands and feet. Devon glanced at the sky and walked faster. Sure enough, moments later fat raindrops hit the street and pounded onto rooftops and carriages. The downpour forced them to refuge in a doorway. He kept an arm around her, shielding her from the worst of the wet. Anne huddled close and didn't demur when he took off his coat and put it around her shoulders.

At last, the rain lessened. Devon lightly touched her nose to wipe away a drop of rain. "Shall we?" She was too cold to do anything but nod. His arm stayed around her as they navigated the now rain-slickened streets. She was glad of his warmth. They reached Cyrwthorn fifty minutes later. Devon led an exhausted Anne up the steps, ignoring Merchant hovering in the doorway awaiting dripping hats, cloaks and coats. He turned and put his hands on her shoulders. "Will you be all right, Anne, or shall I stay?" Water puddled on the marble floor.

"It's kind of you to offer, but, no."

He let his palms slide off her shoulders. "I'll be at home. You'll send if the need arises?"

"I will. And thank you for fetching me." She turned to Merchant when Dev had gone. "He's in the parlor?"

"One worries, your grace, when the dark humor strikes him so deeply."

The parlor door was ominously closed. The implications of her having no fear gave her pause. It seemed amazing, and absurd, that she had ever believed him nothing more than a heartless rogue. She opened the door. The room stank heavily of cigar and the fireplace coals were long dead. Cynssyr sat on an armchair pulled up before the fire, close enough that he could flick his ravaged cigars onto the ashes with minimum effort. A bottle of scotch sat unopened on the table beside him. Without turning to look he said, "Forgive me, Anne. I am not in the mood for company."

She bent down at the fireplace. "I won't disturb you long." With practiced hands, she added more coal and restarted the fire. She stayed by the fire, hoping to take off the chill of her walk. Right now he seemed every inch the man she thought she'd married. Arrogant, harsh, intimidating and beautiful beyond description. She pasted a smile on her face. "There, you see?"

His eyes followed her as she rose. Their sad, faraway expression made her think of faded roses and letters written to parents who would grieve forever after. "How went your interview with Mrs. Withers?" he asked.

"Mostly a waste of time, I'm afraid." Her chest felt tight. She wanted to hold him in her arms and take away his pain, but she could not make herself move. Instead, she said, "Mr. Withers did most of the talking. I dared not ask anything important of her, for with her husband there she would have been forced to lie. Either to me or her husband, and that would not have been fair."

"Always so kind."

"He is too old for her, Cynssyr. I can't imagine why those two would ever have married."

"Yes, well," he said in a voice rich with irony.

The silence lingered. Lord help her, she understood his pain and forgave him. "Have you had dinner or supper?"

"You're wet. Why?"

"It's raining, and Devon and I had to walk home."

"Indeed."

"I'll fetch you a plate of something from the kitchen." She rubbed her hands together, whisking away the inevitable bits of coal dust.

He pulled on his cigar, then flicked it into the fire. "Mrs. Jacobs was nearly murdered," he said softly as she started back to the door.

"Yes. Dev told me. How is she?"

"Clinging to life."

After a moment, she walked to him and put a hand on his arm. "How did you even know where to look for her?"

"After you left, I was on my way to Brooks. Jacobs intercepted me. He had the demand note with him. Two thousand pounds in return for his wife unharmed. I fetched Dev and Ben, and went to some cesspit tavern near the South Road. They watched the place while I delivered the money. A whore met me. I couldn't beat the damn information out of her, though perhaps I should have, for it took me too long to frighten her into telling me anything useful. Fool woman didn't know a blessed thing except there was a lady in her room and she was supposed to be paid a pound to show a gentleman upstairs."

She saw, next to the untouched bottle of scotch, a letter. "Is that the note?"

"Yes." He snatched it off the table and threw the

sheet onto the fire. "For all the good it does. It brings us no closer to Thrale or anyone else."

"A pity the woman was no help."

Flames leapt to consume the paper. "An ignorant thing who cared for nothing but my coin. Even offered her own sweet person." This he said with biting sarcasm. He looked at her from underneath lashes long enough to be the envy of many a woman. "I thought I had him. I really did. We've never had our hands on one of his cohorts before. But the woman knew nothing."

"It is not your fault." She offered her hand, wishing she could take away the anguish he tried so hard to disguise.

"The responsibility is mine."

Without question he believed that to be true. She settled onto the sofa, watching her tall, proud husband staring at the ashes of the letter. "How do you bear it?"

"I am a man." A moment of silence stretched out. "I bear it because I must." To her surprise, he sat beside her, bending his head to her shoulder as if bowing slowly to the sorrow. "I must," he repeated. "There is nothing else."

"You will find him, Cynssyr." Her hand rested on his head, touching his hair, mahogany that felt like silk against her fingers. For some minutes, they sat in the quiet. Then, he lifted his head.

"You were with Devon," he said roughly. "You were with Devon and though I trust you without reservation, I cannot bear the notion of you with him."

"He brought me home, that's all."

"Yes, he did." A spark passed between them, invisible, yet wholly tangible to them both. His mouth came down on hers. Not at all tender, demanding as she buried her fingers in his hair. Roughly, he lifted her onto his lap, bringing her head against his shoulder as his free hand sought to cup her breast.

He made her quiver with longing, a frisson of excitement too intense to survive. Their mouths met again, tongues delving, his hand searching for her, her body offering. After a moment longer, he pulled away, breathing hard. "Why can't you wear those low-cut things like all the other women of fashion?" he complained with a self-mocking smile. "I want to touch you." He took her head between his hands, forcing her to look at him. And she did. She met those peridot eyes and saw her own passion reflected there. "Feel what you do to me, damn you." He sucked in a breath when her hand found the part of him he meant. "Damn you."

She peered at him from beneath half-closed eyes and dared a great deal. Her pulse raced. "Do you want me to kiss you there?"

"God, yes." He laughed softly while she worked at the buttons of his trousers. "Right now." After a moment of her struggling with the front of his breeches, he said, "Bugger it. Stand up, Anne."

She did, and he fumbled at his own trousers only to find himself just as clumsy. "Bugger it again," he breathed. He pulled hard. Buttons popped loose, and he was free. She started to take him in her hand, but he stopped her. "Later," he said gruffly pulling her to him. She felt the length of him pressing against her, the iron heat of his desire between them, the taste of his mouth and despair and desperation unleashed. With a groan, he walked her backward until she bumped against a table. He got her onto it, threw up her skirts and then his body was between her legs, his breath hot against her cheek when he surged inside her. The sensation of being filled made her gasp, and she met that first wonderful thrust of his with one of her own. "God, but you are made for this. For me."

"Cynssyr," she cried, her body already contracting around him.

"When I saw her, Anne," he said as he went deep into her, "I kept thinking, my God, it could have been you." He gasped, almost a sob. "It could have been you."

"Hush," she soothed as she accepted the fierce tautness of his body. "Hush." He took her for some time, silently, fiercely, with single-minded concentration. She moaned as he began to lead her toward oblivion.

"It's not like this with anyone else," he said. His strokes continued, long and steady. "I don't understand why, but it's true."

She arched her back and offered what they both needed, "Harder, Ruan."

He came that much farther and ferociously into her. His hands above her shoulders kept her from sliding away from the urgent thrust of his hips. "Hard enough?" he asked, staring down at her with gem-like eyes.

"No." A pulse of pure sexual desire ripped through her, almost feral. She did not have enough, wasn't yet where she wanted to be.

"No?" he whispered.

"No."

Something changed. She felt the difference. This was not at all like their lovemaking before. Then, he had been tender or passionate by turns, restrained, always, always consummately in control, always leading her, even with his restraint proving his mastery of her body. Not now. They were equals now. She wasn't afraid or intimidated. She burned with the same fire that consumed him. He pinned her hands above her head, and she answered his raging passion with a fury of her own.

"We're going to break the table," he growled. He picked her up, keeping her legs around his hips and him buried deep in her. Then, they were on the floor. He scraped his teeth along her bared shoulder. "I don't want to hurt you," he said. "Tell me if I'm hurting you."

"More," she gasped. "Please, more."

He obliged her, and she went spinning out of her mind. "Anne." Her name seemed to tear from his throat in desperation. "Anne. Sweet Christ, Anne."

Chapter Twenty-seven

Anne stood alone in the dressing room. She kept a small valise hidden here, inside a trunk, covered over with gowns from Bartley Green. In it she'd packed a few clothes, toiletries and some money. Enough to see her to Cornwall. A precaution against heartbreak taken on the night Cynssyr had made such desperate love to her. The night he'd found Mrs. Jacobs and reached to her for comfort, taking her heart and soul away with him.

She gazed at her reflection in the cheval glass. Staring back at her was the old maid of Bartley Green dressed up to suit the fashion. Ivory tulle over amaranth satin with a Morocco belt of a darker hue above her natural waist didn't hide the essential truth. Nor did sleeves fashioned from puffs of satin and tulle. Nor pale red flounces and white lace to match her satin slippers. It was the sort of gown one of Cynssyr's distractions might wear. The truth was she suited neither gown nor husband.

She had herself back in her accustomed place, and her husband in his. Her role was to give him his child, which she would do, and to cause him no embarrassment, which she would also do. All those unsettling feelings he aroused in her were locked away like her valise, to be brought out only if necessary. For now, at least, she was safe from Lord Ruin. He could not destroy her as he had so many other women. She knew how he did it. Unconsciously. Relentlessly. With cruel tenderness. But she was expert at keeping her place; at never wanting more than her due. Reach too high and one got burned. Anne could feel the flames.

Lady Prescott's townhouse blazed with light. There were thirty to supper, an intimate number. Aldreth escorted her tonight because Cynssyr was going to be late. An appointment, he'd said, after the sessions let out. She felt safer yet when Devon arrived.

Even without her husband, she merited a place close to the hostess and had the honor of Sir James's arm on the way to the table. Devon got paired with Miss Fairchild. Camilla's nervous giggles carried throughout the room. John Martin led in Miss Fanny Cooke, but he was seated far from Anne's place. Thrale sat on her left, Devon between Miss Fairchild and Mrs. Cooke. Her father, Aldreth, Lucy, Mary and Emily sat near Anne's end of the table. After supper, when the gentlemen had rejoined the ladies, someone suggested dancing. Once the furniture was moved, two footmen proved themselves able musicians, one on the fiddle, the other on pipes. A young boy kept the beat on a small drum.

Anne never sat down, not even with her sisters for competition. Aldreth partnered her first, then Sir James, himself, and Devon. Julian Durling braved Cynssyr's wrath and asked for a dance. He led with authority so that dancing with him was effortless. She didn't need to think what step was next or what her feet were doing or even much about the music. In consequence, they had a spirited conversation. "You're an outrageous flirt," she scolded him. "How is it a man as charming as you hasn't married?"

He gave her a piquant grin. "It seems I've poor judgment about how to find a wife. I've scoured the ballrooms and salons of London when I ought to have been attending country dances."

Anne laughed. "You see the error of your ways."

"Too late," he said, smoothly coming to a halt. "Alas, too late, for now I'm a hopeless jade." He bowed and handed her to her next partner who happened to be the marquess of Thrale.

Thrale had so far danced exactly three times. Twice with Emily and once with Lucy. This last with Anne made his fourth. He spoke hardly at all of Emily, instead amusing her with a recitation of Lucy's many perceived faults. Her sister, he told her, was a scatterbrained female who wasn't safe even sitting on a chair. Midnight found Anne chatting with Lady Prescott while the two footmen took a well-deserved break from their musical duties. She knew the sessions had let out, for Fenrother and Sather had arrived well over an hour before.

"Bracebridge," said Lady Prescott, extending a bejeweled hand to be kissed when Dev joined them. "Wherever have you been? It's bad of you to have disappeared like that. I've been waiting these past hours for you to ask to me to dance."

He bowed, his unruly curls falling over his forehead. "If I thought your husband would not have my liver on a plate for the presumption, I would."

"Ah, how I do miss your father. You've his silver tongue and the look of him, too, or would have if you'd not gone and ruined your face. I remember when your nose was as straight as his. You were a handsome man then."

"I was never handsome, my lady." He turned to Anne, his eyes serious despite his lighthearted exchange with Lady Prescott. "A moment of your time, Duchess?"

"Of course." Without another word, he led her out of the room. Martin broke off his conversation with Julian Durling as she and Devon passed. Seeing his stare, Anne nodded, then bent her head toward Devon to say, "What is it, Dev?"

He put his mouth near her ear. "Miss Dancy."

Anne's heart leapt. "You've found her?"

"To be precise, she found me."

"Is Cynssyr with her?"

"No." After collecting her cloak, they went to his waiting carriage. Inside, Anne took out her spectacles and put them on her nose. The sudden crispness of her vision startled her. What a relief to be able to see. Devon got in beside her. Without preamble, he said, "She has agreed to talk to you. Only you."

"I wonder why? I mean, why now?"

Devon shrugged. "As of now, you know as much as I."

They drove to an inn near the road to Hampstead Heath, absurdly named the Jolly Duck. Devon took her to a private sitting room on the second floor. A young woman sat on a horsehair sofa, hair as blond as Anne's arranged in what appeared to be a fall of natural ringlets. Her face was pretty, very nearly beautiful, with deep brown eyes and a sensitive mouth.

"Miss Dancy?" Anne said. The remains of her supper had not yet been cleared.

"You are the duchess?" she asked in a soft, anxious voice. She did not stand. "Lord Ruin's wife?"

"Yes, I am."

255

Carolyn Jewel

The girl peeked nervously at Devon. Anne, recognizing the fear that sank hope to her toes, glanced over her shoulder. The look reminded her too much of Polly and Mrs. Featherstone. "He'll wait in the other room, won't you, Devon?" He nodded solemnly and went out. Anne took the only other seat, an uncomfortable and unupholstered wooden chair. "My goodness, you're just a child."

"Nineteen, Duchess." A look of pain flashed over her face. "Last week. Thank you for coming."

"Thank you for seeing me," Anne said.

She clasped her hands over her heart. "I agreed because you're *his* wife," she whispered. "Lord Ruin's." For a moment, Anne thought the poor girl must be in love with Cynssyr. A pretty girl like her would have tempted him. Miss Dancy quickly dispelled that notion, however. "I knew you would understand when I heard why you are married to him."

"Why is that, Miss Dancy?"

She lifted clear brown eyes to Anne's face. "He got caught."

"It wasn't—" Anne meant to say *it wasn't like that,* but the need to keep Miss Dancy talking stopped her. Besides, she knew at least something of what the girl meant, for she remembered her feelings when Aldreth had made her understand what had happened at Corth Abbey. What must it have been like for Miss Dancy, who had suffered immeasurably worse from men without a scrap of humanity or decency? Cynssyr, at least, hadn't acted from hatred or anger, and afterward, he'd done what honor demanded. More, he'd made her welcome in his home, his life even, and he needn't have.

"I knew you would understand."

She reached for Miss Dancy's hand but found the gesture rebuffed. "Will you tell me what happened?"

"There were three of them." Only occasionally did

256

she stop. The details she related differed little from those Anne had already heard from Mrs. Featherstone or Polly Withers. Despite a clear and almost emotionless recitation, the brown eyes told a different story. Anguish leapt from them, a deep and abiding despair and, at certain points, outright fear.

"You know who did it, don't you?" Anne said.

She nodded.

"Who?" Anne tried again to take one of her hands but the girl kept her fists tightly clenched. "Who was it? My husband will see that he pays, whoever it was."

Miss Dancy's pretty mouth trembled. "The marquess of Thrale."

"You actually saw him?"

"He was careful not to let me see his face."

"Then how do you know it was him?"

"I heard his name. They talked about him when he left the room. And I have this." Slowly, she opened her fist. A gold button lay on her outstretched hand, still attached to a bit of blue fabric.

Anne took it and examined the engraving. *"Talbot passant,"* she murmured. Part of the coat of arms of the marquess of Thrale. She couldn't believe Richard capable of such an abomination. Yet the button, ripped from its anchor during a moment of violence, gave silent testimony to the man's damnation.

"I looked it up. It's on his coat-of-arms, that dog."

"Why did you tell no one?"

"I told Papa."

"And?"

"Papa believed Lord Thrale when he claimed he was in Lancashire. He said he didn't come up until late the next day." The girl's chin firmed. "But it isn't true." For the first time, her voice rose with incipient hysteria. "It isn't. How could I have awakened with that in my hand if he wasn't in London?"

257

"There must be some explanation."

"Even you believe him." She gave a half sob, despairing. "But, I tell you, Thrale is a monster. That button doesn't lie." She laughed wildly, scrubbing a hand through her lovely curls. "He should be made to pay for what he's done. He should pay."

"If it's him, he will. Cynssyr will see to it."

"Yes." She drew in a deep breath, calming herself. "Yes, he will, won't he?"

"He's sworn it. I've sworn to it."

"My throat is dry. Please, if you don't mind, something to drink." She pointed to a sideboard on which, along with her mostly untouched supper, there sat an empty tumbler and a bottle of sherry.

"No trouble at all." She splashed a small amount into the glass. The rim was chipped, but after a look at Miss Dancy's frightful paleness she added half again as much more. "Here."

"Thank you." She took a small envelope from a pocket and tipped its contents into the sherry. "For my nerves," she explained. Anne didn't object for, poor child, she looked positively feverish. Miss Dancy's slender shoulders heaved from the unaccustomed taste of so much alcohol, but she drained the last of it.

"May I keep this?" Anne said of the button. "I know Cynssyr would like to see it."

"I meant for you to have it." At long last, Miss Dancy stood, a bit unsteady on her feet. "It doesn't matter anymore."

"Oh, my dear God."

Miss Dancy, unmistakably pregnant, paced before the sofa where Anne sat. "Will you tell Mama that I am sorry and that I love her?" She clasped trembling hands over her chest. "And Edward. Mr. Edward Stephens, that I love him still?" She smiled sadly. "We were to be married."

Too slowly, Anne understood the significance of Miss Dancy's request. Horrified, she jumped up. "What have you done?" She raced to the door but before she got even three steps, she heard a thud as the girl fell to the floor. Anne ran back, sinking to the carpet and pulling the girl onto her lap, terrified. She screamed. "Devon! Devon, help!"

The door flew open, but it was too late. Blue lips worked horribly. "Tell Papa I forgive him." Miss Dancy's hand slipped free of Anne's. "Edward."

"No," Anne raged against her inability to help and for the soul of a young woman who'd lost all hope. "No!"

Devon dropped to his knees and bent over the girl's chest. No breath rose. He shook his head. "Damnation," he whispered, taking up the chipped tumbler.

"I should have known it was poison." A great sob tore from Anne. "I should have known."

"Anne," Devon said, catching her shoulders in a firm grip. He pulled her up and turned her away from Miss Dancy. "Anne. There's nothing we can do." He folded her into his arms. "I'll send for a doctor, but it's too late."

She wanted to be with Cynssyr. Only Cynssyr could help her now. The need to be with him overwhelmed her, flooded through her, rushed in like water freed from a dam, carrying her wherever nature willed. And that was to one place and one place only. Her husband's arms.

"Take me home, Dev."

Chapter Twenty-eight

Words would not come during the drive to Queen Anne Street. Dev, Anne's rock in this storm of misery, stayed mercifully silent, a brooding presence that lent a surprising comfort. "Is the duke home?" Anne asked when Merchant met them at the door.

"No, your grace."

"Has he been home at all?"

"No, madam."

Her heart fell. "Oh." She thought of her secret valise, tucked away in her trunk, and grabbed hold of the meaning of having that particular thought at this particular time.

"I'll see you upstairs," Dev said. Merchant frowned when he handed over his coat and hat, but Anne was beyond caring about Merchant's disapproval. She opened the door to her room. Dev followed.

While she tried to light a lamp, he built up the fire. "Oh, blast it." She gave up on the lamp. Her fingers trembled too hard to manage even the most basic of tasks. He turned from the hearth and went to her. "Here," she said. She pushed the lamp to him and burst into tears.

He gave her his handkerchief and said, "Come now, Anne. All will be well."

"Cynssyr said he would be at Lady Prescott's. He would have to come home to dress for that, and he hasn't." She felt massively insecure. Jealous and adrift. Envious even of whatever woman he'd decided to seduce tonight. "I wonder where he is." With the lovely Caroline North? Mrs. Fairchild? Or some other woman capable of fascinating him? Perhaps he had at last returned to Katie and the arms of the woman he came closest to loving.

"I can't say."

"Why not? You're his best friend," she joked. Her attempt to inject levity into the mood failed. She looked around for a chair and then for a basin. Lord, but fatigue leached her very bones, and she was feeling ill again.

He shrugged helplessly. "That doesn't mean I know where he is every minute, Anne."

She sniffled and blew her nose. "You are right, of course." Devon could take her to Cornwall. The idea flashed over her. He could, and he would. Only, she could not get the words past her throat. They lodged there with stunning firmness. For a moment, he stared at her, sensing her unsettled state. The air thickened, some phantasmal smoke caught her breath and made her disturbingly conscious of Devon's powerful body, aware for the first time since she knew what such feelings meant of Devon as a man. But she felt none of the heat that overtook her when she was with Cynssyr. No shiver of arousal. But, Dev was a man, and she rather thought he had spent his share of time between a

261

woman's thighs. Devon would be an excellent lover. Thoughtful. Caring. Distracting, even.

He drew a breath. "Come, walk with me to the door, Anne." The sinister, crooked smile she had grown to think of as rather dashing appeared. "I dare not stay any longer, you understand." He laughed softly. "Merchant will have my head if I do."

Still off kilter, she did because she thought she might yet find the courage to ask him to help her. The courage never came. She bid Devon good night at the bottom of the stairs. Again, they looked at one another. She saw the question in his eyes, the invitation he would never speak aloud. If she was to seek his aid, it must be now. The thought of Cynssyr with another woman struck like a blow, sharp and painful. As she reached for Devon, Merchant came into the hall.

"His lordship is leaving?" he asked in a hopeful tone, handing over the hat Devon had left at the door.

"Yes, Merchant," he said with wry amusement. "His lordship is leaving." Devon released her hand, and the moment when she might have begged him to rescue her vanished. He seemed to feel the opportunity passing, for he hesitated before slowly saying, "Good night, Duchess."

"Good night, Devon." She watched his broad-shouldered retreat.

"If you need anything," he said, turning back after only a few steps, "anything at all, you know where to find me."

"Thank you."

"Send someone with a note. Or come yourself."

"All right."

He hesitated. "Good night, Anne."

"Good night."

When he was gone, she climbed the stairs to her room. She didn't call Tilly to help her undress. She was used to fending for herself, and she did not want to discuss the evening with her inquisitive maid. Once in bed, she tossed restlessly, images of Miss Dancy in her head, her awful story and the tragic, senseless ending. She wanted to tell Cynssyr what had happened, and his absence was a physical ache. That ache would be with her forever. Whatever happened to her, whenever it was he set her aside in his heart, she would never ever be free of him. She threw off the covers and, barefoot, headed for her dressing room and her trunk of gowns from Bartley Green. Devon *would* help her.

Voices in the hall stopped her before she reached the trunk. A line of light appeared under the door that connected her room with Cynssyr's. Her pulse jumped. The murmur of conversation continued. "You may go, Dobkin," she heard him say. For a moment, silence. Then the door slowly opened. "Anne?"

"Yes?"

"Are you all right?" He stared into the darkness of her room, one arm high on the door jamb.

"Of course," she said. But the words choked her. She was so relieved to see him it broke her heart. She stifled the reaction. The last thing a man like him wanted was a teary-eyed woman clinging to him for comfort. He'd said as much before, and more than once.

"Come here," he said.

Refusal never crossed her mind. She walked straight into his arms. When she rested her head against his solid chest, her arms went around him, touching his shoulders. He felt so right, but she didn't dare tell him so. What she wanted from him, she wanted too badly to take such a risk.

"I came as soon as I heard about Miss Dancy."

"What a hideous waste."

"Yes."

"Is this what you felt like during the war? So helpless and, and horrified?"

"Eventually you stop thinking about it. You must."

"She was a child. Like Polly Withers. Like Emily." She raised her head, and he used his thumb to brush away a tear. "Emily might be next. Or Lucy. Or even Mary."

"I know," he said in a cool voice.

"She was with child, Cyn. That poor girl was going to have a child because of what they did to her."

Ruan drew a sharp breath. In that moment, he hated himself. Hated all his gender. "Are you able, Anne, to tell me about Miss Dancy? Or would you rather wait until tomorrow?"

"Now."

Rather than lead them into her room he turned to his, assuming she would follow. Disposing of her surprise, Anne did. He had, in the meantime, poured a glass of port from a bottle Dobkin had provided in anticipation of a nightcap. The escritoire she'd seen at Corth Abbey sat on a tabletop at the side of the room.

"Have a seat." He held his port in one hand, warming the bowl with his spread fingers. She looked tired. Drawn. And dear to him. If anything should happen to her, he would never recover. He stepped close, intending to embrace her again.

She covered her mouth. "Ugh. Please, Cynssyr, no."

He took away the glass. "Are you unwell?"

"I cannot abide the smell."

"At least sit."

Dutifully she sat on a plush armchair, curling her legs beneath her. Her stomach settled. A fire leapt in the grate, fueled by a fresh measure of coal. The one time she'd been in the room, she'd not been in a state to notice the decor. Not the dauntingly masculine room she'd imagined all this time. The main color was blue with silver accents. Here and there a blaze of color startled the eye; a vase of frigid green on the mantel, a small rug of ivory and crimson lay crosswise over a Turkish carpet of ocean-blue and silver. On the table by her elbow a gold bookmark glittered on the pages of a book, waiting for the duke to pick up where he'd left off. Not translated but in the original Greek. The contrasts of color and beauty made the room far more interesting than it might otherwise have been.

Ruan sat sideways on another armchair. He wore only dark trousers and a shirt open to mid chest. Nothing else. He was barefoot. His boots lay on the floor by the chair. "Every word you can recall." And she did tell him. Everything, leaving Miss Dancy's accusation of Thrale for last. "Mm," he said when she'd finished. "I'd like to see that button." He stopped her from sliding off the chair to fetch it. "Later, Anne. You may show it to me later. It's nearly dawn, and you must be exhausted."

"Is Mrs. Jacobs blond?"

He nodded. "Why?"

"Miss Dancy. Mrs. Withers. Mrs. Featherstone. Miss Leander. Now Mrs. Jacobs. All of them blondes."

"Not all of them." He hesitated, wishing there were some way to stop feeling.

"They are all blondes, Ruan. Every one. That we know of at any rate.

"No." He tugged on his shirt sleeve, then wrestled with his cufflink. "Not all."

"Who else, Cynssyr?"

He lifted his head as if it weighed ten stone. "Katie—" He licked his lips. "Anne, Katie—She was one of the first to be taken."

Her heart shriveled in her chest. Mrs. Forrest. The beautiful, dainty Mrs. Forrest who was his mistress. After a bit, when she could trust her throat to work, she said, "I think, Cynssyr, that I am very tired tonight."

"I know I ought not speak of her to you." He jumped up, swinging his arms and taking short steps first in one direction, then a halt and a stride in another. "I would not hurt you for the world, and yet not to tell you everything in my mind and my heart is unnatural. I would not hurt you, but I will not lie, either." He came to within a foot of her and stopped walking. His arms ceased their frantic motion. "I've seen her tonight."

One half of his cufflink dangled from his sleeve, and Anne reached for it, pushing the bit of burnished gold back through the sleeve while he spoke in a rapid almost staccato rhythm and his fingers curled around her wrist, holding her.

"It's over Anne," he said.

Life and hope came crashing to an end. Her heart stilled in her chest, the blood in her veins slowed to nothing, breath stopped. One thought only remained to her. Thank God, thank God in heaven he did not know he had the power to turn her to dust.

"Katie and I go back years. Before the war. I went to her come-out, a raw boy, full of myself and my own importance. Had I any sense, I'd have married her back then. But I hadn't any. I let her know it was hopeless for us, and she married someone else. Then, after the war, well, I'm afraid I behaved very badly, which you know. I have come to regret my behavior in those days. She wasn't happy in her marriage. She once told me she'd done it just to spite me. We became lovers."

"All this time, you've kept going back to her."

He took a breath. "More than anyone else."

She swallowed hard and by some miracle managed to speak. "How you must regret those lost years."

"No." He stared hard at her, his eyes like green ice. "I regret nothing," he said. "Not my years with Katie. Not even the other women, and I understand now that I often made Katie unhappy. Nor do I regret Corth Abbey." His voice, though low, strengthened. "I regret nothing because all of that brought me here. To this moment."

Turning her back to the fire, she stared at her husband, thinking that when he spoke in the Lords, this must be just how he looked and sounded. Tall and fierce. Determined to have his point admitted and his way his own.

"What of you, Anne?" he said. "I know you have regrets, that you hoped for some other husband than me. But has it been all bad? Can you say nothing redeems our marriage?"

"I cannot say that."

"But naught else."

She closed her eyes and while she saw nothing behind her lids but blackness, she drew a deep breath and shut the door to feeling. When she opened her eyes, she found she could safely look at him. "I should like to go to Cornwall."

"Anne."

"Please. Please, just let me go."

He threw himself onto his chair, legs sprawled, arms dangling over the sides. "I can't. Or, more to the point, I won't."

"Why not?"

Ruan looked away and said, "Because I am in love with you, Anne."

Chapter Twenty-nine

There wasn't any taking back the words. For one thing, they were true. But, he'd said them too soon, he could see that by the way all the color drained from her face, as if he'd just confessed murder. Lord Ruin would have done something to gloss over the awkward confession, make light of it, or, if he were feeling particularly the fiend, continue with feelings fabricated from air, perhaps inspired by some wretched poetry about bedewed bluebells draped about alabaster shoulders. He didn't do any of that. He didn't know what to do. The immensity of what he'd just said paralyzed him.

"You don't mean that."

"I have never lied to you, Anne." He held onto himself, fighting the impulse to go down on his knees and beg her to believe. "You've made me feel again. I ought to hate you for that but instead, I love you. I look at you and see reflected back everything that is wrong with what I became."

"I make a poor mirror."

He reached for his port. "You are kind, and I have not been. You forgive weakness. I never have."

"What of Mrs. Forrest?"

"You are tolerant. I am not. I've always thought myself an honorable man, but where was my honor when I came to Corth Abbey? I acted on my basest impulses and have been rewarded beyond measure. I won't send you away." He gripped his glass. "Still, I show you no honor, for I won't ever send you from me."

"You love me."

"I'm the boy who cried wolf. Now that it's really happened, I'm not believed. Well." He drained his port to the last. "I cannot blame you."

Anne left her chair, slowly walking to him until she stood directly in front of him. "Why?" She accused, and he wondered which question he should answer, why he would say such a thing or why he loved her.

"I don't know why." Her spectacles glinted in the light, and he felt a surge of both desire and tenderness. "I just do." He sat straight, empty glass in hand. "I just do," he echoed with a sort of numb hopelessness. He threw the glass against the far wall where it shattered into tiny pieces. "If I knew," he whispered, "maybe I could do something to stop it."

It was but a measure of his weakness that instead of sending her away, he pulled her onto his lap and kissed her. And Anne, sweet, lovely forgiving Anne kissed him back. Because she was too kind to hurt him with the truth. It was a convenient and effective way to gloss over their impasse.

In the morning, the late morning, Ruan watched her sleep. She lay partly on her side, uppermost leg drawn toward her stomach. A hand clenched into a fist lay on her pillow near the back of her head, the other lax near her chin. Sometime last night her braid had come undone. Flaxen hair spread over the pillow and sheet, a tangled mass. Her chest rose and fell in the rhythm of sleep. Her mouth was slightly open. During the night, the temperature had cooled considerably so the covers hid all but the outline of her shape. Anne was the only woman to sleep in his bed. More, she was the first woman he'd woken next to and found he wanted there again. And again. And again. For as many mornings as a bastard like him had left. She might never love him, but he would make her happy. He'd see to that. She stirred, groaned and opened her eyes.

"Good morning," he said.

She lifted her head, squinting because she did not have her spectacles. Her eyes were puffy from sleep and a crease in the pillow had put a corresponding line down her cheek. He thought if he woke to such a sight for the next hundred years he wouldn't mind one bit. The tightness in his chest eased. She was his wife and that, nothing would alter.

She clapped a hand over her mouth. "Ohh."

He snatched the basin Merchant had tucked away in his room and held her until she stopped retching. She groaned as he bathed her face. With one finger, he moved a strand of hair from her cheek and helped her to sit. "And, by the way, happy birthday, my dear." His heart gave a little hitch at the pleased smile that slowly appeared. You'd think he'd given her a whole casket of jewels, the way she looked at him.

"I didn't think you knew."

"I'll see you at Portman Square tonight." She stretched, and he put a hand on her belly. "Soon, Anne, when I touch you here, like this, even you will agree I feel our child."

Anne lay back. When Cynssyr smiled like that, she couldn't help but return his smile. His fingers stayed on her belly, spreading out in a soft caress that sent fire to her toes and back again. "Our child," she said, pulling him toward her. "I am so grateful, Cynssyr." She was thinking of Miss Dancy and the fate they might have shared. Would she have been tempted to find a similar end?

"For my skill in the marriage bed?" He lifted his head from her throat and gave her a wicked smile.

"What would have happened if we'd not been discovered?"

Ruan froze. When his heart started again, he sat swinging his legs off the bed and holding his head between his hands. A dozen smooth lies came to mind, any one of which would adequately deflect the danger. Any of which he once would not have hesitated to tell. "I would not have married you the next day."

"That's so."

He looked at her, and with the finality born of deep conviction said, "I would have found a way to keep you with me. Hell, the minute I felt your mouth on me, I was planning how I could manage it." Something in his chest eased. "I would have found a way. And I would have fallen in love with you. That sounds like a lie. The very sort I've become infamous for telling, I know, but it's the truth." He gripped her hand. "What frightens me, Anne, is not what might have happened at Corth Abbey, but what would have happened if I had not gone when I did. What if I hadn't ruined you?"

"Ah." Still on her back, she turned her head. He could no longer see her face. "But you are a man who deals in what is. Not what might have been."

"I used to be many things." Dobkin chose that moment to tap on the door. "Blast," he said.

Anne faced him again. "You must show Thrale that ring and the button, too. See what he has to say for himself."

"Right now, I don't care."

271

She slipped out of bed. "If Richard did do this, then he must be stopped. If he didn't, we must know that, too, and discover the man who has." She'd found her nightdress and now stared at it with dismay. He had, she recalled, quite literally torn it off her. From the corner of her eye, she saw his smile of pure male satisfaction. He looked like he wanted to do it again. Oh, but Lord Ruin was a devil. They all believed him. Every single one of them believed he loved her, even Katie had probably believed him. Despite all the past examples against the likelihood, they had all believed themselves the exception.

"My robe is over there." He pointed even though he thought it a shame to cover her delectable self. Another few minutes, and he might be up to a repeat of last night's activity. "We cannot afford to assume it isn't Thrale."

The faint scent of his cologne rose from the folds of silk that swallowed her. For some reason, it made her feel sad. "You are right, of course. Has Devon learned anything more about Richard's household? Disgruntled servants perhaps? Someone who might have taken his coat?"

What would be the harm, she thought, in deciding to believe he loved her? None to him. Much to her when at last she had to face the truth. Would certain agony be worth the brief joy of pretending herself adored by Lord Ruin?

Ruan had half a mind to ask her to come with him, but Dobkin knocked again. "Your grace?" the valet called out. Anne gave the door a wide-eyed look.

"You are my wife. He won't be scandalized to find you here."

"I'm nearly naked."

A grin twitched at his mouth. "Yes, I know. A moment," he replied to Dobkin, but Anne was already scurrying to her room. He wanted to bring her back, ask her when she would be home, when he would see her again, all the horrible, clinging suffocating things women had done to him. He forced himself to stay put. Patience. Patience. And more patience. He would not redeem himself in a day. "Come in, Dobkin," he shouted, irritably running his fingers through his hair. His valet covered any shock at being greeted by a nude Ruan sitting on a bed that had plainly seen active use.

Dobkin disposed of the basin Anne had used. Ruan, standing before the wash basin, gave himself a quick bath of the sort he'd taken in the field.

"Your grace?"

"Hmm?"

"I cannot locate your robe."

He dried his face before answering. "The duchess needed it."

Dobkin concentrated on setting up the shaving kit. "Indeed, sir?" Had Ruan been looking, he would have seen his valet smile. However, he wasn't and so was spared the indignity.

"Clear some space in one of my wardrobes."

"Yes, your grace."

"Enough for a few of Anne's things." Anne might, after all, frequently wake up in his bed. He hoped so. "So she needn't wear my robe when she gets up." Sounded damn practical that way. How could anyone object to so reasonable an accommodation? Not even Anne could argue the logic.

"Yes, sir."

He dressed without paying much attention to Dobkin's choices, agreeing to whatever was selected before dismissing his valet with a careless wave. He gave in to compulsion. He went to Anne's room. There was always time. . . .

Tilly stood in the center of the room, holding Anne's

torn nightdress. "Your grace." She bent a knee, guiltily hiding the ruined garment behind her. Her cheeks flushed pink.

"Has the duchess finished dressing?" he asked. She wasn't here, he knew that even before Tilly's answer. The room felt empty. Bereft.

"Yes, your grace. She's gone to the dower house."

"Thank you, Tilly." He left disappointed and disconcerted by the depth of the emotion. Business at the Justice Courts kept him from calling on Thrale much before three. The proceedings went overlong and bored him nearly to death. He thought to find Thrale at the Lords but came up blank there. No luck either at any of the St. James's Street clubs in which he knew the marquess had memberships. Or used to. He discovered he'd resigned several of them. At last, he ran him to ground at Thrale's Charles Street home.

The marquess greeted him with a somber smile. "To what do I owe the honor of this visit, Cynssyr? Something to drink?" He walked to a sideboard.

"Madeira, if you've got it." He took a seat, admiring the parlor in which Thrale met him. Nothing too fancy. Good-quality furniture, excellent paintings, a Gainsborough among the best. He would have expected something dark and dreary from the man, but bright colors predominated. Whatever financial difficulties the man had didn't yet extend to his London home.

Thrale handed him the wine. "I suppose, like me, you got a taste for it in Spain."

"The only thing I got a taste for in Spain was getting the hell out." He sipped the wine, nodded because it was quite good, then put it on the table next him. "I've been all over town looking for you. Didn't expect to find you here."

He shrugged. "I'm sorry to have inconvenienced you."

"Aren't you usually dogging Emily Sinclair's heels?" he asked. Once, he'd not been able to think of her without a pang of regret. Now, nothing. What a fool he'd been to think Emily Sinclair the woman for him.

Thrale laughed with good-natured chagrin. "I've wrangled an invitation to Portman Square later tonight. See you there, I expect."

"Yes." Hickenson had bought Anne a very expensive silk shawl. A birthday gift that sent no particular message, declared no particular fondness. A nice, safe gift that would not do at all. He glanced at the wall clock. Twenty past six.

"Miss Emily Sinclair is quite a beautiful woman." Abruptly, Thrale left his chair to stand stiffly with his back to the fireplace, hands clasped behind him. "I assure you I hold her in the highest esteem."

"I'm sure you do."

"Mrs. Willcott, too, of course. A great beauty in her own way, though to be frank, I am partial to blondes. Did you know that damned woman, Mrs. Willcott, nearly sent me head first into the Thames the other day?" He shuddered at the recollection. "Might have been the end of me. Wouldn't know it to watch her, but she's quite intelligent. Keeps her admirers too busy watching out for their heads to notice."

"All the Sinclair women are intelligent."

Thrale gave him a sidelong glance. "It's your wife, you know, who beats them all. Never met a cleverer woman. A great beauty in her own singular way."

"I married the best of the lot."

"To be honest, I'd not thought you the sort to appreciate her. Not your style at all. Forgive me if I am blunt, Cynssyr. Surely, you are aware more than one gentleman would champion her if she were made unhappy."

"Including yourself?"

His eyebrows lifted. "Yes," he said. "In fact, I would.

After all, you just turned up married to her amid whispers that you had to. Through no fault of hers." Thrale's eyes turned dark. " 'Tis said you and Bracebridge are at odds over her, which is easy enough to credit."

"How so?"

"Plainly, he loves her, and she's no small affection for him. It's commonly believed Bracebridge wanted to marry her and would have had you not . . . intervened." He shrugged. "Seeing the two of you together, though, I daresay there's more to your marriage than necessity."

"She is a necessity to me."

He nodded once. "Is it true she's expecting?"

"We hope."

"Congratulations." He exhaled. "I was engaged to be married once. Two years ago by now. But then my father died and when, over the course of the months following, her parents got wind of how much damage had been done to the family fortune . . ." He lifted his Madeira, admiring the sun filtering through amber liquid. "The wedding never came off. She married some fellow from Italy, a count or some such, and I have never seen her since."

Curious, Ruan cradled his own wine and said, "You've been nursing a broken heart?"

"No time for such nonsense." He put down his untouched glass. "Too busy pulling myself out of the mess my father left me in. I am not the sort of man who easily lives in debt. It grates on my soul to live beyond my means. A tendency, I assure you, that drove my father to distraction. I never would gamble with him. Nor drink. Had I been a wastrel, he might have had a better affection for me."

"And have you put things right?"

"Yes. I have. Nearly, anyway. At least to the point where I can consider making a marriage for any reason but money."

"I am not here, Thrale, to interrogate you about your suitability to marry a Sinclair sister."

The granite eyes flashed with temper. "Then why have you come?"

"Do you own a signet ring?"

The marquess went still for two heartbeats. "You are here to question me about those women. Even after it was proved I had nothing to do with the Leander girl?"

"Have you a signet ring?"

He examined the back of his hand. "It's disappeared. Had to let one of my footmen go over the incident. Still not sure whether he stole it, but I don't know who else could have. I caught him in my rooms where he had no business. Of what possible importance is that? Ah. I see. You found the ring under circumstances that connect it to those unfortunate women."

"Yes."

"You'd know it for mine the moment you saw it."

"Yes."

"If it were I, I assure you I would not be stupid enough to leave behind such evidence. Credit me with more native intelligence than that."

"There is more." Ruan dug the button from his pocket. "Miss Dancy turned this over to my wife. She claims to have torn it from the coat of one of the men who attacked her."

"Mine," he said slowly. "I don't deny that. Nor can I explain how Miss Dancy could have come into possession of it."

Ruan stood. "Either you are a monster guilty of murder and worse, or someone is out to make me think you are."

Thrale took the accusation with remarkable aplomb. "Murder?"

"Miss Dancy has died."

"Dear God. I am sorry to hear that."

"Her child with her."

Thrale sucked in a breath. "Were her injuries so severe?"

"A suicide."

"May God have mercy on her soul. She did not deserve what happened to her." He offered a grim smile. "There is a reason I am not now married to Miss Dancy, Cynssyr."

"I should like to hear it."

"I am a magistrate in my home parish. On the day Miss Dancy was abducted, I sent a man, a friend, to the gallows for murdering his lover. Indeed, I delayed my return to London long enough to see the sentence carried out. By the time I got to town, Miss Dancy had just been found."

"Easy enough to confirm."

"Nor," he added, "was I in town when Mrs. Withers was taken."

"Have you dismissed any servants recently?"

"A footman. Before that, my valet."

"Perhaps you'll give me their names."

"Clancy Jones and Ned Arrowman. I gave neither a character." Thrale sat down heavily. "It's John. It must be. Punishing me for being the elder. And legitimate."

"How did he get your ring? Your coat?"

"I've no idea."

"If I were you, I'd watch my back."

A wealth of emotion flickered behind Thrale's eyes. Then, he nodded curtly. "I appreciate the warning."

Ruan prayed he hadn't miscalculated, for if he had he'd just put another woman's life at risk.

Chapter Thirty

Ruan's carriage, with its distinctive ducal crest and motto, drew up when he stepped onto the curb outside Thrale's home. Distracted by his conversation with the marquess, he said nothing when he climbed in. Only his coachman's second query caught his attention.

"Portman Square, your grace?"

"Not yet," he replied. Dusk had long since fallen to dark. From the coach window, street lamps flickered over the cobbles. "Jermyn Street first."

"Aye, your grace."

At his destination he threw a half crown to a ragged boy delighted to have the task of standing guard. Ruan pounded on the door. The proprietor of the shop was ten minutes responding to the summons. As it was, he merely raised his window and peered distrustfully down. "What is the meaning of this infernal noise?" Behind him, a light flared, throwing shadows that danced on the glass.

Carolyn Jewel

"Open your store, if you would be so kind."

"In the dead of night?"

"I am Cynssyr."

"I don't care if you're the prince regent. Off with you. We're having our supper." The man made a shooing gesture. Shadows swirled behind him, then settled. His wife appeared next to him, her cap askew. Would there be a day when he and Anne were so quaint a married couple? Ruan stood with his palms outstretched. This was the shop where Hickenson made the purchases with which Ruan had charged him over the years.

"Cynssyr?" the woman repeated, staring down to the street. "Insincere Cynssyr!" She whispered to her husband, but not low enough to prevent Ruan from overhearing. "Lord Ruin himself," the good wife said. "As I live and breathe." She gave her husband a push. "Don't keep him waiting. Go on down."

Ruan stepped into the shop while the jeweler's wife brought in tea and crumpets. He wasn't the least hungry, but he ate a crumpet, not half bad, and drank some excellent tea while the jeweler, Mr. Cowperth, brought out his wares.

"Gift, did you say?"

"Something extravagant." Ruan thought of how Anne had tried to match her ballgown to his eyes. How she'd turned down emeralds because their green was not the right shade. He looked through the jewels Cowperth set before him. Citrine. Topaz. Aquamarine beads. He had all the money in the world, enough to buy every piece he looked at and never feel the pinch. Sapphires, rubies, emeralds. Nothing seemed exactly what he was looking for until he saw the box Cowperth set aside in his search for something truly spectacular.

"That."

"But, your grace!"

"It's precisely what I want."

When he arrived at Portman Square, Anne was nowhere to be found. And neither was Devon. The Bohemian, Laszlo Patok, played an exquisitely lovely tune. He'd heard a storm of talk about a composition for Anne. The tones of the violin were untouchable. Perfect. Likely another piece in her honor, since he did not recognize the music. Thomas Sinclair had bestirred himself to attend his daughter's birthday and even to lose his usual scowl. Ruan knew several of the guests. Lady Prescott. A minister of the Exchequer whose name escaped him at the moment. Lord Sather. Mirthless Thrale, who might or might not be a murderer. Ruan's mother. Julian Durling, of all people. Emily, Lucy and Mary. All were in the parlor. But not Anne or Devon.

"Cynssyr." Mary came to him with a rustle of silk and the scent of fragrant rose. She took both his hands in hers. "I'm so pleased you're here."

"Where's Anne?"

"Somewhere." She looked over her shoulder. "I'm afraid you've missed supper."

He thought of the crumpet he'd eaten. "I've dined, thank you."

"We were just about to start opening gifts, so she can't have gone far."

"I'm glad I haven't missed that." He followed Mary into the room.

She frowned, not seeing her sister. "Where is she? She was with Devon last I saw her."

"I'll find her. Do excuse me, Mary." He moved into the room, the recipient of several surprised stares, most notably one from Benjamin that turned to a smug smile and, honestly, one or two glares. Emily was easy to find. She was, as always, surrounded by a crowd of men even at a party in honor of her sister. Not Thrale though. The marquess sat at the pianoforte, turning pages for Lucy. Emily's lovely eyes opened wide when she saw

Ruan. He was used to parting crowds, so he had no trouble making his way to her. She bent a knee. "Your grace."

"Miss Sinclair."

She exuded polite disdain. "Whatever brings you here? Did you lose your way?"

"Why," he said, with all the innocence he could muster, "it is my wife's birthday." He gave her his arm, and she took it. "Your pardon, gentlemen, my lords, but I must have a word with my sister-in-law."

"Well," Emily said when they'd gone a few feet. "I'll say this for you, you got me away from those awful bores."

With a mock bow, he quipped, "I seek only to serve." He guided her near a window where they might have a modicum of privacy.

She tapped her foot. "What happy accident brings you here?" she asked caustically. "Or was Mrs. Forrest otherwise engaged tonight?"

"You presume too much and know too little."

"Not so. Else I would have done something to prevent you marrying Anne."

"You might have claimed precedence," he said wryly.

It took her a moment to understand, and when she did, she snapped, "If I thought it might have worked, yes."

"Well, thank God it didn't occur to you."

Emily looked at him through narrowed eyes, not at all bothered by the insult. The thought of being married to Emily gave him a case of the frights almost as bad as thinking of Anne married to Devon instead of to him. Emily apparently didn't feel much different.

"You might have come a bit earlier and saved her the humiliation of having to explain why her husband couldn't be bothered to attend the celebration."

"I'm sure she made me an excellent excuse."

"As a matter of fact, she did. And you were not at all deserving of her kindness."

He frowned, too irritated to hold his tongue. "You know, Emily, your sister is a duchess. Her life is not a complete hardship. She will never want for anything." But his heart was not in the rejoinder, and Emily, sensing it, moved in for the kill.

"I don't see that my sister is better off for it, your grace." He knew she was angry because of the insolent way she pronounced the honorific. "You've spent nothing on her for which Mary, Lucy or I haven't been responsible, and I won't count all those clothes nor the diamonds either, for you gave them to her for the sake of your reputation, not for her. You've given her nothing, you ungrateful wretch. Yet, I'll wager Cyrwthorn has never run better since Anne came. Your life has improved immeasurably since Anne. Deny it. Hah. You can't. So, your grace, don't look at me with that holier-than-thou expression."

"If you know the secret to getting her to spend my money, do tell it, for I should like to know. God knows I've tried. She won't."

"Of course she won't. She feels too guilty." He nodded because he knew exactly what Emily meant. But Emily was a woman incapable of leaving well enough alone. She crossed her arms over her chest. "You don't deserve her."

"No," he agreed gently. "But I thank God every day that I have her." In return for the admission, he had the rare pleasure of seeing Emily Sinclair at a loss for a retort. "I am here to find Anne, not listen to a tedious lecture I've already had from Aldreth and Bracebridge both. Where is she?"

"I shouldn't tell you anything at all. You only make her miserable. I know you mistreat her."

"Watch what you say, Miss Sinclair."

Carolyn Jewel

"I've only to look at her to see it's true. Since she married, she's lost weight. She's pale and tired. You've drained her of her strength. I know she was unhappy before, tied to Papa like that, but now—Now it's worse, for she's miserable."

"She's to give me a child."

Emily gaped at him.

"You're a spoiled little brat, Emily Sinclair, and I hope to God one day some man takes you over his knee and soundly beats you. Now, where is Anne? Oh, hell, never mind. I'll find her myself."

"Wait." She caught his sleeve, tugging urgently. "She's with Bracebridge."

His pulse leapt in alarm. "Did they leave together?"

"Not gone. Just out of the room. She was upset." The defiant lift of her chin told him who she thought the likely culprit. She pointed to a door a few steps along the hall. "They went in there." Shrugging, she gave him a look. "That parlor's so small, no one ever uses it."

A few feet from the parlor Emily indicated which, if Ruan correctly remembered, overlooked the back of the house, he realized she'd followed him. He stopped. "Thank you, Emily. Go back to the party. You'll have been missed by now." The door was open, so he had nothing to fear from his wife's decision to absent herself with Devon in so private a manner.

"What am I going to do?" he heard Anne say. "I do not think I have ever been so unhappy in all my life. She loves him. She loves him, and I think he loves her, too. I cannot bear it." Her voice broke. "I can't. Devon, help me. Please, help me."

Stricken by the catch in her voice Ruan took only a step or two inside. Devon sat on a chair that, should he happen to turn his head to the right, would give him a view of the door. And of Ruan. Anne sat on the floor at Devon's feet, her head and arms cradled on his knees while Dev leaned forward, stroking her cheek, a slow and tender caress.

"Darling Anne," Devon said softly, finger gliding along the upper line of her cheek. "If you want to leave him, I will help you." After a moment of silence, he took her hands. "Even if your answer is no, we are not finished, you and I." His voice turned low and sensual. "For now, for another while yet, I will be to you whatever you want. Friend. Polite acquaintance. Enemy. Even lover." His voice dropped another notch to shivery whisper. "Especially that. Be warned, Anne, that when he has his heir from you, I will do anything. Anything at all. Even betray him."

Ruan fully appreciated the moment. His best friend in all the world intended to break his marriage, leaving Ruan with no choice but to trust a woman who had no earthly reason to keep her wedding vows.

"I will protect you. Never fear that I won't." His voice was raw, emotion at the forefront. "Let me love you, Anne. I will give you the happiness you deserve. Whatever the cost."

Ruan heard a sound behind him and turned. Foolishly, he had assumed Emily would do as he told her. Of course, she had not. She stood a step behind him, looking every bit as heartsick as Devon and Anne. Her mouth quivered, and tears pooled in her blue eyes.

Ruan acted quickly. He grabbed Emily by the elbow and pushed her out, walking her halfway down the hall before stopping. "Listen to me," he said harshly. "You're being a damn fool."

That got her attention. She gave him a look of loathing. "How could you just leave them together? Didn't you hear him?"

"You're not a stupid woman. If you have a tantrum over this, you will destroy any hope of making Devon see you as anything but the brat you are."

"Oh, God." That her reaction was despair rather than a cutting rebuke told him Emily's case was near fatal. As bad or worse than his own.

"Even if Anne does love him—" His heart thudded against his ribs. My God, he thought, what if Anne loved Devon? "—she will honor her wedding vows." Which she would do whatever the sacrifice. He had no fear on that score. Nor could he think of anything worse than spending the rest of his life knowing Anne loved someone else.

Emily's chin lifted in quick defense of her sister. "You think I don't know that?" The dratted child might be spoiled rotten, but she had always been Anne's fiercest champion. Despite, it seemed, being hopelessly in love with Devon.

"You understand your sister quite well. As for Devon," he said with a confidence he did not feel, "he'll not stay in love with a woman who will never return his love." Not physically, anyway. The notion sparked a twisting sort of panic. "That sort of passion eventually burns itself out. It must. Bide your time, Emily. Do not press him now."

"I may be a damn fool, as you say, but I'm not a complete fool," she said, dabbing at her eyes. Few women managed to shed genuine tears and still look beautiful. Emily was one.

"There's a good girl."

"Don't you patronize me." But she spoke without her earlier edge. He found himself the recipient of a thoughtful gaze. "You poor man. Have you told Anne you love her?"

Jesus Christ. What was it with these Sinclair women? "She did not believe me."

"I'm not sure I believe it."

"What you believe is a matter of complete indifference to me."

"There is hope, you know," she said, and not without a certain gentleness, though he felt sure any tenderness was for Anne, not him. "Anne admires you. She never speaks of you but to make you a compliment I'm sure you don't deserve." Ruan's heart leaped at that. His entire being grasped at the straw Emily offered. "Why, I cannot comprehend. But she does admire you. You might yet turn it to love."

"How?"

"It's simple," she said archly and with a truly annoying smile. "Lord Ruin must die."

Exasperated, he returned to the parlor door, dragging Emily with him. "I ought to be horse whipped for listening to you."

"You might dispatch the Duke of Sin while you're at it," she added.

"Quiet."

"Insincere Cynssyr, too."

He lengthened his stride and raised his voice. "Anne? Are you here? Ah, just as you said, Emily." Both Dev and Anne were standing when he came in this time.

"Cynssyr," said Anne. She wasn't wearing her spectacles and that made her squint.

Ruan watched Dev, busy straightening the lapels of his coat. The black eyes, when they met his, were unreadable. "Forgive me, Anne. I did not mean to be so late," Ruan said, holding out his arm as she came near. "However, I'm told I've arrived in time for the gift-giving."

She gave him a look, then she smiled, a little sadly. "Shall we?"

Ruan expected Emily, the poor heartbroken child, to wait for Devon to offer his arm, but she didn't. Instead, she walked in front of Ruan and Anne, leaving Dev to bring up the rear. A small victory for Emily, for Devon looked aggravated.

287

Carolyn Jewel

Ruan sat silent while Anne opened her gifts. A bolt of shimmering lavender silk from Mary, a delicate ivory fan from Lucy, a cameo brooch from Emily that all the Sinclair sisters agreed looked very much like one that had once belonged to their mother. Thrale's gift of a sheaf of musical scores by Bach and that young puppy, Beethoven, met with a pleased exclamation. Devon gave her an edition of Shakespeare's sonnets. Ruan could see an inscription inside when Anne opened the cover. What tender words had Devon written for her? Though she scanned the sentences, she did not read them aloud. A small silver rattle came from his mother, for the first of many grandchildren, she said, glancing meaningfully at Ruan.

It was with a certain satisfaction that he drew Cowperth's box from his pocket. A small gift. Inexpensive in the greater scheme of things, but much better than Hickenson's shawl, however lovely, and a shot across the bows of Anne's heart. He almost missed her face when she opened the box because he was watching Devon who had a view of Anne and could see each gift. Her eyes went wide. Devon gave away nothing.

Anne didn't say a word. She couldn't.

"What is it?" Benjamin asked.

"Anne, do show us," said Lady Prescott.

With a trembling hand, she slipped off her borrowed wedding band and returned it to the dowager duchess.

"My dear child."

Ruan reached for the box and the ring inside. One look at Anne's face, and he forgot everything but her. "I should have seen to this ages ago," he said, slipping the gold band onto her finger. "It isn't much, I'm afraid." Tears spilled from her eyes, and he brushed one away. "Hush," he said softly. "Hush, my love. 'Tis but a ring, and a plain one at that." God save his soul, but he'd known that plain gold band would touch Anne

288

more deeply than the gaudiest diamond in creation.

His mother leaned in to examine Anne's left hand. "You have your father's exquisite sense of the appropriate."

He waited until Anne was looking at him, not her hand. "I love you," he said.

At that instant, Anne didn't care if he did or didn't. She leaned toward him, threw her arms around his shoulders and kissed him on a trembling breath. A moment later, his mouth opened over hers, one large hand cupping the back of her head, and she was complete. When at last they parted it was to find themselves the object of everyone's fascination.

"I don't think," remarked a breathless Lady Prescott to Thrale, patting her upper chest, "that I have ever seen a more touching scene in all my life."

Ruan reached for Anne's hand, interlacing their fingers. He told himself it was a statement to Devon that his wife was off-limits, but it didn't feel like that sort of statement. He felt like a man holding the hand of a woman he'd come slowly to adore. She had him tied in knots, no doubt about it, but he didn't mind at all.

Back at Cyrwthorn, Ruan stood beside the carriage waiting for Anne to give him her hand. Movement distracted him when she stepped down. He watched the shadows. Every nerve in his body went taut. The coachman took one of the grays by the bridle. With a soft cluck of his tongue, he started them to the mews. Upon the pretense of adjusting the shawl around Anne's shoulders, he peered into the darkness behind her.

Alarm prickled along his back. There. Something moved. And again. A shadow at the foot of the front stairs deepened, shifted, then coalesced into the shape of a man moving stealthily toward the side of the house.

"Henry," Ruan called softly. The shadow briefly

stepped out of darkness so that Ruan clearly saw the man's face before he turned the corner toward the mews. "Escort the duchess inside."

"Your grace."

"What about you?" Anne said.

"I need a word with the groom." He chucked her under the chin. "I'll be along shortly."

He watched her climb the stairs, then when she reached the door, he walked around the side of the house to find out what the hell Julian Durling thought he was up to.

Chapter Thirty-one

Ruan grabbed Durling's upper arm, ostensibly to steady him, but he didn't want the man disappearing on him either. "What are you doing here?"

"You're a bloody hard man to find sometimes," Durling said.

"You smell like the inside of a tavern. Go home and clean yourself up." Two days worth of beard covered the man's cheeks, he wore no hat, and he still wore a gambler's felt sleeves on his coat.

"I just can't keep away from the hells. Damn shame." Gleefully, he did a drunken jig. "But this time, I won. Enough to cover a good many of my debts."

"Splendid." He leaned back to avoid getting another whiff of stale wine and clothes worn too long.

"Send her away, Cyn." He swayed and steadied himself by catching Ruan's coat sleeve. "Before it's too late, send her away."

"Too late for what?"

"She's next." Durling's bleary eyes fixed on Ruan then crossed. "Lord, but I'm foxed. I've not been this fuddled since university. You're a good man, you know. Really top notch. Even if you weren't a bloody duke." Ruan groaned. He was in for it now. Durling was a sentimental drunk. The man swayed again, tilting his head down as if to lay it on Ruan's shoulder. "You were a class ahead of me. Lord, how we admired you. All of us wanted to be like you, and then you went off to the war. I rowed because you did, know that?"

Ruan grabbed his shoulders and shook him hard enough to rattle him out of his ridiculous nostalgia. "What do you mean, she's next?"

"The duchess," he said in a tender voice. "Lovely, lovely duchess. She's next, Cyn." Durling sobbed. "And I don't think I can stop it."

Ruan's blood froze. "Is it you?"

"Who beats those women? No." He slumped against Ruan's shoulder. "No taste for that sort of violence. Not yet anyway."

"Who is it?"

"Do stop shouting. My head's going to bloody explode." And that was the last thing Julian Durling was going to say for several hours, at least. Had Ruan not caught him, he'd have hit the ground like a sack of stones. Mostly by dint of brute strength, Ruan got Durling to the stables where he and one of the grooms got him into a carriage. He lay sprawled on the seat, snoring.

"You're not to leave him. Not even for a moment," he told the biggest of his grooms. "On second thought, let's get him on the floor. Then he won't have far to fall."

"Your grace."

He met Anne in the courtyard between Cyrwthorn and the mews. "What are you doing out here?" Anyone

could have snatched her where she stood, and he'd have
been none the wiser.

"Looking for you." She sat on a stone bench over-
looking the small plot used for the kitchen garden and
pointed to a spot where someone had planted some pansies. "Not as pretty now as later in the season. It reminds me of home. Look there. Lavender."

Ruan frowned. "You've never seen Fargate Castle,
have you?"

"I meant Bartley Green."

He gave her a sharp look. "Cyrwthorn is your home
now."

"I called on Mrs. Forrest," she said.

His insides seized up.

"She remembers the scent of ambergris. It was her
impression that rape was never intended, but the men
got to drinking and then one of them—"

"Anne."

"Her husband was not kind to her afterward."

"No."

She touched his shoulder. "You say you think you're
dead inside, and I say that's a lie." Her hand moved
from his shoulder to his mouth, gently touching his lips.

"I adore you, Anne." But she wasn't pleased by the
declaration. Damn it all, why not? Every other damn
woman he'd known would have been. Which answered
his question well enough.

"Why?" she asked.

"Why." He wrapped his arms around her. "It's every-
thing about you. It's the way I feel when I am inside
you. How you move with me, the feel of your skin, the
sweet inside of your thighs, the shape of your mouth.
How you moan when I thrust just so. Your bright eyes.
Your arms. Your spectacles send me mad with desire.
But more, in some strange fashion I fail to understand,
I need to give you pleasure. I want you crashing over

the edge even more desperately than I want to fall myself. Anything, so long as you understand you are mine.
So long as I drive the thought of any other man right
out of your head."

"There aren't any other men." She leaned against
him, soft and warm.

"I know." He tightened his arms around her, wanting
to claim her as forever his. "Will you kiss me?"

The kiss soon flamed out of control. He wanted to get
her where he could undress her and reveal more perfection than he had ever dreamed of finding in one
woman. She answered his greed, her arms circled his
shoulders. "We need to get inside," he said into her
mouth.

"I know."

They did not make it off the bench, let alone inside.
By the time she was helping him with the buttons of his
trousers he was painfully aroused and in a state of
wretched longing for her. He dipped his head to take
her mouth in a kiss of searing heat, being very free with
his hands, too.

"The hell with it," he growled. "Here. Right here."
He gathered her into his arms and sank to the ground
with her nipping his ear. Instead of laying her down, he
sat her on his lap, spreading her gown so it billowed
around her thighs while he unhooked her gown.

No other woman could do this to him, make him want
to worship her like some fool boy. He unbuttoned his
trousers and was just about to delve into her when she
pushed him onto his back. Right into the middle of Merchant's lavender. Her hands slid up his arms, bringing
them above his head and holding them there on his suf-
ferance, because although she was tall, she was not tall
enough to truly pin him. Nor heavy enough, either. He
outweighed her by a substantial amount.

"Now," she said, mock serious. "For once you are at my mercy."

For once? Hadn't he always been? "Do what you will, minx." He drew in a breath of lavender pungent with the bruising they'd given it. Her gown was loose enough at the back that he had a thumping good view of shadowed breasts.

She bent her head to his and kissed him, taking control of his mouth. When he started to bring his arms down so he could hold her and put himself inside her as he longed to do, she tightened her grip on him. Her mouth hovered inches over his.

"I want to touch you," he said, thinking of his mouth on the peak of her breast and him inside her. She straddled him so he could feel her heat but not touch its source.

"Why?"

"Because I'll go up in flames if I can't. Because I adore your body. All your sweet curves and that heat inside that's ready for me. Because I love you."

"Love." In the dark, he could just make out the dim gleam of her spectacles. "I cannot stop thinking of all the times you've said that before. To so many other women. Did you mean it before? When you said it to the others? Did you mean it when you said it to Katie?" She laughed sadly. "Is it possible you believed it then and only think you believe it now?"

"I knew I didn't love the others." He worked one hand free and wriggled it under her skirt. He covered her backside, sliding a finger between until he found her core. He could fight dirty, too, when he had to. She gasped but cut off the sound. "I love you, Anne. You're the only one."

"Tell me—Oh, Cynssyr."

"Show me your breasts, Anne. Yes, that's it," he said when she began to pull aside her gown. The two of them were a tangle of clothes and arms and legs. His knees were bent so she could lean her weight against him, his erection, for the moment, conveniently behind her. "There is just no question," he said when she'd managed to bare herself for him. "No question at all that I would have married you on account of these alone." Her arousal and the cool air puckered her nipples. He managed a kiss right there.

"Oh, Cynssyr," she moaned. "Ruan."

"I do love you, Anne. I am your slave, if you would but have me."

She groaned on an intake of breath as his fingers stroked. She wasn't holding herself off him to deny him anymore, but to give him access. "Tell me," she said with some effort, "why I should believe Lord Ruin when he says he loves me."

His other hand was free now, and he put that under her skirt, too, gripping her behind. "Lord Ruin never said he loved you." She moaned again. "It is your husband who loves you. Madly. Truly." She didn't believe him yet. Not entirely. Her head went back, she arched into his hand and came. Hard.

He raised her hips and brought her down on him. "I am home," he said.

Afterward, picking a bit of lavender from her hair, he said, "Forgive me, Anne."

She lifted her head from his chest. "For what?"

"All of this." He raised his hands in a helpless gesture, then helped her put her clothes to rights. "I am sorry you had to marry me. I am sorry for everything I've done since then. I'm sorry you cannot believe I love you."

"Cynssyr," she whispered mournfully.

"You want to know why I love you. You brought light into my formerly gray existence." He touched her cheek. "Until you, I never knew a woman could be both friend and lover. You saved me from the dark. I love you for what you are; strong and brave and kind. When I walk into a room and you are there, my heart lifts. When I'm away, just thinking of you makes me smile. Being with you makes me happy. No one else has ever done that. When I am with you, I am whole. Better than whole, for on my own, I'm a worthless fool."

Reverently, she touched his chest. "If I let myself believe you, I would be on air. Transformed. Delirious with joy. And if ever it ended, I could not survive. Do you even know how many woman you have destroyed this way?" She shook her head. "No, I could not bear it." She curved herself to fit into his arm around her. "I could not."

She wasn't dressed for a cold morning and when a shiver took her, he shrugged out of his coat and slipped it over her shoulders. Already, the sky was turning from black to muted gray. He tucked her against his side. "We were very wild after the war, Devon and I," he said softly. "Our nights were spent in pursuits of no credit to our character. Cards. Drink. Opera dancers, actresses, women of easy virtue. Anything and everything to remind myself I was still alive. That I had cheated death." Her arm crept around his waist, giving rather than seeking support. "After a night of carousing and whoring, I'd come here to watch the sun rise."

She shifted enough to look into his face. "Do you feel alive now?"

He smiled warmly, touching the tip of her nose with the pad of his index finger. "At this moment, I have no doubt I am alive. I never do with you."

The hard edge to her sadness softened. "We are friends, aren't we, Cynssyr?"

"Yes." He nodded. "We are."

"Do you think that's enough? It must be."

Not for him. Not enough for him. In the distance, he heard a wagon rumbling by.

"Ruan?"

"Mm."

"Mrs. Forrest told me she thinks someone's been following her, and I think she's right."

His blood chilled. "Why?"

"From her sitting room, I saw a carriage on the street."

"Nothing alarming about that."

"A gig, actually. Rather shabby. And it was there the entire time. We left together. I told Henry to follow us and we drove in her carriage nearly to Bond Street."

"The gig?"

"Followed us."

Cold fear rippled through him. "The man in the gig. Did he see you get into the carriage?"

"He must have. I'm sure he did."

Ruan sat in perfect silence with his wife, watching dawn turn to morning. The sky softened from gray to silver. Birds began to sing, first just one or two, then more, then a riot of them. Another day begun. And he was utterly without hope.

"Tomorrow," he said, "you must go to Cornwall."

Chapter Thirty-two

Ruan crumpled a letter from some ninny who claimed to have invented a method for turning brass to gold. He tossed it to the floor.

"Bad news?" Hickenson asked from the desk where he'd been taking Ruan's dictation.

"If I had a shilling for everyone who hopes I am a fool, I'd own the bloody world."

"I imagine so. Shall we continue?"

"Finish that last, and we've done for the day," Ruan said even though there remained a dozen letters yet requiring a reply.

Hickenson bowed his head. "Your grace."

Ruan left Whitehall for home and found the silence there unsettling. The void of Anne's absence lay heavier yet on his rooms. With Dobkin absorbed in selecting a fresh cravat, Ruan pulled out his watch, feigning concern with the hour, then threw himself onto a chair and stared at the toes of his boots. Ten past five. Hours now since Anne left. By his reckoning she must be some thirty or forty miles distant from London. He had no desire to go anywhere tonight, though he was expected at half a dozen places. The gaping emptiness of Cywrthorn, of, indeed, the whole of London, without Anne was a small enough price for her safety.

"Your grace?"

He turned his head and saw Merchant at the door. "Yes?"

"An urchin, sir."

"An urchin?"

"A grubby child who claims my Lord Bracebridge sent him."

"Is he still here or have you chased him off?"

"No, your grace. He delivered a message and vanished."

"Which would be?"

"That my lord the earl of Bracebridge requires you to meet him posthaste at the Three Swans."

He shot to his feet, thrilled at the prospect of having something useful to do. "Dobkin!" he shouted. "My coat." He didn't wait for Dobkin's help when the valet appeared. He just grabbed his coat, thrust an arm through the sleeve and was on his way.

A stocky fellow dressed in a ragged black cloak and hat waited outside the hell. He thought he recognized him as one of Devon's men. From his rough dress and scarred face, a companion from the days when Devon had made his living by the expedient of force and wit. "Where's Bracebridge?"

The man performed an awkward bow, sweeping his hat off his head and scraping it inches from the filthy street. "This cove you're after, he had another cove with him who dashed not the quarter hour before you was aware, your grace. A gentleman. Like yourself. A banging dimber, he was. His lordship followed him. You and me can take care of this one, no worries there, he says."

"I say we end this business now and go after him."

"No, no!" The man threw up a palm. "He'll be fly then, and slip out the back for sure. You're not the man to likely blend to the crowd here. There's a fence there, easy enough to climb if a man's in a desperate alarm."

"I'll cover the rear then. You go inside."

"Afraid he's seen my face, sir. Besides, his lordship wants us to bide our time and follow when he leaves. See where he goes to ground."

Devon was probably right about that. "Likely take us straight to the fellow he's working with."

"Aye, your grace. That's as may be."

Ruan settled down to wait, along with his unnamed companion slinking into a dark corner. Three quarters of an hour passed. Tavern downstairs, gaming upstairs, whores up another floor. A steady stream of gentlemen and riff-raff patronized the tavern. They came in cold and left drunk. The gamblers stayed longer, but those who left were just as drunk as the others. "Here's something," said his companion when the door opened to let out another staggering customer. "There he is, by God."

The man who came out had his hat pulled low and a grayish muffler wrapped several times around his throat. Bundled up against the cold, Ruan couldn't be sure who it was. Perhaps Thrale. Perhaps not. "Let's go."

"Right behind you, your grace. Hup! Hup! Watch your step. He's slipping away."

He knew he'd been duped when he looked back after turning several corners onto increasingly dank streets. Expecting to see Devon's man, instead, he saw nothing but swirling fog.

"Damn it to hell." Ahead, the street was only briefly empty. From the noisome mist, a dark shape emerged, coming toward him. The shadow firmed then divided into two shapes. Two men bent on murder, Ruan guessed. He spread his fingers, tensing then releasing them. He drew in a breath and was ready.

The skirmish didn't last long, for, thinking themselves undetected and with the advantage of surprise and number, the men attacked with more enthusiasm than precision. Though Ruan suffered a hard blow to the midsection, he drove the heel of his palm hard into a face. That one staggered back, clutching his nose. He whirled and lashed out with an elbow to the cheek. The other flailed madly, screeching when he saw his companion flee. Ruan got a handful of his coat but the man jerked free and escaped into the dark, leaving Ruan holding only a tattered coat.

Quickly, knowing he risked another attack by staying, he rifled the pockets. He found a knife. Several, actually. He took the sharpest and slid another into his boot. The pound note in another pocket likely represented the man's fee for murder. And, Ruan decided, a fair one for the night's work. Off in the distant, he heard shouts. Whether they came from his attackers screwing up choler enough for another go at the price on his head, he did not stay to discover.

As he walked, he held the larger knife like a man who would know what to do with it. Which he did. He moved as rapidly as the filthy streets permitted. Mayfair was a lifetime away on foot, and he didn't expect he had a prayer of finding his carriage and horses nor any transportation but his boots. No hack who valued his gig would look for a fare in these streets. It'd be an invitation to robbery.

A whore who could think of only one reason for a man of quality to be out alone fell into step with him just long enough to discover her mistake. He brooded while he walked. He'd been tricked on more than one level. Flat out tricked. As for the man responsible for duping him, who but Thrale would even know of his progress in discovering the culprits? He wondered if tonight another woman would pay for his stupidity.

When he stalked into Cyrwthorn, he hardly looked at Merchant. "Has Bracebridge called?" With a flick of the wrist, he tossed Merchant the knife.

"No." He caught the knife handily.

"Aldreth?"

"No, your grace." With equal ease, he snatched Ruan's hat and gloves from the air.

"Any letters?" He refused to think of what might have happened to some young innocent. Not until he had word to the contrary. "Has anyone called? Anyone at all?"

"No, your grace."

"Send three or four men to the Three Swans." Ruan flew up the stairs with an energy borne of pure frustration. Merchant valiantly kept pace. "They're to find my phaeton and my horses. Have them fetch the constable if necessary."

Merchant spoke between gasps. "Your—grace."

"Close up the house."

"Sir?"

"I'm going to Fargate Castle—" Three rapid-fire blows on the front door stopped Ruan in his tracks.

"Are you at home?"

"Find out who it is."

Merchant drew a deep breath and went downstairs. Ruan waited where he'd stopped, nearly to the first landing. He heard voices, recognized Merchant's calm tones. The other he couldn't make out except that it was a man's voice. Another husband or father beside himself with worry?

Merchant returned. "The marquess of Thrale."

"Indeed?" He said the word in a voice so arid desert sands would have seemed moist. As cautious as the marquess had been so far, he would have expected a letter or another boy culled off the street. He wondered what sort of game Thrale thought he played.

Merchant inclined his head toward the front door. "He says he has your carriage."

"Indeed."

"Furthermore, he is under the impression you have been injured, though I assured him you are in perfect health."

"Thank you, Merchant. I'll see him in the Red Salon."

"Shall I bring coffee, your grace?"

"Please." Ruan went to his rooms. When he was dressed in buff trousers—just the sort of daring attire Lord Ruin would adopt—shining boots, white cravat, striped waistcoat, but without the cutaway frac for now, he went to the Red Salon, a man, to all appearances, just in from a night of festivity.

Thrale jumped up. "I must say I am relieved to see you well."

"Why shouldn't I be?"

"How did you get home?"

He lifted a hand. "Why, I walked."

Thrale pursed his lips. "You're not injured?"

"As you can see, I am in the pink." He went to the sideboard. "May I offer you something? Brandy? Claret? Both are excellent." The door opened. "Ah. Here is Merchant with coffee. My cook makes an excellent coffee. *Comme les Turques*, he calls it." He poured for Thrale first then himself.

Thrale breathed in the aroma of Jubert's thick coffee, then took an experimental taste meant to be no more than polite. As Ruan expected, Thrale's eyes opened wide. "Excellent indeed, Cynssyr."

"Why are you here?"

"Well, to be honest, I thought you might have come

to some mischief. You're certain everything's well?"

"More sugar?"

"No."

"May I ask, my Lord Thrale, what were you doing in that part of town?" He forced all emotion from him. There wasn't anyone better at game-playing than the duke of Cynssyr. "I didn't take you for one to visit the hells."

"Hardly a hell." Thrale's eyebrows shot up in what appeared to be genuine confusion. "It wasn't so far from here, as it happens, and—"

"Where, here?"

"The mews behind Lynlear Close. Only saw it by accident. Just caught my eye, the oddness of it, I suppose, and I went to have a look."

"How the hell did my phaeton get there?"

Surprised mid-sip, Thrale made a face. "Not your phaeton. Your coach. Big hulking black thing."

"I'm afraid you've made a mistake, Thrale. You couldn't have found one of my coaches anywhere but here." A sense of foreboding turned his mouth to chalk. "There's some mistake." Ruan rang for Merchant. "Ah," he said when the butler came in. "Thrale here tells me he's found my coach. Who took it out and why?"

"The duchess, your grace."

"Impossible. She's halfway to Fargate Castle by now. In her own carriage."

Thrale put down his coffee with such force the saucer broke in three.

"But, your grace—" Color drained from the servant's face.

"I saw her off to Cornwall this early afternoon."

"Yes. But, your grace, she went first to Portsman Square to make her good-byes to Lord and Lady Aldreth and her sisters. She'd hardly got to Oxford Street when the carriage broke an axle." He drew himself up. "You were at Whitehall by then. I understood, your grace, that you felt she must leave London without delay."

"You understood correctly."

"I took the liberty of sending her your father's carriage."

Ruan spun on his heel and walked a straight line from the fireplace to the exact midpoint of the room. He felt like he'd just walked into a furnace. The sensation was gone in an instant, replaced by bitter cold. He wasn't even aware of his cup hitting the table with a thud. Anne. Oh, God, Anne.

"Cynssyr," Thrale said. "Hear me out. I found two men near the carriage, mortally wounded both. Coachman and postilion. There can be no doubt. They wore your livery. Of your wife, I saw no sign."

"Henry and Gant went as postilions," Merchant said.

"That's three men counting the coachman. Where is the third?"

Thrale shook his head. "I found but the two."

After a rather distasteful description of the injured men Ruan was able to determine Henry was unaccounted for. The door opened and Ruan turned, feeling a surge of relief when he heard the whisper of silk. But it was not Anne. A footmen led Emily into the room. Ruan gave Thrale no time to greet her. "Is Anne with you? Do you know where she is?"

She'd been prepared to give him another lecture, he saw, but his peremptory manner and Thrale's presence brought her up short. "No."

"Have you heard from her?"

"I came here to make you tell me why you've sent her away." She took in Ruan's tense face, Thrale's too-sober nod and Merchant close to having an emotion. "What's happened?"

He knew Emily was too level-headed to panic. "Her carriage has been found abandoned. One postilion gone missing. The coachman and the other postilion gravely injured." He moved toward her, ready to offer aid if she needed it, but she'd already sunk onto a chair.

Emily stared at Thrale. "What of Anne?"

"That is unclear just now," Ruan said gently.

"It's whoever's been snatching all those women, isn't it?" Emily asked. "They've got her."

"Henry," Ruan said not bothering to dissemble, "has probably followed whoever took her. If he is able, he will return with word. Find Bracebridge, Emily," he said, fixing her with a look. He nodded when he was satisfied she understood why he was asking her. It was a measure of his state that he actually hoped Emily would find Anne with his best friend. The alternative was too horrible to contemplate. "If Anne is with him, for God's sake, make haste to tell me. If not, tell Dev what has happened and bring him back here. Merchant, go with her."

"What are you going to do?" Emily asked.

What choice had he? "There is nothing I can do but wait here for a ransom demand."

Thrale rose, but Ruan rapped out, "I'll ask you to stay, Thrale. The better to put a bullet in your head if I find you had anything to do with this."

Chapter Thirty-three

Devon heard a commotion somewhere in the house, but ignored it. Lydia Cooke's arms were still around him while he basked in the afterglow of sexual congress. Better the second time than the first, and the first had been very good. An odd way, perhaps, for a man to celebrate his nuptials, but one thoroughly satisfying. He and Lydia had more or less agreed that within a year he would marry her daughter, Fanny. The noise grew louder.

Annoyed that the staff of his late father's favorite St. James's Street hideaway, whom he paid for discretion above all else, could not keep the quiet, he reluctantly sat up, sliding one leg off the bed. Behind him, Lydia caressed his back, trailing a fingertip along his spine.

The door flew open. His first thought was that Mr. Cooke had found them and there was about to be a distasteful scene. But no enraged husband burst into the room. Instead, Miss Emily Sinclair walked into his private bedchamber. Thunderstruck, he had no words, could only stare at the young woman. A veritable goddess of beauty.

"Thank God," she said.

Every time he saw her, her beauty struck him like a blow. The fate of every man in London, no doubt. She wore a gown in a color popularly called London smoke, cut low after the fashion. With her agitation, a rather magnificent portion of bosom showed. Her mouth, that tender, kissable mouth, quivered. He had just enough wit to be thankful that the sheet, which barely covered him at the moment, at least hid his manly parts.

"My God, Bracebridge," said Lydia, appalled and leaping to a conclusion more than warranted under the circumstances. She dropped her voice to a whisper. "If you've seduced this innocent girl . . ."

Absurdly, Emily bent them a knee as proper as if she'd found them having tea in a parlor. Her lovely eyes quickly scanned the room and settled on something. His shirt, he discovered when she walked over and threw it at him. "Not if I were the last woman on earth, Mrs. Cooke," Emily said. She snatched up his breeches, underclothes and waistcoat, too, moving quickly around the room since he and Lydia had not been careful about where their clothes ended up.

He caught sight of Merchant in the doorway. The man's face was bright red, but he wasn't doing a damn thing to get Emily the hell out of his bedroom. Not with Lydia Cooke naked in the bed. Emily had put Merchant in a fine pickle, walking in as if she expected tea and cakes. "Explain this outrage."

"Merchant thought you might be here," Emily said.

For God's sake, the girl was holding his drawers! "You damned little brat. I ought to turn you over my knee."

"My lord, please." Merchant peeked into the room

and saw him sitting on the bed with only the sheet to cover his lap. "My lord—"

The panic in Merchant's voice brought Devon up short. "What's happened?"

Emily now held nearly all his clothes. The buttons of his breeches winked accusingly in the light. "Cynssyr's coachman is dead," she said. "A postilion, too, another missing." She thrust his clothes at him. "Get dressed, Bracebridge, he needs you. Anne needs you." When he sat without moving, Emily gesticulated. "Did you hear what I said? We haven't a moment to lose."

"Miss Sinclair. I am naked."

"This is no time for modesty." Her eyes, blue as the noon sky, filled with tears.

"Believe me, Cyn can take care of himself." He spoke deliberately to hide his concern. "If they have him they'll soon regret it."

"Not Cynssyr, you dunderhead! Anne. They've taken Anne!" Her breath hitched. "What if something horrible has happened to her, too?"

Lydia slipped out of the bed, lucky enough to have found her chemise within reach. She now appeared next to Emily. "Perhaps, Miss Sinclair, if you would just turn your back?"

But Dev had already come to his feet, and he didn't care if Emily Sinclair saw him naked or not. He saw the quick downsweep of her eyes. In her turmoil, the look was dispassionate. Whatever she felt at the sight of him thrusting his very naked self into his underclothes was put away. Maidenly shock, if any there was, awaited some other time and place.

"Merchant," he said, raising his voice more for the sake of breaking the silence than having the question answered. "What were you thinking to let her in here?"

"She is a force of nature, milord." In the interest of Mrs. Cooke's modesty and reputation, Merchant remained at the door, steadfastly staring down the hall so that he could, in all honesty, say he did not know with whom Bracebridge had been found.

Emily had now fallen to her knees. For a very brief moment an outright evil thought entered Devon's head, heating his blood at the thought of having London's most notorious beauty at his feet. Then she pulled one of his boots from underneath the bed and twisted around to snatch up the cravat dangling from the bedpost. "Come with me," she said. "There isn't time to call for your carriage and ours is waiting outside. Merchant will see your *companion* safely home. Have you a veil?" She didn't wait for a response. She reached for her hat and jerked off the veil. For a woman in crisis, Emily was remarkably clear-headed. "Here is mine. See that you use it, ma'am."

He let Lydia help with his cravat while he buttoned his waistcoat. "I'll need my pistols."

"Unless you have them here, you will have to borrow some from Cynssyr. No, wait, Merchant can stop at Cavendish Square after he's dropped her at some convenient location." Emily glanced over her shoulder at Merchant, still steadfastly staring down the hall. "Did you hear that, Merchant?"

"Yes, miss."

Emily continued. "For whom and for what shall Merchant ask when he gets there, Bracebridge?"

Dev sat on the edge of the bed and pulled on his boots. "Johnson. Ask him for the Pauly. He'll know which one."

"Yes, milord," said Merchant.

Emily gave Lydia a look. "I never saw you here. Nor you me. Is that understood?"

"I shall pray for your sister's safety."

"Thank you."

Devon stood. "Remind me to take you with me the

311

next time I go to war, Em. We could have used a few men like you." He grabbed his coat and followed his intrepid beauty to the carriage.

He sat across from Emily during a surreal ride, feeling as if he were escorting some silly virgin to a party. Only he wasn't. "Tell me what you know." Aside from appreciating Emily Sinclair's beauty, he'd paid very little attention to her except when her spoiled ways forced him to notice her.

Quite wrongly, it appeared, he'd assumed her to be like every other girl put on the marriage block. Young, vapid, naive, and eager to make a match above her station. A beauty like Emily Sinclair, connected now to two noble families, would certainly make a brilliant match. If he hadn't been so preoccupied with Anne, like as not he'd have courted her, himself. Luckily he hadn't. He'd seen the heartless way she treated her suitors. But, there were depths to her, hitherto unsuspected depths.

She spoke quickly, giving only the necessary facts. "Anne came to Portman Square to say good-bye because Cynssyr was sending her away. She wouldn't tell us why. She just gave one of those ridiculous excuses she's always providing for that odious man. I could see she didn't really want to go. The moment I had a chance, I went straight to Cyrwthorn. I thought the man had finally come to his senses about my sister, and I wanted to know how he'd managed to bungle things so quickly." She drew a breath that hovered on the precipice of a sob. "Thrale was there because he'd found her carriage and the servants dead. That is everything I know."

He could see panic behind her eyes, so he did not let the silence linger. "First he jilts you. Now this. How you must despise him."

She shook her head. "Not for this."

"No?"

"He is not responsible for the actions of a man low enough to harm all those women. And, by the way, he did not jilt me. I would have told him no. Yes, Bracebridge, I know about the kidnappings. We women are not as ignorant as men would like to keep us."

"You are hardly a woman," he murmured just to provoke her.

Her eyes flashed. "One might more accurately say you are hardly a gentleman."

Devon was acutely aware of the circumstances under which Emily had found him, of the complete dispassion with which she had looked at his person. The way she was looking at him, he felt naked now. "I know how you feel about my sister," she said surprising him by laying her hand on his. "I am sorry you weren't the one to marry her. You should have been her husband. We all thought so."

It made the hair on the back of his arms prickle to think she understood so much. "We are here," Devon said, glad to be free of her penetrating eyes.

They joined Ruan in the parlor. Thrale had not left. Benjamin stood by the fireplace, a grim expression on his amiable face. Unlike Ruan, who looked like he'd slept in his fancy clothes, Ben's evening dress was still neatly pressed. There were no greetings. Ruan handed Dev a sheet of paper. "As I feared."

"Damn it to hell." Benjamin kicked over the fireplace grate.

Emily sat heavily on the sofa, and Thrale immediately went to her. Fascinated, Devon watched her start to crumble. Her eyes glistened with tears, and her mouth quivered. At that moment, he would have sworn his own heart was breaking, too. Then she straightened her shoulders and gently pushed Thrale from her. Her mouth smoothed. "That's a ransom note, isn't it?" she asked with hardly a trace of emotion.

313

When neither Benjamin nor Ruan denied it, Devon quickly read it. "The diamonds Anne wore at the ball. They're worth thousands!"

Ruan reached into his pocket and when he withdrew it, slapped his hand on the table. "You had an explanation why these did not incriminate you," he said to Thrale, lifting his hand to reveal the ring and button they'd recovered. "Make no mistake, it's your life if it's not so."

"I swear it's not. On my soul, it's not so."

Emily cleared her throat, a dainty cough. "Did you not mention once, my lord Thrale, that you have a new valet?"

"What of it?"

"Does not a gentleman's valet," she suggested prettily, "have access to his employer's most personal belongings? A ring, for example, or, if not the buttons on his coat, the coat itself. I should think a valet would know his master's whereabouts and even his plans. Quite intimately."

"I didn't hire him until after the kidnappings began."

"About the time Cynssyr began to find you a compelling suspect, I expect." She waved a slender hand. "I'd even wager, my lord, that the unfortunate dismissal of your footman wasn't necessary until after your valet began his employment."

"My valet?" Thrale said. "My own damned valet?"

"Caitiff bastard," said Devon.

"Why in God's name did you hire a servant without a character?" Ben said, throwing his hands into the air.

"But he had one. An impeccable one!"

"From whom?"

"Wilberfoss."

Emily stood up and snatched the ransom letter from Devon's hand. "I'm going with you."

"The hell you will," he said, knowing Ruan and Benjamin would back him up.

"Out of the question." Ruan agreed, exchanging a glance with Devon. Benjamin, the coward, bent down to right the screen he'd kicked over. A tumult in the hallway startled them. The door flew open and Henry stumbled inside, followed by one of the footmen who looked horrified and terrified both. Dust coated the postilion's shoulders. An ugly mass of congealing blood covered his temple and ran in a thin, jagged line from ear to cheek.

"Is Anne with you?" Ruan asked with such raw passion that Devon and Benjamin stared in shock. A man who'd withstood the horrors of war now sounded like a man frantic with loss, near to breakdown. Devon had never in all the years he'd known Ruan, heard him sound like that.

Henry shook his head, wincing from the pain. "No, your grace."

"What the hell happened?" Benjamin demanded.

But it was Emily who cut to the heart of the matter. "Never mind that now." She walked to Henry and daintily pressed a handkerchief to his bleeding head. "Where have they taken my sister?"

Henry, the fool, took one look at that angelic face and told her everything. "Bit east of Waltham Abby, near Epping way, miss. Ah, such kind hands to lay on me. A cottage at the end of the lane just after a stand of oaks."

"How many men were there?" she asked serenely.

"Three." Henry visibly melted, thoroughly enslaved to her beauty. "That I saw, miss."

Emily glanced at Ruan. "Have you pistols for Bracebridge and Thrale, Cynssyr? We haven't much time. I am sorry, Bracebridge, we cannot wait for Merchant to return." She called for a servant, completely in

315

charge. No one did a thing to stop her. "We shall want fresh horses." She was too sensible, damn it all. Should anyone countermand her, they'd only have to give the same bloody instructions.

"We?" Devon repeated. He gave her a glare because he had a very unpleasant notion about Emily's willingness to wait patiently or otherwise while they went after Anne. "You, Miss Sinclair, are not going anywhere."

"It's far safer to bring me along than have me follow." She put her hands on her hips. "I will follow. You cannot stop me since I have heard where she is." Her mouth firmed. "She is my sister. She may need me."

Ruan pretended, or at least Devon hoped he was pretending, to humor her. "Ben, go with Emily and Henry in my carriage. If you're game, Thrale, you'll ride with us."

"You can't mean to let her come," Devon protested.

"She will follow, Dev," Ben said in a weary voice. "You've not lived with her for these weeks. A more willful girl there has never been since the day the earth was made. No, don't think for a moment she won't follow."

"Lock her in a room," suggested Thrale, evidently not closely acquainted with Emily.

Emily marched to confront them. Devon couldn't look away from those fiery eyes and didn't imagine Thrale was having any easier a time. "If you succeeded, I would only climb out the window. Or break down the door. I'd remove the hinges if I had to. You won't keep me from this. Anne needs me. She needs all of us."

"I ought to ride," Ben objected. "It'll be faster that way."

"I can't sit in a bloody carriage." Ruan pushed two pistols across the table toward Devon. "Besides, someone has to teach Emily the rudiments of firing one of these."

Chapter Thirty-four

In the concealing shadow of the oaks Henry described, Ruan waited with Thrale and Benjamin, never once taking his eyes off the house. Small as houses went and reminiscent of a hunting box. The two-story structure, built of yellow-gray brick, stood like a once strong man past his prime, hale at the first glance but unable to withstand scrutiny. Peeled shutters, broken newels, a cracked window. Ruan doubted its owner knew anyone was there. A thin curl of smoke rose from the far chimney.

Devon came, silent as death. Ruan felt his approach and turned, watching Dev assess the house. "Easy enough to get in, I should think."

"Ho, there," Benjamin greeted him in the same not-quite-a-whisper voice as the others used. "Emily?"

"Henry's with her. Told her I'd come back for her once we had a look round." Devon gave a grin that was not a grin. "Left her armed to the teeth and itching to shoot someone." His eyes scanned the house, pausing at all the spots Ruan had himself marked as vulnerable. Then he asked a shade too innocently, "Wonder who owns this?"

Thrale glared at them both. "It's not mine."

"One man came out for a look," Ruan said. "He didn't do much, though. Stood a while in the doorway. Drinking."

"The rest are probably drunk on wallop, too."

"With luck."

"Well." Devon stroked his nose. "I'm off. Wish me luck."

While Devon reconnoitered, Benjamin, Thrale and Ruan checked and rechecked their guns.

Moments later—it felt a lifetime to Ruan—Devon reappeared. "Two men downstairs. Drinking. Five horses in the barn, though. Two nags. A dray for the gig. Two thoroughbreds. One almost as fine as yours."

"Anne?"

"Not downstairs, anyway. Upstairs most likely. We ought to assume she is there somewhere."

"No sign of others?" asked Benjamin.

"None."

"Standing guard wherever they're holding the duchess," Thrale said.

Devon gave him a look. "I'll watch the back while the rest of you take on the ones inside. Agreed?"

As it happened, the first of the kidnappers fell easily. Before any of them could move into position, one of the men came outside and wandered over to the oaks to relieve himself. Thrale stepped up and punched him in the stomach. While he struggled to breathe, Dev coshed him and that was that, except for making sure of the knots that secured him to the trunk of an oak. The man sprawled, trousers open, head hanging to his chest. A heavy odor of ale and piss rose from him. He was young, healthy, well-formed and handsome enough to have obtained a good position in the best of households.

Thrale stood over him. "Hell. That's the footman I sacked for theft."

"Give me to the count of fifty to get around back and to the window," Dev said. "Then go in. I'll step in if you need me." He turned back. With a cockeyed grin, he said, "Check you've loaded your guns, milords."

The ruffian they'd overpowered had left the front door ajar. All to the better. Ruan stepped in far enough to make room for Benjamin. Thrale remained behind them, just out of sight. Ruan cleared his throat and took aim.

"That you?" the man said, picking up his lager and taking a long swallow before he turned to the door. He had a barrel chest and arms the size of clubs.

"Twitch and you'll not live to see another day."

The boulder of a man froze, tankard halfway to his mouth.

"Where are they?" Benjamin said. The man pointed upstairs cautiously, in case one of these angry gentlemen took it in his head to squeeze a trigger. "Up you go, Ruan," said Benjamin cheerfully.

"Ned!" The shout was accompanied by the sound of footsteps on bare wood. Ruan first saw low-heeled shoes, then white stockings and black breeches. "It's your watch." The voice came closer. "What the devil are—" The rest of the man appeared. He saw Ruan and stopped dead, one foot poised above a stair.

"You are?" Aldreth said.

With a smile polished as new silver he tugged at the edges of his black coat. "Why, I'm a gentleman's gentleman, milord. At your service." He gave a short bow and then clasped his hands before him as if about to pray. "I am here looking after my employer. At the moment he is not at home. What may I do to help you?"

"I am here," Ruan said, "to fetch my wife."

"Your wife? Oh, I'm afraid there's been some—" Though his smile remained pleasant, his eyes flitted around the room like a starling on the wrong side of a closed door. Then he saw Thrale. "Why, my lord Thrale, here you are hours before you said to expect you!"

"Basset!" Thrale leapt forward, but Benjamin grabbed his arm, stopping him short.

"Your valet, I presume?"

"I'll have your head for this, Basset." The valet's mouth dropped open, a perfect likeness of confusion, but his attention skipped from Thrale to Ben and Ruan and there lingered, and Ruan saw in them not a sign of perplexity.

Basset fled up the stairs, Ruan on his heels. He just missed the man's collar before a door slammed in his face. One kick broke wood, a second shattered the door from its frame. Ruan tore past, frantic at what might have happened during the seconds it took to batter his way in. Basset stood at the broken-down window.

"Where is she?" he demanded when a quick glance around showed him a room empty but for the other man. He lifted his gun.

"I told that coxcomb you'd find him" Basset said.

"Where is she?"

"Kill me, and you'll not find her 'til it's too late."

"I won't ask again."

"Damned fine-looking woman, your wife." He licked his lips and edged toward the window. "He's enjoying himself with her right now, I imagine." He put a hand over his crotch, taunting. "Shall I tell you whether I've had my turn yet? Or perhaps that stallion downstairs?"

Ruan heard himself roar but did not recognize the agonized shout as his own. Basset's eyes opened wide, and he backed against the rotting window frame.

"I ought to kill you." How he had ended with the gun extended to within a foot of Basset's heart, he didn't know, but there it was, and he was ready to pull the trigger.

"Then I'll be dead, no mistake, and you'll be too late to save her. You're too late already."

He let the gun drop to his side. The other man relaxed and stayed that way even when Ruan took a step closer. Ruan pressed the weapon to Basset's cheek. "Start talking." He didn't move the gun.

Basset paled when he saw Ruan's dead eyes and the promise of certain death. "Up there." He tilted his chin toward the ceiling. "With her. Right now." Ruan's hand tensed, and Basset's eyes widened. He launched himself backward shattering glass and wood.

Whether the fall killed him mattered not to Ruan. If it hadn't, he had a lifetime to make sure Basset died while Anne's life could depend on the next few minutes. He ran from the room, taking the stairs three at a time. The door at the top wasn't locked. He threw it open, half-afraid Basset had lied and the room would be empty. It wasn't.

Julian Durling wore only a loose shirt open to the waist, trousers and boots. In eerie silence, he knelt on a pallet of the sort given to servants by skinflint masters, holding Anne close to his chest, a parody of a concerned lover. Light glinted on the wicked blade of a knife in his hand. Her skirts, twisted and torn, exposed one leg to the knee. Rope bound her wrists behind her.

Anne's head flopped back, and Ruan understood why Durling had made no attempt to hide his face from her. She was unconscious. Strands of flaxen hair fell around her face and a bruise rose purple on her cheek. Slowly, Durling turned. A gash from the bottom of his ear to mid-cheek still oozed blood.

"Damn that Basset," Durling said. Ruan's pulse

tripped when he caught the glitter in Durling's eyes. "I knew he couldn't be trusted to follow a simple instruction."

"Not a bit."

Durling softly laughed, a dry and ironical sound. "Somehow, I don't think you brought my diamonds." With a tender motion, he lifted his hand to Anne's face, intending, Ruan understood, to brush the hair from her cheek. His shoulders jumped once, as if seeing a knife startled him. Icy fear coiled in Ruan's gut. The man's sanity stretched thin as a blade. Durling's mouth twisted when he looked at Anne. "No wonder you threw Mrs. Forrest aside. I'd have done the same myself."

"Let her go," Ruan said.

He shook his head as if declining a glass of wine and hauled her upright, one arm clamped tight around her waist. He used her as a shield, knife in his free hand, an awkward position, for she was dead weight.

"Let her go."

"She's a loyal little thing, I'll say that much for her. Wouldn't have me to save her own lovely neck, and I tell you I begged most prettily." He shrugged, sagging against the wall behind him. "Probably do it to save you, though."

"You are dead."

A look of regret flitted across his face. "Undoubtedly the case."

"Do as his grace says, Julian," came another voice from a darkened corner of the room. "And let her go."

Durling's grip on Anne tightened, and he added the support of his other arm. The flat of the knife lay across her waist. "Shoot him, Cyn. Her life depends upon it."

The hair on the back of Ruan's neck lifted. Turning his head, he saw first the gun held unwaveringly, then the man who held it.

"Shoot him, Major," Martin said. He grinned. "Of

322

course. Begging your pardon. Shoot him, your grace. You've a better shot than I." The gun lifted. "Shoot, I say, or it'll be too late. There's no telling what he'll do. He's mad. If you won't shoot him, then step aside and let me do it. Look at him. Can't you see he's mad?" Martin aimed where Durling's ribs would be if Ruan stepped aside. "He owes me money, damn his soul, and I wanted to collect. I went to his house. Saw him leaving, you know, and I followed him," Martin said. "I saw him kill that servant of yours, the one you set on him, following him day and night, and then I followed him here. Managed to conceal myself only just. Now shoot, damn you."

"For God's sake, Cyn, shoot him," Martin repeated. Durling looked frantically from him to Martin. He turned his torso slightly so that Ruan's margin for error became slimmer yet, though he still had a better shot than Martin. "He'll kill her if you don't."

"Hesitate much longer," Martin went on, "and he'll slit her throat. Shoot or step aside. You're the only man I know who could make a shot like that."

Anne stirred and everyone jumped in response. Martin lunged, trying to get around Ruan. In a flash, Durling raised the knife to her neck. "No!" His cry rent the air, rising to a shriek.

Immediately, the ex-soldier backed down. "Cynssyr," he hissed. "Move or shoot, damn you!"

Durling's drawl came back in full force. "I thought I was violent with the women until I saw Martin. He wants her alive, Cyn. And you, for now. He wants you to die knowing what he'll do to her. That's why he hasn't killed you where you stand."

"Madman!" Martin cried. "He's a Bedlamite."

"I wouldn't let him touch her," Durling said. "I couldn't. And here I thought I could stand any depravity. Imagine my shock when I discovered my mistake."

He laughed, and Ruan fancied a touch of madness rang in the sound. Then Anne shifted again, her feet moving as she tried to stand and found she could not. Durling lurched to compensate.

Suddenly, Ruan had a perfect shot. If only his thundering heart didn't throw him off and kill Anne instead. Durling's blade rose, arcing through the air.

Chapter Thirty-five

The back door slammed open with a bang that sent Devon's pulse surging to racehorse speed. One of the men, the larger of the two who'd been downstairs playing dice and drinking, burst out and flat-out ran over Devon, who hit the ground hard enough to knock the breath from him. While Dev gasped for air, the giant man, stinking of ale, recovered his balance and was halfway to the stable by the time Benjamin came in pursuit.

Benjamin tackled him twenty feet from the stable. The moment he managed to pull in a lungful of air, Devon went to Benjamin's aid. The fellow fought with the strength of a man drunk enough to have no sense: graceless and with massive arms flailing. It took the two of them to subdue the ox, as tall as Ruan and wider by half.

Devon fell on him, crushing his knee onto the back of the ruffian's neck. "Where's the other one?" Devon asked with a backward glance.

Benjamin, for all that he'd fought as hard as Dev, looked ready to walk into any London salon. He brushed a bit of dust off his shoulder and grinned with only the faintest chill in his eyes. "Passed out. With a little persuasion from Thrale. Man's got a fist like iron."

The sound of breaking glass fractured their attention. Devon looked up just in time to see a man jump or fall from a second-story window. He made a lucky landing. With a shake of his head, he rolled to his feet and ran like hell.

"I've got this one," Benjamin said, nodding at the man prostrate on the ground. "That's Thrale's valet, Basset," he said. "After him."

Devon took off at a dead sprint. This Basset fellow possessed not an ounce of finesse. He could think of a dozen better ways to escape a house than crashing out a second-story window. But, then, he'd never had Ruan after him, either. The devil headed for the road, taking a straight line through brush and tall grass until suddenly he veered off at an angle. Devon's feet hardly touched the ground. The carriage, with Emily inside, was clearly the other man's target.

Afterward, he was never really sure precisely what happened. Basset leapt for the carriage—Devon nearly on him, certain his chest was going to burst for want of sufficient air—and managed to haul himself onto the seat and tumble Henry backward onto the road. Basset got the reins in one hand and the driver's whip in the other. With a bellow to fairly split the eardrums, he lashed the drays.

Unused to the whip, the startled horses bolted. Dev caught the back of the carriage by the tips of his fingers and damned near had his shoulders dislocated by the jolt. He hauled himself onto the step where a postilion would cling. An undignified yelp came from inside: Emily being knocked to the floor.

"Stay down!" he roared, not knowing if she would hear him over the rumbling, snapping rush of a carriage out of control. The rest was more or less a blur. Dev crawled over the top of the vehicle, he later could not recall that he feared being dashed to his death, though he ought to have, and gave Basset a tremendous blow to the jaw as he snatched for the reins. And nearly got them, too.

By the time he did have them, he was upside down on the seat with Basset trying his damnedest to throttle him. A kick to Basset's chin freed Devon long enough to right himself and haul on one of the reins. The other flapped just out of his reach. The carriage took a stomach-churning lurch to the left. Basset toppled sideways off the driver's seat. He clung to the side, feet dangling inches from the ground and the wheels that would snap his legs like twigs, leaving Devon to stop the pell-mell rush of the horses.

The coach swayed like a ship on a swelling sea. At last, Devon caught the other rein and hauled back until he thought his arms would burst his skin and his feet punch through the boards. Basset dropped off the side but Dev now had the horses stopped, and he threw himself after the man with a shout to bring down all the fiends of hell. In ten steps, he had Basset by the collar and they fell to the ground in a heap.

Basset jackknifed and nearly threw Devon head over heels. Dust choked him, filled his eyes and mouth. Basset landed a punch to his ribs, then he had Dev by the throat. Air became a suddenly precious commodity.

"Stop." A woman's voice.

With a desperate surge of strength, Devon clapped Basset's ears as hard as he could. Roaring with pain, Basset fell back and Dev rolled away, head hanging, gasping. He saw the absurd sight of Emily Sinclair, angelically, daintily beautiful in her pristine gown, pointing

327

a gun in the general vicinity of Basset's chest. She held it like she knew what to do with it, no sign of a tremor, her eye steady. Just as he'd taught her. Blessed girl had the courage of twenty men.

"If you move, sir, I will shoot you. Bracebridge, are you all right?"

Basset, alas, underestimated the enemy. Laughing, he leapt for Emily and the gun. Just in time, Devon covered his ears. Basset spun around and hit the ground, writhing and screaming like she'd got him in the balls instead of the shoulder. Devon staggered to his feet.

Emily scowled at Basset. "Need you make quite so much noise? I ought to shoot you again, just to shut you up." Devon couldn't help himself. He laughed, a very ungentlemanly sound. About then, the blood began pooling in the dust beneath Basset. Emily turned several shades of white. "Good heavens, he's bleeding."

"Of course he's bleeding." He roared with laughter. "You bloody well shot him, Em."

Her eyes went big as saucers. "I shot him."

Devon bent over Basset to inspect the wound. Blood seeped steadily but didn't spurt. "I don't think you nicked the artery. Be dead by now if you had."

"Dead? Is he going to die?"

"I can't say. He needs a surgeon." He used Basset's shirt to make a bandage, tore off another two strips to bind his hands and feet and hauled him inside the carriage. He secured the door and turned, surprised to find Emily close behind him. Grinning, he said, "The world lost a great soldier when you were born a female."

"I am glad I'm not one." She held out the gun. "I do not care for shooting people. It's disagreeable."

"Just the right touch of humility." He winced when he took the gun from her and slipped it into his pocket.

328

That sharp pain up his shoulder meant he'd be in a good deal more discomfort tomorrow.

"Are you all right?"

"Of course." He saw immediately he'd spoken with unnecessary curtness. She was already turning away from him. "Here, now," he said, contritely, grabbing her upper arm. "I'm sorry." Somehow, he pulled a little too hard, because her face ended up scant inches from his. Like Anne's, the dark lashes were absurdly thick. Eyes the color of the sky opened wide, viscerally, sweetly vulnerable. He knew when a woman needed to be kissed, and Emily Sinclair needed to be kissed. Emotions already raging, he reacted on pure instinct, which in his case proved disastrous. His instincts had never been very proper.

He lowered his head to hers and kissed her. Not a platonic kiss, but as a man does a woman he intends to bed. Raw lust, primal and demanding of satisfaction, filled him. He ravished her mouth, parting her lips, delving, touching her teeth and tongue. He backed her toward the coach, and when she could go no farther he held on to the door and pressed himself against her, flattened his groin against her, grinding in imitation of what he would do when he had her naked and was between her thighs. The image of her underneath him danced in his vision. And Emily, the little witch he thought he so thoroughly disliked, wasn't resisting at all.

Her bosom rose and fell against his chest. The moment her back hit the carriage, her arms went around him, hanging on for dear life. With all his soul, he wanted to grab her hand and bring it down to where his erection bulged against his trousers. Whatever common sense he possessed evaporated and he would have sworn he heard the sound of his control snapping like a twig. He tugged at the neckline of her bosom, cradling the bare skin above her gown because he wanted the peak of her breast between his teeth.

"Milord?"

Moments and inches from his goal, Devon forced his eyes from the creamy flesh of Emily's bosom and looked over his shoulder. Henry stumbled toward them.

"Milord, is she all right? Has the bastard hurt her?"

Emily suddenly went limp against him. He grabbed her waist to keep her from hitting the ground and found she had swooned, quite deliberately and falsely, in such a fashion that it was possible for him to remove his hand from her bosom without Henry seeing direct evidence of what he'd interrupted. Her eyes fluttered open when she felt both his hands around her waist.

"She is overcome with emotion." He faced Henry, thinking if he'd been half as cold-blooded during his thieving days as the woman in his arms, Corth Abby would be twice its size. Hell, if he'd had Emily with him, Corth Abby would be a bloody great palace. The sound of a distant shot took all their minds off the present.

Emily straightened a bit too hastily for a woman overwhelmed by sensation. "Anne."

Chapter Thirty-six

The hilt of Durling's knife struck the floor with a thud then spun wildly across the planks until it hit the toe of Ruan's boot. Anne's eyes flickered open, and she moaned. In a voice so triumphant with rage that Ruan felt the curse rather than heard it, Martin screamed and aimed his gun at Durling and Anne.

Durling could have saved himself. He could have done nothing and probably kept himself entirely out of harm's way. But he didn't. Instead, he shoved Anne to the floor and launched himself at Martin. The shot slammed into his chest. Durling staggered back and hit the wall. He clapped his hands over his chest but nothing stanched the red flow. The smell of gunpowder slowly sharpened in the air.

"Now," Martin said, his chest a bellows fanning whatever fire burned in him. He aimed straight at Ruan's head and grinned. "Before I kill you, where are the damn diamonds?"

331

Anne's eyes popped open. She stayed motionless on the floor.

"Anne was right about you," Ruan said, willing himself not to look at his wife lest Martin see she was awake and aware. She wasn't near enough to reach the knife.

"The money, your grace."

"When Anne is safe."

"Oh, but I am not finished with her. I was about to find out what's had you so worked up since you got married when Durling, the poor lamented fool, interfered." Martin nudged Anne with the toe of his boot. She moaned and rolled. Her head lolled limp on her neck. And now she was close enough. "He was right, though. You'll die knowing what I'm going to do to her."

Anne's fingers closed around the knife.

"Why?" Ruan asked, desperately afraid Martin would see her. "Why this?"

Martin swiped the back of his hand across his forehead. "I've often wondered about my compulsion. Why does one man drink to excess while another gambles away his fortune? Why is one a glutton and another a gourmand? I have decided the answer is a simple one. It's how I am made, and I do not care to stop. Not even if I thought I could."

Anne saw Ruan's face slide into the same ice that seemed to have frozen her fear and stopped her heart from beating. He meant to shoot Martin and he would surely be shot in turn. She coiled her fingers around the knife and raised herself up on her knees, facing Martin. With both hands tight around the hilt, blindly she brought the blade down with all the force her aching arms could muster.

Everything happened at once. Steel slipped into flesh and grated against bone.

Martin howled.

A gun fired.

Something fell on her, pinning her to the floor. Pain shot along her shoulder and the side of her head.

"Good God!"

She tried to roll away and could not. Someone moaned, a pitiful sound. She forced herself to open her eyes but saw little but dark fabric. That pathetic noise was coming from her. The weight on her shifted, and suddenly she could see.

"Anne?" Aldreth bent over her.

Ruan stood over Martin, both hands gripping his pistol like he intended to fire again. His eyes were twin coals in a face devoid of emotion. Ludicrously, she noticed her husband was not his habitually immaculate self. He looked like he'd slept in his clothes. Lord, he wasn't even wearing a coat. His white shirt hung partially loose from his trousers.

"Are you all right?" she asked Ruan. "Are you hurt?"

Aldreth gathered her in his arms. "Don't look, Anne."

The warning came too late. Anne saw Martin sprawled on the floor, his open-eyed gaze glassing over. Beneath his head and shoulders, a crimson pool slowly formed, burning into her memory. Ruan moved, distracting her.

When she looked at her husband he was inspecting his gun with a quite casual expression. As if killing a man were commonplace. He did look like he'd slept the night in his clothes. His jacket was rumpled and the crease of his trousers less than perfect. And his collar, which she had never seen less than meticulously arranged, was wildly crooked. He'd probably been terrorizing the staff, she thought. Aldreth brought her to her feet while Ruan used one hand to tuck his shirt into the waistband of his trousers. As Aldreth lifted her, she saw Julian Durling, half-sitting against the wall.

"Thank you," she said to him.

Finished adjusting his clothes to his satisfaction, Cynssyr looked over. "He is dead."

"He saved my life. He kept Martin away from me."

"Are you all right?" Cynssyr asked softly. His green eyes were bleak. The gun disappeared into his coat pocket.

"Fine," she said, even though her knees went to water when Aldreth loosened his grip on her. "The child, too," she said in answer to his unspoken question.

"Good God."

"Here." Cynssyr handed her something. Her spectacles. They were bent, and when she put them on they perched unevenly on her nose. "You are covered in blood," he said.

Anne looked. Red spattered her gown, some even on her hands. "I should like to go home. Very much." She refused Aldreth's arm, but Cynssyr insisted on taking her elbow.

"You were brave," he said approvingly. "You kept your head."

"I knew you would come." In all honesty, she wasn't sure if she spoke or if the words remained thought. Not for a moment had she doubted he would come. Cynssyr said nothing at all, so she supposed she hadn't spoken. She needed his strength just to walk. The bent frames of her spectacles meant she saw well only through the right lense, a disconcerting feeling that impaired her already precarious balance. He carried her down the stairs, but set her down at the bottom.

Aldreth cleared his throat. "I'll just go fetch Devon. See to the carriage. Have it brought round. Thrale's taking care of the others, by the way. Good man to have in a crisis." He hurried out the rear entrance, leaving Cynssyr the unenviable task of walking with her to the front door.

"What day is it?" she asked, surprised to see it was

light outside, late morning even. Fixing on such mundane details helped her maintain her sanity. Whenever she closed her eyes she saw Durling's empty stare or else the icy green of her husband's eyes.

"Thursday."

She didn't realize she'd shivered until he put his coat around her shoulders. "It seems Thursday ought to have come and gone already." She took a wobbly step toward the open front door. But for his steadying arm, she would not have made it.

Outside was quite a scene. Devon sat on the driver's seat of a carriage, holding the ribbons like a coachman born. Emily sat on one side of him, Henry, pale and looking none too well, on the other. Thrale bodily lifted one of her captors into another carriage. Aldreth appeared from around the side of the house, shouting something indistinct to Devon before intercepting Thrale and helping him with another man, the one who'd started the vile talk about sharing her between them. He'd talked of having his turn after Durling and Wilberfoss were done. She shivered again, turning away so that she would not even accidently see those brown eyes again.

Though Cynssyr steadied her with an arm around her waist, descending the front stairs took an overwhelming effort. She had been tried enough. To the very limit of her soul's endurance. More than anything, she wanted to collapse into his arms, but she held herself in check. She had to. He expected no less of her.

"Anne." Emily clambered over Devon and slithered down the side of the carriage without a thought to propriety or decency. She gathered her skirts in both hands and ran to her. "Are you hurt? My God, you've blood all over you. Cynssyr, what have you done to her?" She pushed him hard enough to make him take a step backward. "Oaf, clod, bumpkin, you bloody great lout—"

Carolyn Jewel

Heedless of Anne's grimy clothes, Emily threw her arms around her, hugging her tight and bursting into tears. "I'll not forgive him for this. I won't." She glared behind her. "What a fool I was to think you'd changed!"

"Emily, you're being a perfect goose. He saved my life," said Anne, watching Devon walk slowly toward her. Dust coated him from head to toe, and he limped. She held out her hand.

"I was so afraid for you," Emily cried, still embracing her. "Were you hurt? Why are you covered in blood? Cynssyr, why is there blood?"

"Emily," Devon said, coming close enough to take Anne's hand. "All will be explained in good time. Right now, however, your sister needs to go home."

Emily bristled. "I know that."

Devon raised Anne's hand to his lips and kissed the back of her hand. "Are you well?"

All she could manage was a nod, and that was more effort than she cared to admit. Oh, Lord. She was safe. Free. Overwhelmed. Perfectly incapable of putting together two rational thoughts, let alone one.

Aldreth reappeared leading two horses, Cynssyr's sorrel gelding and his own dun. He tied them to the back of the carriage. "I'll drive," he said, looking askance at Devon and his dusty clothes. "Henry, move over."

The drive home was peculiar. Devon and Emily, sitting on the opposite side from her and Cynssyr, stayed as far from each other as it was possible to get, taking such care to avoid looking at one another that the more usual glaring daggers would have been an improvement. Bursts of conversation in which everyone spoke at once came crashing to a self-conscious halt. Even worse, during each of the silences Anne found herself leaning closer to Cynssyr's solid warmth. Eventually, though, she heard enough disjointed bits and pieces of how she'd come to be rescued that she sat straight, though without quite leaving the protective circle of his arm.

"Emily, you—" Her voice cracked. "Emily, what were you thinking? You might have been killed."

Cynssyr drew her close. "All is well, Anne," he murmured. "You are safe. Emily is safe." His breath stirred her hair, and he kissed the top of her head. "You are safe, and all is well."

The remainder of her protest lost a good deal of bite because for some reason that inconsequential kiss nearly undid her. She swallowed hard against the lump in her throat. "What were the three of you thinking to let her come? And Richard, too. He ought to have known better."

"Quite true," Cynssyr said.

Devon gave Emily a queer look. "The woman is a force of nature. Nothing could have stopped her." Another of the silences fell with Devon staring at his boots and Emily out the window. Peculiar. Most peculiar. When she wasn't feeling like a noodle too long in the water she would reflect on the oddness of their behavior.

Ruan's arm was around her shoulder, and she allowed herself the briefest moment of relaxation against him. No tears. There must be no tears. She must be strong for his sake. For now, it was enough to have him next to her. Or perhaps too much. He would send her to Cornwall, and she'd already learned how it felt to be apart from him. The trap had closed long ago, if only she'd had the eyes to see. In truth, whether she left or stayed, her heart was already broken.

Her eyes drifted closed, and she didn't wake until he carried her up the front stairs. She was hardly conscious, fatigue burned her eyes, pulled her lids down so that several times she opened her eyes to the sudden realization that she'd very nearly been asleep. "The duchess is fine," she heard Cynssyr say as he swept past Merchant and the rest of the servants. "She'll need a bath," he said, raising his voice to be heard over the applause, raucous cheers and even a few sobs. "Send one of the maids to her. And have a physic look after Henry."

"Yes, your grace," was all Anne heard before Cynssyr was heading up the stairs and into her room. He deposited her gently in the bathing room. One of the upstairs maids came in by the far door. Behind her were two footmen with a tub and two more with buckets of steaming water.

He gave the young woman an impenetrable stare. "Look after her. And call me if—anything should happen."

She bent a solemn knee. "Your grace."

Anne was glad to have her ruined gown off and even gladder to hear someone mutter something about throwing it directly in the fire. The bath felt marvelous. She barely made it to the bed before she fell asleep for a second time. When she woke she was alone in her bed. Blessedly clean. Bruised ribs made breathing something of an exercise in restraint, but she managed to pull on her dressing gown. Bent over like an old woman, she crept down the stairs. Voices from the French parlor told her where to look for Cynssyr, and the open door invited entry. If she was to have a broken heart, she might as well give in to her weakness. She just hoped Ruan would let her stay once he'd grown tired of her.

A horribly familiar scene met her.

Mrs. Forrest and Cynssyr.

"Do not turn away from me, Ruan," Mrs. Forrest pleaded. "Please, I am here for you. As I have always been. As you once were for me." Cynssyr's mistress stood in the center of the room. From the doorway, Anne had a view of her exquisite profile. As for Cynssyr, she could not see him. Not directly, for he stood at the fireplace, his back to the door. His face, however, was perfectly reflected in a mirror on the opposite wall from where Anne stood.

His lip curled, whether in disdain or amusement she could not tell. "Really?"

Mrs. Forrest went to Cynssyr. "Darling," she said, touching his back with one dainty hand. "Darling, I heard the most awful rumor. I came here the moment I heard." He bowed his head so that Anne could no longer see his face. "My God, is it true, then?" Facing him, Mrs. Forrest put her arms around him, pulling him close. "She is dead?"

He did not accept her embrace. "Not dead. But lost to me, Katie. Lost. After all I've done, it's only just. What I deserve."

"Just?" Mrs. Forrest repeated with a trace of indignation. "She is not suited to you. Lord knows she is not your equal in any way, but, darling, what happened to her was not *just* for anyone."

"Nothing that's happened to her has been just." A note of despair rang in his voice. "I never told you the circumstances of the marriage. Did she tell you?" Mrs. Forrest shook her head. "Of course she wouldn't. She was forced to marry me."

"Never say any woman was forced to marry you."

"Those rumors are true."

"I don't believe it. Why, even if I believed you'd take an instant's interest in her, she'd not give in. Not even to you. She's not a drop of passion in her. You can see that just looking at her. There is only duty in that one."

"She had no choice. We had no choice but to marry. I took her without her consent. Do you understand? Without her consent, and I was caught out." Mrs. Forrest gasped, but he continued. "I got her with child that night. My God, if you could have seen her face when she told me." He lifted a hand, then let it fall helplessly to his side. "She was shattered. You see," he said bitterly, "she had hoped I would divorce her, and she knew a child made that impossible."

Mrs. Forrest gazed into his face, earnestly puzzled. "But she never seemed unhappy. In fact, I would have said quite the opposite. I thought she loved you. Like all the others have."

A smile like a ray of sunshine appeared on Cynssyr's face. Anne and Mrs. Forrest both caught their breath at the sight. "That is her singular beauty. She is good. Inside, deep in her soul, she all that is good and kind and right in the world."

"You love her." Mrs. Forrest took a step back.

"Yes."

The impact of his answer shot through Anne like a thunderbolt. Her legs trembled, and she clutched the door post for support. A part of her did not want it to be true. It meant the potential for loss. Surely, her life would be safer without his love.

"Have you told her?"

"Several times."

"Oh, Ruan. Darling Ruan. She does not believe you, does she?"

"No."

"You will convince her."

"How, when she loves someone else?"

"I do not believe that. Who?"

"Devon."

"No! Oh, Ruan, no. She does not love him. How could she when she is married to you? Ruan, no."

Anne could imagine being married to Devon only in the vaguest way, as a poorly sketched drawing, and like Mrs. Forrest, she wondered at Cynssyr believing such a thing.

"When she is well, she will have her freedom from me." Ruan caught Mrs. Forrest's hand and drew her toward him. "Will you have me back, then, Katie? A divorced man in love with another woman?"

She brushed his cheek, an intimate, tender caress that made Anne hate her for the intimacy and grateful for her tenderness. "I would have you back under any circumstance. But what nonsense you're talking. If you love her, there can be no question of giving her up."

"Christ!" Cynssyr gave an anguished cry. "She does not want me, Katie. Don't you understand that? I cannot live with that. I can't. She must be free of me or she will come to hate me." Abruptly, he turned away from the fireplace and Mrs. Forrest. He took one step, saw Anne and came to a halt. Instantly, his face cleared. "What are you doing out of bed?"

"Looking for you." She wobbled a little when she let go of the door post, and Cynssyr rushed to support her. She lurched into his arms, and for the first time in days, she felt at home.

"Don't ever give me such a fright," he said, holding her close and stroking her hair. "You should have called for a servant when you woke."

She, too, ran a hand over his head, feeling the hair thick and silky under her fingers. "I wonder I managed to sleep at all. I was sure I never would again." Her heart swelled in her chest, filling her. Her legs trembled. A lump in her throat the size of all outdoors stopped her from speaking. Her feelings, now too immense to contain, insisted upon freedom. "Ruan," she whispered, clinging to him.

"Exhaustion." He tapped her temple with a gentle touch that turned to a caress. "Mental and physical. I've seen it happen to soldiers."

"I love you," she said, before she lost her nerve.

"Please, Anne, do not say that unless you mean it."

"I love you. Not Devon. You." She felt her heart expand in her chest. "Ruan, I love you. Beyond thought and life, I love you."

Neither of them noticed Katie Forrest slip from the room, a sad and bittersweet smile on her lovely face.

Ruan started to speak but caught himself short then began again. "Are you certain?"

"I have never been more certain of anything."

"After all I've done to you? God, don't answer that." He touched her cheek. "You have my heart, Anne," he said softly. "You know you are my heart."

"And you are mine." Her finger traced along his lower lip. "I do love you." She savored the rightness of that. "Yes, I do." With a wry smile, she shook her head.

"You shall have to practice telling me so."

"I will." She laughed, a sound of pure joy. "I cannot get enough of touching you. I love you. I love you. I love you." With each word, her fingers caressed, smoothed and moved on, marking him as hers. "Goodness, if I'd known what a relief it would be to finally tell you, I'd have done it a sight sooner."

He gave her that incandescent smile of his. "I must say, I wish you had."

She pulled his head down to hers and gave her husband the kiss for which he'd been longing. The kiss of a woman who loves the man she holds in her arms.